Educated at Bedales and in the US, Arnold began his career as a graphic and industrial designer. He specialized in the development of creative play and learning materials, and these were exhibited in a one-man show at New York's Museum of Modern Art. He served as a consultant to publishers of educational materials, toys and games and wrote several books and a newspaper column on education, widely syndicated in the US, Canada and Britain.

Arnold's interest in learning and the culture of childhood led to his gathering an important collection of early toys, games, learning materials, children's books, and books about early childhood education. He became involved in systems analysis and cybernetics as a result of his interest in game and learning theories. Arnold was Director of New York's Workshop School, has served as a Fellow of Boston University and was a Leverhulme Fellow. He lives in London and is writing his next book, in addition to his work as a systems analyst.

D1077324

# ARNOLD ARNOLD

# The Corrupted Sciences

Paladin
*An Imprint of HarperCollinsPublishers*

Paladin
An Imprint of HarperCollins*Publishers*
77–85 Fulham Palace Road
Hammersmith, London W6 8JB

Published simultaneously in hardcover
and paperback by Paladin 1992

ISBN 0 586 09239 0
ISBN 0 586 08891 1 (paper covers)

Set in Baskerville

Printed in Great Britain by
HarperCollins Manufacturing Glasgow

**For Alison**

# Acknowledgements

I owe a debt of gratitude to everyone who has read and helped clarify what I have written; also to those who programmed aspects of my discovery of the pattern structure of primes and their composites and who found errors they helped me correct. Further mistakes may have escaped their and my detection and I would be grateful to any reader who points them out.

Alison Pilpel went over my original MS with a fine-tooth comb. In more than one sense she is my collaborator – I benefited enormously from being able to bounce ideas off her and getting back critical responses. Her help was crucial as far as style and expression are concerned. I rewrote again and again until what I wrote was clear to her. This book was made more simple and readable, thanks to her intelligent insights and swingeing use of a red pen.

I want to acknowledge valuable help and criticism from knowledgeable friends who gave their time freely to read my MS, including Audrey Adams, Dr Geoffrey Kolbe, Ian Kurston, Richard Pickard and Carolyn Rodney. I also received invaluable advice, help and criticism from Richard Pickard and Thomas Sippel-Dau who, since 1985, programmed and tested right and wrong turnings on the way to formalizing my discovery of the pattern structures of primes and their composites. Those who helped me in one way or another by being good friends include 'Puck' Dachinger. My thanks go to Bob Barkany for the photographs he took of me, and to

Armando del Torto for providing me with copies of his late brother's writing. I am most grateful to the Leverhulme Fund for supporting my application of the neural network principle to learning (see Chapter 6) with a 1984 Fellowship. Last but not least, I want to thank Ian Paten, editorial director and my editor at Paladin, without whose sympathetic understanding and help this and my previous book *Winners and Other Losers in Peace and War* might never have seen the light of day.

# Table of Contents

# Foreword

This, and my previous book *Winners*, are the result of more than twenty years' work. Both books describe what is, up to a point, a first – a new way of looking at the world that is derived from fundamental mathematical principles. These are given in the Appendices to both books. However, no mathematics are required to explain or understand what all of this means.

Knowledge and understanding are evolutionary, like everything else. The same is true for the technologies. Without all three I would not have been able to present coherent – if unorthodox – solutions to world problems within a relatively short period of time. For example, while I have worked on the now-resolved prime-number problem during a period of about eight years, the actual time that I spent on it was probably less than a year. I could not have done it without the help and co-operation of my associates, and certainly not as quickly without computers. Foremost, I could not have done it without first making a more fundamental discovery: for I seem to have discovered 'the theory of everything', known in physics as the 'Grand Unification Theory' (GUT). The path to this theory does not appear to lie in physics. Instead, the human central nervous system and the totally objective logic it makes possible are the twin keys. But this discovery also depends on having the correct feelings. Feelings and logic must match or there is something seriously wrong with one or the other.

I understand the consequences of what I have done. Soon anyone will be able to understand them equally well and apply successfully what I have discovered to whatever interests them most. For my discovery may herald an age of common sense and uncommon men and women who think for themselves and act as individuals. Both qualities are in short supply today.

Given this new tool, everyone can be a master craftsman or a Nobel prize-winner if they try. By this I mean that everyone can try to achieve the greatest qualitative success possible in whatever they attempt, given sufficient interest, effort, time, cooperation and resources. All of this could lead to the world's spiritual, material and economic recovery.

The impossible (like artificial intelligence), to which I devote a part of this book, has been attempted for far too long. Such attempts make life needlessly complex. Solutions to genuine problems are always simple, despite the intricacies of life. The most gratifying results depend on a reduction of complexity to its simplest common factors, and that takes a great deal of work and time. For example, I have discovered that the principles that hold true for chess are also true for noughts and crosses and human behaviour. Many people find this a difficult concept only because few manage to see through apparent complexities. Simplicity and perfectibility go hand in hand. The exercise of both leads to eventual perfection in whatever we try to do.

But this poses two critical problems. The first consists of a psychological re-orientation for those who have let themselves become conditioned to believe falsehoods. They alone may feel threatened by what I have discovered.

The second problem concerns applications. My knowledge is as limited as everyone else's, and so I can only apply this theory to whatever I know and can learn. The same is true for everyone else. So far I have applied what I have discovered to as many previously unsolved or partially solved problems as my knowledge and time have permitted.

Hopefully, I can extend all of this further, given sufficient time and the co-operation of others.

Contrary to what some academics may think, this is not the end of anything. It could represent a new beginning for them as much as for me. Many people have intuitively felt such a need for generations. All I have done is prove them right. Others may go to their deaths insisting that they are right, no matter how wrong they may have been. That also is nothing new. It has happened again and again in the past. Such people cannot benefit from any of this. For we could stand on the threshold of an age of certainty, peace and a science of life if at least some of us apply principles and methods that lead to the best results.

Everyone – the whole human tribe – is invited to use these tools. I did not invent them. They were always there for anyone to find. If understood they will make for survival, love of life, perfectibility and eventual perfection in art and craft, science, and anything else to which they are applied. Clearly none of this will happen overnight. It calls for changes in how people feel, think and behave in all the games we play seriously and for amusement. The correct intuitions could not often be proven in the past. Now we can prove them in all the ways there are. Only then may most of us make lasting agreements to agree as to what is right or wrong; that life can be rich, infinitely varied, beautiful and productive rather than governed by chance, conformity, perpetual agreements to disagree, arguments about everything, and wars.

For the rest, this and my previous book speak for themselves.

# Introduction

'If a man will begin with certainties he shall end with doubts; but if he will be content to begin with doubts he shall end in certainties.'                     Francis Bacon

Much of modern science is tainted with eight deadly sins, each of which is related to the others. The first is an exclusively mechanistic and materialistic orientation, largely inherited from conventional religions; the second consists of a preoccupation with operations ('*how*' things work) to the exclusion of causes and consequences ('*why*' things work); the third is excessive specialization unrelated to global concerns; the fourth consists of passing on 'revealed knowledge' by means of operant conditioning of one sort or another; the fifth is a catering to vested interests and fashions; the sixth is a dedication to acquiring credentials – to publish or perish; the seventh consists of the pretence that science is value-free; and the eighth is that most of today's science, like Western religions and philosophies past and present, is not human-centred.

This book makes a number of claims that may evoke reasonable and unreasonable scepticism in the general reader to whom it is addressed, and even more so in specialists in various fields. I have therefore divided it into two parts: one for the general reader and a second (the Appendices) for those who are interested in geometric demonstrations.

It is easy to make contentious statements or to propose new theories and quite another to demonstrate them. Here I have tried to do both. What I say is not intended to be the last word. On the contrary, these may merely be the first steps towards a more logical and subjective reassessment of the scientific method and how science is learnt, taught and practised. What I have to say can be summarized as follows.

- All of nature works on the basis of the laws of cause and effect. The operations – the main concern of modern science – only describe what takes place in the gap between both. Meanings – in other words 'why' events in nature occur – depend on all three.
- Principles are always simple and underlie the seeming complexities of life and existence.
- Omniscience is clearly impossible. But principles are all-important. Once any principle is found to be broadly true, the details will take care of themselves.
- Principles are discovered by establishing causal–consequential relationships between facts, old and new.
- Without hindsight there can be no foresight and without foresight there can be no hindsight.
- A basic geometry underlies the whole of nature.
- Nature can be said to be self-organizing inasmuch as a large number of redundancies (identical repetitive sequences of events) are likely to recur again and again in the short run, even in the most random systems. This fact becomes apparent only once the operations of randomness are analysed causally, consequentially and hence semantically (i.e. 'why'), rather than merely operationally (i.e. 'how'); combinatorially (in terms of relationships), rather than merely permutationally (in terms of sequence).
- A geometric, three-dimensional and valuative method of analysis seems more efficient than the techniques currently used to solve complex problems because it apparently mimics the operations of the human central nervous system.

- The human brain is unique and is a far more powerful problem-solving mechanism than any machine or computer.
- Induction (i.e. making things happen experimentally or modelling anything from cause to consequences) should precede deduction (i.e. inferring causes from consequences), for causes come before consequences. Or, to put this another way, if deduction alone is used it is likely that the wrong causes may be extracted from observed phenomena and events.
- Making the correct conditional value judgements and choosing benign goals are prerequisites to true learning and freedom.
- The object of learning is to understand the meanings of what you know rather than merely to accumulate knowledge.
- We do not live in a world governed by chance or one in which the future is predetermined by God. Instead, the universe is conditionally deterministic (i.e. determined by circumstances that prevail at a particular place and time).
- Our universe, including time and human behaviour, can be modelled three-dimensionally.
- The arrow of time is irreversible and moves perpetually into the future.
- The cosmos seems to be eternal and apparently consists of an infinite series of finite universes.
- Our universe gives us all the options there are. It is our obligation to choose the right ones. Choosing the correct options defines survival.
- Subjective and valuative truths should predominate in the sciences as much as in everything else because we can perceive the micro- and macrocosm only through human senses – and not the other way round.

In one sense all of this is an elaboration in a different context of the conclusions demonstrated in my previous book *Winners and Other Losers in Peace and War* [AA], in which I exploded many cherished ideas in the social and behavioural sciences.

There I discussed what no Western philosopher, logician, mathematician or scientist had ever considered: the 'draw' principle that defines the concepts of co-operation, balance and creativity in nature. I also showed that our ideas about randomness, chance and order in human affairs are in conflict with mathematically demonstrable facts. Here I deal with related ideas as treated in religion, philosophy and the 'hard' sciences, and show how a prevailing illogic runs through many of these ways of looking at the world because certain premises and conclusions in all three are distorted by beliefs and prejudices.

Since time immemorial a great many theories have been proposed about mankind's relationship to the universe; about predictability, time, the nature of fundamental particles and the implications of the concept of 'man a machine'. Most reflect the methods of the day and not laws of nature.

The ideas that underlie today's sciences affect our everyday lives and thoughts far more than we realize. Clearly modern beliefs – religious, philosophical or scientific – shape our existence and future, just as they have in the past. For example, if we believe that everything is predetermined (by God) or is indeterminate (chance), then either becomes the basis on which we view nature and conduct our lives. If we decide that we are nothing but machines, then that is how we will behave.

In the past, religions have provided supposedly literal and subjective accounts of the beginning and end of the universe and of right and wrong. Philosophies claim to bridge feelings and logic. However, the sciences presume to explain nature objectively, solely on the basis of observing its operations (i.e. the observed symptoms of whatever seems to be happening). Heisenberg's uncertainty principle, big-bang and chaos theories are typical examples. But this process is, in fact, only relatively objective and hence incomplete because it excludes essential subjective manifestations. Any resulting conclusion is bound to be mechanistic and flawed. Obviously we have benefited from advances made in this manner. Yet they have not proven to be unqualified blessings.

Many of today's technologies are certainly useful, yet their uncritical uses have resulted in long-term ecological, economic and social problems that may prove far more damaging than the short-term benefits they bestow. For example, the mechanistic and purely technological approach posing as science has given us audio-visual media and computers which are largely responsible for undermining our children's abilities to read and be numerate. Medicine can now treat the symptoms of many diseases from which former generations suffered, but the treatment of symptoms does not provide cures and has been instrumental in causing problems that will increasingly impoverish the quality of life. Mass production and rapid transport have contributed to excessive urbanization and the destruction of community life. The technological approach to science may have improved personal and social hygiene, but we now suffer from an inability to rid ourselves of our wastes to an extent that threatens our future. As a result, the balance of nature on earth is hopelessly out of kilter with foreseeable consequences, despite the best efforts of those with a 'green' orientation to reverse these trends.

Modern sciences and technologies are corrupt not because they are evil in themselves – this is not an anti-science or anti-technology book – but because many perceptions in, and methods of, science are wrong in theory and in practice, and because many scientists refuse to face the consequences of their work or make value judgements about its possible applications. Such an attitude makes technicians out of those who profess to practise science.

The theories I propose and the claims I make in this book have a sound mathematical foundation. For example, my geometric analytic method can now be shown to underlie hitherto unsolved problems – for example, how we learn, or the pattern structure of prime numbers and their composites – using valuative methods that fly in the face of modern scientific perceptions. The prime-number solution, as far as it goes, also demonstrates that without hindsight there can be no foresight and vice versa. These are far from trivial results for they have profound practical, mathematical, philosophical, scientific and behavioural implications that will take some time to be digested. They reflect a paradigm shift of considerable proportions towards predominantly subjective, human-centred sciences. This is, or should be, the global and ecologically aware approach to the sciences of the future.

In one sense this book is a celebration of common sense, with which science, philosophy and religion are often in conflict. For, contrary to the myth that modern sciences are solely devoted to seeking truths about ourselves and the universe, many ideas expressed in their names have their roots in mysticism, religious fundamentalism or science fiction. These can be as prejudiced and superstitious as those of witch doctors and shamans. Others are incomplete theories, costly half-truths, delusions or frauds.

My discovery that randomness limits chance demonstrates that, contrary to the tenets of modern science, we live in a universe that can only become predictable with valuative analysis. In other words, once we try to understand causes and consequences (the 'why') the options for the future become increasingly predictable and certain. With this and other demonstrations I show that in the evolving inorganic and organic portions of the cosmos a fundamental order and purpose are implicit. To speak of chance mutations is therefore as absurd as to believe that randomness creates chance when you shuffle a pack of 52 playing cards. The discovery of the mechanism of randomness and its meanings alone should affect our perceptions in all branches of the sciences for some time to come.

Despite the prevailing beliefs in today's sciences, we may live in a purposive, and not in an indeterminate and purposeless or pre-determined universe. If so, then life does appear to have an overriding and eternal purpose – not to allow us to get into heaven or avoid hell – but simply to learn. Apparently that is why we are here.

NOTE: To avoid repetition, the AA superscript refers to my previous book (see References).

# 1
# The Question

'What is the ultimate truth about ourselves? Various answers suggest themselves. We are a bit of stellar matter gone wrong. We are physical machinery – puppets that strut and talk and laugh and die as the hand of time pulls the strings beneath. But there is one elementary inescapable answer. We are that which asks the question.'

Sir Arthur Eddington[1]

We can see the quality of today's world deteriorate socially, politically and ecologically despite seemingly rapid scientific and technological progress. This decline is brought about by prejudiced value judgements that govern most of our perceptions. This deterioration is so drastic from one year to the next that even the very young are aware of it. Further, a perpetually accelerating accumulation of actual and spurious information makes it difficult for anyone to keep up with or evaluate most of what is going on in the world of science and the technologies.

In my last book I dealt with erroneous concepts about why and how people win, lose, draw or achieve stalemates in games of strategy and chance, in science, politics, business, war, peace and personal relationships. I showed that many of our ideas in psychology and other behavioural sciences are based on false premises. I also demonstrated that randomness and chance in a human context are not what they are believed to be. These findings are extracted from a geometric model of the central nervous system that I call the 'combinatorial neural network'. The logic behind those findings discloses the relationship between man-made and universal laws and defines the meanings of rules as they apply not only to games and their outcomes, but to nature and human nature.[AA] I have upset the conventional wisdom in these matters and here I do the same to related misconceptions.

## The Scientific Method

The scientific method as applied today involves observation and quantitative analysis (i.e. measurement of size or quantity) with the object of discovering natural laws. Once such observations are made theoretically or practically and confirmed by experiment, they are then considered demonstrated as far as anything can be. This method is considered objective by modern science. As a result, most scientists claim to limit themselves to descriptions of 'how' things work to the exclusion of 'why' they work, usually ignoring any possibility of valuative analysis. In other words, they believe that the sciences and technologies are value free. But that is a value judgement in itself – albeit a wrong one – because value judgements should depend on an understanding of causes and consequences. Whenever these are ignored, as, for example, in aspects of medicine, the sciences can only deal with superficial symptoms. They ameliorate rather than cure; describe rather than explain. The myth of a value-free scientific method has had consequences that affect the technologies and our very lives.

Orthodoxy in religion, philosophy, science and the technologies aims, in effect, to control man and nature and to manipulate the operations of both on a stimulus/response, input/output basis. The object is always a 'win'. But the first rule of nature seems to be that the draw – a balanced, error-free game played *with* rather than *against* one another or nature – is the creative approach to autonomy, responsible freedom and learning. While life is certainly not a game (especially when it comes to consequences), games of strategy and chance turn out to be the best analogies we have for explaining otherwise impenetrable laws of nature – and human nature especially. Foremost among the conclusions demonstrated by analysing these analogies is that ethics (i.e. values) are not man-made nor God-given but are governed by the laws of cause and effect. It is my object here to show why the observation of processes and symptoms alone (i.e. 'how'), without qualitative analyses (i.e. asking 'why'), leads to incompleteness and distortions in our understanding of the laws of nature. These flaws in method seem to have affected the 'hard' sciences like physics and biology as much as the 'soft' ones like psychology and sociology.

This lack of valuative analysis appears to be a vital flaw in the scientific method as applied today. As stated earlier, to deny the need to make value judgements as part of the scientific method is a value judgement in its own right, something that many scientists are loath to admit.

## Technologies and Machines

Originally, technological improvements – fire and the wheel – were the result of observation, trial and error. Later ones came about as a result of a mechanization of human actions (for example a hammer as a substitute for the human fist; the knife as a substitute for teeth; water and wind power as substitutes for muscles). The technologies served human needs. But at a later stage there came a shift in emphasis. Man, instead of making the machine his slave, became an adjunct to the machine, enslaved by it and by those who controlled it. This concept has been expressed by many humanists, but the philosophical and practical implications for the sciences are not always appreciated.

Today the technologies are, by and large, practical applications of the sciences. But they have lost their way. Whatever can be done will be done in both, regardless of long-term consequences. But while in the sciences it is worth *thinking* about even what may seem impossible or dangerous, there is no excuse for experimental testing or applying whatever may seem theoretically possible without making human value judgements. Were it otherwise you could justify the 'scientific' medical experiments conducted with concentration camp victims in Germany or with prisoners of war in Manchuria by the Japanese during World War II. Such atrocities perpetrated in the name of science are possible only when the differences between man and machine become blurred.

Any system can be called a machine when the output is determined entirely by external input (i.e. stimulus/ response). This is even true for components of organisms that behave in a relatively mechanical manner (e.g. the heart or kidneys) and that can be replaced by mechanical analogues. But the fact that aspects of human biology are pseudo-mechanical does not mean that we are machines.

The widely-held belief that organisms – and especially humans – are nothing but machines is therefore a typical example of value-free judgements made on the basis of a relatively objective, purely quantitative yardstick rather than on totally objective ones that must include the 'why' as well as the 'how'; subjective as well as relatively objective criteria. This is the only way to achieve absolute objectivity.

The value-free criteria alleged to apply in the sciences have spilled over into the technologies. This attitude is reflected in a prevailing belief that the universe and mankind are subject to purely mechanical (i.e. statistical, non-valuative and probabilistic) rather than conditionally deterministic laws (i.e. determined by time, place and circumstances). In other words, today's sciences and the technologies are mutually self-reinforcing at the expense of human values and the quality of life.

## The Anthropic Principle

There are two ways of looking at the world. The first

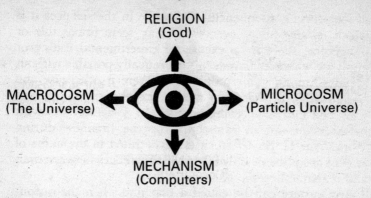

RELIGION
(God)

MACROCOSM
(The Universe)

MICROCOSM
(Particle Universe)

MECHANISM
(Computers)

*Diagram 1*: The anthropic perspective

is to recognize that the cosmos is accessible to us only through human senses and an understanding of human experience – the anthropic view (see Diagram 1).[2] This places man at the centre of the universe but at the same time enables him to step outside and regard it with total objectivity, recognizing its predominantly subjective characteristics.

This seems the most promising way of looking at nature, provided our value judgements are correct. These depend on accurate assessments of the chief characteristics of human nature: self-knowledge and an understanding of our own sense impressions and behaviour. For example, ideas like balance and conflict or randomness and chance in nature must first be understood in a human context before we can impose the meanings of these states onto any cosmology. Thus the micro- and macrocosm are filtered through human perceptions and value judgements.

The second, most common, approach is to interpret existence piecemeal and in terms of rival theories concocted by specialists in religion, philosophy or science and filtered through the distorting lenses of purely materialistic, 'spiritual' or expert dogma. Here definitions of nature and human nature depend on pockets of expertise in fundamental particle physics, astronomy, religions, the technologies,

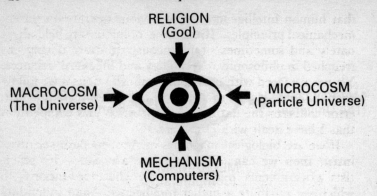

*Diagram 2*: The external, inward-looking perspective

or in other subjects (see Diagram 2) that may be unrelated to direct human experience.

The anthropic view is regarded as simplistic by most modern scientists largely because this was the method employed by the ancients, East and West, and by primitive cultures. While their knowledge was limited, many came closer to fundamental truths than we do despite our greater knowledge or perhaps because they were not overwhelmed by facts and theories. Clearly an anthropic orientation is preferable subject to the stated conditions, for it is easier to know ourselves than to be certain of the operations of the universe, many of which are inaccessible to direct experience. If, as in today's sciences, we speculate about ourselves from a limited external position, based on insufficiently objective criteria and observations, we are likely to assign the wrong meanings to our own perceptions and behaviours. This 'specialist expert' outlook is relatively objective (i.e. it excludes subjective components) and has led to misunderstandings epitomized by four self-contradictory conceptual errors that run through much of twentieth-century science and philosophy.

The first of these errors consists of the belief in an indeterminate, purposeless universe governed by chance; the second that our future is pre-determined; the third that human intelligence and behaviour operate on purely mechanical principles. These three 'opinions' are held alternately and sometimes simultaneously and are deeply entrenched in philosophy, psychology and the 'hard' sciences. Yet we are faced with untenable contradictions if we follow each of these ideas to their logical conclusions. (The fourth error concerns the nature of co-operation and competition that I have dealt with elsewhere.[AA])

If we are biological machines as most modern scientists insist, then we can only do as we are told – by scientists, governments, our genes or by whatever authority to which we attribute a higher intelligence – and individual responsibility goes out of the window. If nature is purely deterministic and mechanical, then past and future are pre-ordained and the conditions would be identical to a universe created by God. If the universe is indeterminate and governed by chance, then predicting the future would depend on the throw of symbolic dice and on forces of nature that modern science believes to be purposeless. In that case the processes of evolution, human behaviour or perceptions could not affect our future in the least. In other words a cosmos ruled by God, by purely mechanical laws or by chance must lead to similar conclusions – abrogation of individual responsibility.

The prevailing orientation in the sciences throughout the past four hundred years reflected the ideological climate of the times and was more often than not a product of dogma or fashion. For example, what passed for science was dictated by the Church until the sixteenth and seventeenth centuries. Dissent was a heresy often punished by death. Many philosophers, like René Descartes who is credited with being one of the first to employ the scientific method, avoided such a fate by disguising their views. Descartes is also reputed to have been one of the first mechanists, but he held quite different views from those popularly attributed to him, as I show in Chapter 3. On the other hand, Descartes's contemporary Blaise Pascal was a firm believer. He married an unqualified religious determinism to an unqualified belief in the mechanism of chance, based on an amalgam of faulty logic and religious fervour. In his correspondence with Pierre de Fermat he claimed that randomness creates chance, but in his famous wager he insisted that the toss of a coin must always come up in favour of the existence of God. This is equivalent to saying, 'Heads I win; tails you lose'; still a common position in religion, philosophy and science.

The desire to manipulate and control nature and human nature pre-dated Descartes by centuries. Science inherited these anti-human tendencies from political and religious institutions. Whenever neutral or anti-humanistic principles prevail in religions, philosophies and the sciences, the technologies degrade the quality of life. It is amazing that so much technological progress has been made despite this. But many scientific discoveries and theories are incomplete or speculative – half-truths that can be more damaging than outright fabrications – and many of our technologies are short-term solutions. They may work for a while, but this is no test of long-term value, efficiency or truth.

Classical and neo-Darwinism illustrate how the sciences have been tainted by society's false norms. Darwin's humanism was corrupted by Herbert Spencer's competitive and materialistic nineteenth-century outlook, the consequences of which we still suffer. For many modern ideas about evolutionary biology and the study of human and animal behaviour are products of an anthropomorphic (i.e. attributing human characteristics to animals) and malicious interpretation of the theory of the 'survival of the fittest', propounded by nineteenth-century theorists, politicians and economists.

The interpretation of Pavlov's work is another example of how prejudiced social ideas have corrupted the sciences. Pavlov is commonly thought to have discovered operant conditioning with reinforcement (i.e. carrot-and-stick training). For the sake of simplicity and because it is merely the other side of the same coin, I do not distinguish here between the carrot (conventional operant conditioning with reinforcement by reward) and the stick (reinforcement by punishment). Both methods have been used since time immemorial to control and manipulate individuals and populations. It is the basis of the stimulus/response, input/output approach in all sciences. Pavlov just showed scientifically how it works in a behavioural setting. But he made it possible for twentieth-century psychologists like F.W. Taylor, J.B. Watson, B.F. Skinner and Hans Eysenck to disguise their authoritarianism with scientific jargon, thus rationalizing long-established methods in education that stupefy perfectly intelligent people. Pavlov's studies led directly to behaviourist psychology, perhaps the most corrupting influence in the social sciences because it institutionalizes conformity and group-think – the enemies of independent thought and reason.

If carrot-and-stick training (stimulus/response) were the best way to learn, as is believed even by those who claim to oppose the behaviourist school of psychology, then we must certainly behave as if we were machines. But if we learn freely to reach self-originated goals within self-rewarding, socially responsible but ever-expanding limits, we have every opportunity to realize the best of what it means to be human. Humanness is therefore a conditional state of mind that colours our perceptions and is a precondition for the evolution of a humanistic science. We are unique as a species in so far as we can pick the right or the wrong options for our future, individually and together. We can predict and choose those that allow us to be at one with ourselves, one another and the universe, and to create whichever future is possible and most desirable. Or we can surrender to chaos and its inevitable consequence: authoritarian control.

Current scientific ideas about randomness, chance and predictability are derived from sixteenth- and seventeenth-century mathematical studies of games of chance by Galileo Galilei, Girolamo Cardano, Marin Mersenne, Blaise Pascal and Pierre de Fermat. Their speculations led to misconceptions that persist today, cloaked in the respectability of mathematics and enshrined on the altar of science. As a result, our ideas about the operations of randomness, chance and predictability turn out to be largely wrong.

One aspect of quantum theory based on these misconceptions – the uncertainty principle – illustrates my point. Quantum theory is a cornerstone of twentieth-century physics. It evolved in two parts: the discovery by Max Planck that light consists of discrete packets of energy called quanta that have both wavelike and particle characteristics, and Heisenberg's 'uncertainty principle' (discussed in Chapter 5). Only the latter is questioned here for it defines imprecision in the method of measurement rather than in the behaviour of fundamental particles. Without going into great detail, the uncertainty principle exemplifies a process whereby human transactions are misinterpreted in science and the results imposed on the supposed behaviour of fundamental particles of which the universe is made.

Physicists have likened the movements of such particles to what happens when a pack of playing cards is shuffled mindlessly. But their mistake is to assume that all future arrangements of the cards are entirely unpredictable. Suspicions have been voiced in recent years by David Bohm[3], Ilya Prigogine,[4] Benoit Mandelbrot[5] and Roger Penrose[6] that a fundamental order must underlie randomness and that the universe is creative and self-organizing, yet they do not explain of what such an order, creativity and self-organization might consist. The effects of randomness and its inevitable reduction of chance have not previously been demonstrated successfully in any of the sciences. The same is true in philosophy. Indeed until now no Western philosopher with whose work I am familiar – from Thales to Alfred J. Ayer and Karl Popper – no theologian or scientist has correctly identified the operations of randomness relative to chance and certainty in human affairs or in inorganic nature. Only the earliest Chinese Taoists intuited the truth about the operations of chance some 2,500 years ago, but their insights eventually became corrupted by superstition. As a result the effect of randomness on particle affiliations in nature as much as on biological mutation and evolution are misunderstood in our day. (The actual causes and consequences of randomness are explained in Chapter 5.)

In chaos theory, one of the more recent fads in science

(a more current one is 'self-organizing criticality',[7] a refurbished version of 'catastrophe theory'), the claim is made that the movements of fundamental particles are governed simultaneously by chance and by a theoretical 'fractal' order (fractals are patterns generated on a computer screen by mathematical formulae. In magnification they show repeat patterns that continue to infinity). Chaos theoreticians have proposed that we exist in a paradoxical universe of infinite order and simultaneous disorder. Science becomes meaningless when such self-contradictions are left unresolved. As a result, much of modern science has no firm foundation and is built on quicksand.

A different but related version of pseudo-scientific doublethink was provided by the Soviet agriculturalist Lysenko and illustrates how science is influenced by dogma of any kind.[8] During the heyday of Stalinist Russia he insisted that the genetic structure of grains and other plants could be altered by artificially manipulated environmental conditions, and that these new characteristics could be inherited by future generations; a theory that flew in the face of what was even then known about genetics. Russian scientists who disagreed with Lysenko were liquidated or sent to Siberia with Stalin's approval. Belief in this theory set back Russian agriculture and genetic research for decades. Lysenko and his colleagues got their ideas from the Communist dialectic which suggested that environmentally manipulated changes in human behaviour are genetically heritable. Lysenko claimed to have altered the genetic characteristics of cereals and vegetables by what would be equivalent to operant conditioning in a human context. In a behavioural and cultural sense (but not in a genetic one) Lysenko was correct, for those who allow themselves to be manipulated without thinking for themselves turn into quasi-vegetables or robots.

Western scientists were up in arms over the Lysenko affair without realizing that they were guilty of similar sins for different but equally disastrous ideological reasons. Some aspects of today's behaviour modification (for example, Delgado's attempts to alter human behaviour by means of electronic brain implants[9]) are derived from the same power-madness that motivated Lysenko. The history of what is known today as artificial intelligence similarly dramatizes how the wish to control man and nature can misdirect and pervert the legitimate aims of science (see Chapters 2 and 8). These are just a few of many examples of science and the technologies gone wrong.

A topsy-turvy approach to the sciences has succeeded in constructing a cosmology that is often divorced from human logic and reason. Additionally it has rendered mankind unaccountable rather than helping it to become individually and collectively responsible. Our ways of thought and behaviour are usually attributed to factors beyond our control like original sin, the ill will of the gods, chance, our genetic heritage or the environment. The present state of the ecology – a potentially fatal consequence of greed, an inappropriate use of the technologies, a disregard for organic realities and absurd attempts to 'conquer' nature – is one consequence of these misconceptions. Here, as in other matters, what counts are fundamental meanings deduced in an unprejudiced manner from the examination of causes, consequences and the operations that bring both about, relative to time, place, circumstances and behaviour.

The scientific view that man is fundamentally nothing but a programmable machine is rooted in religion. The same is true of other aspects of 'scientific' thought, like what is supposed to have happened prior to the big bang. Here science is silent for it claims that the scientific method breaks down at that point. Religions and philosophies have sought to resolve this question, yet their answers remain undemonstrable. All three methods of looking at the world have regarded mankind and the universe from an external, piecemeal and purely materialistic point of view, despite claims to 'spirituality' in religion, 'mind' in philosophy, and expressions of humanism in the sciences. There are huge gaps in our understanding, and confusion prevails as a result of the illogic that runs through much of our established knowledge, from the relatively trivial and mundane (for example, why and how we win at noughts and crosses or chess) to the most profound (why we exist).

So when in our search to understand the cosmos, as distinct from human nature, we attribute characteristics to the latter that are believed to apply to the former, we may erroneously conclude that both mankind and the universe share characteristics with machines and are manipulated by externals like gods. For, if we believe that man is a mechanism created by God or nature, then this becomes the universal standard. Roger Penrose, a mathematical physicist, provides yet another example of this kind of purely mechanistic science. He suggests that the human central nervous system may operate on quantum principles.[10] Signals may indeed arrive at nerve junctions (synapses) in 'packets', but the uncertainty principle could not possibly be operative here. If it were true then we could never be certain of anything. Equally disastrous is when we misunderstand human behaviour – for example, what happens when we shuffle a pack of cards mindlessly – draw the wrong conclusions from this experience and then attribute them to the operations of the particle universe. This again illustrates that our universe can be understood only in a human context and must first be filtered through human senses – the anthropic view. The universe may or may not be as we perceive it, yet all we can know and understand depends on our perceptions.

To question the established wisdom should be the business of everyone who has any concern for the future. For we ourselves are to blame for the rapidly declining quality of life and the prospects of a dismal future. A cultural and scientific inheritance based on pure materialism and self-delusion threatens our social, physical and intellectual existence. The poisoning of our globe by nuclear waste is a technological symptom of these trends. It has been known for more than forty years that tailings from uranium mines, waste from the production of nuclear weapons and energy and the factories that produce both, once they become obsolete, are lethally radioactive for millions of years. No containers or safe storage places can last that long and these wastes will inevitably leak into soil and sea. Rather than stop nuclear weapons and energy production, scientists have encouraged its proliferation in collusion with governments. Energy producers – public and private – have made fortunes by building factories that may eventually make large sections of the planet uninhabitable for tens of thousands of centuries.

Even now many of the earliest nuclear plants are being dismantled for permanent storage. The rest will need the same treatment sooner or later at an infinitely greater cost than the benefit of the energy that was produced. Some of this waste is presently stored in leaky containers. Those who financed the original plants profited in the short term. Now taxpayers must defray the cost of storage and pay with their health and lives for increasingly dangerous radioactive pollution until a way is found to neutralize nuclear waste. Even if such a technique were to be discovered, interim storage will become incredibly unsafe and expensive. The responsibility belongs to nuclear scientists, technologists and their political and industrial masters, many of whom blinded themselves to the causes and consequences of their work or knowingly accepted high salaries and profits for promoting policies that are ruining the ecology.

So this is how our social attitudes impinge on the sciences and the technologies and affect our daily lives. Conditioned thinking in one affects the others. This can be seen not only in Western societies but becomes even more obvious in former Iron Curtain countries. Instead of freeing themselves from their conditioning, many former dissidents who believe that they have been liberated from the tyranny of the left are reverting to that of nationalism, factionalism or fundamentalist religions. Each ethnic, scientific or political group seeks to win at the expense of the rest. A better world – and better science – is impossible for as long as these attitudes persist.

The failure of classical Communism – the dictatorship of a bureaucracy that is solely motivated by self-interest but that pretends to speak for the masses – is one of the signs of our times. Conventional capitalism – a dictatorship of greed and perpetually increased profits obtained by unfettered free enterprise – is equally a failure that has yet to be faced. Democracy as understood today suffers from related flaws. Like politics, the sciences operate on the basis of control, operant conditioning (rule by carrot and stick), stimulus/response, input/output and a preoccupation with symptoms and operations. As a result most scientists play a mechanistic, quantitatively (competitive winning and losing) rather than qualitatively competitive (i.e. co-operative and organic) game. Although this process has gone on for centuries, we seem to be approaching a climax.

No options other than those we exercise at the moment seem to have occurred to anyone, but they exist. Because of our blindness to alternatives and their meanings we appear to be coming to what some believe to be the end of history. But like those who prophesy the end of anything – the world or, as in the 1960s, the death of God – they could be in for a disappointment. We face a possible new beginning: a future that could consist of what should be, rather than what is. The opportunities for such a development have never been greater. But if they are not grasped we may remain stuck in our current dark age of superstition for a very long time, repeating a disastrous history, and possibly do irreversible damage to ourselves and our world.

If we are indeed that which asks the question, as Eddington correctly stated (see the quote that heads this chapter), then we have the capacity to think and learn independently, are responsible for our actions and create our own fate. But do questions concerning our destiny and their possible answers matter? And, if so, why and to whom? Why should anyone care whether or not we are biological machines? Would answers to questions about whether we are heading for heaven, hell, Armageddon, nirvana, or a perpetual increase in the entropic rate change anyone or anything of consequence? What if we discovered a factual basis for the belief that some invisible reality governs our existence – call it soul, mind, psyche, God, a self-organizing, creative universe or any other abstraction? What if it can be demonstrated that there is a purpose in nature? Would such ideas affect us individually and our relations to one another?

The answers to such questions are certainly 'yes'. What we know factually or believe intuitively concerning the nature of nature is affected by and affects how we think and feel about ourselves and each other; how we learn and educate our children; the meaning of freedom; the rights of the state over the individual and the latter's rights and obligations; the purpose and future of work, social and political organization, justice, morals and ethics. These in turn affect the sciences. Answers to puzzles like the meaning of life, determinacy and chance are bound up with fundamental questions concerning the mechanical or other-than-mechanical nature of man and the universe.

The logic that emerges from the propositions suggested here concerns relative predictability. Our present knowledge defines the horizon of our future; one that can be pushed further and expanded with perpetual learning and understanding. In other words, the more aware we are – perceive, know, learn and understand – the further we can see into the future, recognize options and analyse the past with perpetually enhanced precision. Armed with such an understanding we can correctly interpret our often regrettable history and have the power to choose a better future out of the welter of possibilities.

Neural network analysis – the model or paradigm-generator on which this book is based – provides a path to creative diversity rather than oppressive conformity; to responsible freedom rather than anarchy; self-control rather than control from without; consciousness rather than unawareness. It suggests that there is a far greater number of options than were previously imagined. All of this permits us to redefine human purposes and meanings: how we learn; why we think and behave as we do; whether we do so mechanically or organically; whether we choose our future, or hope for the best and continue to repeat the mistakes of the past. Our future depends on whether we come to understand which choices we have and what each choice means.

The questions dealt with here include those relating to the nature of the smallest particle; the origin of the universe and its possible end, or indeed whether there was a beginning or might be an end; the relationship between the relatively objective and subjective aspects of time and existence; and whether there might be more than a single universe. These subjects are discussed here in as much detail as space permits. My object is to outline ideas that are logically and philosophically tenable. Some are amenable to mathematical demonstration. Others may, in time, be demonstrable experimentally. As I have said, the ideas expressed here are derived from an analysis of principles on which our central nervous system – the filter of our perceptions – operates. Nothing exists for us outside what human beings can perceive, know and imagine. There may be other realities in the universe but they are not accessible to us, at least at this stage of our evolution. We can therefore safely ignore them until we can call upon new knowledge.

The perspectives that emerge from a reconsideration of beliefs and supposed facts resolve some of the paradoxes and absurdities that are found in science, philosophy and religion. A growing disenchantment with the established wisdom is made apparent by the legitimate cynicism of students; a general, justifiable distrust of authority; a questioning of current scientific and philosophical perceptions, of the technologies and ideologies of the right, left and centre; the number of those who turn to esoteric cults; a proliferation of gurus who promise imminent nirvana or predict the end of the world; a resurgence of superstitions like astrology; a New Age liturgy derived from ancient belief systems, and a return to fundamentalist beliefs by Jewish, Christian, Muslim and other fanatics. A search for ancient values or a new paradigm has been in the making for some time – often confused and misdirected – but a search that must eventually lead to a world view that differs from present-day ones in significant respects if we are to survive and prosper.

# 2
# Nothing but a Machine

'The purposive aspects of reflexes, especially in the higher organisms ... have given biologists the impression that the organism is a "machine" ... But in their somewhat hasty enthusiasm for this comparison the mechanists have forgotten that every machine is constructed for a given end, and that it presupposes a mechanician who has designed and constructed it.'
Eugenio Rignano[1]

A machine's output is pre-determined by the input (i.e. stimulus/response). In practical terms, a machine is a substitute for brute-force muscular activity (like a crane), or for rote mental skills (for example, a calculator) that can out-perform human labour in certain respects. A machine can also mechanize work that would otherwise be impossible (a sewing needle, for example). As man constructed ever more complex machines that mimicked, facilitated or supplanted human effort, philosophers began to view human behaviour in purely mechanical terms. Indeed, once wedded to this convenient and erroneous idea, they characterized all of nature and human nature as operating on nothing but mechanical principles; a concept that has shaped our social and learning behaviours as well as the course of the sciences and technologies.

In later chapters I elaborate some of the religious,

philosophical and scientific origins of this misconception. Here I confine myself predominantly to its technological history because it is a blatant, sometimes unintentionally funny, and more often tragic example of the confusion of values that underlie the man-machine debate.

## Automata

The technologies have always represented power. The Egyptian priests claimed to be able to predict the annual flooding of the Nile by a ritualistic communion with the gods. This seeming magic enthralled believers who were unaware that their spiritual leaders consulted secret reservoirs built underground that enabled them to measure with precision the annual rise and fall of the river. The same was true of religious statues that appeared to move on their own or to speak. The principles learnt from these frauds led to the development of hydraulic mechanisms like the fountains and mechanical toys of Hero of Alexandria in about 100 A.D.[2], and the waterworks and windmills of medieval Europe[3]. The originally ritualistic, mystical and later playful origins of machines were followed by the evolution of useful ones like corn threshing and grinding machines, mining equipment and, eventually, mechanical clocks.

The Chinese developed sophisticated machines and water-clocks centuries before they were discovered in the West. But early Chinese philosophers were aware of a key difference between man and machine that is not often appreciated even today. For when a machine is taken apart it can always be reassembled to function as before, whereas dissection of an organism destroys it permanently. A Chinese record of the third century B.C. tells the story of a presumably legendary craftsman, Yen Shih, who had invented a mechanical man in the time of King Mu of Chou. It illustrates the point I have just made and the superior logic of early Taoists.

'Who is that man accompanying you?' asked the king. 'That sir,' replied Yen Shih, 'is my own handiwork. He can sing and he can act.' The king stared at the figure in astonishment. It walked with rapid strides, moving its head up and down, so that anyone would have taken it for a live human being. The artificer touched its chin, and it began singing, perfectly in tune. He touched its hand, and it began posturing, keeping perfect time. It went through any number of movements that fancy might happen to dictate. The king, looking on with his favourite concubine and other beauties, could hardly persuade himself that it was not real. As the performance was drawing to an end, the robot winked its eye and made advances to the ladies in attendance, whereupon the king became incensed and would have had Yen Shih executed on the spot had not the latter, in mortal fear, instantly taken the robot to pieces to let him see what it really was. And, indeed, it turned out to be only a construction of leather, wood, glue and lacquer . . . Examining it closely, the king found all the internal organs complete – liver, gall, heart, lungs, spleen, kidneys, stomach and intestines; and over these again, muscles, bones and limbs with their joints, skin, teeth and hair, all of them artificial. Not a part but was fashioned with the utmost nicety and skill; and when it was put together again, the figure presented the same appearance as when first brought in. The king tried the effect of taking away the heart, and found that the mouth could no longer speak; he took away the liver and the eyes could no longer see; he took away the kidneys and the legs lost their power of locomotion . . .[4]

Not until the fourteenth century did machines and automata (clockwork-operated animal and human-like robots) become the prevailing analogy for intelligent life in Europe. Perhaps the most famous examples dating from this time are the animated apostles that march round Strasbourg Cathedral's clock when it strikes the hours. (The primitive belief in the lifelike characteristics of machines is basically the same as that of modern scientists who believe that computers are potentially artificially intelligent because they mimic certain human behaviours.) By the eighteenth century the mechanistic world view had become so prevalent that it was believed as an article of faith in and outside the sciences. 'Proof' seemed to exist everywhere. A man named Jacques Vaucanson was said to have 'invented' life in a form described in his handbills distributed in Paris in 1738 as: 'An artificial duck made of gilded copper who drinks, eats, quacks, splashes about on the water, and digests food like a living duck.'[5]

Vaucanson was hailed a genius by monarchs, philosophers and scientists wherever his marvellous duck performed. It quacked and waddled realistically about the gilded drawing-rooms of eighteenth-century Europe, pecking grain spread before it. But far more miraculous was that after apparently having digested what it had eaten, this duck expelled genuine duck turds from an orifice at its rear on to the Persian carpets and Sheraton table-tops on which it performed, to the amazement of royalty and commoners. How could Vaucanson have achieved anything other than the creation of mechanical life, when his duck clearly quacked, moved, ate, digested and eliminated like any living creature?

Vaucanson, a believer in the man-machine myth, had come from Grenoble to Paris in 1735 with the intention of discovering the secrets of mechanical life. This proved to be rather more difficult than he anticipated and he ran out of money. An entrepreneur as well as a mechanic, Vaucanson refinanced himself by making lifelike automata and exhibiting them to paying audiences. Far from his goal, Vaucanson pretended that he had already succeeded (like many of today's researchers in artificial intelligence, expert systems and neural networks), and felt justified in fooling the public because he was certain that he might succeed eventually.

Admiring audiences flocked to pay for the privilege of being deceived. Vaucanson fared equally well with a mechanical flute player and other automata he built before he vanished from popular sight, devoting himself to the design of programmable power looms. He never managed to create mechanical life (and neither will anyone else for reasons given in later chapters). One of Vaucanson's automata survives at the Musée des Arts et Métiers in Paris, but his duck disappeared towards the middle of the nineteenth century after a distinguished commercial career.

Early in the eighteenth century, Jonathan Swift, like many satirists before him and since, foresaw the consequences of adopting the machine as an analogy of life. In his satirical novel *Gulliver's Travels* he describes Gulliver's experiences in Laputa where he encountered the forerunner of the 'intelligent' computer.

> After salutations ... he [the first Professor] said [that] ... by his Contrivance, the most ignorant Person at a reasonable Charge, and with a little bodily Labour, may write books on Philosophy, Poetry, Politicks, Law, Mathematicks and Theology, without the least Assistance from Genius or Study. He then led me to the Frame ... composed of several bits of Wood ... linked together by slender Wires ... covered on every Square with Paper pasted on them; and on these Papers were written all the Words of their Language in their several Moods, Tenses, and Declensions, but without any Order ... The Pupils at his Command took each of them hold of an Iron Handle ... and giving them a sudden Turn, the whole Disposition of the Words was entirely changed ... and where they found three or four Words together that might make Part of a Sentence, they dictated to the four remaining boys who were Scribes ... The Professor showed me several Volumes ... of broken sentences, which he intended to piece together; and out of those rich Materials to give the World a compleat Body of all Arts and Sciences, which however might still be improved, and much expedited, if the Publick would raise a Fund for making and employing five hundred such Frames ...[6]

Other well-known automata are worth describing for, like Swift's imaginative 'contrivance', they mirror almost exactly the claims made for the computers and robots of today and tomorrow. One of the more extraordinary automata described by Brewster, the nineteenth-century inventor of the kaleidoscope, concerns a mechanical toy made for Louis XIV when he was a child. This mechanism, if it existed as described,

> ... consisted of a small coach, which was drawn by two horses, and which contained the figure of a lady within,

with a footman and page behind. When this machine was placed at the extremity of a table of the proper size, the coachman smacked his whip, and the horses immediately set off moving their legs in a natural manner, and drawing the coach after them. When the coach reached the opposite edge of the table, it turned sharply at a right angle, and proceeded along the adjacent edge. As soon as it arrived opposite the place where the king sat it stopped; the page descended and opened the coach door; the lady alighted, and with a courtesy presented a petition, which she held in her hand, to the king. After waiting some time she again courtesied and re-entered the carriage. The page closed the door, and having resumed his place behind, the coachman whipped his horses and drove on. The footman, who had previously alighted, ran after the carriage, and jumped up behind into his former place.[7]

In 1748 the Marquis of Worcester, infected by the popular infatuation with automata, offered to develop numerous mechanical inventions provided he was subsidized out of the public purse (like today's AI researchers):

> . . . in his Address to the King, Lords and Commons, that he had try'd and perfected, and humbly offered to perform, for the Service of the King, Advantage of the Kingdom, and Profit and Pleasure of every individual Subject . . . How to make a brazen or stone-head, in the midst of a great field or garden, so artificial and natural, that, tho' a man speak never so softly, and even whisper into the ear thereof, it will presently open its mouth, and resolve the question in *French, Latin, Welsh, Irish, or English*, in good terms, uttering it out of its mouth, and then shut it until the next question be asked.[8]

This was but one of a long list of 'intelligent' automata for which the Marquis requested 'R&D' support from His Majesty. The Government, evidently wiser then than today, declined to fund this universal translation machine which linguists and computer scientists in the EEC, Britain, Japan and the United States are still seeking, supported with huge amounts of public money.

Eighteenth-century accounts of automata were often more inventive than Swift's satire or machines that actually existed. For example, it was reported in 1754 in *The Gentleman's Magazine* that:

> There is shewn at the hotel of *Monaco* at Versailles, an automaton of the figure of a man, larger than the life and painted the natural colour, placed on a tun, which pronounces most distinctly a considerable number of words and sentences, the letters of the alphabet, and the months of the year; wishes the company good morrow, etc. To put it in motion there are required only a bellows and a cylinder. This most envious machine has been seen with admiration by the whole court.[9]

The story of the Great Turk Chess-player, invented by von Kempelen in the eighteenth century, is detailed elsewhere[AA] and does not bear repetition, but its originator did not stop there. He continued his colourful career, as reported in another issue of *The Gentleman's Magazine*: 'Three automatons are now exhibited at Paris – the first writes the names of persons; the second copies drawings; and the third, which is a *chef d'oeuvre*, speaks and articulates distinctly. They were made by an ingenious mechanic, named KEMPER.'[10] It seems hardly possible that this could have been anyone other than von Kempelen, alias Kempett, who had sold the Great Turk Chess-player to a man named Maelzl. The latter allegedly added it to his stock of automata, according to the *British Register* of December 1808:

> M. Maelzl, a German mechanist, is at present exhibiting an Automaton of a singular construction. The figure represents a trumpeter in the uniform of the band of the French Imperial Guards, and at the word of command raises a trumpet to his mouth and plays some exquisite pieces of martial music. The whole of the mechanism is contained within the chest of the Automaton: its feet rest upon a board to which casters are affixed, and the proprietor moves it from place to place, in the exhibition room, to shew that there is no communication with any other apartment. In this respect it is superior to the celebrated flute-player of

Vaucanson, which once made so much noise in Europe. The latter figure reclined against a wall, behind which some complicated machinery was supposed to be placed. The most wonderful part of M. Maelzl's Automaton, is the effect produced by the lips of the figure upon the trumpet, which are made to exhibit all the delicacy of touch peculiar to the lips of the human body. No jarring or creaking sound of the machinery is to be heard, although the ear is applied close to the body of the Automaton, nor can any musical sound be emitted unless when the trumpet is applied to the mouth. At the conclusion of the exhibition, M. Maelzl sits down to a pianoforte, and his trumpeter performs an accompaniment to several pieces of music, with all the precision of a first-rate performer . . .[11]

If this was not a hoax like the Great Turk, then Mr Maelzl could have taught a thing or two to today's American, European and Japanese computer experts.

## Robotto Okaku

Japan has its own history when it comes to automata, reflected in its Shinto, Bushido and Samurai warrior cults. Japan proudly refers to itself as *robotto okaku* (the kingdom of robots), an apt description of its feudal culture that has not changed in essence through the centuries, although cracks are now appearing in the traditional image that Japan has of itself.

An influx of Western technology began when Portuguese Jesuit priests arrived in Japan in 1543 and brought with them the first clockworks seen there. The Japanese were astonished by mechanisms that seemed to reflect some of their cultural characteristics, but with which they were entirely unfamiliar. Western technologies must have seemed like magic to the Japanese who first encountered them, but they are a highly skilled people with a long tradition of craft. It is therefore not surprising that then, as today, they efficiently copied many of the inventions of the 'barbarians', improving them and substituting local materials for European ones.

In following centuries, with intermittent isolation and a return to traditional crafts alternating with frantic efforts to emulate and surpass the West technologically, the Japanese converted their feudal and militaristic *robotto okaku* into a post-World War II, economically combative robot kingdom. For this the Japanese pay a heavy price. Frederik Schodt provides the details of this historic evolution,[12] starting with the first Japanese imitation of a European clockwork automaton – *karakuri*, a tea-serving doll – that became a traditional Japanese artefact. It was described in 1675 by the poet Saikaku Ihara. Other presumably erotic automata were exhibited in Osaka's red-light district as early as 1662. Ingenious variations – *hanare karakuri* (freely operating automata consisting of spring-driven acrobats that fly from one trapeze to the next without visible controls) – became classic Japanese festival toys. It is but a short step from excessive conformity and mechanistic private and public behaviour to an infatuation with mechanical toys and to the enthusiasm with which Japan has embraced computer-controlled robots as culturally compatible and economically advantageous tools.

The relatively unchanging Japanese character and its preoccupation with imitation and robotics is of special significance in the context of this book. A statement made in 1982 by Yasuo Kato, senior executive at Nippon Electric Corporation, reflects and indeed seems to praise this conditioned psychological orientation towards non-originality, competitive imitation and machine-like conformity: 'We are not so creative because the creative mind is peculiar, and we Japanese don't like anything peculiar. We believe that everyone should be the same.'[13]

Not even the importation of Buddhism or the earlier humanistic Tao philosophy of original Chinese settlers in the Japanese archipelago prevented the evolution of the warrior cults of Bushido and Shinto, both of which celebrate machine-like obedience. This paradox seems to have been resolved by recent anthropological discoveries. It is now believed that the earliest Chinese invaders, rather than destroying the combative Ainu aborigines of Japan after defeating them in battle, employed them as military guards for the ruling caste. The Chinese aristocracy intermarried with their Ainu servants, thus inheriting certain physical characteristics and adopting some of their cultural traits. Japan's ruling families still share physical characteristics with the Ainu that are not found in the rest of the population. These developments in Japan's prehistoric past are now believed to account for many of the contradictions in Japan's modern culture.

The part-Chinese and part-Ainu aristocracy is said to have kept alive the latter's warrior-cult attitudes (now transformed into principles of economic warfare and imperialism) in which robotic and excessively controlled behaviour was transmitted from one generation to the next by ritualistically enforced conditioning. It imposed conformity in war and peace to an extent that seems extreme to non-Japanese. It has also fostered an absolutism that tends to crush creativity and individuality but encourages perfect imitation – the characteristics of machines. Even Japanese cultural rituals, pleasing as they are, tend to reflect mechanistic virtuosity and have at times been automated to be performed by *karakuri*. (This explanation of Japan's cultural history is not popular among Japanese, although in time they may accept it.)

The introduction into Japan of lifelike mechanisms – *karakuri* dolls or computer-controlled industrial robots – that Japanese craftsmen copied from the West and at times improved, served as a fatal reinforcement of the worst features of Japan's mechanistic culture. Absolute obedience (programmed instruction) is the only form of co-operation Japanese know in their military, social, political, economic and educational lives. During World War II this attitude produced willing *kamikaze* pilots, the brutal fanaticism of Japanese soldiers (similar to that of certain Muslim groups), and the inhuman treatment of prisoners of war, who were regarded as inferior human machines undeserving of compassion. It has also conditioned Japanese employees to be willingly exploited and to work under often intolerable or excessively paternalistic conditions. The same mindless brutality (overlaid with a deceptive ritualistic but meaning-less politeness, born of a mechanistic approach to life) is a formidable weapon in Japan's economic competition with the rest of the world. Such competitiveness inevitably leads to the economic and political corruption which has surfaced in recent years. It may prove just as costly and disastrous as the military and nationalistic competitiveness that led to Japan's attempted domination of Mongolia and the Pacific before and during World War II.

Japan's educational system has become more competitive and dictatorial as a result of the mechanization of thought (produced by pitiless operant conditioning that frequently drives more sensitive students to suicide). Japan's academics and students may know more than those in the West but they understand less – least of all the psychological effect of a competitive, mechanistic outlook and the robot technologies to which they have become addicted. None of this is said in the spirit of anti-Japanese paranoia currently felt in the US and the EEC. It is an analysis of the historic reasons for prevailing Japanese cultural attitudes.

But what of Japanese art? It would be inaccurate to say that this is uncreative because there are two forms of human creativity: origination and arrangement (as, for example, in a musical composition or that of flowers and rock gardens). Ideally a creative individual originates and then works out variations and arrangements that seem most aesthetic or appropriate, but that is not always the case. Original or innovative creation is discouraged in Japan because of the mechanistic orientation of its culture. For that reason, arrangement is its dominant art form and this determines the quality of its crafts, technologies and social life.

The difference between Japan and the rest of the world lies in its uniform society, which none the less adapts foreign technologies and makes them its own, with few humanistic or humane concerns. Isolated and primitive tribes have shared similar cultural profiles, but few survived once they were penetrated by foreign invaders because, unlike the Japanese, they lacked the means to copy and better their conquerors' technologies. Japan, alone among technologically advanced nations, has never experimented with any philosophical orientation other than its own nationalistic, mechanistic and exclusive one. When penetrated by subjective foreign ideas (e.g. Buddhism), Japan has always converted them into relatively objective ones (Zen Buddhism). The belligerent forms of Japanese martial arts – Judo and Karate – are very different from Chinese defensive ones like Kung Fu.

## Human Robots

Japan's modern mechanistic culture is clearly unlike that of China and the West. But there are similarities. Historically, China has fluctuated between an essentially Taoist, humanistic orientation and one that has been at times as brutal and mechanistic as that of the Japanese or our own, as attested by the 1989 Tiananmen Square massacre. Further, original Tao principles were modified and altered by Confucians who provided a philosophical framework for a tradition-bound, moralistic culture.

Today's China shares the social and political dilemmas of former Iron Curtain countries. They want democracy, self-determination, economic freedom, freedom of expression and a caring society. Yet they tend to confuse these with Western materialism and consumerism. The consequences are lack of self-discipline, irresponsibility and the wrong forms of competition. This is the psychological malaise of the West that causes economic instability, despite superficial well-being. Carrying out a policy of reduced industrialization in favour of rapid agricultural and labour-intensive industrial expansion, the Chinese Government seems to have fallen once more into the trap of using its own population as a substitute for machines (as during the Cultural Revolution); a pre-industrial mechanistic orientation in a modern setting that is as damaging to individual freedom and initiative as is quantitatively competitive free enterprise. That paradox, found in all Western societies (and in Japan), is one to which the Russians and East Europeans are starting to awaken now that the euphoria and confusion caused by their new-found freedom has worn off. Gorbachev seems to recognize this problem, but few in the East or the West appear to share his understanding.

## Clocks and Souls

The founders of modern scientific thought – Nicolaus Copernicus, Johannes Kepler, Galileo, Pascal, Pierre de Fermat, René Descartes and Isaac Newton – attempted to wed supposedly non-materialistic Judeo-Christian theologies to a new world view that dealt with what were believed to be objective facts uncovered by scientific methods and applied technologically. They tried to divide the world of knowledge into two categories – subjective (religious) and objective (scientific and technological) – each ruling over separate domains. Inevitably these two worlds were perpetually at war with one another, as evolutionists and creationists are to this day.

Descartes, like many before him and since, sought to bridge these two categories of thought, perhaps for reasons of self-preservation. You could be excommunicated or killed if you did not genuflect to the religious orthodoxy of the day. But Pascal, his contemporary, certainly acted on the basis of convictions brought about by his conversion to Jansenism in his middle years. However, he failed to harmonize his religious and scientific beliefs and he was a mechanist at heart. Descartes, disguising his humanism, was said to believe that human beings are machines superior to animals because we enjoy God's gifts of speech, thought and reason. But in fact he was essentially an atheist, as is revealed by a proper translation of his statement, 'Cogito; ergo sum' (see Chapter 3). Descartes's sometimes ambiguous views are summarized by the following:

> The only difference I can see between machines and natural objects is that the workings of machines are mostly carried out by apparatus large enough to be readily perceptible by the senses (as is required to make their manufacture

humanly possible), whereas natural processes almost always depend on parts so small that they utterly elude our senses. But mechanics, which is a part or species of physics, uses no concepts but belong also to physics; and it is just as 'natural' for a clock composed of such-and-such wheels to tell the time, as it is for a tree grown from such-and-such seed to produce a certain fruit. So, just as men of experience of machinery, when they know what a machine is for, and can see part of it, can readily form a conjecture about the way its unseen parts are fashioned; in the same way, starting from sensible effects and sensible parts of bodies, I have tried to investigate the insensible causes and particles underlying them.

This may give us an idea of the possible constitution of Nature; but we must not conclude that this is the actual constitution. There might be two clocks made by the same craftsman, equally good time-keepers, and with absolute similar outsides; and yet the trains of wheels inside might be completely different. Similarly, the supreme Craftsman might have produced all that we see in a variety of ways . . .[14]

. . . it seems reasonable, since art copies nature, and men can make various automata which move without thought, that nature should produce its own automata, much more splendid than artificial ones. These natural automata are the animals . . .[15]

But to Descartes human beings are very different from what he believed animals to be. He attributed this difference to the human soul, an undefinable entity that gave rise to what today is called Cartesian dualism (the relation of body to soul) or the mind-body problem. Pascal appeared to be in agreement with Descartes except in degree, because he believed that while man was a machine, he enjoyed God's grace. I will return later to the differences between the views of Descartes and Pascal. What concerns us here is that ever since, many scientists and philosophers who are religiously inspired as much as those who are agnostics or atheists have believed in a universe that functions like a clockwork. Religious scientists disagreed with the others only in so far as they regarded man as nothing but a machine into which God had infused 'spirit' by endowing him with a soul, without changing his fundamentally machine-like characteristics.

Lewis Mumford understood much of this, although he dwelt almost exclusively on the history of mindless (rather than intelligent) mechanization. Unfortunately he also perpetuated the conventional misinterpretation of Descartes's writing.

> Descartes's original recognition of the lifelike qualities of clockwork, which exhibit a highly advanced form of mechanical organization, tempted him to introduce the extraneous form of mechanism into his analysis of organic behaviour . . . To account for the orderly behavior of living beings Descartes introduced the concept of the machine which, more than any conceivable organism, is the product of design from start to finish. Even more than Newton's divine organizer, the machine model introduced teleology or finalism in its classic form: a purposeful organization for a strictly predetermined end. This corresponds to nothing whatever in organic evolution.
>
> By accepting the machine as his model, and a single unifying mind as the source of absolute order [i.e. God], Descartes in effect brought every manifestation of life, ultimately, under rational, centrally directed control – rational, that is, provided one did not look too closely at the nature and intentions of the controller. In doing so, he set a fashion in thought that was to prevail with increasing success for the next three centuries.
>
> On Descartes's assumptions, the work of science, if not the destiny of life, was to widen the empire of the machine. Lesser minds seized on this error, enlarged it, and made it fashionable.[16]

Descartes was never guilty of the sins attributed to him by Mumford and others who were misled by mistranslations and misinterpretations of his work and did not understand what he really meant. De la Mettrie, an eighteenth-century author still quoted as Descartes's authoritative interpreter, was one of the earliest to twist his writings to suit his own prejudices.

## Man a Machine

Julien Offray de la Mettrie had fallen under the spell of what was attributed to Descartes (rather than what he actually meant) and of a mechanistic explanation of life. In 1748 he wrote a book called *L'Homme Machine* (*Man a Machine*)[17] which had intriguing consequences that reached well into the twentieth century.

De la Mettrie's book became an instant success and was translated into English in the year following its first French publication. That same year also saw the first work written in opposition, followed by several others respectively titled *Man More than a Machine*,[18] *Denial of Man a Machine*,[19] *On Man's Machine and Soul*[20] and *Refutation of Man a Machine*.[21] The first of these critical rebuttals declared on its title page that it 'contradicted and disproved the abominable opinions' of M. de la Mettrie, but that work is reputed to have been written by de la Mettrie himself to heighten controversy and increase the sales of *Man a Machine*.

De la Mettrie was born in St Malo in 1709. He studied theology and logic in Paris under the tutelage of Jansenists, the fundamentalist Christian sect that Pascal had joined in the previous century. However, de la Mettrie decided not to enter the Church and instead studied medicine at Rheims where he graduated in 1733. He continued his studies in Leyden until 1742 when he returned to Paris to practise. Falling ill and near death he underwent a conversion of sorts, deciding that living beings were nothing but machines and publishing his first book, *Natural History of the Soul*.[22] As a result of the clerical uproar caused by publication of this book (similar to today's protests by Muslim fundamentalists against Salman Rushdie's *Satanic Verses*) and a number of other anti-theological satires he had written, de la Mettrie hurriedly left Paris and returned to Leyden in 1746 where he published *Man a Machine*.[23] Once again he created a furore that forced him to flee to Prussia where he joined the Academy of Sciences and the Court of Frederick the Great as Frederick's protégé, personal physician and philosopher.

Frederick was captivated by de la Mettrie's philosophy. This Prussian soldier-king found the man-machine image to his liking. Frederick was a confirmed mechanist himself; perhaps the first to insist on 'close-order drill', a method of conditioning soldiers to become mindless robots still favoured in most of the world's armies (and codified later by von Clausewitz[AA]). In the eighteenth and nineteenth centuries it resulted in soldiers lining up and kneeling in ranks to fire on their opponents who, having fixed targets, mowed them down like sheaves of wheat. These methods led to blind military obedience and a barbaric increase in combat casualties. Frederick's military philosophy has prevailed since then with few exceptions. The following are quotes from *Man a Machine*:

> Man is a machine so composed, that it is impossible to form at first a clear idea thereof, and consequently to define it ... Even Galen knew this truth ... In diseases the soul is sometimes as it were eclipsed ... Sometimes the noblest genius in the world sinks into stupidity, and never after recovers. Farewell, then to all those noble acquisitions of learning obtained with so much labour.[24]

The author then sets out to prove that man's thoughts, feelings and intentions depend on his physical state of the moment, using the following as an example. He was obviously convinced that we are no more or less than what we eat and that our psychology is at the mercy of our appetites, a view not dissimilar to that held by Sigmund Freud 170 years later, who believed that most human behaviour is dictated by sexual fantasies, fulfilment or frustration.

> There was, in Switzerland, a magistrate called Monsieur Steiguer, of Wittighofen: this gentlemen was, when fasting, the most upright and merciful judge; but woe to the wretch who came before him when he had made a hearty dinner! He was then disposed to hang every body, the innocent as well as the guilty ...
>   I shall only conclude what evidently follows from these incontestable observations: first that the more savage

animals are, the less brains they have: secondly, that this organ seems to be greater in some measure, in proportion to their docility: thirdly, that there is a constant and very surprising law of nature, that the more is gained on the side of understanding and wit, the more is lost on the side of instinct.[25]

De la Mettrie also anticipated evolutionary principles that were not elaborated until later in the century by T. R. Malthus, J.P.B.A. Lamarck, Erasmus Darwin, and in the nineteenth century by Darwin's grandson and author of *The Origins of Species* (Charles Darwin), who suffered from the influence of his friend Herbert Spencer: 'The transition from animal to man is [in] no way violent . . . What was man before the invention of words, and the knowledge of language? nothing but an animal of this kind . . .'[26] (It must be kept in mind that de la Mettrie, like Descartes, believed animals to be pure machines.)

But then de la Mettrie also foresaw the approach of behaviourist psychologists of the twentieth century and defined their views of operant conditioning with reinforcement (carrot-and-stick training) as the best and only method of education:

Words, language, laws, sciences, and the liberal arts were introduced [by and to mankind] in time, and by them the rough diamond of our understanding was polished. Man has been broke[n] and trained up, like any other animal; and he has learnt to be an author, as well as to be a porter. Geometricians have contrived to make the most difficult demonstrations and calculations, just as a monkey to put on, or take off his little hat, or jump upon his tractable dog . . . Nothing, we see, is so simple as the mechanism of our education! All is reduced to sounds and words, that from the mouth of one pass thro' the ears of another, into the brain . . . Let us enter into a sort of detail of those springs which move the human machine.[27]

Like many twentieth-century psychologists, de la Mettrie in the eighteenth century confused automatic, genetically conditioned responses like eye-blink and heart-beat with conditioned psychological traits and beliefs on the one hand and independent learning on the other. He seized on Vaucanson's automata that had just then made their first appearances in Paris as the analogy for human behaviour:

> [since] it required more art in Vaucanson to frame his mechanical musician, than in making his duck, sure then it must require still a greater degree of skill to form a speaking machine, which, perhaps, may not be altogether impossible . . . In the same manner we must suppose it necessary, that nature should make use of more art and preparation in the formation of a machine, which for a whole age is able to mark the throbbings of the heart . . . It can be no mistake if I suppose the body of a man to be a clock, though a stupendous one . . .
>
> To be a machine, to feel, to think, to be able to distinguish good and evil, as well as the eyes can different colours, in a word, to be born with an understanding and moral sense, yet at the same time, to be but an animal, or machine, in all this there is no more absurdity than in asserting that there is a Monkey, or Parrot, both of which are capable of giving and receiving pleasure. Here I may take the opportunity to ask, who at first could have imagined, that one drop of the seminal liquor which is discharg'd in copulation, should be the occasion of such extatic pleasure, and afterwards spring into a little creature, which in time, certain conditions being suppos'd, should itself feel the same transports?[28]

Aside from his misinterpretation of Descartes's writing, de la Mettrie's assumptions were understandable given the state of knowledge in the eighteenth century, the strong influence of clocks and automata on popular perceptions and his own limited understanding of biology and psychology. But, wrong as they were, his ideas were valuable because they suggested variations on the clergy's explanations of the human condition. At best he provoked discussion of the prevailing orthodoxies. Theologians used de la Mettrie's arguments to defend their own brand of materialism (as did Joseph Needham in his defence of the Communist dialectic nearly two hundred years later). The man-machine debate was even then tied up with issues like the original cause of the universe and the purposes of life about which philosophers and theologians still argue today.

By the middle of the nineteenth century the man-machine issue faded into the background as Darwinism took centre stage. The burning question – and the main conflict between science and religion – took the form of evolution: whether or not man had descended from animals in general and apes in particular, and the question of the survival of the fittest. The evolutionary principle has become accepted in this century by most lay people and theologians. But the adaptive process and whether it depends on the survival of the fittest (i.e. by means of intra- and inter-species competition) or on symbiosis (i.e. co-operation) is still a subject of debate.[AA] Even deeply religious philosopher-scientists of the twentieth century like the geologist-priest Teilhard de Chardin, the physicist Schrödinger and the biologist Thorpe endorsed and never questioned the competitive, relatively objective and therefore mechanistic interpretation of Darwinist evolution or of their own religious beliefs.

The mechanistic view of life enjoyed a considerable revival in the 1920s, due to an uncritical acceptance of social Darwinism; the Russian Revolution of 1917 and the spreading of a purely materialist interpretation of Karl Marx's dialectic; European and American capitalist materialism that felt threatened by Communism, and the after-effects of World War I in which millions of human beings had been used as if they were nothing but machines. The definitive book on materialism by F. A. Lange, published at that time, had nothing but praise for the mechanistic/materialist explanation of life given by de la Mettrie almost two hundred years earlier, and heaped scorn on his critics:

> Julien Offray de la Mettrie . . . is one of the most abused, but one of the least read, authors in the history of literature . . . Whoever came into unfriendly contact with Materialism attacked him as its extremest representative; and even those who approached to Materialism in their own views, protected their own backs against the worst reproaches

by giving de la Mettrie a kick. And this was the more convenient, as de la Mettrie was not only the earliest of the French Materialists, but was the first also in time.[29]

## Man not a Machine

The year after Lange's book was published, Eugenio Rignano, a philosophy professor at the University of Milan, wrote what may seem like an answer to Lange although he probably did not know about his book's existence. The title of Rignano's book was *Man not a Machine*[30] and in it he attempted to refute de la Mettrie's views that had become once again the centrepiece of philosophical and scientific perceptions. Rignano made regrettable errors in some of his explanations and laid himself open to justified criticism as being a 'vitalist' and a 'Lamarckian' (i.e. believing in the heritance of acquired characteristics). Elsewhere, however, Rignano's demolition of the man-machine myth was apt:

It is absolutely unthinkable to entrust the construction of an organism to the mere play of fortuitous variations, in which the organism would take no active part, and which would come to it as a gift from heaven, even though this chance play were aided by an incessant, and most active selection. For the construction of an organism means the construction of a mechanism more complicated and more perfect than our machines, one which answers a well-defined purpose, and which represents the most absolute antithesis to processes left to pure chance . . .

Every toxin, whether mineral or produced by bacteria, that invades the organism, causes the organism itself to produce precisely and exclusively that antitoxin [i.e. antibodies] which is capable of neutralizing its effects . . . Whence does the living substance derive this marvellous property of persistence . . . which has so distinct a purposive and providential character . . .

The behaviour of even the lowest organism is substantially differentiated from that of brute matter; an animal moves by its own inward forces; it is autonomous in its movements, and while it lives it never abandons itself passively to the play of external energies, like a piece of wood left to the mercy of the waves . . .

The purposive aspect of reflexes, especially in the higher organisms, is so pronounced that they more than any other manifestation of life, have given biologists the impression that the organism is a 'machine', in which every smallest element is carefully studied so as to co-operate with all the others in fulfilling its functions . . .

There is no escaping the dilemma: if we hold that the organism is a machine in which only physio-chemical forces are active, we must then grant the 'clock-maker' of Voltaire, who has designed and constructed this delicate and perfect mechanism; or if we do not wish to grant this creator, we must then have recourse to some fundamental property of living substance capable of taking his place.[31]

Joseph Needham, then an Oxford biochemist, felt himself challenged and replied in a scathing book of his own with the less than original title *Man a Machine*,[32] in which he not only sought to refute Rignano but lent his unqualified support to de la Mettrie. Needham's other achievement is a seven-volume encyclopaedia on *Science and Civilization in China* from its earliest beginnings.[33] He will go down in history as a twentieth-century Diderot and, like Diderot's work,[34] his own will remain a classic for all times to come. But Needham, like Diderot, is a mechanist. Despite his deserved reputation, Needham suffers from ideological confusion. He is, by his own confession, a Marxist, a member of the Church of England, a humanist and a Taoist.[35] Humanism and Taoism are complementary; it is even possible to reconcile them with some of the rest of his beliefs. But it is impossible to marry them to Marxism, Christianity and his firm belief that man is nothing but a machine. Needham's views had already been aired in 1925 in a book that he edited and to which he made the following contribution:

The mechanistic theory of life is not new. Its history as a theory goes back as far as the first speculations on the nature of life and the universe . . . Once natural science was clearly founded on such fundamental hypotheses as the belief in the uniformity of nature and such orientations of mind as that which dealt witchcraft its death-blow, then the field was clear for the attempt to see whether living beings would indeed conform to the principles of a mechanistic physiology. In 1527 Paracelsus of Hohenheim, lecturing at Basel, gave biochemistry its charter when he said: 'The body is a conglomeration of chemical matters; when these are deranged, illness results, and nought but chemical medicines may cure the same . . .' And all through history it [the purely mechanistic explanation of existence] has evoked the condemnation of the theologians, the mystics, and the idealist philosophers . . .[36]

It seems extraordinary that Needham was unable to distinguish between the purely physical and psychological aspects of existence. Witchcraft, which he deplores, is of course one form of mechanistic manipulation. It is evident that he believed, and perhaps still believes, that the human psyche, like the human body, operates on the same mechanical principles. Needham quotes de la Mettrie:

'The body may be considered a clock . . . Let us conclude boldly then that man is a machine, and that there is only one substance, differently modified, in the whole world. What will all the weak reeds of divinity, metaphysics, and nonsense of the schools, avail against this firm and solid oak? . . .'
[Needham insists that] There had always, even in the crests of the movement, been a small minority of the older type of vitalists. Very late in the nineteenth century they found a leader in the person of Hans Driesch, and another in that of Haldane, who elevated the banner of neo-vitalism which has had a considerable number of books to its credit, but few supporters.[37]

Convinced mechanists like Needham are fond of calling all those who disagree with them animists, vitalists, religious fanatics, scientifically ignorant, romantics, primitives, eccentrics, idealists or lunatics. They find it impossible to imagine that there might be any way of looking at existence other than their own. In *Man a Machine* Needham attempts

to refute Rignano on the basis of what he claims to be
superior scientific knowledge, yet ultimately he rests his case
on poetry:

> The mechanistic theory of life needs a Lucretius, a poet
> inspired to a red-hot enthusiasm by the inflexible laws of
> the atoms, by the unshakable determinism of physio-chemical
> explanations, and by the exquisite harmonies and adjustments
> of which pure physio-chemical systems are capable. The
> beauty of the living organism by which he will be caught
> up will not be that loose and mysterious charm touched with
> emotion which appeals so much to the old-fashioned student
> of 'natural history' but rather that
>
> > '. . . keen
> > Unpassioned beauty of a great machine'
>
> which Rupert Brooke described.[38]

Needham continued to espouse the cause of dialectic
materialism (a logical form of materialistic reasoning proposed by Hegel and adopted by Karl Marx) in a later book,
*Order and Life*:

> The new point of view ensures that we shall not forget
> the extreme complicatedness of the living system, while
> at the same time forbidding us to take refuge in pseudo-
> explanations. The older vitalism could hardly be acquitted
> of leaning toward romantic animism; it hoped that rigid
> causal analysis would fail, whereas mechanism hoped it
> would win. If science wins . . . the world will prove to be one
> in which man is thrown wholly on his own resources, skill,
> and self-control, on his courage and strength and perhaps on
> his ability to be happy by adjusting himself to pitiless fact. If
> science fails there is room for the childlike hope that unseen
> powers may come to the relief of human weakness. If science
> wins, the world is the necessary consequence of logically
> related facts, and man's enterprise, in Huxley's figure of
> speech, *the playing of a game of chess against an opponent who
> himself never errs and never overlooks our errors . . . The motivation
> of biological mechanism was thus progressive, vigorous, and youthful,
> a seeking for independence and mastery* [my italics].[39]

## Control from Without

Needham revealed himself and his approach to life in these few sentences. He was perhaps unaware of the meaning of what he was writing. But he was not alone. On the contrary, he represented what is still the majority view.

The advent of the electronic computer lent additional support to the classic mechanistic stance in philosophy and the sciences. For once more, as during the seventeenth- and eighteenth-century automata mania, the emulation of life by machines is believed to be a good possibility, if not now, then in the imminent future. (Some computer scientists insist that this has already been achieved, acting on the principle that if it looks like a duck, quacks like a duck, eats like a duck and excretes like a duck it must be a duck, even if it is only a clever imitation.) But during the first quarter of this century some doubters besides Rignano began to question the common madness. Not the least of those was the biologist Haldane, himself a convinced socialist and atheist:

> The structure of a living organism has no real resemblance to that of a machine, since the parts of a machine can be separated without alteration of their properties. All of these properties are also independent of whether the machine is at motion or at rest. In the living organism, on the other hand, no such separation can be made, and the structure is only the appearance given by what seems at first to be a constant flow of specific material, beginning and ending in the environment. We have seen that the apparent flow has a persistence and power of its own, which we cannot account for by mere constancy in the physical and chemical environment.[40]

C. M. Joad, a British philosopher of that same period about whom more is said later, was also an atheist and a champion of the anti-mechanist school in his early years. But he underwent a later and quite remarkable religious conversion. Dissenters from the mechanistic world view are still rare. An American academic, Joseph del Torto, was one of the few who voiced his objections in 1951:

The new industrial revolution of electrical and atomic power, of robot-factories, thinking-machines, and thoughtless men, is at hand. To use, for the moment, the now-obsolete mechanometaphors, it is an iron-bound, copper-riveted, lead-pipe cinch. This is no intergalactic joy-ride by those modern mechano-cowboys, the hot-rod boys and ray-gadgeteers, the Science Fiction kids. An age of servo-mechanisms looms up through the open door of history. In America it signals a complete victory for the cult of the machine *against* man, instead of in his service. In place of the promised largesse and leisure, an ironically reversed enslavement is prepared. The Machine is humanized and worshipped. Man (at best) is mechanized . . .

If a machine performs the same functions, acts, operates as a man, then logically they are equal, not to say identical. If a machine played chess, then the machine is a chess-player. If the 'built-in' logic of a computer does the work of faltering human logic, then the computer is a 'brain'. The equation is more than metaphorical. Do machines learn? Certainly, says Professor [Norbert] Wiener . . . The equation has always been reversible. Man is a machine: the machine is man.[41]

Yet the mechanistic and absolute materialistic view of man and the universe has by now permeated every aspect of science and philosophy, swamping the few voices of sanity like that of Mary Midgley, former senior lecturer in philosophy at the University of Newcastle-on-Tyne, who takes conventional religions to task for promoting a mechanistic view of mankind:

. . . we are liable to get the picture which Calvin sometimes presented, of a clockmaker who designs, builds and winds a clock, and then punishes it for striking. [Calvin has indeed much to answer for in promoting the religious version of 'man the machine'.] He taught that God had predestined each man before birth to salvation or damnation and that no heroic virtue a man might show or no vile crime he might commit could alter that pre-natal verdict. A man was an automaton with no moral choice.[42]

Mary Midgley is equally critical of Richard Dawkins's mechanistic version of biological evolution that goes hand in hand with social Darwinism and conventional religions. Dawkins writes in *The Selfish Gene*: 'We are survival machines – robot vehicles blindly programmed to preserve the selfish molecules known as genes.'[43] Midgley answers Dawkins's attempted excuses with: 'Complaints are met by the claim that this is just a metaphor. But a chronic, unvarying metaphor cannot fail to be part of meaning.'[44] Since writing his unfortunate book, Dawkins has partially reversed himself in a revised edition of *The Selfish Gene*,[45] borrowing ideas from a book by Robert Axelrod, a US psychologist (who claims to have discovered the wellsprings of co-operation by misinterpreting an interesting computer program written by Anatol Rapoport, discussed in *Winners*[AA]).

Historically, human beings were used by religious leaders and rulers as machines or as adjuncts to machines from the dawn of civilization to the present. They became figurative human robots – unfortunate social, economic and military products of a manipulative and mechanistic approach to life: slave labour, conscripts pressed into the world's armies and navies to serve as cannon fodder, concentration-camp guards and bureaucrats who blindly obey orders. They were turned into agricultural and industrial serfs and in our day into compulsive consumers – another form of slavery. Lewis Mumford accurately traced these historic developments in two books: *The Condition of Man*[46] and *The Myth of the Machine*.[47] It is unnecessary to repeat his observations here.

The purely mechanistic explanation as a world view has become a self-fulfilling prophecy. What began as a religious concept – God as the master-mechanic, inventor of the universe and creator, whose will we must obey or suffer the consequences – has determined the course of Western philosophies and sciences. It is reflected in the authoritarianism of those who wish to deny responsible freedom to the rest of mankind and who seek to impose their controls on us from without, while hypocritically paying lip-service to slogans like freedom, democracy and unconditional love.

# 3
# Stubbing Your Toe on the Philosopher's Stone

'... I have often noticed that highly intelligent persons to whom I have explained some of my views and who seemed to understand them distinctly at the time, have almost completely transformed them when reporting them, so that I could no longer acknowledge them as my own ... I would beg posterity never to believe what is ascribed to me if I have not published it myself.'   René Descartes[1]

We are all philosophers. The philosophy to which we sub-scribe – our own or that which we have been conditioned to believe – determines our *Weltanschauung* (an apt German term for world view). How we regard ourselves and the world determines how we think, learn and behave.

Much of philosophy deals with the invisible aspects of life – like human will, awareness, attention, intentions, ethics, values, learning, meanings and other subjective intangibles. Philosophers seek by means of rigorous logic, geometry, mathematics, reason, intuition or 'feeling' to discover meanings and purposes that the religious claim to receive direct from God and that scientists insist can never be demonstrated objectively. Philosophers believe that the methods they employ are the products of mind, which is defined explicitly by some and implicitly by others as a mechanism. (But if the 'mind' works on mechanical principles we can have no purposes other than those programmed for us by our genes or by God.)

Philosophy and science are intimately related. But today's science is limited to demonstrating the operations of what are believed to be natural laws. It does not seek to explain them or define their meanings. As I stress repeatedly, science only asks 'how?' and philosophy 'why?' But to obtain a true picture of our universe both the how and the why must be considered. A scientist who is not concerned with causes and consequences is a technician. A philosopher who does not consider the operations that bring about causes and consequences is divorced from reality. Any failure on the part of either to consider all three criteria renders their conclusions meaningless. Or, to put this in another way, science and philosophy should be inseparably intertwined. As elaborated elsewhere,[AA] science (or philosophy) should establish totally objective criteria and definitions that wed our perceptions of the relatively objective external world to an equally and possibly more significant internal, subjective reality. This is a precondition for learning, enabling us to internalize our experience of the external world, to become aware of principles and to discover meanings.

## How and Why

As I said, the definition of meanings (the 'why') is regrettably the exclusive business of philosophy and is largely ignored in the sciences. As a result, meanings are believed to be matters of opinion or dogma. But they should be defined by methodical (i.e. scientific) analyses of causes and consequences and the operations that bring both about, relative to time, place and circumstances – in other words by asking both how and why. Human behaviour and senses are essential parts of the circumstances. Once these criteria have been satisfied we can be certain of the meanings of ideas, concepts, transactions and principles. Only then can definitions be matters of indisputable fact. This is not as difficult as it may seem. For example, in the modern world the majority of people believe that survival is the sole purpose of existence. But that depends on how survival is defined. It can be interpreted as 'the survival of the fittest' – as perpetual competition for territory and the means of subsistence. Or it can be viewed as a co-operative enterprise, depending on a symbiotic relationship between human beings and nature.[AA] Only then can we arrive at some measure of certainty.

Certainty is considered a form of arrogance today. But each of us should be certain about the meanings of everyday concerns like survival and death, love and hate or peace and war – common experiences about which we need to make value judgements if anything is to make sense. A valuative analysis of ideas viewed in the context of human experience allows us to be certain of generalizations that seem to be universally true.

## All Generalizations are False

Most philosophers insist that all generalizations are false – including this one. However that is an unfinished sentence. The complete statement should read: 'All generalizations are false, including this one, unless it happens to be the right one.' The best way to test this is to apply it by analogy to universals.

Let us imagine a planet in a distant galaxy on which sentient life-forms have evolved that are very different from any with which we are familiar. They could perhaps thrive on sulphur rather than oxygen. They might move about and sense their surroundings in ways that we cannot even imagine. (There is no evidence that such species exist except in science fiction, but that does not matter for the purposes of our analogy.) The physical matter of which such other-worldly species are composed – it might perhaps be silicon – will eventually disintegrate. Such creatures must have evolved and reproduced in some fashion. They would have to live in a social world in which competitive or co-operative relationships between members must be possible. For without social intercourse no species can survive, even if its members were hermaphrodites. Without some means of reproduction such a species would have appeared or evolved out of nothing. Its members certainly could not live for ever unless the second law of thermodynamics did not apply to them. For if such a species operated on the basis of laws that do not apply to us, it would exist in a universe that is not accessible to us by application of any scientific method, philosophy or logic with which we are familiar. We could not even make any aesthetic judgements about it. All of the foregoing may seem like a circular argument and it is just that, because once we exhaust all possibilities we can only go back to the beginning.

From the foregoing we can conclude that evolution, reproduction, material existence and death, competition, co-operation, self-defence, friendship, love, enmity, feelings and intentions are universal characteristics of any self-, other- and globally-aware species that we can speculate about, no matter how they are constituted or where they might exist in the universe.

It is therefore obvious that we can make correct gener-alizations whenever principles can be tested logically and factually. Philosophers are often reluctant to accept new generalizations based on logic and fact, yet they will accept traditional ones even when logic and facts contradict them. The best examples I can think of that demonstrate this are the questions of randomness and its relation to chance, and the relationship of competition to co-operation. Here phil-osophers and scientists, past and present, have persistently ignored the facts and yet have made sweeping and erroneous generalizations. (I go into the randomness/chance problem fully in Chapter 5. The competition/co-operation question is discussed in my previous book.[AA])

As I have shown by example, false generalizations in philosophy or science can be discovered by analysis and corrected by applying rigorous causal-consequential logic to any given situation. Once such logic is applied it would seem to follow that we live in a conditionally deterministic universe governed by the laws of cause and effect, no matter what many Western philosophers may feel or believe. (The concept of conditional determinism is equivalent to Einstein's theory of relativity applied in the widest possible context, as explained in Chapter 5.) Therefore analysing experience in a totally objective way (i.e. considering both relatively objective and subjective aspects of existence under various conditions) can provide philosophers and scientists with greater or actual precision and certainty.

## Knowledge

The history of philosophy, like that of religions, is far too complex for a detailed description here. But it is possible to refer to comprehensive works on the subject like those written by Will Durant,[2] Bertrand Russell,[3] the philosophical comments made by James Jeans[4] and Heisenberg[5] and representative works of some of the philosophers they discuss.

As I said earlier, philosophers aim to discover meanings, purposes, origins, means and ends. Some, like Anaximander, Plato, Voltaire or Immanuel Kant based their opinions on logic and reason; others, like Henri Bergson, on intuition. Some believe in God or the gods; others in nature and science, and a few in humanistic principles. Still others, like René Descartes, Baruch Spinoza and Gottfried Wilhelm Leibniz, relied on geometry and mathematics. Oriental schools of humanist philosophy, like Taoism and early forms of Hinduism, base their conclusions on common sense and the laws of cause and effect.

Western philosophy had its beginnings in Greece about 500 B.C. and Thales was among the first philosophers about whom anything is known. It is remarkable how close he and others like Pythagoras, Socrates and Democritus arrived to certain absolute, conditional truths, limited only by the knowledge of their day. At about the same time as the earliest Greek philosophers, and well before the opening of the silk route to the West, Chinese philosophers had reached a similar plateau of wisdom.

Greek philosophy declined under Roman rule. After the fall of Rome it was kept alive by groups of Arab, Moorish and Jewish scholars who, living in Sicily and Spain, rescued what would otherwise have been lost for a long time to come. Only the philosophy of Aristotle prospered during the early days of Christianity. But Aristotle was a theorizer who refused to look at nature's evidence for himself – a common error even in our day of empirical sciences. Philosophy only began to blossom again when the dogmatic grip of the Church on thought and reason lessened, first under the aegis of a more relaxed Christianity (e.g. St Augustine and St Thomas Aquinas) and later by lay scholars who revived the early Greek tradition.

Between then and now philosophy has teetered back and forth between reason and belief. Various schools of philosophy have attempted to establish a bridge between science and religion, straddling rather than resolving the same questions asked since the beginning of human societies.

Two main divisions now exist in modern philosophy, characterized on the one hand by the Cambridge school of philosophy that believes in logic, and on the other by the US Essalen school that believes in feelings. Both fail to consider that either depends on applying the correct logic and having the right feelings. Neither school has found conclusive answers to questions of profound importance. They seem unable to conceive of a possibility that there might be a tangible, scientific way of settling philosophical, subjective questions about life and the universe.

It is therefore ridiculous to insist, as many philosophers have done, that feelings or intuitions alone are enough to achieve philosophical wisdom or, as is common in science, to say that whatever 'works' is correct. For some people feel good about tearing the wings off flies. Some learn the wrong lessons from their intuitions or experiences. And even what works is not necessarily a test of truth. For example, operant conditioning certainly works in the short run. It works with a vengeance. In the long term it often makes those who allow themselves to be conditioned subscribe and conform subconsciously to wrong values and standards. Thus, thanks to their wrong conditioning – and their tacit agreement to be conditioned – people become less intelligent (i.e. they do not think or behave appropriately in all circumstances) than they would be if they thought independently. If people thought for themselves they would become aware of causes and consequences and of their own and of other people's contradictions.

## Self-contradictions

The resolution of paradoxes and the removal of internal and external contradictions should be cornerstones of philosophy and science. Any inconsistency is a warning to be sceptical. For example, the late Konrad Lorenz objected to Immanuel Kant's principle of *a priorism* – that certain concepts are innate and exist prior to birth and experience.[6] But Lorenz was a champion of the fact that organisms are born with Innate Release Mechanisms (IRMs). This knowledge is *a priori* (i.e. it exists before birth) and is embedded in our genes. It was therefore absurd for him to argue with Kant's *a priorism*. This contradiction can be traced to Lorenz's admiration for one of his university professors who was fanatically prejudiced against Kantian philosophy.[7] No knowledge Lorenz subsequently acquired could shake his conditioned belief, even when his own experience showed that it was wrong. Such is the power of wrong conditioning.

Before looking critically at aspects of philosophy, two cautions are in order. The first concerns theories and opinions. An undemonstrable truth lies in the realm of speculation and may be unrelated to the facts. Such a theory can be a possibility or it can be pure fiction. In the absence of facts one can of course express opinions or propound theories provided they are tentative and ignorance is acknowledged. But ignoring known facts or logic can be due only to conditioned blindness, prejudice and unconscious or deliberate distortion. Logic and known facts are often stretched to fit a theory that flies in the face of reason (e.g. in game theory the belief that winning in games is due to superior strategy and fault-free play[AA]).

Knowledge is never a matter of knowing everything,

even within any narrow speciality; we can never know all the facts because there are simply too many. Expertise should not be confused with pretended omniscience. This is true for knowledge about our central nervous system, the possibilities generated by the DNA or anything else. We only need to know and understand enough to establish principles and that means making selective value judgements from the start. All of this is amply demonstrated by the misconceptions about the mainsprings of human behaviour that have prevailed in science and philosophy for thousands of years. Typical is the deeply rooted, but false idea that human nature is essentially competitive and that nature operates on this principle.[AA]

The second problem concerns the misinterpretation or mistranslation of a philosopher's ideas. That can have complex consequences. Descartes was very much aware of this when he wrote the words that head this chapter – they proved prophetic when it came to later interpretations of his writings. Whoever misinterprets or mistranslates so that original ideas conform to the fashions of the day can assure himself of immortality by being quoted again and again until someone notices the discrepancies between his version and the original.

## I Think therefore I am

One of the best examples of this kind of error is Descartes's famous statement: *cogito ergo sum*. This is still mistranslated to read, 'I think; therefore I am'. It misrepresents the essence of Descartes's philosophy because most philosophers now regard the process of thinking as a kind of invisible mechanical action (i.e. stimulus-response). Historians, philosophers and many scientists have repeated this mistranslated phrase for more than three hundred years. But Descartes meant something entirely different, as can be discovered only when *cogito ergo sum* is read in context. But before I provide a correct translation, it is worth dwelling briefly on the mistranslation and its meanings. The 'I think; therefore I am' statement does not make sense. It is unlikely that Descartes, who was a first-rate geometer and logician, would suggest that human 'beingness' is proven no matter what we think – for example, if we think that the moon is made of green cheese.

The Latin word *cogito* can mean 'I think', 'I know' or 'I am aware'; *ergo* always means 'therefore' in any context. However *sum* can mean 'I am' or 'I exist'. To suggest that 'I know; therefore I am' would be wrong, for it is possible to accept wrong knowledge as correct (e.g. that winning is superior to losing or that randomness creates chance). If Descartes's *Philosophical Writings*[8] are read in context, it becomes obvious that he was concerned with awareness rather than with thinking or knowing and with existence rather than with being. Descartes's famous phrase, properly translated, should therefore read: 'I am aware; therefore I exist' – a subjective rather than a mechanistic generalization. No machine can be self- or globally aware (see Chapter 7), no matter how many sensors may be attached to it. Spinoza translated *cogito ergo sum* as 'I am conscious, therefore I exist'. Even that is wrong, though it comes closer to the truth than the conventional translation. For consciousness means something rather different than awareness, as we shall see later.

It is disturbing that the 'man is nothing but a machine' idea was consciously or subconsciously attributed to Descartes by successors who latched on to a mistranslation which has since served to support the mechanistic orientation of writers like de la Mettrie, Joseph Needham and many others. (I do not know who the original translator was, but future PhD aspirants could find this a rich vein to mine.) In his writings Descartes stated the obvious: that physiological functions are pseudo-mechanical. But he also insisted that man was much more than a machine because of his subjective awareness of the self and of the universe. He implied that the other-than-mechanical and subjective portions of existence consist of self-awareness, global awareness and an ability to create artificial symbols – qualities that no other species possesses. With present-day knowledge, awareness can be shown to be mainly a matter of degree in all species. More about that is said later (see Chapter 7). Still, Descartes was correct about the inability of animals to invent artificial symbols.

> . . . if there were machines with the organs and appearance of a monkey, or some other irrational animal, we should have no means of telling that they were not altogether of the same nature as those animals; whereas if they were machines resembling our bodies, and imitating our actions as far as is morally possible, we should still have two means of telling that, all the same, they were not real men. First, they could never use words or other constructed signs, as we do to declare our thoughts to others . . . Secondly, while they might do many things as well as any of us or better, they would infallibly fail in others . . . so it is morally impossible that a machine should contain so many varied arrangements as to act in all the events of life in the way reason enables us to act.[9]

The fact that Descartes thought of animals as machines is excusable, given the state of biological knowledge in his day. His terminology (e.g. his use of the word 'soul') may seem metaphysical but understandable given the power of the Church at that time. What is inexcusable is that twelve generations of philosophers and translators misrepresented what Descartes actually wrote and used this to further their own ideologies.

## 'Darwin among the Machines'

In many instances such misinterpretations may be subconscious (i.e. due to wrong conditioning). But the subconscious can be a product of either full understanding backed by sufficient knowledge, or of operant conditioning. In either case and once we believe that we know and understand anything perfectly or nearly so, even when we are totally wrong, there is likely to be a suspension of critical thought. We then have no opportunity for discovering or admitting possible errors. Absolute certainty and absolute operant conditioning (i.e. stupidity) can become reflexive and work positively or in a negative sense. Fear of admitting a mistake and being found out becomes a form of self-conditioning that can also lead to a deliberate or subconscious falsification of facts. Reflexive responses can be due to certainty and self-assurance or to self-delusion and fraud. One example of the latter is Cyril Burt, the British psychologist who falsified research results to substantiate his prejudices.[10] Another is the misinterpretation of Samuel Butler's anti-mechanistic attitude by many who write about the future of computing. Butler's satirical letter, titled 'Darwin among the Machines', was published in 1863:

> We refer to the question: What sort of creature man's next successor in the supremacy of the earth is likely to be . . . In the course of ages we shall find ourselves the inferior race . . . If they [machines] want 'feeding' (by the use of which very word we betray our recognition of them as living organisms) they will be attended by patient slaves whose business and interest it will be to see that they shall want for nothing . . . until the reproductive organs of machines have been developed in a manner which we are hardly yet able to conceive, they are entirely dependent upon man for even the continuance of their species. It is true that these organs may be ultimately developed, inasmuch as man's interest lies in that direction; there is nothing which our infatuated race would desire more than to see a fertile union between two steam engines . . .[11]

When such an obvious parody is taken seriously as it was by Geoffrey Simons, then editor-in-chief for the National Computing Centre in Manchester, the results can be hilarious. The following is an excerpt from a 1982 issue of the *Guardian* in which Mr Simons made prognostications for the future of artificial intelligence, something Samuel Butler derided well before the advent of robotics. Mr Simons and those who share his views cite Butler (and Descartes) to corroborate their mechanistic fantasies in order to substantiate untenable premises: 'The reader may speculate what will happen when, as seems highly likely, machines may be able to reciprocate human emotions. We may even prefer machines to human beings for purposes of intercourse.'[12] The author does not leave us in any doubt as to what he means by intercourse:

> For female robot lovers to be responsive they would have to possess an abundance of tactile sensors controlling robot behaviour via feed-back signals – and this . . . puts us well on the way to creating artificial emotions . . . It is easy to envisage a robot system with a complex of control micro-electronics including a cluster of silicon chips to comprise the cerebral neural net, not to mention highly sensitive skin and other features. Most of this is well within the scope of modern computer technologies.[13]

Such female robots already exist in many of the world's bordellos. They are called flesh-and-blood whores, a subject on which Mr Simons has written extensively.[14] To prove his humanistic concerns and social consciousness he continues: 'As far back as 1972, William G. Lycan suggested [in "The Civil Rights of Robots", a lecture at Kansas State University] that it might be appropriate to regard the robots of the future as persons, and he coined the term "robot-person" to link the artificial and biological worlds.'[15]

There is an apocryphal story about Descartes that could be construed to lend support to such absurdities. Descartes was said to have created a convincing female automaton which was lifelike in all respects that matter which he carried about with him on his travels in a large trunk. During a sea voyage he supposedly displayed his mechanical companion to the ship's captain who, being superstitious and fearing for the safety of his ship and crew, ordered it thrown overboard.

These and similar fairy tales are taken seriously in various guises even by today's 'reputable' scientists and science writers. Rather than reflecting technological or biological expertise, such bizarre ideas are representative of a purely materialistic philosophy that excludes subjective reality.

Misconceptions like these are sincere inasmuch as they are fervently believed (i.e. conditioned), no matter how ludicrous they may be. Believers and their hangers-on make extraordinary efforts to misrepresent facts, misquote or fabricate evidence in order to justify claims made for the impossible, for what is demonstrably wrong or to capitalize on a current fad. The scientific and philosophical frauds and delusions of our day are no better or worse than the magical, mechanical and religious superstitions of former ages. All are directly related to and derived from the same common psychological malaise: the intention of some to win at the expense of the many, the willingness of believers to allow themselves to be conditioned by deceptions and self-deceptions, and by a preoccupation with materialistic and mechanistic ideas.

## Wisdom

We obtain knowledge by gathering information, but wisdom can come only from a careful analysis of the latter. One reason why certain ancient Greek and Chinese philosophers seem to have understood more than we do, despite their limited knowledge, was because they believed that mankind was the model of their universe (i.e. they had an anthropic perspective). Hence generalists abounded at that time as they did once again during medieval times, the Italian Renaissance, and the seventeenth century's so-called Age of Enlightenment. The philosophers of those times were often ordinary, self-educated men and women who were globally aware within their world, limited though their factual knowledge may have been. Few were academics or had credentials from institutions of learning. The same was true of early mathematicians and what would today be considered scientists. They were free-thinkers and relatively unconditioned, able to think independently. For whoever discovers anything new must ignore conventions and step outside the established wisdom. That was Socrates's crime, for which he was condemned to death.

Medieval philosophers and alchemists, side by side with charlatan sycophants at the royal courts of Europe, were preoccupied with the search for the philosopher's stone (i.e. rearranging matter so that base metal could be turned into gold), the supposed source of all wisdom. There is a correspondence between the analytic philosophy of that day and today's science that seeks similar ends – the discovery of the smallest particle that is believed not only to provide unlimited energy but also to enable physicists and biologists to re-create everything in the universe. Somehow it was felt, then as now, that the discovery of the material basis of the universe would provide us with wisdom – not only with the 'how' but also with the 'why'.

This search began in the days of Anaximander and Democritus when attempts were made to define the smallest indivisible particle. Democritus thought he had found it and named it an atom. His was a philosophical rather than a scientific discovery and in his wisdom he anticipated modern science by more than two thousand years.

The reason why the definition of the smallest indivisible particle is important is that it is directly connected with original causes (or, as some philosophers prefer to put it, final causes) and with quantum, big-bang, chaos and fundamental energy theories discussed later (see Chapter 5). That in turn relates to questions concerning materialism as opposed to the soul or mind, what each means, and the roles they play in existence – a debate that began thousands of years ago and continues today. Here, as elsewhere, there is a close connection between religion, philosophy and science. All three attempt to deal with what religions have tried to spiritualize, science considers in terms of matter, and philosophy seeks to approach via the 'mind'.

## The Brain as a Precision Instrument

The task of science and philosophy is to do things as precisely as circumstances allow. It is frequently believed that science is more objective than philosophy because it uses instruments of measure. But the healthy human brain is the most precise measuring instrument we have – far more precise than any mechanical or scientific one. Therefore philosophers should be more precise than scientists whose instruments are precise only to plus or minus

.5 of whatever unit of measure is employed. Since the micro- and macrocosm are accessible to us only through our senses, it seems absurd to postulate a universe that operates on laws that differ from those that apply to human thoughts and perceptions. This would seem to affirm the validity of the anthropic view of man and the universe. Aristotle said something quite similar, yet I cannot agree with his conclusion that, because the universe we perceive is potentially contained within ourselves, there is therefore no need to observe it.

In the scale of things, we could position the human brain about halfway between the microcosm (the smallest particles of which our universe is composed) and the macrocosm (the cosmos – see Chapter 1, Diagrams 1 and 2). Today it is still believed by many scientists and philosophers that different laws apply to these three aspects of our universe. Others subscribe to the idea that the nature of human nature can be discovered by applying to ourselves what we believe to be the various laws that are thought to govern the micro- or macrocosm. Still others, like Stephen Hawking, hope to discover a unifying principle for both the micro- and macrocosm that would include human behaviour. In his book *A Brief History of Time* Hawking makes the following statement:

> We already know the laws that govern the behaviour of matter under all but the most extreme conditions. In particular we know the basic laws that underlie all the chemistry and biology. Yet we have certainly not reduced these subjects to the status of solved problems; we have, as yet, had little success in predicting human behaviour from mathematical equations![16]

The microcosm (which concerns particle physics) is believed to work on the basis of non-causal laws and uncertainty; the astronomical universe (the macrocosm) is thought to operate on the basis of causal laws. But human behaviour is at times believed to operate on the basis of one and at other times on that of the other. There is no coherence or logic in these beliefs, so no wonder scientists and philosophers are constantly at loggerheads or promote contradictory theories.

The human brain – the neural network – operates on binary principles. Neurons either fire or they do not. They are either on or off. It may require a number of impulses arriving at the same nerve junction from different directions before they are translated into thought, feeling or action. But the basis on which they fire does not depend on random discharges of quantum packets of information, nor do they fire unconditionally. The brain functions on the basis of relative certainty based on genetic or experiential conditioning, on feelings, intentions, will or thought, even when any of these turn out to be wrong, when conclusions are biased or even when indecision predominates. In essence the answers the brain provides consist of 'yes' or 'no', 'right' or 'wrong', or 'I know' or 'I don't know as yet'. The 'perhaps' or 'maybe' states are also governed by a binary decision-making process because they represent a vacillation between yes and no. In everyday terms these grey areas represent a lack of knowledge or commitment.

## Memory

In Chapter 5, I define memory as possibly being the smallest particle in the universe and in Chapter 8, I discuss it in terms of information theory and the computer technologies. Here I deal with memory as a philosophical concept. The possibility that memories are the fundamental, one-dimensional components of two-dimensional information is not yet fully appreciated, although it is a very ancient idea. In one sense it was first proposed by the Greek poet Simonides, as recounted by Cicero. Since then the art of memory has become part of the Hermetic tradition elaborated during the Middle Ages by Ramón Lull and Giordano Bruno. Frances Yates details the history of the art of memory in considerable detail.[17]

We build up a picture of the outer world within ourselves by conscious or subconscious remembering or imagining visual, aural, tactile, verbal or other experiences and symbols. We then manipulate them by what is called the mind. When we speak of 'recall', that is what we do in a literal sense when we remember. We bring memories back from wherever they are stored and make associations by relating one set of memories to others. The transmission of memories – genetic, experiential and cultural – from one synapse to the next in our central nervous system is a process that is not yet fully understood. Memories would appear to be electro-chemical during the process of transmission and their flow is accepted as a physical reality in neurophysiology and bio-chemistry. But what memories are and what directs their flow in one direction in preference to another still lies in the realm of philosophy where it is claimed that the direction of this data flow is governed by the mind. It is therefore essential to define what the mind might be and how it works.

## The Subjective Mind

The term 'mind' encapsulates a whole series of concepts – attention, concentration, awareness, consciousness, intentions, choice and will – that are usually undefined or imprecisely defined. Here and in following sections of this chapter I establish relationships between these ideas that may help clarify what they really mean. It is important to remember that when we speak of mind and other subjective concerns, we are not talking about any visible, material reality or, as is sometimes claimed, a mechanism that we can see, touch or experience. It has never been demonstrated that any organ makes up or produces awareness or attention. But we do use our central nervous system and other organs to focus our attention and express awareness. These and other qualities, like will and intentions, are usually attributed to the mind. They are therefore part of an invisible transactional reality; something that Plato believed to be true, but which has been the subject of debate among succeeding generations of philosophers.

Just as the mind or psyche apparently satisfies the quest

for an invisible mechanism that accounts for personality and intentions in philosophy and science, so does the 'soul' appear to explain the same phenomenon as far as theologians are concerned, supposedly distinguishing man from animals and inert matter. No one as yet has found any explanation of how the mind (or soul) might work. For Descartes the material body consisted of an aggregation of matter that differed from the stuff of the soul, but he never explained what this 'mind-stuff' is. Philosophers like John Locke, Bishop Berkeley and David Hume proposed that the universe is a figment of our imagination and that it and the world around us have no physical reality, but are products of mind. If Locke, Berkeley and Hume were correct then mind would be a product of mind and that is impossible. Leibniz's monad theory proposed that body and mind were made of the same material and in this he was largely correct if the mind deals with memories. The creative energy that recalls, combines and determines the direction of the flow of experiential and cultural memories in our central nervous system makes up our mind in a literal sense, just as the DNA preserves and transmits genetic memories.

Plato suggested that, 'There is no special organ for existence and non-existence, likeness and unlikeness, sameness and differences, and also unity and numbers in general.' Plato also believed that, 'The mind contemplates some things through its own instrumentality, others through the bodily faculties.'[18] The question of how the mind does these things and what if any mechanism is involved is, however, evaded by Plato as it is by all other philosophers with whose work I am familiar.

Bertrand Russell wrote: 'The distinction between mind and matter, which has become a commonplace in philosophy and science and popular thought, has a religious origin, and began as the distinction of soul and body.'[19] He showed that Aristotle believed the soul to be the final cause of the body and that mind, being less bound to the body, is higher than the soul. Plotinus, one of the forerunners of the Gnostics (who disappeared with the Christian domination of the Roman world) and perhaps the last of the true philosophers of that era, came closer than most in defining the human mind as *nous* – the essence of oneness that 'has the desire of elaborating order on the model of what it has seen in the Intellectual-Principle'.[20]

Grey Walter, the neurophysiologist, took exception to the common usage of the word mind: '. . . no sane physiologist would look for a mechanism identifiable as Mind . . .'[21] It is, however, one thing to deny the material reality of the mind and another to claim that the process of minding the facts cannot be modelled. Description of non-material processes like 'minding' by other than mechanical means (i.e. without a model) is a practical impossibility. Yet that is attempted in every textbook on science, philosophy and psychology.

## Attention and Concentration

The question remains: how can mind be defined? Mind, while certainly not a mechanism, describes a concentration of energy and memories. We speak of 'paying mind' to something, doing things 'with a purpose in mind', being 'mindful' of something or someone, 'changing our mind', or doing something 'mindlessly' (i.e. inattentively). Therefore mind is a process and the term should be used in the sense of a transaction rather than as a transactor. Minding establishes the relationship between our material (relatively objective) and other than material (subjective) selves, and between the self and the larger environment. Minding is certainly purposive, yet not in any way that is explained by conventional philosophy or science.

To 'pay mind' provides a filter for our perceptions. It makes possible classification, analysis, synthesis, understanding and generalization of the facts. It is that which enables us to recognize original causes and ultimate purposes, the conditions and processes that bring them about, and the consequences to which they lead. Human attention is that which minds the facts, interprets and gives them meanings. To pay mind or attend to the facts and their meanings makes us consciously aware of them. Minding is that process which focuses our attention, will and intentions.

It gives them direction, as is plain when we speak, for example, of a change of mind that in essence redirects our intentions, behaviours and energies by means of an act of will.

The end product of changing one's mind certainly involves a reversal of thought or behaviour (i.e. the dataflow in our central nervous system), but whatever brings that about is something other than mechanical. You may change your mind about picking up a burning coal with your fingers as a result of the pain it causes (i.e. stimulus/response). But the same causal/consequential relationship (in the given instance by paying attention to a pain-avoidance reflex) is not involved in preferring baroque to rock music, or a draw to winning in a game of chess. Mind your step, mind the baby or the shop refer to concentrating energy on a particular subject to the exclusion of others and focusing your attention on it alone because you are aware of the consequence if you don't. But you will not suffer serious consequences as a result of making any purely aesthetic judgement (unless you happen to be a professional artist, writer or musician). Minding therefore consists of a discrete selection of subject matter on the basis of a conscious awareness of causes and consequences (the 'why') and the operations (the 'how') that bring both about, as a result of a conditioned reflex *or* by making a value judgement.

When we focus our conscious attention on something external or internal to ourselves and mind it sufficiently in an awake state in order to act – crossing a busy street, writing a book or baking bread – we hypnotize ourselves in effect. We render ourselves momentarily unconscious of irrelevant distractions and thereby consciously gain a heightened awareness of certain events to the exclusion of others. We pay mind only to what matters at the moment. The process of minding therefore consists of giving purposive directions or redirection to internal, neuronic processes involved in thought or intentional behaviour. The exclusion of certain internal (e.g. hunger or pain) and external experiences (e.g. noise or other distractions) serve to heighten concentration on and minding of what is momentarily important.

There is ample evidence derived from neurological and hypnotic experiments that no mechanism exists for mind. Neurosurgeons like Penfield have shown that with electro-stimulation it is possible to locate portions in the brain where memories can be dredged up involuntarily and mindlessly that appear to have been forgotten.[22] However, in order to remember without electric stimulation of the brain or without hypnosis one needs conscious minding (i.e. selective remembering). This can occur only when attention is focused intentionally on a given event. It is done by every individual on an other than mechanical basis whenever a transactional value judgement needs to be made (i.e. focusing on what is momentarily important while ignoring everything else). So, if it is possible to stimulate memory mindlessly or by an act of conscious will, where does the mind-mechanism fit into thought and behaviour? (Penfield was convinced that a non-mechanical process governs the process of 'minding'.[23])

As the brain was explored in ever greater detail, even the loci at which intentions are processed were identified.[24] But why, how or where they originate or the biological causes for intentions cannot be found anywhere. All that can be said about them is that they can be conditioned. The seat of passions can be located in the brain – anger, violence or sexuality – and stimulated to extraordinary excesses or anaesthetized. Yet I have never heard of any neurosurgeon who has electrically stimulated an excess of reason or reasonableness or a minding of new facts with deliberation. These are innate potentials that exist in all organic systems to a greater or lesser extent. They can be misdirected or stifled by conditioning, drugs or lobotomy, but only the self – either by deconditioning or by stubbornly clinging to the innate potential within each of us – can be mindful of (i.e. pay attention to) natural laws of cause and effect in any given context. Healthy individuals in full possession of their faculties can only be or become reasonable intuitively or as a result of awareness, by an act of will, by using their reasoning powers, by exercising self-control and by paying mind to whatever is known, can be discovered and understood. Those are the criteria for minding and they are the bases on which existential, conditional and rational value judgements are made.

Only with deconditioning can all available possibilities be considered with total objectivity (i.e. considering facts in both relatively objective and subjective terms). The same applies to purposive, self-originated learning and discovery of relationships. Goal-oriented deconditioning (acquiring an open mind about things that interest you) sharpens reasoning powers and feeds back to the self. Ignorance, dogmatic closure (i.e. a closed mind which has the wrong goals or none at all) and the wrong forms of conditioning lead to unreasonableness, boredom, passivity and mindlessness.

## Consciousness

Minding describes states of consciousness – another invisible, non-material phenomenon. Medically the word 'consciousness' refers to awake attention, self-awareness, awareness of others and awareness of the external environment. But can it be properly applied to states of sleep, drug-induced torpor, electrical stimulation of cortical areas, hypnosis, or when an individual is awake but unable to control the act of remembering? Does it apply even to those states in which there exists a near-total concentration on (or minding of) internal processes? Is sleep mindless? What produces dreams but has no material reality? Is a sleeper unconscious? Is sleep identical to coma or anaesthesia? Answers to such questions must be qualified conditionally, although these phenomena share common characteristics. The sleeper, anaesthetized patient, comatose or hypnotized individual or drug addict is absorbed by his or her inner world to the near total exclusion of external reality. That is the minding by which we attend to internal processes. But these are very different forms of minding from those we exercise in the awake states when we are fully conscious of ourselves, of others and the external world.

What we call consciousness becomes visible only as a result of our actions. For, as I have said, there is no tangible mind any more than there is an organ that is responsible for intentions or will. Consciousness of externals can be dampened or suppressed by sleep, hypnosis, drugs, mental disorder or surgery. But it cannot be heightened by anything other than greater awareness – a psychological rather than a physical state of minding. Our intentions, attention, concentration and will – or their lack – determine the direction of the data flow within our central nervous system one way or another. There is no material or electro-chemical mechanism for deciding that we intend to win when playing games, lose, play at random, for a draw or a stalemate, or refuse to play. These are questions of goal-definition, purpose and conditional freedom – psychological process and not mechanism, unique to biological systems of a high level of complexity. A mechanism can only react; it cannot act autonomously as we can. A computer can reach conclusions, but it needs a human being to make *a priori* (advance) and *post facto* (after the event) value judgements as to whether a decision is appropriate and error-free. Computers are never conscious and cannot pay attention selectively, extract or be aware of meanings or find errors spontaneously. They can do only what they have been programmed to do. But they can do one other thing. They can produce variations on a theme by means of optional branching in their circuits. But they cannot make conscious (or even unconscious) value judgements that can cause a change of mind, or exclude whatever may be extraneous, irrelevant or wrong.

## Mindlessness and Creativity

A musical analogy demonstrates the difference between minding and being mindless. A synthesizer, given an infinity of time, could mindlessly (without attention or conscious awareness) churn out all possible variations and arrangements for a musical composition. But only a human being can write the original score and make a selective arrangement. Musical composition and selective arrangements can be subjective, creative acts or they can be relatively mechanical ones. Even when musical arrangements are made by a synthesizer within practical limits of time, a human being must first define the rules that limit the synthesizer's search for variations. A computer could not set these limits for itself (i.e. make its own rules). At best it could generate all possibilities if programmed to do so, given enough time. It could not autonomously choose those that seem to fulfil the composer's intentions. Computers are therefore mindless just like human beings who blindly follow orders and instructions, who shuffle the possibilities without thought or self-imposed limits, who try to exhaust all possibilities (i.e. trying everything once), or who do their work solely for money.

The imaginative (i.e. foresighted) part of the score should be written by a creative human being on the basis of intentions, feelings and craft. Aesthetic judgements should limit the possible variations and arrangements. None of this applies to computer-generated music, except in so far as arrangements are concerned. Unfortunately in music today, with the availability of synthesizers, the creative (mindful) and mechanical (mindless) aspects of musical composition and arrangement have become confused. At best these are creative acts. At worst, composition and arrangement can be the work of hacks with or without computers.

## Purpose

If human beings must be consciously attentive to be creative, then how can nature be creative since the particles of which it is composed move about and affiliate at random and in a mindless manner? Here it is necessary to refer to the randomness/chance problem discussed in Chapter 5, for there we discover what at first seems like a paradox: purpose in mindless, random nature. But, as we shall see, randomness reduces chance and assures the short-term recurrence of events with greater frequency than in an ordered universe. In the longest run there is virtually no difference between a random (chaotic) and systematically arranged (consciously ordered) universe. The mechanism of randomness therefore implies an order and purpose of a special kind. When viewed combinatorially (in terms of relationships) rather than merely permutationally (in terms of sequence – see Appendix A), the meanings and purposive aspects of nature are demonstrated by a preponderance of subjective feedback when the sum of all possibilities is classified. Therefore randomness, even when mindless, can have the effect of purposiveness provided there exists a species with aware consciousness that can isolate and appreciate this fact.

Such purposiveness seems to apply also to biological evolution. While mutations, like particle movements and affiliations, are certainly random, their very randomness limits rather than creates or increases chance. Natural selection reduces chance still further. On the highest branches of the evolutionary tree, systematic human ordering can bring about whatever possibilities we want in the short as much as in the long term by limiting them to those that are benign. We can thus avoid and eliminate chance for most purposes in situations in which we have sufficient knowledge provided we think and act creatively, logically and systematically. All of this depends, of course, on our 'paying mind' to the facts.

## Materialism

Even invisible processes like minding must be definable in symbolic terms or else they do not lend themselves to demonstration. Once you employ symbols you are already in a material world. However, materialist philosophers and scientists, like Needham and Russell, and *spiritual* theologians equally insist that symbolic modelling of non-material (i.e. subjective, spiritual, psychological or mental) transactions is impossible.

The word 'materialism' has been much abused. It seems

to be an Aunt Sally designed to discredit those who
do not subscribe to vague notions like soul or mind.
Even the most ardent spiritualist or psychic would not
deny the existence of material reality. Nor can the most
hidebound materialist deny the existence of an invisible
reality that consists of feelings, intentions, will, learning,
value judgements or attention. One of the problems of
philosophers has always been the difficulty of making the
invisible aspects of life and existence sufficiently visible and
symbolically real so that anyone can understand what they
mean.

All of existence can only be experienced directly in
material ways. Our bodies, of which the central nervous
system is a part, are made of material stuff. We must eat,
digest, convert foodstuffs into mechanical energy (as differentiated from psychological energy) and eliminate waste.
These are material and relatively mechanical processes. It
is therefore absurd to ignore the importance of the visible
and material aspects of existence.

The philosopher F. A. Lange attempted to classify some
of the important aspects of materialism[25] summarized
here:

- Economic – winning and losing, competitive – materialism (e.g. capitalism).
- Scientific materialism: quantification of material aspects
  of existence, concurrent with a refusal to admit any
  possibility of a quantification of qualities.
- Mechanical (i.e. technological) materialism: attributing
  exclusively mechanistic characteristics to organisms and
  the universe.
- Dialectic materialism: viewing man solely as an economic
  production unit subject to the dictatorship of the prolet-
  ariat (e.g. Communism).
- Ethical materialism as expressed in conventional religion: e.g. it pays to be free of sin because then you
  receive your reward in heaven, or if you sin you receive
  your just desserts in hell, unless you tithe or confess.

The wrong forms of materialism, by now global phenomena, hardly require elaboration. Yet, if I read him correctly, Lange seems to have made no distinction between what is conventionally considered to be crass materialism (e.g. capitalism, consumerism, Communism and Fascism) and conditional materialism (long-term enlightened self-interest – the draw principle[AA]).

None the less, Lange points to a representative example of longer-term interest instead of the short-term materialism usually attributed to Adam Smith (believed to be the father of modern capitalism):

> All the time, this market of interests was not with him the whole of life, but only an important side of it. His successors, however, forgot the other side, and confounded the rules of the market with the rules of life; and even with the elementary laws of human nature ... This simplification consists, however, only of this, that men are conceived as purely egoistic, and as beings who can perceive perfectly their separate interests without being hindered by feelings of any other kind.[26]

Lange stresses that all knowledge is sensory, peculiar to ourselves, reflecting only human reality. He misses the point that no other reality can exist for us and that only what we can imagine or experience constitutes the sum total of what is accessible to us. Thanks to modern technologies that magnify physical and biological phenomena we can also experience what would otherwise remain invisible and inaudible.

Indeed, no reality other than our own need concern us. It may be modified, modelled and magnified by the technologies or explained by analogy. But our senses provide us with the momentary limits to our understanding, just as our bodies aided by today's machines define the limits of our strength and speed. Tomorrow we may be able to sense more, travel faster or lift greater loads, but none of this should affect our understanding of fundamentals. There may in future be other ways to experience or express reality, but not at this stage of our evolution. Any reality other than our own should therefore be of no consequence to science or philosophy.

The possibility of life, its goals and whatever allows us to pay them mind must exist from the very beginning, if indeed there was a beginning. The ever increasingly complex, if random, combinations of sub-atomic and atomic particles would seem to lead to the evolution of life, self-aware organisms, intentional learning and adaptive behaviour wherever the conditions for such possibilities exist. If that is the case, the stuff of existence is contained as a future potential in the random combinations of the smallest particles in the universe, but not necessarily within the particles themselves. As Chapman Cohen, a convinced atheist and materialist, wrote in 1927:

> The lower unit always becomes the basis of the higher unit, becomes as it were the stepping-stone to the next stage. Thus the earlier simple structure of the atom becomes the unit for the molecule; the molecule for the crystal; the complex of molecules for the cell; the complex of cells for the higher organism ... But while this newness, this creative novelty arises everywhere, it is at two stages in particular that something utterly new and wholly different in kind and nature arises from the union of pre-existing elements; these are the stages where so-called life and mind appear.[27]

There is, as I have said before, a way of looking at the world in which subjective processes (perpetual feedback and the anthropic principle) predominate. From that perspective the possibility for self-organizing affiliations of energy and matter that lead to life would be present as a potential even at the lowest stages of inorganic evolution. They could therefore be inherent in the simplest structures in the universe. This principle has some followers in philosophy and in the sciences, yet it has not been previously demonstrated in a form that is scientifically acceptable.

As I show later, the initial conditions for the evolution of life from inorganic matter depend on a high rate of redundancy in random affiliations of particles and matter. This very redundancy causes repetitions of every possibility to occur in short bursts, assuring that the combinations of particles that can lead to life eventually 'take' when the conditions are right. Like most processes in nature this seems to be a combinatorial rather than a purely permutational process (see Appendix A). It appears to be the life principle, reflected even in inorganic nature. The invisible relationships within and between ourselves and the environment can be experienced and expressed subjectively (by means of intuitions and feelings), by analogy (e.g. the game metaphor), or by totally objective geometric modelling, classification, synthesis, analysis, quantification and eventual generalization (i.e. the combinatorial neural network model;[AA] see also Appendices A and D).

To believe that such a geometric model cannot reflect the subtlest processes of nature because it was never done before is to limit the explanation of subjective experiences to aesthetics, the supernatural, the metaphysical, religions and philosophies. But, contrary to current scientific beliefs, subjective realities are accessible not only on the basis of feelings and intuition but also on the basis of common sense, inferential logic and pattern recognition. The last should be the most reliable method because a geometry of one sort or another underlies every pattern in nature and every geometry is amenable to mathematical and algebraic analysis and generalization. This is as true for human behaviour as for everything else.[AA]

The fact that invisible and non-material subjective processes can now be modelled in material ways does not mean that we live in a purely materialistic universe or that we are nothing but machines. This would be a simplistic, reductionist view of nature and existence. But material demonstrations are needed to show that the invisible reality has substance (see Appendices A–E).

## Invisible Reality

Chapman Cohen, whom I quoted earlier, also wrote:

'[The] general meaning [of materialism] ... stands as the challenge of Naturalism to Supernaturalism. Against the operations of nature as being determined by so many independent volitional powers, it asserts the possibility of explaining everything as a consequence of the composition of forces.'[28]

Forces (like gravity and electromagnetism) are the binding principles of visible and material, as well as of invisible, non-material processes in nature. Yet Cohen never comes to grips with the nature of the invisible forces he postulates. What are they? What causes them? On what principle do they operate? To attribute an invisible reality to them simply begs these questions. It is like saying that the wind blows. But that is just a non-technical term for atmospheric heat exchanges, just as the word mind is a metaphor for the processes of attention and awareness. We never actually experience heat exchanges except as changes in temperature, moving clouds or the rustling of trees bending to the wind. But symbolic isobars model atmospheric pressures that are invisible, causative forces of nature. We can no more see what causes the wind to blow than we can see what causes subjective intentions, will or creativity. But we can take the temperature of the atmosphere and model it in two or three dimensions, just as we can now symbolically represent and quantify the cause and effect of subjective behaviours like learning (see Appendix D), creativity,[AA] or time (see Appendix C). Thus models can give material, three-dimensional reality to invisible phenomena.

In a footnote Cohen warns that: '... A law of nature is a formula devised by man to express his experience of things. It is well to bear this consideration in mind, so as to make the case for supernaturalism rest upon a misunderstanding, or an overlooking of this fact.'[29] But he was wrong; the laws of nature are not human inventions. Cohen, like Wittgenstein and many philosophers before him and since, failed to define or distinguish between man-made laws (e.g. the rules of games) and those of nature. The limitations on the sum of all possibilities define the laws of nature and of man, but only those of nature are immutable.

All of this comes down to Bishop Berkeley's absurd paradox of the tree in the forest. He proposed that a tree falling in the forest does not make a noise if man is not there to hear it. Bertrand Russell suggested an equally ridiculous paradox: that if you look at a house from across the street you cannot tell that the house is still there when you look away.[30] These are amusing word games but they obscure common sense, for every event, object or qualitative process has reality and consequences whether human beings exist or not. Coal deposits affirm that trees existed and fell long before human beings inhabited the earth, and experience tells us that they made loud noises as they crashed to the ground. As far as Russell's paradox is concerned, he needed only to run headlong into the house he hypothesized, even while looking away, to ascertain its existence. We – or any other species – may be imprisoned by our sense organs, muscles and technologies. But reality, no matter how it may be perceived and even when large segments lie beyond our present capacity to perceive them, always depends on affiliations (co-operation), collisions (conflict) or evasions (separation), not only as far as we are concerned but for all particles that make up our universe (see Chapter 5).

The processes of affiliation and disintegration are as true for purely psychological or aesthetic phenomena as for physical, material ones. Experiences and events are affected, impinge on or interfere with perceptions, feelings and matter of any kind. What is true for the material world seems equally true for the unseen one. This does not mean that everyone is moved, touched or interfered with by the same experiences. However, whatever is felt by any human being anywhere lies within a spectrum of experience and feelings common not only to all of humanity but also (in principle if not in detail and to a greater or lesser degree) to all life-forms.

It is here that philosophy touches on the province of science and both become inseparably intertwined, as the physicist Eddington realized. For he felt intuitively that human behaviour and the behaviour of inorganic particles in nature are intimately related:

We have busied ourselves with the processes by which the electric particles widely diffused in primeval chaos have come together to build the complexity of a human being: we cannot but acknowledge that a human being involves also something incommensurable with the kind of entities we have been treating of. I do not mean to say that consciousness has not undergone evolution; presumably its rudiments exist far down the scale of animal life. But it is a constituent or an aspect of reality which our survey of the material world leaves on one side ... On the one side there is consciousness stirring with activity of thought and sensation; on the other side there is a material brain, a maelstrom of scurrying atoms and electric charges. Incommensurable as they are, there is some kind of overlap or contact between them.[31]

Eddington was on the right track (see Chapter 7). Yet he, like the biologist Haldane and other free-thinking scientists who felt that there was more to existence than conventional materialistic values, was accused of religious fanaticism by the majority of scientists of his day. Even so, Eddington was sceptically cautious, bound by the conventions of his time:

... we no longer have the disposition which, as soon as it scents a piece of mechanism, exclaims, 'Here we are getting to bedrock ... This is the ultimate reality ...' We all share the strange delusion that a lump of matter is something whose general nature is easily comprehensible whereas the nature of the human spirit is unfathomable ... In comparing the certainty of things spiritual and things temporal, let us not forget this – Mind is the first and most direct thing in our experience; all else is remote influence ...[32]

The most hidebound materialist would acknowledge the existence of non-material manifestations and relationships within and between organic and inorganic matter, information and memories. They find expression in muscular, cellular, electro-chemical, gravitational, atomic or sub-atomic interactions and behaviours within any given environment.

In organisms these activities are governed by intentions whenever they are not regulated genetically or by randomness. In the past, randomness and intentionality could be demonstrated only on the basis of behaviour and its consequences. Now it can be modelled on the basis of totally objective criteria and analytic processes that mimic those of the human central nervous system.[AA] The same method enables us to analyse and solve any problem about which we have enough information (see Appendices A–E). The discovery and modelling of these processes and what they make possible are reflections of an invisible reality that underlies all of existence. It does seem possible, Eddington's reservations notwithstanding, that we can get down to bedrock although some of the details may escape us as yet.

## The Quantification of Subjective Behaviour

Today's philosophers and scientists deny the possibility that subjective processes can be modelled and quantified scientifically. This stance is exemplified by Joseph Needham, who stated:

> I suppose I might stand as an example of a pronounced mechanist; but I by no means accept the opinion that the phenomena of the mind are not amenable to physio-chemical description. All that we shall ever know of them scientifically will be mechanistic, expressed in the language of determinism, and related as closely as possible to physio-chemical facts obtained from observations of cerebral metabolism. The experimental psychology is the only scientific psychology. I find no great difficulty in regarding all the events of our mental life from a mechanistic point of view.[33]

But elsewhere he contradicted himself: 'Mental processes cannot possibly receive explanations or descriptions in physico-chemical terms.'[34]

Bertrand Russell summed up the mistaken philosophical belief in the impossibility of scientific quantification of subjective qualities when he wrote:

There remains, however, a vast field, traditionally included in philosophy, where scientific methods are inadequate. This field includes ultimate questions of value; science alone, for example, cannot prove that it is bad to enjoy the infliction of cruelty. Whatever can be known, can be known by means of science; but things which are legitimately matters of feeling lie outside its province ... Philosophy, throughout its history, has consisted of two parts inharmoniously blended; on the one hand a theory as to the nature of the world, on the other an ethical or political doctrine as to the best way of living ... [35]

As stated earlier, Stephen Hawking says virtually the same thing: 'We already know the laws that govern the behaviour of matter under all but the most extreme conditions ... we have, as yet, had little success in predicting human behaviour from mathematical equations!' [36]

But, as shown in *Winners*,[AA] the neural dataflow, including intangibles like intentions and will, can now be modelled and quantified. It is therefore possible to predict and demonstrate subjective processes (the 'why') and the operations (the 'how') geometrically and quantify them mathematically – in other words scientifically.

To summarize: intentions, goals and learning are expressions of choice, will and manifestations of invisible subjective processes (i.e. feedback to the self). In the past philosophers despaired of discovering any method of quantifying and establishing conditional absolutes for subjective processes like learning. Now they can be modelled successfully. But to suggest that intentions, will, choice, paying mind, learning or making value judgements are products of some mechanism within the central nervous system, as many philosophers have done, means assigning the production of an invisible reality to a non-existent biological mechanism. To believe that these are matters of the soul, spirit or mind is to provide poetic, aesthetic, religious or philosophical explanations for what can now be demonstrated scientifically (see Appendix D).

# 4
# In the Name of God

The famous Bishop South was once complimented by
Queen Anne on a sermon to the delivery of which she had
just listened. But, she added, 'It was very short.' 'Madam,'
replied the Bishop, 'it would have been shorter had I had
the time to make it so.'                    Chapman Cohen[1]

The reason why I discuss religions here is that they have had
a profound influence on the evolution of modern sciences. It
seems to make no difference whether we take the Old or New
Testament, the Koran, or any other such document literally,
regard it as garbled verbal history or as symbolic allegories
and myths. Some religions when analysed logically contain
important kernels of natural law (for example, nine of the
ten commandments) formulated by generations of wise
men in prehistory. But, as we shall see, the characteristic
attributes of the conventional God are such (for example,
God seen as the master-mechanic of the universe whose
commands we must obey) that they are clearly manipulative
power ploys by organized priesthoods who want to control
rather than enlighten their congregations.

I lost my faith in God at the age of four. Each night
I was made to pray by my mother who assured me that
God answers every prayer. More than anything else I
wanted a pocket knife but gave up on God after weeks

of entreaties when I never found one on awakening. I gave Him subsequent chances without success. The last straw was when, at about the age of nine, I asked why God allowed the babies of the poor in slums to be bitten by rats, while those of the rich were safe in their cots. If there was a God He seemed prejudiced in favour of the children of the well-to-do and had it in for those of the indigent. The argument that these were the consequences of human sins, though true, should not apply to God, for to hold babies responsible for the sins of their fathers carries punitive retribution too far. The promise of heaven to the destitute and everlasting hell for those who have every opportunity to enjoy life did not seem much of a consolation.

While the loss of my faith may seem simplistic, I was, none the less, convinced then as now that life is meant to be fair, that nature is indifferent to our wishes but not to our actions, and that the world in which I grew up was upside down, as it still is. If there were a paradise, its realization should be on earth rather than elsewhere. The intervention by man rather than God seems to be needed to create heaven on earth or, at the least, to give it less the flavour of hell.

Like philosophy and the sciences, theology professes to offer ultimate answers to what are universal questions but, like both, provides what are essentially mechanistic explanations of man's relation to the universe. The very concept of God as the designer and creator of man is a mechanistic idea. It is embedded in religions ancient and modern, as is the demand that man must unquestioningly obey religious dogma and conditioning (i.e. programming) which certainly means treating man as a machine. All religions with which I am familiar are self-contradictory and, like science fiction, ask us to suspend logic and reason much of the time. On the one hand believers are expected to subscribe to the concept that God or the gods created the universe. On the other, no logical explanations of such a creation are ever offered and you are expected to accept this as a matter of faith and feeling. No human being would buy a car based on that principle. Christian and other religious sects profess to teach universal love and 'turning the other cheek' while encouraging adherents to fight figuratively and literally, not only in self-defence but also aggressively to defeat any 'enemy' who disagrees with their beliefs.

Religions, like states, become corrupt because in order to protect their power-base they create exclusive and supposedly superior hierarchies whose sole claim to authority is their proximity to God. These cults and priesthoods insist on privileges based on spurious expertise. They guard their trade secrets like any craft guild and prevent such mysteries from being shared by those to whom they supposedly minister. This is the classical winning and losing game.[AA] They pretend communion with God or the gods, insist that they possess secret knowledge and act as if they were the sole conduits of revealed truth, demanding our trust and allowing no dissent.

Such priesthoods exist as much in philosophy and science as in religion and politics. While science is dedicated to discovery, many of its practitioners insist on an exclusive right to dictate unchanging traditions (i.e. what is known today as the scientific method) and lay claim to a higher understanding that is actually a product of belief, myth, operant conditioning, prejudice or superstition. Scientific and religious priesthoods bow to belated change only as a result of extreme pressure – the benefits of birth control, for example, fought even now by some religions, or nuclear energy promoted by influential sections of the scientific establishment. They persuade their flocks that they know best and that the lay public lacks expertise and is therefore inferior and must do as it is told. Theologians, academics and politicians thus use identical techniques to crush independent thought and dissent. My object in discussing religion in what is a critique of the sciences is less to examine various beliefs than to show that religious fictions dominate much of modern scientific thought and that its promoters are often motivated by the same intentions as the most primitive witch doctors.

## In the Beginning

God, if He exists, could be known only by what He does. In

the following I propose to consider one by one some of the characteristics attributed to Him by various religions and sects which have resulted in confused and contradictory ideas. For example, in the King James version of the Bible, the first sentence in the Gospel according to St John states that, 'In the beginning was the Word'. If that were so, then God is the word. Individual words are arbitrary inventions agreed to by all who speak the same language. But the *meanings* of the ideas for which words stand are fundamentals. This version of the Gospel must therefore be a mistranslation or wrong or, more likely, theologians would have us believe that because 'the word' comes first and was God, we must believe whichever meaning is assigned to it by the Church. I suggest that this sentence should actually read, 'In the beginning there was meaning'. For, as I have said, meanings depend on an understanding of causes, consequences and the operations that bring them about.[AA] This even applies to God, for an uncaused God can have no meaning and a meaningless God is an absurdity.

God as represented in theology would have to be all-knowing, all-powerful, representing the highest principles of ethics, creativity, peace and understanding, demanding unconditional love. However God the creator as conventionally defined poses logical difficulties. Like Aristotle and St Thomas Aquinas, Pascal saw God as the 'unmoved and immovable mover' who set the universe in motion. If this concept is meant to be interpreted in a physical sense then He could not be eternal, for eternity is a time concept (just as infinity is a spatial one) and without motion there can be no time.

It is also said that God brought order out of chaos. In that case chaos preceded the conditions created by God, or He created chaos before creating order. We will see later why either possibility runs counter to the operations of nature.

Next let us consider God as the creator. As such He would have to be a materialistic rather than a spiritual conception; the original clockmaker who, having wound up the universe, is its master mechanic and manipulator.

His free will would rule supreme. Our choices would be limited by the program He gave us and hence we would lack free will. A God-given soul (or program) would only make us special-purpose machines (as is indeed sometimes proposed). The Judeo-Christian-Islamic religions insist that God created man in His image, thus achieving a double purpose. The first was to allow mankind to assume some of the attributes of godliness; the second to attribute many of man's characteristics to God. This would make us inferior imitations of God, just as wind-up dolls are poor imitations of ourselves.

One of the other puzzling characteristics of the conventional Judeo-Christian, Islamic or other God is that His intentions seem inconsistent, cloaked in mystery, magic and ill will. Any departure from the path laid out for us by the master mechanic goes against the original blueprint and is presumably punished. We are warned to do only as we are told. When we refuse to do God's bidding we are consigned to the scrapheap (hell). But those who follow the dictates of their master's will are rewarded with an eternity of bliss (heaven). This would be carrot-and-stick training on a cosmic scale.

The meanings of this God's confused and confusing intentions become clearer when we consider the so-called original sin and fall of Adam and Eve. In the Bible and the Koran God is said to have warned Adam and Eve not to eat from the tree of knowledge. If this warning applied to carnal knowledge one must question God's intentions in having equipped Adam and Eve with sexual and reproductive organs in the first place. It would seem that God wanted his creations to remain ignorant even of their bodily functions. Framed symbolically and in a larger context, the question remains as to why God should give us the ability to reproduce, be curious and learn and then insist that we remain barren and ignorant. These are questions that no religion (or God) has ever satisfactorily answered.

The machine analogy is especially apt here, for if God's creations were to learn independently they might come to be His rivals as far as knowledge and the exercise of free will are concerned. But this is impossible if we are programmed machines that lack the autonomy and conditional freedom to choose for ourselves. Acquiring knowledge would be an original sin if the Bible is to be believed. It would therefore follow that we could regain God's grace and the Garden of Eden only if we revert to our original ignorance – if not, we are damned for ever. God therefore teaches by punishment and reward. In psychological jargon, that is known as 'operant conditioning with reinforcement'. Pavlov formulated this as a scientific principle but it had been practised since time immemorial by priests, teachers and leaders who presumably learnt these methods from God. In computer terms operant conditioning is equivalent to programming.

This demonstrates that religions, far from being spiritual, are essentially mechanistic and manipulative and that they share this characteristic with modern science. By this token intelligent computers would be a possibility and, by a *reductio ad absurdum* those who design and program them are would-be Gods.

Pascal, although far more religious than Descartes (if the latter's religiosity was real rather than feigned), believed in the purely mechanistic explanation of the universe's origins for conventional theological reasons: 'For we must make no mistake about ourselves: we are as much automaton as mind . . . Proofs only convince the mind; habit provides the strongest proofs and those that are most believed. It inclines the automaton, which leads the mind unconsciously along with it.'[2] Pascal's famous wager about the existence of God depended on the toss of a coin and his insistence that it must come up in favour of the Deity. He also believed that any refusal to wager on the existence of God was in itself an admission of His existence. By an even greater convolution of logic he proposed that the need for the Redeemer is proven by the 'fact' that nature is corrupt, for without such corruption and the fall of man there would be no need for Christ. Why an omnipotent God would allow such corruption to occur in the first place is not explained.

It is said to have come about due to Adam and Eve's fall
from grace because they were curious, disobeyed orders
and ate from the tree of knowledge – the first instance
of deconditioning (i.e. thinking for yourself) in the biblical
history of man. For God to have wanted man and woman
to remain permanently ignorant, while convenient for the
established Church, is a denial of the meaning and purpose
of life, once it is realized that both can be summed up in a
single word – learning.

The philosopher Leibniz subscribed to the idea of man
as a God-created machine: 'Each body is thus a divine
machine or a natural automaton . . . Thus the final reasons
of things must be in a necessary substance, in which the
variety of particular things exists only eminently, as in its
source; and this substance we call God.'[3]

Spinoza disagreed with Leibniz, and differed in other
respects with him and with most of his contemporaries and
predecessors, Jewish and Christian. Unlike conventional
religionists, he correctly intuited that the concept of man's
free will is inconsistent with a God-created universe:

> I hold that God is the immanent, and not the extraneous,
> cause of all things. I say, all is in God; all lives and
> moves in God . . . Like substance, God is the causal
> chain or process . . . the will of God is the sum of all
> causes and laws, and the intellect of God is the sum of
> all mind.[4]

In essence, Spinoza says that if God has free will, man's will
must be limited because he would then be a God-created
machine. If man had free will he would be God's equal.

The following are representative examples of variations
on the mechanistic ideology common to theists and atheists
alike, together with a few rare dissenters from the popular
wisdom. Robert Boyle, although a confirmed deist, insisted
that whatever the outcome to the debate between science
and religion might be, man's obligation was to keep asking
these vital questions: 'I judge it erroneous to say in the
strictest sense that every thing in the visible world was

made for the use of man, yet I think it more erroneous to deny, that any thing was made for ends investigable by man.'5

Joseph Priestley summed up the infinite regression problem that is central to the creationist mystique as much as to science:

It is very true, that no person can satisfy himself with going backwards *ad infinitum* from one thing that requires a superior cause, to another that equally requires a superior cause. But any person may be sufficiently satisfied with going back through finite causes as far as he has evidence of the existence of intermediate finite causes; and then, feeling that it is absurd to go on *ad infinitum* in this manner, to conclude that, whether he can comprehend it or, not, there *must* be some *uncaused intelligent being*, the original and designing cause of all other beings. For otherwise, what we *see* and *experience* could not have existed. It is true that we cannot conceive *how* this should be, but we are able to acquiesce in this ignorance, because there is no *contradiction* in it.6

Isaac Newton, perhaps the greatest mechanist of his time and a contemporary of Leibniz, corresponded with a Doctor Bentley and set forth a number of arguments in 'proof' of the existence of God.7 But Holbach, Newton's contemporary and an atheist, thought otherwise:

If a faithful account was rendered of man's ideas upon the Divinity, he would be obliged to acknowledge, that for the most part the word *Gods* has been used to express the concealed, remote, unknown causes of the effects he witnessed; that he applies this term when the spring of natural, the source of known causes ceases to be visible: as soon as he loses the thread of causes, as soon as his mind can no longer follow the chain, he solves the difficulty, terminates his research, by ascribing it to his gods; thus giving a vague definition to an unknown cause, at which either his idleness, or his limited knowledge, obliges him to stop ... Can it be possible we are acting rationally, thus eternally to make Him [our God] the agent of our stupidity, of our sloth, of our want of information on natural causes?[8]

Yet William Paley still insisted on the classical theological idea of the creation, exerting an influence on the world view of Cambridge scholars and students well into this, the twentieth century:

> Were there no example in the world, of contrivance, except that of the eye, it would be alone sufficient to support the conclusion which we draw from it, as to the necessity of an intelligent Creator. It could never be got rid of: because it could not be accounted for by any other supposition, which did not contradict all the principles we possess of knowledge; the principles, according to which, things do, as often as they can be brought to the test of experience, turn out to be true or false.[9]

The atheist idea of 'the death of God' popular in the 1960s was symbolic of that hedonistic era and a direct consequence of its purposelessness and rejection of learning as the life principle. It was inevitable that such beliefs, in America at least, led to massive learning failure, to a totally materialistic and mechanistic lifestyle and, simultaneously, to a revival of the most primitive forms of religious fundamentalism and West Coast cults of consciousness-raising. Today, everyone in America and elsewhere – scientists and non-scientists alike – is looking for a redefinition of 'values' without the slightest inkling of what these might be or how to find them.[AA]

## Why are We Here?

The most common view in the sciences is that life has no purpose except physical survival and that we live in a purposeless universe. If this were true, all art and science would be meaningless and a total waste of effort. Thomas Huxley, Charles Darwin's champion against the religious anti-evolutionist establishment, addressed himself to – yet failed to answer – this vital question:

The teleological [i.e. purposive] and mechanical views of nature are not, necessarily, mutually exclusive. On the contrary, the more purely a mechanist the speculator is, the more firmly does he assume a primordial molecular arrangement of which all the phenomena of the universe are the consequences, and the more completely is he thereby at the mercy of the teleologist [i.e. those who believe that evolution has an end in view], who can always defy him to disprove that this primordial molecular arrangement was not intended to evolve the phenomena of the universe.[10]

Since life's purposes and meanings seem inaccessible to present-day science, many people can only hope to find them in religion, metaphysics, art, literature, poetry and music. This means, however, that the God principle is admitted to be an aesthetic analogy which provides the inspiration for art in all its forms and serves as a symbol of what some people can only feel but do not really know or understand. This seems to them an immanent and transcendental experience that rises above logic and reason. Despairing of finding the answers in science, a few scientists, like the twentieth-century physicist Schrödinger, turned once again to God because, as he said: 'Most painful is the absolute silence of all our scientific investigations towards our questions concerning meaning . . .'[11]

Thorpe, Schrödinger's contemporary and an Oxford biologist, was troubled by the same questions and came up with similar answers for identical reasons:

I see science as a supremely religious activity but clearly incomplete in itself. I see also the absolute necessity for a belief in a spiritual world which is interpenetrating with and yet transcending what we see as the material world . . . Similarly I believe that anyone who denies the validity of the scientific approach within its sphere is denying the great revelation of God to this day and age. To my mind, then, any rational system of belief involves the conviction that the creative and sustaining spirit of God may be everywhere present and active; indeed I believe that all aspects of the universe, all kinds of experience, may be

sacramental in the true meaning of the term . . . I cling
to the hope and belief that a natural theology will in time
become possible . . .[12]

Thorpe also cites Paley (quoted earlier) in support of
his own religious interpretation of the causal, purposive
and semantic (meaningful) aspects of our universe, taking
exception to the biologist Jacques Monod's belief in chance
and necessity:[AA]

The main argument of [Paley's] book [required reading at
Cambridge in the 1920s] was that if one were walking on
a desert shore or a new and supposedly uninhabited world
and found, say, a watch or a clock, one would be forced
to assume that the world must, at one time, have been
inhabited by an intelligent being. The book emphasized
throughout the clockwork-like or mechanical nature of
much of the natural world, arguing from this that the
world had been designed by a 'Creator'. This book was
in fact the most widely known popular example of the
'Argument from Design'.[13]

Thorpe quotes Alfred North Whitehead who, in contrast
to Bertrand Russell, his erstwhile co-author, mistakenly saw
the universe in a metaphysical, if not theistic frame of reference: 'Metaphysics is an endeavour to frame a coherent,
logical, necessary system of general ideas in terms of which
every element of our experience can be interpreted.'[14]
Thorpe believed in the big-bang theory of the universe's
origins yet felt that something must lie beyond that concept,
as some of today's physicists suspect:

It is now generally accepted that our universe originated in
a 'hot big bang' anywhere between ten and twenty billion
years ago. But far more than this, it now appears that the
essential nature and development of the universe must have
been determined (perhaps 'programmed' is not too strong
a word) during the first micro-seconds of this cataclysmic
event . . . Indeed one can say that the 'Argument from
Design' has been brought back to a central position in

our thoughts, from which it was banished by the theory of 'evolution by natural selection' more than a century ago. There seems now to be justification for assuming that from its first moment the universe was 'ordered' or programmed – was in fact Cosmos, not Chaos . . .

Many process philosophers are of the conviction that their studies eventually bring them to the point at which some form of theism is seen to be inevitable. This is a viewpoint which I share; for surely the belief in an all-encompassing process, purpose, or design must inevitably be theistic.[15]

This view was shared by physicist Werner Heisenberg who, after happily collaborating with the Nazi anti-theological structure for as long as it seemed to be 'winning' (he worked on the development of the A-bomb for Hitler during World War II), had returned to Christianity after the end of the war. Robert Augros (a philosopher) and George Stanciu (a physicist) are among the most recent crop of American academics to escape into religious fervour. Having discovered that nature is essentially a co-operative enterprise, they are so overwhelmed that they can only attribute it to the creative act of a manipulative God: '. . . the reality of purpose . . . argues a Mind behind nature since things lacking intelligence do not act for a purpose unless directed by a separate intelligence [i.e. God] . . .'[16]

But no one has ever learnt anything by being a believer; by following the dictates of God or man without question; by doing as one is told without independent thought or value judgement; by accepting the dictates of anyone as to what is right or wrong without agreement as to fundamentals and proof of his authority; by being conditioned by the carrot or the stick; by enjoying unconditional freedom or practising unconditional love. To do so or to allow that to be done to them reduces humans to the level of robots.

It is a coincidence (i.e. a certainty) that operant conditioning with reinforcement (i.e. carrot-and-stick training) is the method that is closely related to total freedom, for total freedom without goal-definition leads to total conditioning by the shortest route. The belief that operant conditioning is the only way to learn, endorsed by God and his delegates, has caused computer scientists to conclude that computers can learn and will eventually compete with human beings. They would, if programming were a learning method (see Chapter 6).

Some computer and other scientists are convinced agnostics and atheists, ready to discount the views of anyone who differs with them as being religiously inspired. Yet they themselves subscribe to educational principles that are applied by the most dogmatic religions. Thus both religionists who believe in the biblical creation and anti-religious scientists, social Darwinists and behaviourist psychologists use identical methods. They are thorough-going mechanists as far as learning is concerned, even when they may disagree among themselves about everything else (see Chapter 8).

It is perhaps asking too much of poetic and religious conceptions to be logical, internally and externally consistent and subject to the rules of induction and deduction. Believers insist on the one hand in an unconditional concept of God who needs no proof, yet on the other challenge disbelievers to 'disprove' His existence by deduction. I have done so up to a point. But it would require a book of its own to enumerate the fallacies of religious absolutism by this method for, as we shall see later in this chapter, all absolutes are conditional, especially those that are attributed to God. Deduction and induction provide conditional proof in science. But if I could demonstrate God's existence and creation by induction I would be God and I am certain that I am not.

## Meanings

The common denominators of philosophy, science and religion are attempted prediction and a quest for meaning. Thus they deal with original causes and final ends; reconciliation with the fact that all of life ends in death, the difficulties caused by unrepented error and guilt and a search for purpose in a life that is disorienting without worthwhile goals. In the case of the latter, fears and doubts can be assuaged by, or find release in, pure materialism as much as in metaphysics and theology.

A search for values plays an important role in our psychological evolution for as long as uncertainty haunts the human condition. There are two kinds of uncertainty: uncertainty about principle and uncertainty about detail. Ignorance about detail is inevitable but we can be certain of principles at least. Religion should therefore bear the same relation to science as art does to factual information, the former representing intuitive prescience as far as the correct principles are concerned (i.e. cause and effect) and an aesthetic insight into what science attempts to define later with relative precision. There should therefore be no conflict between religiosity in a true sense and science although, as we know, there is a great difference between what should be and what is.

No responsible, imaginative and foresighted individual needs any external authority to spell out the principles and meanings of conditional, ethical behaviour and the correct forms of co-operation, competition or the relationship between relatively objective and subjective reality. Meanings, like ethics, are governed by the laws of cause and effect embedded in our very genes and in the universe at large. They are merely amplified by experience and learning. Morals are something else again. They are of a purely cultural (or religious) nature and often conflict with natural law. It is up to each of us to adapt to or reject conventional morality on the basis of what is fair, just and in accordance with ethics and aesthetics and the rituals in which we choose to participate.

## Ritual

The world's religions fall into different categories of belief: animism, theism, totemism, shamanism, ancestor worship, shintoism, witchcraft and magic. Taoism, Hinduism and Sufism are not religions but humanistic ways of life. Yet Western religions share a common ground with those of African, Pacific and American Indian tribes, even to the extent of possessing similar legends (for example, the Adam and Eve myth). Some societies seem to have felt no need for a formal religion, yet still subscribed to beliefs that sought to explain the origins of the universe and of man, of a superhuman law-giver, of purpose and meaning, of good and evil, health and illness, birth and death, the seasons and the weather, chance, causation and consequences. They also sought to avert or ameliorate the effect of cataclysmic events through ritual, sympathetic magic and sacrifice to the gods.

Rituals are the threads that bind all the world's religions, irrespective of belief. They come in two basic forms. The first is all-inclusive, ecumenical and subjective. It is found in 'ways of life' that celebrate the fellowship of all mankind and the unity of nature. Such religions require no elite priesthood and no one is excluded. They tend to be global, holistic and legitimately hierarchical in outlook (i.e. any member, male or female, who performs best earns a position on the top branches of the hierarchical tree). Here ritual stands for a universal oneness. The second kind of ritual celebrates exclusivity, conflict and domination by the elect in the causes of competition, nationalism, sectarianism and spurious elitism. No distinction is usually made between these two forms of ritual.

In most societies, ancient and modern, the rites of birth, passage from adolescence into man- or womanhood, marriage and death were conducted by priests who made sure that the correct rituals were followed. However, in Christianity the training of the young was shared with lay members of the Church – teachers who adopted the methods of their spiritual leaders. This education, rather than leading to independent learning, assumed the forms of operant conditioning. Rote learning, rites of passage, passing examinations, acquiring credentials and 'doing as you are told' became its principal features: the rituals of training, propaganda and programming rather than of interest-based learning. They can be applied with equal success not only to human beings but also to animals and machines. But while such programming makes it possible for machines to function or animals to be domesticated, it turns human beings into robots; believers rather than 'that which asks the question'. Operant conditioning makes perfectly intelligent people increasingly machine-like and dependent.

Most religions, while preaching universal love, exclude non-believers. Yet ritual should be the aesthetic expression of a non-sectarian sense of community with, and the celebration of, the co-operative principle that predominates in nature. Religiosity in this sense can therefore be convergent with a humanistic science and philosophy.

The anthropologist Malinowski understood the co-operative principle embedded in ritual, although he did not distinguish between the two forms I have defined:

> First of all, social co-operation is needed to surround the unveiling of things sacred and of supernatural beings with solemn grandeur ... In the second place, public performance of religious dogma is indispensable for the maintenance of morals in primitive communities ... The endurance of social ties, the mutuality of services and obligations, the possibility of co-operation, are based in any society on the fact that every member knows what is expected of him; that, in short, there is a universal standard of conduct.[17]

## Aesthetics

As we have seen, the twin aspects of co-operation and competition reflect the conflicts within and between conventional religions, and account for their internal and external contradictions. These religions have alternately inspired a creative and unified vision of the cosmos and the most horrendous forms of divisiveness, competition, destruction and cruelty. On the one hand, religions have been responsible for the co-operative creation of magnificent edifices and works of art in the name of God or the gods – for example, the Egyptian pyramids, the Parthenon, Chartres Cathedral and the music of Vivaldi and Bach. On the other hand, they have been guilty of great cruelty, like human sacrifices and the tortures of the Holy Inquisition, as well as immense psychological damage. Athanasius Kircher, a polymath, was among the few who tried to bridge this chasm.[18] He gave us a system of musical classification (Kircher numbers) and attempted a unification of knowledge and belief that, flawed as it was, has seldom been matched before or since. He worked in the tradition of Hermetic principles sought by Ramón Lull[19] and Giordano Bruno.[20]

The vision born of an awe inspired by nature's variety and power and expressed symbolically in religious terms is not to be disparaged. It can find expression in the highest forms of art and science as much as in everyday life. There is no need for everyone to be a mathematician, scientist or philosopher any more than there is a need for everyone to be a butcher or baker. Each can approach and understand the laws of nature (or of God) in his or her own way because they are universals.

## Holiness and Holism

The principle of holism is not new but is seldom defined as well as it was by Jan Christiaan Smuts, the late Prime Minister of South Africa.[21] In a humanistic frame of reference God and nature represent the creative principle and method. Neither punishes, rewards or teaches. Such an orientation leads to holism (i.e. being whole and able to consider problems globally in a philosophical or scientific sense) and 'holiness' in a truly religious one. Will Durant, an American historian of philosophy, showed that this concept was understood among the early Greeks:

> Earlier civilizations than the Greek had made attempts at science; but ... their science was indistinguishable from theology. That is to say, these pre-Hellenic peoples explained every operation in nature by some supernatural agency; everywhere there were gods. Apparently it was the Ionian Greeks who first dared to give natural explanations of cosmic complexities and mysterious events: they sought in physics the natural causes of particular incidents, and in philosophy a natural theory of the whole ...[22]

The interpretative history of religion, ritual and myth remains to be written, although Bettany's *Encyclopedia of the World's Religions*[23] and Frazer's *Golden Bough*[24] have attempted just that. Frazer's book suffers from the fact that he did not stir from his study and relied exclusively on the classics. Bettany depended for the most part on nineteenth-century reports from often unreliable travellers and prejudiced missionaries. Anthropologists have since added to the folklore of ancient religions. But their works tend to be fragmented, and more recent studies are of dubious value because Western cultures have irreparably corrupted indigenous ones. There is, however, a clear distinction that must be made in theology between those cultures in which people stood unafraid but in awe of an infinite and eternal universe, and those of the mechanists who find manipulative levers in religion and use them to inspire fear, guilt and conflict. Lewis Mumford describes the latter:

> All the boasted inventions of our modern technology first erupted in audacious Bronze Age dreams as attributes of the Gods or their earthly representatives: remote control, human flight . . . and the wholesale extermination of large urban populations by fire and brimstone . . . If you are not familiar with the literature of Egypt and Babylon, you will find sufficient data in the Old Testament of the Bible to testify to the original paranoia of the Power Complex in the dreams and early acts of the gods and kings who represented that power on earth.[25]

# Belief

The loss of faith at an early age is as interesting as the sudden conversion of unbelievers at a later one, like that of St Paul on the road to Damascus. There are perhaps four reasons for this. The first may come from ecstasy caused by a feeling of oneness with the universe that, when not induced by drugs or hysteria, can trigger a religious experience. It can also be felt by those who achieve qualitative and aesthetic excellence, yet believe that they are ordinary men and women in receipt of 'the grace of God'. It can seem to them that some external agency is responsible for their creativity, rather than their own independent efforts. Similar, but far less rational, are the experiences of those who believe that they hear the voice of God when they are merely talking to themselves. The second reason can be an injustice that can convince the innocent or ignorant that there must be a compensatory higher justice. The third is based on fears of failure, pain, old age, death, loss or disaster. The fourth is the belief that we can never understand the purpose of life and that we are therefore in the hands of God.

The religious conversion of the philosopher C.E.M. Joad is a typical example of the discovery of God after years of atheism. Joad was a philosophy lecturer who enjoyed great popularity in Britain during the 1920s and 1930s. He wrote best-sellers, appeared frequently on the BBC and delighted audiences with his erudition and wit. In post-war years his popularity suddenly declined and he became a convinced member of the Church of England. He also seems to have lost his sense of humour. The apparent reason for his religious conversion was the result of his fondness of cheating the railways out of their fares. He was finally caught, prosecuted and found guilty. Joad's public never forgave him and it was then that this sinner repented. His fate was a tragedy because he was a first-rate popularizer in the tradition of H.G.Wells and Hendrik van Loon, and much of what he said prior to his discovery of God was rational and entertaining, especially when he wrote scathingly about sudden religious conversions:

There seem to be no beliefs which human beings, if put to it, are incapable of holding . . . [One reason is] that misfortune of any kind indicates that God exists and is good. A study of the past suggests that nothing so effectively promotes the belief in the goodness of God as a first-class calamity. Let men's crops be destroyed by drought, their cattle washed away by floods, their towns be demolished by earthquakes, their communities be smitten by pestilence and wasted with famine, [or let them be caught committing a crime] and they will be seized by a robust and lively religious zeal which sends them flocking into the churches, in order to entreat God to avert further calamities in the

future and to thank Him that he has not made them any
worse than they are in the present. It is not recorded that
this procedure has had any particular salutary effect; in
some cases very much the contrary . . . Being charitably
disposed towards the Almighty, I do not propose to accept
the obvious inference of an ironic malignity [on God's part]
– for example, the presence of active volcanoes in Italy and
the absence of drains in the Middle Ages . . . I am not, God
knows, an admirer of the Church. I know too much of its
record . . .[26]

Joad then cites the Church's dogged eighteenth-century
fight against smallpox vaccinations because clerics believed
that inoculations were 'an offence to God', and their
nineteenth-century opposition to anaesthesia in childbirth
because 'had not God laid a primeval curse upon women?'
They had also inveighed against steam engines and light-
ning conductors as 'unnatural', to say nothing of Bishop
Wilberforce's objection to the theory of evolution; just as
early in this century the established Church crusaded
against legitimate labour strikes for living wages. Joad
at his best and during his agnostic days had discovered
Taoism and Confucianism and considered his own way of
life a mixture of both. But by 1951, and with his downfall,
we suddenly find Joad among the converted: 'The following
book is an account of some of the reasons which have
converted me to the religious view of the universe in
its Christian version. They are predominantly arguments
designed to appeal to the intellect.'[27] The absurd mishmash
of reasons Joad gave for these new convictions included his
fear of atomic war; the population explosion; the need to
keep a calm temper in the face of disconcerting distractions
'when compelled to listen to the clack of women's tongues
against a background of radio light music in a hotel lounge
in which [a man] is trying to write'; the success of an
inferior tennis player who wins against a superior one; the
eventual end of the universe proposed by the astronomer
James Jeans which suggested to Joad that there must have
been a creation; that life is a mixture of good and evil; the
supernatural significance of morality; the mystery of man's

fall from grace and his inherent sinfulness; that Christ died for our sins, and Joad's belief that Dr Rhine, a discredited American parapsychologist, had proven the existence of telepathy.[28]

Anyone can change his mind as he goes through life, but there must be some coherence in what a self-styled professional philosopher believes even after a religious conversion. Joad is only one of many examples illustrating the internal and external inconsistencies common to 'believers', be they religious or agnostic, lay or professional, academic or amateur. For a belief-system based on anything other than rationality and the available facts is born of fantasy, opportunism or desperation and sometimes of all three.

## Father Teilhard's Error

There are true believers from St Augustine to Teilhard de Chardin who are persuaded of the existence of God because no other explanation for original causes and purposive existence seems possible to them. I have chosen to consider Chardin's beliefs in some detail because he was both an unusually liberal theologian and a scientist. A Jesuit, Chardin was a respected palaeontologist who tried to establish a convergence between his scientific knowledge and deeply-felt religious beliefs.

Chardin hoped to establish *unity*, which he ascribed to the smallest particles of matter; *homogeneity*, by which he meant the uniform nature of these particles; and *collectivity*, a term he used to describe the affiliation of particles by means of a binding energy. His conclusions are mechanistic because he was a theist (i.e. he believed in God and therefore that we are mechanisms created by God), despite his insistence that there is more to the universe than physical matter and his awareness of the relationship between the internal (invisible) and external (visible) facts of existence. According to Chardin, both the world of matter and the matter of ethics are the work of God, and by this attempted unification he approaches the oneness – the unity of which he speaks – that is a fundamental law of nature. Yet there are serious flaws and contradictions in what he writes because he denies the uniqueness of the individual (who is uniform and homogenous) and because of his belief in a final *victory* of the forces of God (his Church) over unbelievers – the religious competitive winning and losing game.[AA]

Chardin's viewpoint, like that of all theologians and believers, postulates an absolutely deterministic universe that has a beginning and an end. Instead, in the conditionally deterministic universe that it seems more likely to be, life can evolve from non-life as a continuous and eternal process wherever the conditions are right. These conditions need not exist at a particular beginning. Only a coincidence of combinatorial and realizable possibilities must occur at advantageous moments in time. Then life is an inevitable and recurrent consequence given the operations of randomness, the arrow of time and the direction of the evolutionary process. Thus today's scientific views of a beginning and an end (i.e. the big-bang origin and the suggested eventual heat death of the universe; see Chapter 5) seem as untenable as the religious explanation which also suggests an original cause and an eventual end. Instead it seems that evolutionary processes tend to progress eternally from the inert to the organic, resulting eventually in conscious and purposive existence (see Chapters 6 and 7). But – and this provides legitimate religiosity with credibility – evolutionary purposes, meanings and ethical laws of cause and effect appear to be implicit in such an eternally existing and evolving universe.

Like Schrödinger and Thorpe, Chardin searched for an original cause and a final end. To him God's bidding could be the only beginning. But religious and scientific beliefs notwithstanding, there does not need to be a beginning or end in the universe – the purpose of existence and its meanings could be eternal and stretch infinitely into the past and future. Should we ever reach an end we may find that we have merely arrived at a new beginning on the circumference of an ever-expanding circle. This explanation would suggest that the universe exists without infinite regress or the big bang, and would do away with traditional religious and scientific speculations about its origins or ends.

Chardin does not question the evolutionary process: 'That there is an evolution of one sort or another is now . . . common ground among scientists. Whether or not that evolution is directed is another question. Asked whether or not that evolution is going anywhere at the end of its transformation, one biologist out of ten will say no, even passionately.'[29]

What Chardin attributes to the soul and to God are indeed the hidden variables that define the relationships between the inner and outer world, between matter and process, facts, value judgements and ethics. These relationships can now be modelled and made visible (see Chapter 6). There is nothing esoteric or mysterious about them. They were hidden only for as long as we failed to find a symbolic way of defining subjective realities as scientifically demonstrable facts.

## Peace through Conquest

It seemed inconceivable to Chardin that only unbiased knowledge and understanding can lead to unanimity (in terms of the game analogy this is one aspect of the dynamic draw state, perfectibility and perfection[AA]). And this leads him into a fatal error – the belief in the superiority of the victor:

> A new domain of psychical expansion – that is what we lack. And it is staring us in the face if we would only raise our heads to look at it . . . *Peace through conquest . . . waiting for us beyond the line where empires are set up against other empires . . . in the unanimous construction of a spirit of the earth* [my italics].[30]

Such a stance is not unique to Jesuit Catholicism. It is the theme of proselytizers, bigots, extremists, dictators and fundamentalists of every stripe, and is expressed as often by politicians, philosophers and scientists as by theologians. Alice Kehoe, a US anthropologist, has gathered expressions of this idea in theology in an unpublished work from which I quote:

> Casting the world into antitheses is simple. If you are not with me, then you must be my enemy. If I am on God's side, but you are not with me, then you must be on Satan's side against God . . . [She quotes St Augustine's *The City of God*]: Every man seeks peace by waging war; [and Martin Luther]: He who will not hear God's word when it is spoken with kindness must listen to the headsman, when he comes with his axe . . .[31]

No doubt Chardin hoped that his faith would conquer the world and seemed unaware that this could only lead to a perpetuation of the winning and losing game or the endless stalemates and paranoia it engenders. On the other hand, he believed that:

> Love in all its subtleties is nothing more, and nothing less, than the more or less direct trace marked on the heart of the element by the psychical convergence of the universe upon itself . . . Love alone is capable of uniting living beings in such a way as to complete and fulfil them, for it alone takes them and joins them by what is deepest in themselves.[32]

Here we find the fundamental contradiction between professed peace and waged war, the love for like-minded co-religionists and hatred of non-believers implicit in all fundamentalist beliefs.

## Unconditional Love?

Chardin suffers from the paradox created by all believers in an exclusive theology that professes unqualified, universal love and peace imposed through conquest, where conflict and violence are inevitable. There is a further logical contradiction here, for this means 'love thy neighbour' even if he seeks to destroy you. Fundamentalists demand universal love from those they wish to dominate or destroy; the pseudo-charismatic dream of every autocrat throughout history, who as often as not acts in the name of an all-powerful God or some other messianic ideal. It seems to make no difference whether this is a Judeo-Christian, Muslim or other religious fundamentalist utopia, or a nationalist, capitalist, Communist, Fascist or democratic one. The result is always the same – heightened conflict as a result of victory sought over others who do not share the views of the enlightened.

The notion of God as the symbol of love should incorporate ecumenical, conditional co-operation and yet it has nearly always led to an authoritarian and competitive society in which you are none the less expected to love God, king and country unconditionally. Parents are expected to love their children and all children their parents, no matter how hateful, dishonest or murderous they might turn out to be. But only babies and the infirm are entitled to unconditional love because they are totally dependent.

The altruistic dogma of unconditional love professed in and outside established religions has caused a great deal of needless guilt and has enabled the few to dominate the many. For no matter how terrible and punitive God, the state, a priesthood, parent or offspring past the age of dependency may be, you – the true believer – must still love him, her or it if you are to enter the kingdom of heaven. Religious principles thus become tools for manipulating or enslaving those who have allowed themselves to be conditioned to believe in unconditional love or in any other convenient fiction.

To insist that only believers of the true faith are eligible to enter the circle of the enlightened and that all others are the enemies of God is the basis of fundamentalism and the height of arrogance. Historically and in all cultures and religions, beliefs are designed to enforce unity through conformity and dogma by means of operant conditioning with reinforcement – all of which are mechanistic processes. With institutionalization ideas of any kind tend to fossilize. Institutionalization inevitably leads to exclusivity and competition with other ideas and sects and are their eventual undoing.

Chardin's theist ideas, while framed in a twentieth-century scientific context, go back to the expressions of religiosity in antiquity. But they are also reflected in today's sciences and science fiction:

> Every culture has its tales explaining the world's beginning and man's creation, among them the biblical story of God creating Adam, and the Greek story of Prometheus creating man . . . we see how the science fiction imagination never takes anything for granted. It keeps . . . raising new questions, such as: Is man the final form of intelligence, or will another evolve? Does alien intelligence exist somewhere out there in the mysterious cosmos, and if it does, what will be its form? Could it be machine intelligence? Could God be a machine? Could a machine have created man? . . .[33]

We can therefore see how mechanistic concepts evolving from the idea of a God-created universe were adopted by the philosophies and empirical sciences in the West. They embraced materialistic and mechanistic perceptions embedded in theology since earliest times, as Descartes realized in the seventeenth century.

Any serious discussion of religion requires that genuine and deeply-felt beliefs be separated from the institutions and individuals that propagate them. Only then can religiosity in the true sense be one of the approaches to universals, provided it is humane. Humanness and humaneness are the keys to all knowledge and understanding. The failure of today's religions is attributable to a lack of subjectivity and to the mechanistic, relatively objective principles to which they adhere and which they share with modern science. Those who manage to be totally objective and therefore recognize that the correct forms of subjectivity predominate in the cosmos (i.e. perpetual feedback to the self and to everyone else in an ever-growing universe of discourse) cannot subscribe to conventional religious dogma.

In order to discover the principle of God's or nature's creativity we must first understand human creativity.[AA]

To understand God's will (if there were such a thing) we must understand the potential of human will. For, as I have said earlier, the behaviour of anything – of a hypothesized God or of inorganic particles – can only be extrapolated from an understanding of human behaviour rather than the other way round. The measure of all things is man, given the limitations and potentials of human senses and sensibilities.

## True Religiosity

To summarize the function of religions it is necessary to define the meaning of God. Whatever else He may be He would have to be the original cause of everything and therefore could not be caused by any preceding event. But the characteristics of God change dramatically once He is equated with an eternal nature that represents the sum of all combinatorial possibilities. But by doing away with the concept of God as the creator and original cause we are left with the question, 'Is there a purpose to the universe and to man's existence?' As is obvious, every machine created by man has a purpose. If that is true for man, so conventional theists argue, it would require a master mechanic (God) to create man in order to answer His purposes, whatever they might be. They believe that in the absence of God there would be no purpose to life and the universe. Yet what could be the purpose of a construct for which no expressed purpose existed from the beginning except to do its creator's bidding? That again is the definition of a machine (see Chapters 2 and 8).

If we redefine God or nature as generators of the sum of all possibilities, and considering that either would be biased in favour of ethics and the reduction of chance, the purposes of both become clear. The logic of either must lead to adaptive and sentient life sooner or later and the purpose of life is to learn and discover meanings (i.e. causes, consequences and the operations that bring both about).

None of the foregoing debases the aesthetic ideal of God or detracts from the ethical principles for which

He supposedly stands. But it shows that His existence is a logical impossibility and irrelevant. Whenever the creative principles attributed to God or nature are defined in non-manipulative, non-retributive and non-exclusive terms, or when He or it provides us with free will, all the options there are and conditional freedom to choose for ourselves, then religion, philosophy and science are as one. Religiosity can provide intuitive knowledge, aesthetic and ethical feelings and beliefs; philosophy can offer reason and logic; and science could produce replicable demonstrations of the same phenomena. Instead of differences, there would then only be agreement concerning principles. With those precepts in mind it makes no difference whether any of us are religiously, aesthetically, logically or scientifically inclined. We could then find an endless variety of truths – an agreement-to-agree as to the fundamentals of nature – or a wholly benign God if we prefer to think of these ideas in truly religious terms.

The only 'religions' with which I am familiar that define man and the universe in humanistic terms are oriental ones: the Tao, aspects of Hinduism and one Sufi sect. As I have said before, rather than religious belief-systems, they are ways of life. Such humanistic belief-systems are non-exclusive and define ethics and meanings as natural laws of cause and effect. Those who subscribe to them are intuitively aware of an eternal universe and 'the wheel of life'. A few religions and belief-systems of isolated and primitive tribes all over the world were variations on this theme until they were penetrated by missionaries and traders. These superimposed Western competitive, mechanistic, theological and political ideologies on to people who originally had the correct subjective intuitions.

## False Gods

No proselytizing, no missionary faith forced down the throats of supposed infidels, no sectarian dogma that pretends to be the sole arbiter of truth or insists on a reserved place in heaven for believers and everlasting damnation for those who dissent, and no one who demands from or gives unconditional love to healthy adults can lay claim to aesthetic or ethical legitimacy. Any priesthood (religious or psychiatric) that offers dispensation from sin by means of confession, analysis, drugs, penances and indulgences, deprives man of the dignity, responsibility and self-determination that are our birthright. Exclusive cults thrive on separatist rituals rather than on those that serve to foster a humanistic unity and communion with nature. No missionary faith that seeks converts gains followers except by coercion, threats or empty promises. Its gods are false – power symbols exploited by priesthoods and governments, or refuges for those who wish to absolve themselves of individual responsibility. Such faiths are the enemies of knowledge, science, reason, true religiosity and true love, rather than a parallel way of appreciating nature's wonders and the best works of man.

Karl Marx defined religion as the opiate of the masses and in a sense he was correct. It is also the opiate of authorities which are similarly addicted. Anyone – including Marx – who thinks in unconditionally deterministic ways cannot understand that ideologies (including Communism, capitalism, Fascism, nationalism, racism or feminism) are exactly like classical religions in so far as they insist on dogma that is less than totally objective. Each belief-system claims that it has a patent on the 'truth' or, like liberal dogma, that everything is a matter of opinion. Absolute conditional truths do not exist for them. In promoting the idea of a mechanistic or value-free universe, as much as one created by God, believers stop thinking along any other than party, nationalistic or sectarian lines. Hence these are purely materialist and manipulative philosophies (i.e. they are based on principles of external control), even when they are cloaked in spirituality.

Only by applying totally objective criteria (i.e. by considering all possibilities within any given context) can it be shown that conditionally absolute truths predominate in the universe. Both subjective and relatively objective criteria must be applied if we are to understand and appreciate the fundamental laws of nature. Any God representing a wholly benign, supreme power or self-organizing nature does not create the universe or reveal it to us. We are meant to discover it and its meanings for ourselves. Such a God does not expect us to believe anything except what we can learn and demonstrate. At that point we do not need religious institutions. But the conventional believer in religion as much as in philosophy and science surrenders his freedom to a higher authority and thereby loses the autonomy needed to learn. However, even the freedom to learn is conditional. It depends on a choice of benign goals. We can be free only at a point at which learning with a purpose becomes the purpose of life. We are then free to reach such goals by any legitimate means. It makes no difference whether we believe that such truths come to us from God or whether we discover them through logic, by observation or by experiment.

To summarize, true religion is a pre-scientific recognition that fundamental laws of nature rule our existence and perceptions. These laws can be codified and expressed by feelings, beliefs and ecumenical rituals to celebrate what could not formerly be demonstrated in scientific or philosophical terms. All genuine religions share common archetypal roots embedded in natural law, truth and ethical behaviour. The dominance of subjective realities in nature, like ethics, in which relatively objective ones play only a minor role, are embedded and perpetuated by means of ritual in the world's great religions, prior to their corruption into exclusivity and control of believers by priesthoods and governments.

For as long as subjective processes and their meanings remained inaccessible via the scientific method, they could be approached only via art, poetry, philosophy and religions. However, now that we can model and demonstrate how subjective processes work in geometric, mathematical terms (including those that apply to human behaviour) we can relegate an uncaused and eternal God to the realm of fiction. True religions can none the less continue to serve a useful purpose in so far as poetic truths always precede the discovery of scientific ones, even when the former are merely elegant metaphors for what eventually turn out to be laws of nature.

# 5
# The Blinkered Sciences

'Scientific theories have blundered in the past; they blunder
no doubt today; yet we cannot doubt that along with the
error there come gleams of truth for which the human mind
is impelled to strive.'                          A.S. Eddington[1]

As suggested earlier, modern science and the technologies
influence our perceptions to the same extent that fundamentalist religious ideas formerly ruled most people's
lives. Today we *believe* in science as once we believed in a
literal heaven and hell. Science is the religion of our day.
Indeed our convictions concerning the meaning of life, or
whether life has any meaning, can be traced directly to
religious beliefs that have filtered down to today's sciences
in new disguises. Some of our beliefs about the origin or
end of the universe, randomness, chance, time, our ideas
about natural laws, predictability, learning and human
behaviour and whether or not we are biological machines,
stem from the current wisdom promulgated in the name
of sciences which are still affected by erroneous religious
and philosophical concepts of the past. This is not often
appreciated.

In my previous book[AA] I showed that many of our
opinions about human and animal behaviour are based on
wrong premises and pseudo-scientific misconceptions. As
demonstrated there, human behaviour can be defined and

predicted geometrically and mathematically; something that was previously thought to be impossible. The discovery of an analytic, geometric pattern structure that appears to underlie human behaviour demands that we reconsider how we regard ourselves and the micro- and macrocosm. Identical methods can be used to examine other aspects of the universe about which we have sufficient knowledge. These appear to confirm certain current scientific theories and call others – especially what is known as the scientific method – into question.

It is not enough to disagree with scientific theories. It is equally important to show why they and the prevailing scientific method may be questionable. It is then necessary to provide revised methods and definitive results in branches of science in which one or the other does not stand up to logical analysis. For this reason I elaborate in the Appendices new findings and the analytic techniques that enabled me to make them. These model the combinatorial neural network (see Appendices A and D) that defines how we think, learn, perceive the universe and make predictions. This approach is not a new paradigm but a paradigm generator that enables us to examine critically any paradigm – old or new – and make value judgements about it.[AA] As demonstrated, when events are analysed permutationally (in terms of sequence) as is done today, the sum of possibilities is inadequate. But when any known sequence of events is analysed combinatorially (i.e. in terms of the relationships between sequences), their meanings can become clear and the facts can be put into perspective. Anything else lies beyond our current knowledge or understanding. That is the best we will ever be able to do in science, philosophy, art or anything else.

Demonstration and prediction are the chief aims of the sciences. But, as stated earlier, the sciences ask *how* but not *why* and claim to be value-free. To demonstrate how we (or fundamental particles) behave is not good enough. To understand and predict behaviour we must also know why we – and they – behave in given circumstances. Scientists who insist that their methods should be limited to operations and quantification (the how) to the exclusion of qualitative analyses (the why) are mere technicians, doomed to perpetual tinkering and uncreatively churning out statistics. This is why many of the sciences are mired in mechanistic, relatively objective and therefore *faulty* ways of looking at man and the universe. Dissident scientists who make value judgements are usually accused of straying into the realms of theology, philosophy or politics and are severely criticized by their peers. So let us begin by examining some of the prevalent beliefs in the sciences about how the universe is thought to have begun, how it is supposed to end, and of what it might be composed.

## Is the Universe Open or Closed?

The methods of modelling used for defining the universe and quantifying its particle components are determined by what we believe to be natural laws. They turn out to be the same methods that apply to the analyses of human behaviour. Further, today it is often suggested that our current methods of describing nature are natural laws themselves (e.g. that the universe is governed by the laws of statistics) – a highly questionable proposition. The first question I discuss here is whether our universe is open and infinite or closed and finite. (It will become apparent later why this is an important question.)

Since the 1920s and Edwin Hubble's observations at Mount Wilson Observatory, we have known that the universe expands spatially. In other words, all galaxies are rushing away from us and each other in every direction. This means that the universe is larger (and cooler) today than it was yesterday and that it was smaller (and hotter) in the past. But, as the general theory of relativity seems to indicate, the expansion of the universe could take three different forms, depending on the characteristics and force of gravity.

1. The universe is closed, contains a finite number of particles and expands until it dies a heat death.

2. The universe is closed, perpetually creates particles out of nothing and expands perpetually.

3. The universe is open, but exchanges particles with other parallel universes, expanding and contracting rhythmically over eons of time.

In the first instance it is assumed that the number of energy and/or matter particle components of the universe remains constant; in the second, that the particle components of the universe are variable; in the third, fundamental particles might be eternal or they might be formed in a manner that is not yet understood. Whether or not these ideas are correct hinges on a number of unknowns, for example whether our universe conforms to relativistic or quantum principles or a combination of both, as Stephen Hawking suggests;[2] or whether so-called invisible 'dark matter' and 'virtual particles' form a substantial background to the visible and tangible universe. These and other possibilities are discussed in an interesting book by Lawrence Krauss[3] who postulates the existence of a 'fifth essence' that, while suggested by the available evidence, seems to have eluded identification so far. Krauss, an astro-physicist, claims that this invisible and intangible background makes up between 90–98 per cent of all particles in the universe. But Krauss also believes in the big-bang origin and eventual heat death of the universe. On the other hand, Hawking, one of the former subscribers to the big-bang theory, now has his doubts about it and its implications.

If the universe were closed it would have a beginning and an end; if open it might be infinite and eternal. The assumption that the universe was once smaller than today is indisputable, given its current expansion. But this does not necessarily mean that it started with a big bang. It could expand up to a certain point and then contract periodically, or it might expand indefinitely. It could be closed at any moment in time yet open to future input, like other systems with which we are familiar (e.g. numbers can be said to consist of an infinite number of finite sets). If the universe pulsated (i.e. periodically expanded and contracted), the arrow of time would still point to the future (i.e. time would be irreversible, as now), for elapsed time would continue unabated even during periods of contraction. Also, and as admitted in physics today, the scientific method breaks down when considering anything that preceded the hypothesized big bang. But what might have occurred before the big bang must still be subject to logical analysis, as shown later.

As I have said repeatedly, any process is meaningless for which we cannot define causes, consequences and operations. The big-bang theory is mostly concerned with operations and ignores original causes and long-term consequences. It is therefore logically meaningless. If it occurred without any evident cause, the big bang would be a random event and a product of chance or an act of God. If the universe were ever to destroy itself without a trace then its history and operations are inconsequential. But such a concept does not hold up, given my redefinition of randomness and chance which has a sound mathematical basis (see below).

If our universe is uncaused, or came about due to unknown causes or as a result of God's creation, is finite (as far as particles are concerned), but expanding (as far as space is concerned), then statistical methods for determining the number, velocity or position of component particles might be appropriate, although misleading. This is the kind of particle universe described by Heisenberg's uncertainty principle. It is worth reiterating that it is paradoxically believed in today's sciences that fundamental energy particles (of which all matter is composed) operate on principles of uncertainty and the macrocosm (the actual matter, bodies and galaxies) on relativistic (i.e. conditionally deterministic) ones. This is an irreconcilable paradox that Stephen Hawking has tried to resolve, unsuccessfully so far. In theory and in practice it is a practical impossibility because conditional determinism and the uncertainty principle are incompatible, as Einstein knew.

Heisenberg's uncertainty principle merely describes a current standard of measurement – the yardstick we employ and not what is measured. Yet, as Stephen Hawking believes: 'Heisenberg's uncertainty principle is a fundamental, inescapable property of the world.'[4] Heisenberg's theory describes limits dictated by current methods of quantification rather than the characteristics of actual events. If Heisenberg's uncertainty principle were a fundamental, inescapable property of the world, as Hawking suggests, then the same would have to be true for a randomly shuffled pack of playing cards. But combinatorial methods of analysis demonstrate that this is untrue (see below and Appendices A and D).

Statistical methods of analysis might suffice for particle behaviour in a finite universe in which all the facts can be theoretically or actually accounted for, when the future is identical to the past, and for events taking place between precisely defined marks. They appear to work when the number of possibilities is too immense to lend itself to precise quantification. So we can say that probabilistic methods of calculation can be adequate for particle behaviours when no better methods exist, but not otherwise.

I have shown that human behaviour is an open system and is best described and predicted by combinatorial (i.e. relativistic) methods.[AA] Any statistical calculation for human behaviour has no predictive value unless all future conditions remain identical to those that obtained in the past or unless what is predicted is limited to a finite environment. Statistical methods can never be predictive for human behaviour except in an unchanging world. However, change is the first rule of existence.

The claim that nature operates on the basis of statistical laws is therefore highly questionable. We may favour or have no better methods for making calculations. But, if my redefinition of chance has any merit, much of modern science is vulnerable because it postulates that nature operates on principles of uncertainty, probability and chance (rather than on the basis of conditional determinism) when in fact chance seems to be largely a question of time and human ignorance.

On the basis of neural network analysis it seems likely

that our universe is finite at any moment, yet open and expanding. Or an infinite number of parallel universes may exist with which our universe exchanges particles in both directions. Hence, in either case, it may expand perpetually, or expand and contract alternately over eons of time. The infinite future of the universe would thus be guaranteed, tending towards a dynamic (and not a static) balance and order in the long run. In that case, and as I have suggested before, our universe would be eternal. Its fundamental particle components would still combine and recombine at random, like a perpetually shuffled pack of playing cards, but their number might in- or decrease periodically.

If it turns out that we do not live in a closed and ultimately finite universe, then different methods of modelling and calculation would have to apply to it than those we now use. It seems absurd to insist that the particle universe is indeterminate because Heisenberg's theory seems to describe it successfully for current practical purposes, or that it is governed by chaos principles because that is the latest fashion in science. To sum all of this up, it is important to recognize that the methods we use to describe what seem like natural laws are not necessarily natural laws in themselves. A map is not the terrain, no matter how convenient a representation it may seem to be.

The dynamic *relationships* (the coincidences) between aggregations of fundamental energy or matter particles are at least as and probably more important than their number, position, velocities and permutations. These relationships cannot be accounted for statistically or by considering the permutations only. But combinatorial modelling – in which classification reveals the unique characteristics of every individual permutation – makes possible a detailed analysis of all relational possibilities between individuals and groups (i.e. the solution to the many-body problem in physics).

It is also not enough to look at these relationships in a relatively objective manner (i.e. within a limited frame of reference), for this means that you cannot see the problem in its totality. Total objectivity can only be achieved by stepping outside the system and regarding it as a whole. It is obviously impossible to do this for the universe, except theoretically. But when we use combinatorial methods it is possible to demonstrate conclusively that subjective processes (i.e. feedback – a balance between energy and matter and the first law of thermodynamics) predominate in the universe. Similarly it can now be shown that relatively objective processes (closure – the second law of thermodynamics and the rush towards perpetual increase in entropy; the idea that all systems keep running down with ever greater speed) are temporary and purely local phenomena.[AA]

The evolution of modern science from its religious and philosophical origins represents a swing to extremes from absolute and unconditional certainty to uncertainty, and from pre-determination to indeterminacy and chance. It does not seem to have occurred to many modern scientists to question their beliefs in a universe governed by chance any more than religionists questioned the laws of a universe laid down by God. On the basis of what follows I hope to show that we live in a conditionally deterministic universe in which optional branching provides vast evolutionary choices in which chance plays only a limited role in the short run and virtually none in the longest run.

For these reasons I deal next with the twin concepts of randomness and chance because these are central to our understanding of how the universe works and because both are misunderstood in modern mathematics, physics and biology. There are dissenters like David Bohm[5] and Ilya Prigogine,[6] but they do not seem to have demonstrated their contentions in specific terms.

If the concepts of modern mainstream philosophy and science were correct and if our universe were to operate on principles of uncertainty, probabilities and chance, then life would be an accident of nature and our existence uncaused and without consequences (i.e. meaningless). The same would of course also be true for science, a proposition that most scientists would dispute even while clinging to the belief in an essentially purposeless and chancy nature. However, many scientists insist that we are nothing but machines – a *mechanistic* outlook (i.e. viewing portions of the universe from a purely materialistic and deterministic perspective; see Chapters 1 and 8). But then they also claim that we and the universe are products of indeterminacy and chance. Such contradictory and paradoxical stances are untenable when held simultaneously or when they are examined in combinatorial terms.

The sciences are therefore caught between two mutually exclusive contradictions: a universe governed by chance and, at the same time, by purely mechanical principles (i.e. pre-determinacy, because a machine must be the product of someone's design). None of this makes sense unless the universe is a fruit machine designed by God. But even the randomized program of a fruit machine repeats itself once all possibilities are exhausted and thus becomes deterministic in the long run. So, even if the universe operated like a one-armed bandit, one of the fundamental concepts of particle physics would be wrong because chance is virtually non-existent in the longest run.

To be a generalization a theory should apply to the infinitely small and the infinitely large; to the inorganic as much as to the organic, considered globally. But, as pointed out earlier, any analysis of the cosmos in macrocosmic terms must remain theoretical because it is impossible to step outside it physically or to consider the sum of its combinatorial possibilities (e.g. the relationship of every atom or particle combination to all others). For, as the philosopher-mathematician Pierre Laplace suggested, if this were possible then everything in the universe would be predictable: 'An intelligence that, at a given instance, was acquainted with all the forces by which Nature is animated and with the state of the bodies of which it is composed . . . nothing would be uncertain for such an intelligence, and the future like the past would be present to its eyes.'[7]

We are thus limited to understanding principles that can be verified by observation and demonstrated by experiment, analogy, deduction or by means of a simplified model.

Our knowledge of detail is likely to remain incomplete in subjects more complex than the game of noughts and crosses or a pack of playing cards. It is therefore only possible to make generalizations based on principles that apply to whatever is known. Theory and practice must match and be internally and externally consistent, work inductively and deductively and be infinitely replicable – the philosopher Braithwaite's definition of proof – if analysis is to lead to accurate generalizations and forecasts. Even so, any generalization must be open to modification through learning, or else we might lock ourselves into perpetual error.

As I have said before, beliefs in science that have no basis in fact are perpetuated by operant conditioning as are those in religion and philosophy (see Chapter 6). It is this which makes for further corruption in the sciences as much as in every other human activity. Once a method or an idea is established, becomes fashionable and is believed – no matter how wrong it may be – it becomes a universal or near-universal standard, taught as gospel in schools and universities and perpetuated without being sufficiently questioned. Any deviation is considered a heresy and actively discouraged by practitioners who have a vested interest in maintaining the current orthodoxy and status quo. As a result, people lose the ability to think independently. This leads to a dictatorship by a self-appointed academic elite that crushes individuality, responsible freedom and creativity.

## Randomness in Our Universe

The 'scientific' idea that man and the universe are products of chance goes back to the seventeenth century.[AA] But well before that time certain native American tribes believed that originally the gods played dice for possession of the earth. (It seems from today's perspective that the winner was a loser.) Equally, and as I have said before, the concurrent belief that man and nature operate solely on mechanical principles is a concept inherited from the religious notion that we are the creations of God's design. Any belief – theological, philosophical, scientific or political – which is without factual and logical foundation is a religious or quasi-religious one, no matter how hard agnostic or atheist scientists, philosophers or politicians try to deny it. Thus we and the universe are simultaneously (or alternately) believed to be accidents of nature and nature's (or God's) purpose-built machines. Many unresolved contradictions in science, philosophy, and religion therefore hinge on the following questions:

- Are all things in our universe pre-determined, or are they products of the laws of cause and effect or of chance?
- What is the cause of chance?
- What is the nature of coincidence?
- Are accidents chance events?
- Does randomness (i.e. chaos) create, increase or reduce chance?
- Do the universe and existence have meaning and purpose?
- What defines meanings?
- What is the purpose of existence?
- Is our universe mindless, or does there exist a duality consisting of the physical (matter) and some other invisible reality (for example, Cartesian duality, soul, mind, spirit or psyche)?

Because chance is a basic tenet in the sciences, the uncertainty aspects of quantum theory seemed attractive for they suggest that all is indeterminate in the microcosm (but not in the macrocosm), that probabilities rule in the particle universe and that organic life is an accident of a purposeless nature or an act of God. Any of these are convenient stances that, despite obvious self-contradictions, seem to appeal to scientists who are atheists, agnostics, materialists or anti-materialists and even to many with strong religious convictions. Manfred Eigen, a German physicist and a devotee of Heisenberg, wrote a book about the relationship between supposed aspects of chance in the games we play (including purely strategic ones in which chance should play no role whatsoever)[AA] and the chancy and uncertain aspects of a quantum-bundled particle universe.[8]

Therefore it seems that we have invented contradictory ideas like unqualified chance (i.e. accidents) and a deterministic God (i.e. predetermined certainty) to avoid thinking and acting rationally and responsibly. For example, if the origin of the universe or of life is a chance event, then the same must be true of its consequences. The evolution of mankind would have to be an accident of nature. But in the absence of man there can be no accidents because only man interprets events in such a fashion. Accidents can be caused only by human ignorance, inattention, a refusal to assume responsibility and think or act appropriately, or when we are overwhelmed by events that are beyond our control. Or, if there were an original cause for the universe (God or the big bang), the future would be pre-determined by the initial conditions. In a God-given or big-bang universe there could therefore be no accidents. Conversely, in the absence of original causes all events in organic and inorganic nature could only be accidents; otherwise, as insurance companies and theists prefer, they would have to be 'acts of God'. In science as in theology and philosophy the reasons for believing that accidents in any consciously aware, behavioural setting are caused by blind chance are primitive superstitions. In the inorganic portions of the universe there can also be no accidents, for even there every event has a cause or a cluster of contributing causes.

If nature operated on principles of chance then any purposive intervention by mankind would merely be ameliorative or in vain. Life would be an insignificant event in a more-or-less unpredictable scheme of things. This idea must also lead to bland materialism, as indeed it has, because then it would not matter what we do as long as it pays (either in cash or by getting into heaven). In the long term we will all be obliterated, so during our brief stay on earth we might as well get as many of the world's goods as we can (or hand some of them back as acts of charity so as not to take a chance on frying in hell for eternity); do as little as we can get away with, assuming no responsibility for anything; or wait until nirvana arrives, as it may, given an infinity of time. If you believe that existence is a matter of chance or the result of a one-time creation by God, then there is no need to plan or do things systematically and in a craftsman-like fashion. You might just as well give up – as many people have done.

Clearly there is a conflict in these perceptions between purpose and purposelessness; chance and certainty; between organic life and inert or dead matter; between an inorganic universe that keeps running down like a clock and a God who originally is supposed to have wound it up. All of this is reflected in how we think about the universe and ourselves. Organic behaviour is clearly different from, yet related to, inorganic behaviour inasmuch as it can slow or in some respects halt the second law of thermodynamics (the law that states that all systems run down perpetually), rewinding the eternal clock. These conflicts are resolved only once we recognize that we live in a *conditionally deterministic* (relativistic) universe. Conditional determinacy (i.e. where the conditions we impose or perceive determine the outcome) can therefore be the most likely alternative to a universe directed by chance or by God. This definition of the universe (or of human behaviour) does not seem to have occurred to anyone other than Albert Einstein or the early Taoists, Hindus and one Sufi sect. Instead, Western science has become infatuated with unconditional chaos. Even here conditional determinacy rules, for we always get what we want, create, or perceive to be true.

To understand the relationship of randomness to chance, philosophers and physicists usually use the analogy of a pack of playing cards. A mindless and random arrangement of playing cards is an apt metaphor for the random movements of particles in the universe. Obviously, in the absence of human beings, there is no one around who could compare the evident randomness of the particle universe to a pack of playing cards or make comparisons between a randomly shuffled pack and one that is ordered and reordered systematically. For that matter, without us there would be no playing cards. Human existence and awareness are therefore essential preconditions for distilling order out of apparent chaos, a quality previously attributed only to God.

Philosophers, mathematicians and scientists have repeatedly used, but never understood – and have therefore persistently misrepresented – this useful analogy, for they believe that no sequence in a pack of cards is ever likely (or is most unlikely) to repeat itself with random shuffling.[AA] In other words, physicists use the shuffled playing-card analogy to claim that there is a perpetual increase in disorder among random particle affiliations in the universe. However, they have never directly compared what occurs in a randomly shuffled pack of cards to an infinite number of packs arranged as they come from the shop or to one that is reordered systematically in combinatorial terms (see Appendices A and D). It is essential to do this to understand what takes place in a randomly shuffled pack of cards, before applying the results to the particle universe.

Chance depends very much on a 'coincidence' (the coinciding of two or more events and the frequency of repetitions) of identical cards, particles, events or other combinations, their order and recurrence in a random universe. Coincidences are conditional certainties, as Brian Inglis demonstrates.[9] But our understanding of chance also depends on which analogy we use. As in Heisenberg's uncertainty principle, the methods used (i.e. the premises) to measure and describe the universe or anything else usually determine the result. For example, Stephen Hawking uses the example of pieces of a jigsaw puzzle, jumbled and shaken up in a paper bag to define the meaning of randomness.[10] Obviously, no matter how hard or for how long you shake such a bag, the pieces will never reassemble into the picture that was originally jig-sawed into irregular, but tightly fitting components. They must be reassembled by hand so that each irregular shape fits precisely into adjacent ones to form a single, pre-determined picture. But since this cannot occur at random and without human intervention it is an inappropriate metaphor. The puzzle will always be jumbled, no matter how long you shake the bag, although occasionally one or another piece might find itself locked temporarily into a neighbouring one by chance. Fitting pieces together by hand is a matter of attention and trial and error and never of chance. By using the wrong metaphor Hawking comes to the wrong conclusion that randomness creates chance. However a pack of playing cards is an appropriate metaphor for a random universe because it can form all possible combinations by any kind of mindless shuffling (e.g. being shaken up in a bag, shuffled by hand or the wind) or by deliberate sorting.

The physicist Paul Davies presents the 'classical' view with some variations of his own and provides a summary of what mathematicians, physicists, biologists and game theoreticians of the past and present have written about the relationship of randomness to chance.

> The effect of the molecular collisions is akin to the random rearrangement of a deck of cards. If you start out with cards in a particular order – for example, numerical and suit sequence – and then shuffle the deck, you would not expect that further shuffling would return the cards to the original orderly sequence. Random shuffling tends to produce a jumble [i.e. chance and chaos]. It turns order into a jumble, and a jumble into a jumble, but practically never turns jumble into order . . .[11]

But then Davies introduces a variation that is no less wrong than the conventional wisdom:

> . . . so long as the shuffling is truly random, jumbled sequences will be produced much more often than ordered sequences – because there are so many more of them. Another way of expressing this is to say that a sequence picked at random is far more likely to be jumbled than ordered . . . there is a fundamental *statistical* element

involved. The transition from order to disorder is not *absolutely* inevitable; it is something that is merely *very probable* if the shuffling is random. Clearly, there is a tiny but non-zero chance that shuffling a jumbled card sequence will transform it into suit order. Indeed, if one were to shuffle long enough, *every* possible sequence would eventually crop up, including the original one ...

It seems then, that an inexhaustible shuffler would eventually be able to get back to the original ordered sequence [as he would if he rearranged the cards systematically and once he had exhausted the sum of all permutational possibilities. But then Davies asks:] Is the arrow of time therefore an illusion here? Not really. We can certainly say that if the cards were initially ordered and then shuffled a few times, it is overwhelmingly likely that the deck will be less ordered afterwards than before. But the arrow clearly does not come from the shuffling as such; rather, it owes its origin to the special, orderly nature of the initial state ... These ideas carry over in a fairly straightforward way to the case of a gas ...[12]

Stephen Hawking suggests that the same is true for fundamental particles:

Suppose a system starts out in a small number of ordered states. As time goes by, the system will evolve according to the laws of science and its state will change. At a later time, it is more probable that the system will be in a disordered state than in an ordered one because there are more disordered states. Thus disorder will tend to increase with time if the system obeys an initial condition of high order.[13]

Knowledgeable gamblers would object to these 'scientific' beliefs, but they usually do not read books on quantum theory, particle physics or biology. Gamblers derive their ideas about chance from experience. Scientists who base their theories on conventional game theory do not appear to understand what really takes place when a pack of cards is shuffled and so their beliefs concerning randomness and chance are wrong. Personal experience illustrates the fore-going. Travelling to France by ferry from Dover recently, I asked the on-board blackjack (vingt-et-un) dealer how long she had worked in her job. 'Six months,' she replied, 'and before that I was a cocktail waitress.' 'Tell me, then,' I said, 'does shuffling the pack of cards create or increase chance?' 'Neither,' she answered. 'Shuffling reduces chance. That is one reason why gambling casinos increase the natural odds in their favour or else they would go bankrupt.' I asked this question of the manager of London's fashionable Claremont Casino – also no scientist or philosopher – and he gave me the same answer. It should therefore be obvious that casino employees know far more about the practical relationship between randomness and chance than most academics. They learn from experience and pay attention to the facts instead of wasting their time creating elegant but erroneous theories and generalizations.

As a result of such faulty methods of analysis it is generally believed in physics and biology that randomness creates or increases chance in so far as a shuffled pack of playing cards, the movement of gas molecules, sub-atomic particles and mutations are concerned. Thus it seems to most scientists that God plays dice with the universe – an idea suggested by Heisenberg's uncertainty principle to which Albert Einstein objected. The fallacies concerning chance that prevail in today's science become obvious when the relationship of randomness to chance is re-examined in combinatorial terms. (The detailed mathematics that apply are given in an appendix to *Winners*[AA], but the process is explained simply and in non-mathematical terms below and in Appendix A. Even this explanation may necessitate several readings because these processes are subtle and run counter to current beliefs.)

The *internal* and *external* repetitions of all permutations in a randomly shuffled pack of playing cards over periods of time can be discovered only by systematic combinatorial sorting. These repetitions remain hidden when the pack is considered statistically, permutationally or in any other way. What really takes place is obscured by random shuffling and can only be unscrambled combinatorially. In other words, a mindlessly shuffled pack consists of a combinatorial (showing the relationships between sequences) rather than a permutational (purely sequential) series. The actual relationship of randomness to chance was never previously appreciated because combinatorial mathematics was imperfectly understood until now. As in other branches of science, the answer lies in a correct choice of method.

As a result of an application of the combinatorial method one can predict that any and every sequence of cards (including the pack as a whole) is likely to recur quite frequently at indeterminate intervals in the short term in a randomly shuffled pack. In the longest run there will be very little or virtually no difference between the repetitions in a combinatorially arranged infinite series of packs and an infinite randomly shuffled one. What holds true for packs of playing cards is equally true for fundamental particles.

Were fundamental particles ordered systematically by God or nature, evolutionary processes that lead to life might occur only at extremely rare, regular intervals. Randomness ensures that all possible combinations repeat in irregular bursts anywhere in the universe where the environmental conditions are right. Even these depend on randomness for the frequency of their repetitions. So to return to Einstein and Heisenberg, if God had played dice with the universe He would have done so to enhance the certainty of the evolution of life.

The sum of combinatorial possibilities explodes at an exponential (i.e. geometric) rate with every increase in factors (i.e. added cards or particles) for reasons explained in Appendix A and in *Winners*.[AA] As systems grow larger the repetitions increase in predictable ways. For example, partial permutations increase at the greatest rate. As systems grow larger chance decreases further in certain respects. Chance is therefore a conditional factor that decreases in random series in proportion to the increase in the number of factors. In other words, the randomly shuffled pack of cards would seem to be equivalent to a combinatorial rather than a purely permutational micro- and macrocosmic universe.

The only difference between a pack-of-cards universe and our own is that the latter may fluctuate if, as I suggested earlier, additional particles are created or exchanged with parallel universes at unpredictable intervals.

## The Reduction of Chance

The question of randomness and its relation to chance is fundamental to any understanding of the scientific method. This issue can be illustrated by a mathematical analysis of relatively small systems. As I have stated, the pack of playing cards example is perhaps the most accessible one.

There are four ways of considering order, randomness and chance in a pack of playing cards:

1. The order in which packs of cards come from the shop – thirteen cards each in four different suits, arranged from the two to the ace (see Diagram 3) – is established by convention. Such a pack is finite. Eventually the pack will be restored to its original order if you move every card in succession from the top to the bottom of the pack. If you continue this process indefinitely this is equivalent to an infinite series of the same pack placed side-by-side (see Diagram 3) in which the original order repeats *externally* in every next pack.

*Diagram 3*: An infinite series of finite, identical packs of cards
Here every stack represents a pack of ordinary playing cards as it comes from the shop. Any other agreed-to or known order might be an equally good starting point. This is an infinite series of identical packs of fifty-two playing cards, each representing a finite series. It is easy to see that the King and Ace of any one suit repeat only once in each pack. They will repeat *externally*,

*indefinitely and at predictable fifty-two-card intervals* for as long as the cards in each pack remain in the same order. Mixed suit sequences cannot occur.

2.　When such a pack of cards is re-arranged as described above, permutations (i.e. sequences of cards) like those containing a mixture of all four suits (e.g. two and five of hearts, three of spades and four and six of clubs as in a 'straight' in poker) can never occur, unless each pack is rearranged permutationally or randomized.

　　The complete and partial permutational possibilities (i.e. all possible sequences, including those of mixed suits) within the pack of fifty-two cards can be established mathematically or by physical rearrangement until all possibilities are exhausted. As shown in Appendix A, this is an inadequate calculation. The sum of all permutations for all cards in a pack is 52! (or 52 × 51 × 50 . . . × 1). But when all permutations are exhausted and if this sorting process is continued, these sequences will also repeat – another form of *external* repetition. Therefore external repetitions are guaranteed if we have an infinite series of finite packs of cards or if we rearrange the same pack more than once permutationally.

*Diagram 4*: Permutations
The permutations of cards in the pack consist of all possible whole and partial sequences within the whole pack (including mixed suits), into which they can be arranged systematically. With continuous systematic arrangement and rearrangement, after all permutational possibilities have been exhausted, the full and partial permutations also repeat *externally*. Thus the permutational repetitions follow the same principles as any

other conventional rearrangement of the original order (see Diagram 3 above). Here only the twenty-four suit permutations (hearts, spades, diamonds and clubs) are shown to demonstrate the principle.

3. A third method of rearranging the finite pack involves *combinatorial* sorting that systematically analyses what shuffling brings about mindlessly and at random. This generates a finite sum of:

$$52 \times 2 \; \frac{52(52-1)}{2} \; \text{possibilities.}$$

Here every combination of cards repeats *internally* within every single pack a calculable number of times in relation to the rest of the pack. This is what occurs when a pack of cards is turned into an infinite series by being shuffled mindlessly. In play and after shuffling (i.e. mindlessly disordering the original order) the pack is dealt – which, in effect, is a further form of shuffling. Previously it was believed that it is then impossible to isolate and calculate what seems to occur with random shuffling, except statistically. However, as we shall see, statistics can be very misleading especially in an infinite universe of discourse, and even in a finite one when they are not derived from combinatorial calculations.

When a single pack is arranged and rearranged combinatorially and systematically, every single card and every whole and partial permutation of the pack and the pack as a whole will repeat *internally* as often as there are combinations in the rest of the pack before all possibilities are exhausted (see Diagram 6). Successive packs will also repeat internally with continued combinatorial sorting. Thus both *internal* and *external* repetitions will recur again and again with predictable frequency and order when the pack is viewed combinatorially in a systematic manner. When shuffled mindlessly, the pack will generate the *internal* and *external* repetitions in bunched sequences in the short run. In the longest run there will be virtually no difference in the number of repetitions in the original ordered combinatorial infinite series and the randomly shuffled one. Thus randomness actually reduces chance in the short term and reduces it to zero in the longest run, except for the periodicity and order of recurrences.

The number of whole and partial permutations in a pack of cards is very large, but the number of internal combinatorial repetitions is astronomical. The difference in percentages of repetitions in permutational and combinatorial series becomes comprehensible when each is compared to the other in a pack involving just a few cards. So, for example, when there are only five cards in a pack, and when these are arranged and re-arranged permutationally, there can only be 120 permutational sequences, each of which differs from all others. There are no *internal* repetitions.

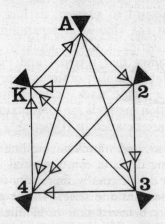

*Diagram 5*: Systematic combinatorial analysis. One of 5,120 combinatorial possibilities for five cards of one suit

With systematic combinatorial sorting (rather than just per-mutational re-ordering), it becomes obvious that the King-Ace combination of the same or any mixed suit (or any other combination) will recur internally as often as there are combinatorial possibilities in the rest of the pack. Even the pack as a whole will recur internally in its original order a calculable number of times when the combinatorial sum of all possibilities is considered systematically. Then the true number of *internal* and *external* repetitions becomes totally predictable, including when they occur and in which order. None of this can be discovered unless combinatorial geometry is used. Diagram 5 shows how often the King-Ace sequence will occur, relative to a five-card pack or sequence. It repeats *internally* 1,220 times (23.8%) and the whole series of five cards repeats 160 times (3.125%). In a randomly shuffled pack such facts remain hidden. Certainty is therefore a question of method.

But when a pack of five cards is arranged systematically in a combinatorial way, there will be 5,120 possibilities, 160 of which (3.125%) are *internal* repetitions of the original five-card series, to say nothing of partial sequences. These percentages are slightly reduced with every increase in the number of cards in the pack, but the internal repetitions grow in number. The same is true for external ones. It is therefore absurd to suggest, as has been believed for centuries, that the chance of repetition of any sequence in a random series is nil or unlikely. Instead, it is an absolute certainty that internal and external repetitions occur a calculable number of times, depending on whether we consider a single pack or an infinite series. (Note: The classification methods for combinatorial geometry and mathematics are detailed in *Winners*.[AA])

4.  The random and mindless shuffling of a pack of fifty-two playing cards is combinatorial by its very nature and turns the originally finite fifty-two-card pack into a disordered, infinite series. In the past it was always erroneously believed that randomization creates total unpredictability in which the possibility of repetition is remote or impossible. It is true that we cannot predict in which sequence the cards will be arranged at any moment in time, or when which repetitions will occur. But we can make conditional predictions about short-term, and near-absolute ones about long-term occurrences, recurrences and consequences.

    It is predictable that, when the pack is shuffled at random, an incalculable but high number of *internal* and *external* repetitions of every whole or partial series in the pack is likely to occur in bunched sequences at irregular frequencies in the short run. In the longest run (i.e. in terms of astronomical time-spans that apply to galaxies, to the universe as a whole, and to evolutionary processes) there will be hardly any difference between an infinite series of combinatorial, systematically ordered and re-ordered packs of cards, and an infinitely randomized one. The number of recurrences in a combinatorial, systematically ordered universe would be totally predictable; those in a mindlessly randomized one, nearly so. The main difference between them is due to the unpredictability of which sequences will repeat when, and in which order. But repetitions of every sequence and their relative frequency are certainties.

*Diagram 6*: A randomly shuffled pack of cards
This diagram represents one pack of fifty-two cards shuffled mindlessly and continuously. It is an infinite, randomly shuffled combinatorial series.

Let us assume for the moment that the number of shuffles involves as many cards as an infinite number of packs arranged as they come from the shop (as shown in Diagram 3). Although only a single pack is shuffled here at random (i.e. in a mindless, unsystematic manner), we are in effect combining the first and all future packs, treating them as if they were a single one. Therefore we are mindlessly combining more or less the same number of *internal* and *external* repetitions of cards and permutations as those that would exist in an infinite series of finite, combinatorial, systematically arranged packs. Thus in short-term bursts, the King and Ace (or any other combination of cards, including the pack as a whole) are likely to recur far more often in the short run in the mindlessly shuffled pack than in a series of ordered ones (as they come from the shop or ordered permutationally), with unpredictable frequency and with greater or smaller gaps in between. In the longest run, almost the same number of repetitions of every card and sequence (including the pack as a whole) will occur in both situations. This is what occurs in shuffled packs of playing cards, in the particle universe, in genes that are subject to random mutations, and in every situation where randomness prevails.

What has further obscured these demonstrable facts, as far as mathematicians, physicists and biologists are concerned, is that in card games only certain combinations of cards have artificially assigned 'winning' values. All others are said 'not to count' and are therefore ignored. Both the 'winning' and 'worthless' combinations remain hidden, more often than not, in portions of the pack that remain undealt or in other players' hands. But, unless they are analysed in a totally objective, combinatorial manner, artificially imposed values can hide the 'natural' ones in all card and other games of so-called chance, in life and in the universe at large. In card games winning combinations are established arbitrarily, but in nature they are conditionally determined because only certain combinations lead to life and have survival value in particular environments. The patterns, sequences, combinations, variations and their recurrences that make life, sundry species and their survival possible can only be understood as a result of a semantic awareness of internal (subjective) and external (relatively objective) combinations and conditions.

This discovery has profound implications as far as fundamental concepts in physics, biology and mathematics are concerned. It calls into question some aspects of quantum theory and genetics and upsets the conventional wisdom concerning predictions based on statistical methods.

In any infinite, temporarily closed or perpetually open universe and in the longest run, chance would eventually be reduced almost to zero when particles are shuffled at random. Then *external* and *internal* repetitions will occur almost as often as in an infinite combinatorially ordered particle universe. We know that this is true for an infinite series of randomly pitched pennies, except that in this case there are only two options – heads or tails. With combinatorial ordering (of cards, dice, prime numbers, particles, amino-acid combinations or anything else) by human beings able to make valuative analyses, every possible sequence – including the whole series – will occur and recur again and again with predictable frequency. This constitutes an ordered, infinitely recursive, conditionally deterministic universe in which all occurrences and recurrences can be predicted precisely, limited by knowledge of and attention to the facts and time. Only human beings can create such order out of seeming chaos and discover the relationship of randomness to chance. Then even what can occur in a random universe in any short- and long-term future can be predicted, although not necessarily when or in which sequence.

Chance can therefore be reduced to an absolute minimum or eliminated entirely once conscious and self-aware behaviour evolves with learning, knowledge, in time and when ordering becomes possible (e.g. the systematic classification of combinatorial possibilities). Then, and as a result, we can discover the pattern structure and order that underlie randomness.

We have now arrived at a definition of the difference between consciously aware (i.e. selective), organically adaptive learning, and unconscious, inorganic, random behaviour. From this we can conclude that even without active intervention on the part of God, our universe is essentially purposive. For the effect of randomness is clearly to reduce chance and that of human learning to eliminate it nearly so or entirely, in principle at least. The prime number solution demonstrates all the foregoing conclusively.

To reiterate: in the inorganic portions of the universe where no consciously selective awareness exists, chance is automatically reduced by randomness as far as conditional branching, options and the number of irregularly spaced, bunched short-term recurrences are concerned. The average frequency of permutational repetition can be calculated by systematic, combinatorial sorting. In the longest run there is then only a very small difference between random and combinatorial, systematically ordered series as far as the frequency of repetitions of permutations are concerned. This is a difficult idea to express and it can only be demonstrated geometrically[AA] (i.e. as regards dataflow possibilities and optional branching in any closed universe, or mathematically in an open one; see Appendices A and D). The difference between randomness in an inorganic universe and order in an organic one consists mainly of unconscious (i.e. inorganic), sub-conscious (i.e. intuitive or instinctive), or conscious (aware) pattern recognition (i.e. learning). The last can make us aware of causes, operations and consequences. The game analogy – using what happens and why when games of chance and strategy are played – demonstrates this conclusively.[AA]

Eventually and with mindless shuffling *ad infinitum*, an equivalent to near-absolute order emerges. In the shortest run there will be continuous change and variation in most open systems or those that include so many variables that we can take only a limited number into consideration. But even within such an ever-changing, self-organizing, continuously modified system there will be precise repetitions over unpredictable periods of time. Permutationally redundant series will recur quite frequently in unpredictably bunched sequences. Many of these will be individually unique because of the options provided by the external dataflow (e.g. as a result of changes in environmental conditions). In other words identical internal permutational repetitions (i.e. identical sequences) may differ because of the large number of options provided by the external environment (see Appendix D). This is especially important in the analysis of complex systems that contain a high order of internal and external optional branching, like the human central nervous system, fluid turbulence or the weather. These optional variations endow each of us and many identical events with individual uniqueness.

This also means that combinatorial methods verify the conjecture of some biologists that evolution can take place as a result of longer or shorter *jumps to conclusions* (because of the higher rate of repetition of incomplete permutations compared to complete ones that have the same outcome) in short-term bursts. The discovery of the relationship between randomness and chance demonstrates that the same innately purposive combinatorial processes apply in the hard sciences, like physics and biology, as in those that are currently considered 'soft', like the study of human behaviour and learning.

The demonstrations I give of the conditionally deterministic nature of even the most random processes should affect our perceptions in philosophy, the sciences and technologies for the foreseeable future. It is absurd to speak of a non-purposive, meaningless universe once the underlying order relative to randomness and chance over periods of time are appreciated. Our understanding of the particle universe, the behaviour of genes and of human beings depends on it.

## The Three-dimensionality of Time

Einstein proposed in his special theory of relativity that time is relativistic (i.e. conditionally deterministic). He stated that human perceptions of time depend on the velocity and direction of motion of the observer, relative to the velocity and direction of motion of whatever he or she observes. But this definition of time is often misunderstood, possibly due to a mistranslation (Einstein wrote in German) or misinterpretation, to mean that time is a 'fourth (and hence an invisible) dimension' in a geometric sense and reversible at or near the speed of light. Contrary to what is ascribed to Einstein and as he probably knew, time is simply an additional factor to be considered, relative to our three-dimensional universe. It is certainly not an invisible fourth geometric dimension. It can even be modelled as an extended three-dimensional aspect of space, relative to motion. Further, time's arrow always points to the future and is irreversible, even when special conditions appear to slow clocks or to reverse them (see Appendix C).

Stephen Hawking speaks of the one-directional aspects of time, yet he seems confused about the meaning of four-dimensional space-time. He writes: 'It is often helpful to think of the four coordinates of an event as specifying its position in a four-dimensional space called space-time. It is impossible to imagine four-dimensional space. I personally find it hard enough to visualize three-dimensional space!'[14]

Heisenberg even claimed that modern physics lies beyond 'visualization' (see Chapter 6), thus putting science beyond 'imagination', foresight and prediction. However, a science that lies beyond any of these is a non-science or, to put this more precisely, a nonsense.

Light can be viewed either as a linear stream of particles or as moving like ripples over a lake into which a stone has been thrown. The characteristics of light have also been compared to a comb whose teeth when seen from one angle look like individual bits but when seen from another appear as wavelike packets called quanta. This means that according to the uncertainty principle you can only predict or establish the approximate position or the velocity of a given particle at any moment in time, but never both simultaneously. Like all statistical analyses, this works for the past or in permanently closed environments. It works well enough in the short run and up to a point, but creates severe long-term scientific and philosophical difficulties.

Quantum theory, because it concerns the position of particles in space relative to motion and time, is linked to navigation and mapping theories, both of which work adequately for all practical purposes. Despite satellite and other electronic methods, pin-point mapping, navigation and targeting have not yet and may never be achieved due to instrumentational imprecision. The point is that, until now, navigational precision has not even been achieved theoretically. Most of the world's coastlines are mapped only to an accuracy of about 12–35 yards. Long-range missile targeting or satellite navigation is correct to about the same measure and needs perpetual error correction. The aiming circle achieved by these means is small enough for all practical purposes when it comes to laser-guided missiles, but its size depends on method as well as the inherent error in measurement found in all instrumentation.

To establish the position of any particle in space depends, like navigation, surveying, mapping and targeting, on the definition of an x:y coordinate matrix (e.g. longitude and latitude) relative to motion in time and space, given points of departure and destination, to say nothing of the earth's or spatial curvature and distortions caused by gravity. For example, beyond the earth's magnetic field severe distortions can be caused by gravitational forces generated by large bodies that *bend* space around them. On earth, mapping and targeting must make allowances for the earth's speed of rotation, its course round the sun, the flattening of the polar regions and other irregularities, as well as its magnetic and gravitational fields in addition to innate instrumentational inaccuracies.

Local time in space can be established only by means of at least one external, theoretically fixed reference point relative to elapsed time and motion. The fact that the universe and all of its components are in perpetual motion and that there is no fixed point anywhere is immaterial. If a star or planet is located sufficiently far away in space it will seem stationary for all practical purposes and in the past served as an external reference for navigation. But by applying a three-dimensional x:y:z matrix to time relative to long- and latitudinal motion, we can do away with the need for any external reference point other than that required to establish speed and heading (i.e. direction of travel). This confirms what Einstein stated – that time is *conditional* and *relativistic*.

It is important to remember that any instrument or

yardstick can be precise only to plus or minus .5 of whatever unit of measurement is employed. Therefore, although the new relativistic time theory promises absolute theoretical precision, in practice it will be no better than the precision of the instrumentation that is used.

Had the time-based mapping and navigation principle been understood in three-dimensional terms, Einstein's relativity theory would never have been misinterpreted. But before I summarize the three-dimensional solution of the mapping and navigational problem (see Appendix C for a more detailed description), it is useful to quote at some length what the astronomer James Jeans had to say about the relation of quantum theory to navigation:

Imagine a ship crossing the Atlantic from New York to Southampton [today Jeans might have chosen radio-beacon or satellite navigation, but the principles would have remained the same because it is admitted that our knowledge of mapping and navigational principles is incomplete]. The first day out, the ship's position would normally be determined by taking the altitude of the sun at noon; the navigation officer would then mark the position on the ship's chart.

If the sky was too cloudy for the sun to be seen [or if modern electronic navigation systems had failed], it might be necessary to calculate an approximate position by dead reckoning; the officer would know the approximate speed of the ship, or the distance it had travelled through the water as recorded by the log, and could make a rough allowance for the motion superimposed by currents in the sea. He might in this way be able to fix his position to within, say, 5 miles. He could not mark a cross on his chart to fix his position, but might draw a circle 5 miles in diameter [known as the aiming circle]; this, like the waves of the undulatory theory [concerning sub-atomic particles], would represent his knowledge of his position.

As the ship progressed on its journey, we can picture this circle travelling over the chart like a wave travelling through space, at a speed representing the speed of the ship. As new uncertainties accumulated, the circle would continually increase in size. If the sun was still invisible on the next day, it might be necessary to indicate the ship's position by a circle 10 miles in diameter. If the sun could not be seen throughout the voyage, the uncertainty as to the ship's position would continue to increase, until, by the time the ship was close to land, it might have been represented by a circle 50 miles in diameter.

Suppose, that when such a circle had been marked on the chart, half of it was found to lie over the Cornish coast. As the ship could not be on land, this half of the circle could at once be ruled out; this bit of knowledge would at once reduce the extent of the uncertainty by half – just as happened in the experiment [concerning light falling on a thinly coated mirror, postulated by Einstein and Ehrenfest]. If the Lizard was sighted a few moments later, the further knowledge thus provided would reduce uncertainty practically to zero, and the ship's position could now be marked by a point.

This analogy explains a more general orientation in other respects. We know how in practical life one uncertainty leads to another [that errors tend to be compounded and increase in time]; for instance, the uncertainty which prevailed as to the ship's position when it was one day out continually increased; this uncertainty made it impossible to allow exactly for the currents [and winds, tides, drift, and variations of the ship's speed] encountered on the second day's run, and as the voyage proceeded uncertainty was piled on uncertainty. The wave-picture of radiation faithfully reproduces this cumulative uncertainty in knowledge, because it is an inherent property of a group of waves always to spread out, and so to occupy more space.

In this analogy the ship represents a photon [or a W or $Z^o$ particle], the sea represents the space in which the photon moves, and the land represents barriers . . . [or a target like Einstein's mirror] which prevents the photon moving through the whole of space. The sea, land, ship and photons all exist and move in the ordinary space of everyday life; indeed this is what we mean by ordinary space – the space in which we see things through the impact of photons on our retina, and travel by ship. But the waves which represent the navigator's knowledge of his ship's position do not travel through ordinary space, but over a nautical chart, which is a sort of diagrammatical representation [i.e. a geometric model] of ordinary space.

In precisely the same way, the space traversed by those waves [of probability] which represent our knowledge of photons is not ordinary space but a mathematical representation [model] of ordinary space ... In brief, the space of photons [travelling as individual particles] is ordinary physical space, while the space traversed by the waves of the undulatory theory is a conceptual space [ever-increasing aiming circles of uncertainty until a target is reached]. Indeed, it must be, since the waves, as we have seen, are mere mental constructs and possess no physical existence.[15]

My three-dimensional redefinition of time relative to the mapping-navigational-surveying-targeting problem provides a theoretical method by which exact local time – and hence position – can be established beneath any plane, ship, land-vehicle or particle with pin-point precision (up to the nearest micro-second). Of course such precision is impossible in practice because of the instrument problem. But theoretically it can be done by establishing long- and latitudinal time co-ordinates, relative to velocity and direction of travel from any given point of departure. For some reason the geometric and dynamic space–time relationship on earth does not seem to have been worked out before, relative to the earth's rotation, a vessel's speed and elapsed time of travel from point to point from any given location relative to heading, disregarding countervailing influences. Once such a dynamic, three-dimensional time- and space-co-ordinate grid is established, the intersection of long- and latitudinal time provides theoretical positional precision. The rest depends on reliable data concerning wind, currents, tides, speed and other variables and the instruments used to obtain this information.

The same kind of theoretical grid can be established for any body or particle anywhere in space, demonstrating that time can be represented three-dimensionally like everything else in the universe. Had early navigators understood this principle, even though they lacked modern instruments of navigation, they might have reduced their aiming circle by one- to two-thirds using conventional dead-reckoning methods.

There are obvious scientific implications for establishing the position of any particle or body in this manner. For one thing, the uncertainty principle is hereby severely limited as far as theoretical position-finding, relative to time, mass, direction, velocities and position of fundamental particles or other bodies in space are concerned. This theory also provides one of the best and most efficient ways to ameliorate the jet-lag syndrome – perhaps a trivial spin-off, but one that could be of value to many of today's long-distance air travellers (see Appendix C).

# The Big Bang

The foregoing redefinitions of chance and time suggest that we exist in an eternal cosmos. This would affect our perceptions of the three laws of thermodynamics,[AA] because it dethrones the second as the primary law of the universe. The second law of thermodynamics is a cornerstone of modern science. It states that the universe is running down with increasing momentum (by a perpetual increase in disorder – i.e. entropy) and will eventually destroy itself. Most physicists believe that just prior to this point there must be a static balance and an even distribution of fundamental particles. This would mean the heat death of the universe. Thereafter the universe would collapse into an infinitely dense particle of matter swimming in a cosmic void. So much for such a postulated ultimate end. Now let us look at what modern physics suggests was the beginning.

The universe is believed in modern physics to have been caused by the sudden explosion of an infinitely hot fireball. In the following few micro-seconds, that fireball supposedly turned into diffused radiation that, as it began to cool, solidified into clouds of cosmic gases. These, as they cooled further, are said to have formed all matter in the universe. This is the big bang of which echoes are claimed to be audible even now. Some physicists like Stephen Hawking, a contributor to black-hole theory, are, however, beginning to have their doubts.[16] Others, like Fred Hoyle,[17] have rejected the theory so that by now there is no consensus on this question.

If this theory were correct, one possibility that is not usually considered would be that the universe might perpetually reincarnate over eons of time in a circular and recurrent process of renewal (in the form of the big bang) and self-destruction (in the form of a periodic heat death). But the possibility most frequently accepted in conventional physics, as in most religions, is that the universe is a one-time event. But this seems improbable because the scientific method is unable to explain how the postulated fireball came into being.

Suppose that the universe has just died a heat death and collapsed. Or, if you prefer to view the universe as a singularity, the fireball, surrounded by absolutely nothing, would have existed for all eternity until it suddenly and unaccountably exploded. In either event, if indeed anything had preceded the fireball it would have had to have been an infinitely dense, infinitely cold and infinitely small nugget of matter existing in the void. At absolute zero temperature there can be no motion and hence no time – not even eternity. Further, since the residual nugget of matter is infinitely small and dense it must be a singularity and not an aggregate of smaller particles with spaces between them or external space between the nugget and the void, either of which might permit some sort of motion and hence time.

A trigger that might be responsible for any future explosion of such a nugget could therefore not be internal to this infinitely dense, non-existing particle swimming in a cosmic void. It would have to be external. The only possible external factor to trigger the big bang might be God, but it is highly unlikely that creation would consist of such a violent act. Somehow none of this seems in character with any useful definition of God or nature.

Given these seeming impossibilities, it is extraordinary that anyone should ever have dreamt up the big-bang theory merely on the basis of the expanding universe, that people should have believed it, or insist that they hear its echo via the dishes that have been built to catch cosmic radiation emissions. That seems equivalent to claiming to hear the roar of ocean waves as you hold a conch shell to your ear, when what you hear is background noise or the blood rushing through your own veins. Cosmic radiation certainly exists, but it does not have to be an echo of any 'big bang'.

## Chaos

Hard on the heels of the big bang comes chaos theory, the latest fad in science widely touted as the answer to everything. It is a catch-all term for methods that range from Edward Lorenz's 'butterfly effect' weather model, to Benoit Mandelbrot's fractals. Chaos theory is said to have been applied successfully to fluid dynamics, biology, meteorology, astrophysics, medicine, politics, economics, linguistics, game and communications theories, mapping, war, physiology, oil prospecting, polymer studies, the stock- and commodities markets, snow-flake pattern analysis, schizophrenia, artificial intelligence, chemistry, electrical engineering and jet lag (among other subjects).

In any theory or experiment, analysis ultimately comes down to pattern recognition. But as far as pattern recognition in chaos theory is concerned it seems that, as Ludwig Bemelmans wrote in his children's book *Madeline*, 'The crack in the ceiling had the habit of sometimes looking like a rabbit.' The failure of chaos theory to establish the relationship between randomness and chance – its main claim – discredits it as a fundamental concept. To understand just how confused and opportunistic perceptions in science can be, it is useful to quote some of what James Gleick has written about chaos theory:

Where chaos begins, classical science stops . . . [Since the early 1970s] chaos conferences and chaos journals abound. [US] Government program managers in charge of research money for the military, the Central Intelligence Agency, and the Department of Energy have put ever greater sums into chaos research and set up special bureaucracies to handle the financing ... the laws of complexity hold universally, caring not at all for the details of a system's constituent atoms.

... Had he [Edward Lorenz] stopped with the Butterfly Effect, an image of predictability giving way to pure randomness, then Lorenz would have produced no more than a piece of very bad news. But Lorenz saw more than randomness embedded in his weather model. He saw a fine geometrical structure, order *masquerading* as randomness ... Nonlinearity means that the act of playing the game has a way of changing the rules.[18]

Changing the rules according to how you wish to play the game is known as cheating, for, as I explain in *Winners*,[AA] rules define limits in games, science, nature or anything else.

... [Lorenz's weather-mapping system] traced a strange, distinctive shape, a kind of double spiral in three dimensions, like a butterfly with its two wings. The shape signaled pure disorder, since no point or pattern of points ever recurred. Yet it also signaled a new kind of order ... Chaos is ubiquitous; it is stable; it is structured.[19]

What Lorenz demonstrated is a truism that is hardly novel. He shows that if you start with different initial conditions (and the difference might be minimal), the evolution of events may run nearly parallel in the short term but is likely to diverge in the longer run for a number of reasons, so that predictability ultimately dissolves into chaos. So if you are not certain of causes or attribute different ones to the same set of events, then the short-term consequences may in all cases be nearly the same but will diverge increasingly over longer periods of time. However, with a clear understanding of initial conditions (i.e. causes), consequences and a knowledge of operations (i.e. the meanings), anything about which we know enough would be highly predictable in the short and the long term. Since I have shown that chaos theory does not work in cases for which its efficiency has been claimed and that combinatorial methods work and give rather different results (e.g. in game theory, jet lag, psychology and on the stock-market),[AA] most of the edifice of chaos theory would seem to collapse.

Additionally, and especially when it comes to weather prediction, internal and external variables and unknowns that may change the course of events (i.e. internal and external optional branching and dataflow) do not become apparent unless combinatorial modelling methods are used. In other words, lack of knowledge, uncertainty about initial conditions (i.e. causes) and the use of wrong methods may lead to eventual chaos. Chaos theory therefore seems to describe the consequences of itself rather than processes of nature.

Edward Lorenz states that while short-term weather forecasts made on the basis of a three-dimensional linear matrix can be reasonably predictive, chaos theory supposedly demonstrates that long-term prediction is impossible. His non-linear theoretical weather model, one of the cornerstones of chaos theory,[20] was based on only eleven variables. It generated perpetually changing, long-term unpredictable patterns. But combinatorial methods show that his results are worthless because Lorenz's technique assumes uncertainty about initial conditions. It does not allow for greater certainty derived from learning or the use of better methods.

Eleven variables, considered in terms of combinatorial relationships, generate $11 \times 2^{55}$ possibilities, each of which is individually unique despite recurrent, permutationally identical sequences. The uniqueness of each is defined by the options produced by variations in the external dataflow (see pack of playing cards example given earlier). Predictability in any dynamic (i.e. perpetually changing) system therefore demands separate predictions for every possible initial condition (i.e. causes). Each must be examined combinatorially within boundaries defined by a ratio between internal and external, domain-defined variables over periods of time within a dynamic, ever changing universe of discourse. Only combinatorial methods (those that model relationships between internal factors and their permutations relative to a given external environment) can predict possible consequences,[AA] given sufficient information and time, as for example in genetics. Stochastic, non-linear methods like those used in chaos theory cannot establish or predict these possibilities in the long term because they ignore combinatorial relationships. As with uncertainty theory, not only is there insufficient knowledge of the facts, but the method of modelling the known facts is wrong.

So far, chaos theory has depended on the creation of abstract computer models. Anything can seem convincing when represented in isolation on a computer screen, as when scientists test a hypothesis without taking into account contributing, contingent, internal and external factors or their ratios, relationships, optional branching possibilities and periodicities. Chaos, like uncertainty theory, can therefore be faulted on a number of grounds: poorly understood initial conditions; wrong definitions of randomness, chance and time; a disregard of internal and external effect and ignoring the differences between organic and inorganic behaviours. As I said, any discovery of relationships and qualities requires three-dimensional combinatorial forms of modelling that facilitate one's making transactional value judgements. But most scientists claim that their work is value-free and does not require value judgements to be made. This means that they are not sufficiently objective, for with total objectivity it becomes obvious that subjective elements (i.e. feedback) predominate in our universe. That oversight alone invalidates much of modern science.

What holds true for physics is true for biology where the function of randomness, chance and time are also usually misunderstood. I have shown that current biological concepts of species-survival are derived from social Darwinist prejudices for which there is no shred of factual evidence.[AA] That error was derived from scientific anthropomorphism (i.e. making the wrong generalizations by attributing momentarily prevailing human characteristics to animals). A linear, three-dimensional combinatorial analysis of games shows that the co-operative (symbiotic and subjective) principle predominates in nature and that competition (relatively objective behaviour) plays only a minor role. This means that biological precepts based on conventional game theory (i.e. games of strategy and chance) and probabilistic mathematics are wrong as a result of erroneous and prejudiced value judgements about human behaviour that have persisted for centuries.

Richard Dawkins was carried away by these ideas and a clever computer model that he devised in order to demonstrate a concept that is closely related to chaos theory.[21] Using an algorithm (i.e. a mathematical formalism) he shows the random, spontaneous evolution of an artificial creature on the computer screen. John von Neumann attempted a similar feat in the early 1950s, of which Dawkins seems to be unaware. Dawkins, like von Neumann, tried to demonstrate that nature knows no purpose, that we are nothing but biological machines and that evolution is governed by blind chance. But he ignored or is ignorant about the effects of randomness over long periods of time, external (environmental) influences, and internal ones like IRMs (Innate Release Mechanisms that trigger instinctive animal behaviours), natural selection, adaptation and learning.

When chaos principles are applied to strategic situations like human behaviour or to the commodities markets (that are affected at least as much by speculation and the creation of artificial shortages as by the weather), then the absurdities of chaos theory become increasingly apparent.

... when Mandelbrot sifted the cotton-price data [from 1900 to 1960] through IBM's computers, he found the astonishing results he was seeking ... Within the most disorderly reams of data lived an unexpected order. Given the arbitrariness of the numbers he was examining, why,

Mandelbrot asked himself, should any law hold at all? And why should it apply equally well to personal incomes and cotton prices? . . . Order in chaos. It was science's oldest cliché. The idea of hidden unity and common underlying form in nature had an intrinsic appeal, and it had an unfortunate history of inspiring pseudoscientists and cranks . . . Several chaos-minded cardiologists [heart specialists] found that the frequency spectrum of heartbeat timing, like earthquakes and economic phenomena, followed fractal laws . . .[22]

Doyne Farmer, a US academic, and a number of colleagues had spent years unsuccessfully trying to discover a mathematical way to beat roulette at the Santa Cruz campus of the University of California before he and they discovered chaos theory. James Gleick cites Farmer after he joined the Theoretical Division of the Los Alamos National Laboratory: 'The idea that all these classical deterministic systems we'd learned about could generate randomness was intriguing . . .'[23] Whereas Mandelbrot, like the physicist David Bohm, claims to have discovered that an implicit but unspecified order underlies chaos, Farmer, employing the methods of chaos theory, suggests that order breeds chaos. Whom are we to believe?

As I showed earlier, combinatorial methods of analysis demonstrate that randomness generates an order that is not very different from absolute order in terms of the frequency of repetitions and recurrences of events in nature, viewed in cosmic timescales. But such an order is not a characteristic of chaos, but of randomness in a combinatorial universe.

Mandelbrot's fractal theory breaks down as soon as it is examined in terms of his geological-geometric frames of reference. Claims that measurements of coastlines can be refined indefinitely depending on the scale of particles are absurd. That is like the medieval, ecclesiastic conundrum concerning how many angels can dance on the head of a pin. The answer depends on whether angels – or fundamental particles – have dimensions. Their number is finite even if they have only one dimension (see Appendix C). This holds true for gross measurements of geographic features as much as for those between pebbles on a beach, fractals, atoms, neutrinos, quarks or $Z^o$ particles. Though every instrument of measure contains an innate error, the distance between marks is always finite. Only an interval of time is infinitely divisible. Thus Mandelbrot merely restates Xeno's famous paradox that holds true for time but not for space (Xeno, a Greek philosopher suggested that if you divide a line running from A to B at C and keep halving the residue, you will never get to B – an obvious absurdity).

Finally, chaos theory's non-linear mathematical basis has a linear substructure that its proponents choose to ignore. Even the most compound shapes, curves, turbulences and random processes can be defined on a linear x:y:z graph. All problems and their solutions can thus be expressed in linear, three-dimensional form.

In this bizarre branch of theoretical science no distinction seems to be made between organic and inorganic systems and behaviours. If chaos theory applied in all specialist subjects in which it is claimed to work, then it would indeed be a grand unification theory (GUT), far broader than any that Einstein had in mind or the one that I seem to have discovered. Fashions of the moment, like chaos theory, demonstrate the corruption in modern science. Chaos theory is an idea born out of the belief that academics must publish or perish. It is a good example of how the creation of a scientific fad leads to generous research funding by politicians who hope to win future elections by claiming that they have supported spectacular scientific discoveries, or by the military who are always on the look-out for magic (see Chapter 8).

## The Smallest Particle

A belief in magic is apparent in much of modern science – for example, that fundamental particles can suddenly appear out of nothing or vanish into the void. This is no different from the medieval belief that spontaneous generation of insects and small organisms in manure is possible, because at that time microscopes had not yet been discovered and microscopically small eggs, larvae and spores could not be observed.

The law of conservation of energy states that energy or its equivalent in mass cannot be destroyed. Hence no particle can vanish absolutely. One may only turn into another. Matter is always three-dimensional. Space/time can be modelled two- or three-dimensionally (see Appendix C) but energy may be one-dimensional. Before we consider the smallest particle and what it might be, it may be useful to consider one-, two-, and three-dimensional aspects of nature in terms of their meanings.

Three-dimensional matter is what we can touch. Two-dimensional representations have no physical substance, are invisible and when represented symbolically consist of information. But two-dimensional information is made up of one-dimensional components that I call 'memories', to borrow a term from neurophysiology and information theory. From this we can postulate a universe made up entirely of one-dimensional memory particles that by being joined, one to another in two-dimensional chains, form information and, by their eventual affiliations, three-dimensional matter. Symbolic models of natural laws can also be two- or three-dimensional. Thus particles like neutrinos that are thought to have no mass may, in affiliation with others like themselves, form the informational matrices that underlie all three-dimensional energy and matter. Thus no visible particle could ever disappear. Instead, it could dissolve into information. With a further disassociation it may perhaps turn into one-dimensional energy/memory particles – the invisible dark matter or fifth essence that supposedly makes up 90–98 per cent of all particles in the universe of which Lawrence Krauss speaks.[24] Such a concept might describe evolutionary processes in terms of information theory and appears to explain what seems inexplicable and is unexplained by the current scientific method (see Appendices).

The computer technology provides us with a useful analogy. A *bit* would then be equivalent to the smallest, one-dimensional energy particle. It has no meaning until it is affiliated with other related ones and becomes a *byte*. One-dimensional memories and two-dimensional information remain invisible until they are encoded (e.g. the letter 'b' can be viewed as an undifferentiated memory that, until affiliated with the letter 'e', does not constitute a word or actual information). All of this is totally convergent with the Turing machine (see Chapter 8) and might provide a useful model of the invisible and most profound aspects of our universe and of human existence.

None of the foregoing is as far-fetched as it may seem because the search for dark matter (i.e. the invisible matter in the universe) has been on for some time. If dark matter could be shown to exist physically (by particle bombardment that might measure the loss of an invisible quantity from three-dimensional matter), then what I suggest may be confirmed by scientific methods. If I am correct, rather than considering the universe solely in terms of so-called objective reality, we would have to begin to reconsider everything in subjective, philosophical and qualitative terms. Perhaps this is the way towards a science of the future. Memory, conceived as the smallest invisible particle in the universe, would provide a jumping-off point not only for a new cosmology and physics, but also for the framework for a general theory that applies to everything.

According to the anthropic principle, what holds true for the smallest particle should also hold true for human consciousness and awareness. For, without memory and informational components, the DNA, the central nervous system, human reason and logic would be inconceivable. Instead of existing in a universe described by what is now known as the scientific method, we would exist in one that follows principles of pure informational logic – a merging of philosophy and science. As I have said earlier, the smallest particle as a philosophical concept was recognized by the early Greek philosophers. It could be a fundamental principle that has practical implications for the science of the future.

In my previous book I showed that our very intentions (i.e. the relationship between invisible memory components of the human psyche) can be modelled as a two- or three-dimensional directed, combinatorial graph (see *Winners*[AA] and Appendices A and D). This graph models the possible relationship between one-dimensional *memory* nodes and their affiliation with others to form two- and three-dimensional networks, similar to the human central nervous system. Such a representation defines its self-organizing creative potential. Every variation in the direction of the dataflow indicates a change of conditions or of mind.[AA] These processes seem to hold true for all processes of nature. Meanwhile it is gratifying that some physicists are beginning to concern themselves with invisible particles that are no less real than consciousness, awareness, will, intentions and time. But what they do not consider is that these and other invisible processes of nature can only be expressed graphically, verbally or mathematically as two-dimensional information or modelled three-dimensionally in combinatorial terms.

## Implications

Natural phenomena can be divided into relativistic, inorganic and organic, open and closed systems. Randomness itself is conditionally deterministic inasmuch as it reduces chance, as I have demonstrated. Inorganic and organic systems differ in many respects and yet have common characteristics. Some are predictable and others are not. For example, quantitatively competitive organic behaviours like playing to win in games, in economics and politics will always remain unpredictable. You win only by inducing and taking advantage of an opponent's errors that can never be predicted. Qualitatively competitive organic behaviours (i.e. essentially co-operative and creative ones) in any setting are orderly and lead to predictability.[AA] The inorganic and random universe generates a kind of short- and long-term order that can only be perceived as such by us, using our reason and systematic synthesis. Thus meanings, order and purpose are implicit throughout the cosmos and it is evidently our responsibility to discover which kind of order prevails under what circumstances.

Indeed form itself determines predictability, depending on symmetries. For example, the molecules of water are symmetrically arranged under certain conditions. Once water is frozen 'symmetry breaking' occurs. New symmetries appear in the shape of snow-flakes and ice crystals, no two of which seem alike. But with the onset of organic evolution systems become increasingly asymmetrical and yet predictable, despite increasing complexity in detail. It is impossible to arrive at these conclusions statistically when analysing highly complex systems. One must first analyse relatively simple ones combinatorially, like packs of playing cards, before we can begin to understand the simplicity that underlies complexity, randomness, order, symmetry and asymmetry.

Even the most random (asymmetrical) systems share characteristics with ordered (symmetrical) ones once they are analysed combinatorially. This requires a three-dimensional mapping of known facts, the possible relations between them and the choices for internal and environmental dataflow in both. Most of this remains hidden and enigmatic when stochastic (statistical and probabilistic) or permutational methods of analysis are used, making prediction impossible except in a very limited context (e.g. when the initial conditions are fully understood, or when they fall within well-defined limits, or when the future is simply a repetition of the past).

The illogic inherent in many 'scientific' theories is a product of operant conditioning in fields where fashion and opportunism have taken over from a search for lasting values. Catastrophe theory is yet another that is easily disproven. Obviously, apparently catastrophic events occur in nature (e.g. stellar explosions, implosions and temporary 'closure'). However, these are evolutionary and not revolutionary events. The only catastrophes in the universe are human inventions (e.g. wars, nuclear weapons and ecological despoliation). When it comes to such theories the laws of cause and effect are simply ignored. Indeed much of science insists that nature violates common sense – a conventional religious position. Thus some of the difficulties caused by non-causal, probabilistic reasoning implicit in many scientific theories are conveniently overcome. But this also causes problems in explaining or predicting the behaviours of simple and complex phenomena and makes it impossible to define their true meanings.

## Hindsight and Foresight

As I have said before, prediction is one of the main functions of the sciences. Value judgements limit the sum of all possibilities. Therefore all prediction is based on value judgements (even when scientists categorically deny this), for the sum of all possibilities is too great without limits (i.e. valuative rules) being imposed on it. Furthermore, if the universe is infinitely expanding and recursive, it could be compared to and modelled as a perpetually enlarging, self-organizing feedback loop that has no beginning or end. It would then consist of an infinite series of finite systems. Or, to put this in another way, the cosmos may consist of an infinite series of new beginnings and ends. In that case there is no need to fear an end – death of the species or of the universe – for while the first may lead to temporary oblivion, both are endless evolutionary series, each end leading to a new beginning; the principles of perpetual evolution, rebirth and learning.

Any combinatorial definition of past and future[AA] shows what the limits of predictability are. For example, the outcome of a purely strategic (i.e. complete information) game played to be won can never be predicted, except that it will be lost sooner or later. Chance reigns in the short run with such a *winning* orientation. With repetition, even an infinite series of strategic games played to be won must ultimately lead to a draw. The latter is also true for randomized games of chance (for example, the tossing of a coin). But with sufficient attention and awareness and when a purely strategic game is played between equals, a draw can be predicted and achieved immediately. The future is therefore very much in our hands, not only in strategic situations but in any for which intentional choices determine the outcome.

The inorganic universe provides a vast preponderance of balanced outcomes (i.e. creative draws), all of which are predictable in principle if not in practice. For predictability depends on an understanding of principles (e.g. the relation between randomness and chance), aware and valuative selection, the number of known factors that can be considered at any one time (complexity), and whether they are arranged systematically or at random. The event-horizon of any foreseeable future consists of a matrix limited by the sum of all combinatorial possibilities. It is generated by an existing, but ever-increasing store of information. Every additional factor of which we become aware pushes that horizon further into the future, making the latter increasingly predictable, sharpening our hindsight and increasing future options and certainty, depending on the choices we make in the present. In such a paradigm the past is of relatively little consequence, except to establish how we came to arrive at our present options.

In the inorganic universe the sum of all possibilities plays itself out, limited only by unconscious and mindless relationships between its components and the options these provide. In the organic portions of the universe, adaptation, valuative intentions, free will, systematic choice and learning should perpetually reduce uncertainty. Thus there is a thrust towards increasing dynamic balance and certainty in nature until a stage of evolution is reached at which life and consciousness evolve. No special act of creation is required because the universe seems most likely to be eternal. Nature is perpetually creative (i.e. it tends towards dynamic balance in all possible variations – the first law of thermodynamics). That creativity is its chief characteristic and source of subjective energy. Therefore self-organization, purposive direction and ethical principles are in-built and implicit characteristics of nature. Even in inorganic portions of the universe and in the absence of any kind of consciousness there seems to exist a potential for goal-oriented life and self-aware intelligence.

The past and future are part of a perpetual continuum of growing awareness and consciousness wherever life evolves (i.e. from reflexive and instinctive awareness to conscious learning). That evolution is a certainty when the conditions are right. The present does not exist, for as soon as it is experienced it is already in the past. The present is a moving point between past and future and a consequence of the options that have been exercised in the past. The details of that past are far too numerous to be fully reconstructed. However, given an understanding of first principles, the conditionally deterministic nature of the past reveals its causes.[AA] We suffer or enjoy the consequences in the present, leaving many – indeed most – possibilities not yet exercised from our current, earth-bound perspective. The past is unalterable, but its unrealized possibilities can be discovered. They emerge as we learn and accumulate old and new information that provides us with an ever-growing sum of options for the future.

The future therefore depends on a constant reconsideration of past and existing options and the discovery of new ones, entered on the matrix of the sum of all possibilities. This can be represented as an event cone within which there is increasing optional branching as it reaches into the future. We can never consider all of these options because there are too many. Therefore we must make valuative choices as to which are the most appropriate (i.e. intelligent) and promising ones. Certain future events like earthquakes, volcanic eruptions and hurricanes may as yet be largely unpredictable due to lack of knowledge. But what is currently uncertain may become increasingly certain in time as we learn more about ourselves and the processes of nature, and apply the best available analytic methods.

To summarize: the choices for our future depend on energy, intentions, adaptation, learning, combinatorial analysis, valuative classification, synthesis, will and time. In other words, both the inorganic and the organic portions of the universe are not pre-determined or governed by chance. They provide us with all the choices there are. We choose the right or the wrong ones. The options we recognize or choose determine the future up to the event-horizon of our current knowledge. We can therefore choose the best or worst options for our future, or abandon it to chance or to time. Chance is the ruling factor for as long as human misunderstanding, lack of knowledge, wrong intentions, inattention and wrong analytic methods prevail. But despite any of these, time neutralizes chance in the long run.

The laws of evolution, natural selection, adaptation and learning leave room for enormous future creativity and new knowledge in the sciences. Valuative forecasting of the inorganic and organic processes of nature (including human behaviour) therefore consists of four strands:

- The creative, originating draw principle (i.e. symbiosis, balance and co-operation) that predominates in nature in all its ramifications and subtleties.
- The systematic and valuative arrangement of existing knowledge and possibilities based on a model that provides conditional branching of the dataflow (i.e. the combinatorial model).
- The discovery of unrealized possibilities and options in the past that can bring about a new understanding for the future.
- The combination of and variations on old and new knowledge that pushes the horizon of predictability ever further into the future.

These are the preconditions for discovering, understanding and explaining the causes, consequences and operations (i.e. the meanings) of the universe. As pointed out earlier, there are in science five main ways of looking at the universe: in microcosmic, macrocosmic, religious, mechanistic and human terms (see Chapter 1). The first concerns itself with the atomic and sub-atomic world, the second with astronomy, the third with God, the fourth with mechanism, and the fifth with life and organic behaviour. Until now there existed unbridgeable gaps between the theories believed to hold true for the micro-, macro-, theological, mechanical and psycho-physiological aspects of the universe. The missing link consists of a true understanding of organic, human behaviour. For until we understand ourselves we cannot expect to understand the rest of the universe. We can discover the truth about both only when what holds true for us is matched to what seems to be true for the cosmos. Our central nervous system is therefore a model of the universe, at least in so far as we can perceive it. None the less, unqualified and unconditional chance may continue to rule the universe until a massive change in orientation takes place in our understanding of organic and inorganic processes and behaviours, especially when it comes to learning.

# 6
# You Can Take a Horse
# to Water

'My image in some places is of a monster of some kind who wants to pull strings and manipulate people. Nothing could be further from the truth. People are manipulated; I just want them to be manipulated more successfully.'

B.F. Skinner[1]

The methods by which we learn are of crucial importance in the sciences which supposedly deal with facts rather than opinions. How we learn is therefore as and possibly more important than what we learn. Education has usually been in the hands of those who feel that they have the right to manipulate others (see the quote that heads this chapter). Rulers, politicians, priesthoods, academics, technologists and educators have insisted through the ages that their credentials give them the authority to control people and nature. Thus control and manipulation became the techniques used in education and the sciences. As a result, mechanistic principles now underlie education nearly everywhere. They victimize practitioners as much as those they manipulate. For whatever works, even if it works only in the short run, tends to become embedded in a belief system that eventually destroys the ability of both teachers and students to think critically and to learn.

Prevailing misconceptions about how we learn best have

affected physics and biology as much as the social sciences. These ideas are historically rooted in religio/political practices and their consequences reach into every walk of life. Not only the process but also the purpose of education has been largely misunderstood, for rather than training people to *believe* or do as they are told, it should foster independent thought and action.

## Evolution and Learning

As I suggested earlier, memories may be the eternal stuff of which we and the universe are made. The linking of related memories is the basis of information. It could also underlie the evolution of inorganic and organic processes. Evolution in inorganic nature is an unconscious process that, given the redefinition of the operations of randomness, is, as I have demonstrated, innately purposive, leading towards ever more complex combinations of matter. The same may be true for the evolution of life, consciousness and learning.

Species evolve in a direction of increasing awareness of the self and of nature. This in itself seems purposive because the evolutionary process has led to the human capacity to decode information. But we can discover the purposes of nature only once we become aware that meanings (i.e. causes and consequences) underlie all of nature's processes. This is, or should be, what learning is all about. The development of language, the sciences and the technologies are all subject to evolutionary principles. Learning is therefore the overriding purpose of life. By learning and culturally passing on what has been learnt to future generations we achieve psychological and cultural evolution; a form of immortality that is denied to other species.

Animal awareness concerns adaptation and short-term survival. An animal species' capacity to survive is nearly totally conditioned by its genetic program relative to any environment in which it can exist. Its adaptive capabilities are far more limited than our own. Animals behave in ways that are predominantly reflexive and instinctive rather than reflective. They reproduce as a matter of course and as

territory and opportunity allow, feed, shelter themselves
and their young and are prey for species on higher branches
of the evolutionary tree (in other words all predators eat
'down', rather than 'up'). But they are not consciously
aware of long-term survival (i.e. survival of the species) or
evolutionary possibilities in a genetic, symbolic or cultural
sense. Their learning abilities are restricted to the present
and are variations on their instincts (see Chapter 7). Yet
animal adaptation is a precursor to human learning because
what is initially reflexive and instinctive evolves eventually
into conscious reflection.

As the biologist Thorpe writes:

> ... from the philosophical point of view the central
> problem of ethology is the relation between purposiveness
> ('purpose' here has the usual meaning – a striving after a
> future goal retained as some kind of image or idea) and
> directiveness. All biologists agree that the behaviour of
> organisms as a whole is directive, in the sense that in the
> course of evolution at least some of it has been modified
> by selection so as to lead with greater or less certainty
> towards states which favour the survival and reproduction
> of the individual ... So for the ethologist the question is,
> 'How much, if any, of the animal's behaviour is purposive,
> and what is the relation of this behaviour to the rest?'[2]

It seems unlikely that the first birds to build nests above
ground did so to lay their eggs and rear their young in
safety. Birds do not have a long-term memory. They built
nests because they could. The first nest-building efforts
must have been fuelled solely by a genetic and physiological potential. Those who built nests adapted, prospered
and reproduced. The rest developed other self-protective
strategies, were eaten, domesticated or became extinct.
Their genetic potential allowed some to adapt and survive
in particular ways. No actual learning was involved. But to
act in a human, long-term purposive manner requires an
awareness of future generations and an ability to learn. All
species are conscious of their environment, but only mankind is aware of the long-term future and its possibilities.

Only we have the freedom to think and learn autonomously, to adapt to and create our own environment within very broad limits, or to invent language, artificial symbols and tools that evolve through generations of experimentation and use. Lamarck, the eighteenth-century naturalist, erroneously believed that a species can genetically pass characteristics acquired through use on to following generations. This is clearly impossible. The young of many animal species expand their genetically acquired reflexes and instincts by copying the behaviours of their parents or by trial and error. But animal experience can only pass from one generation to the very next and is limited to physical survival skills. We alone among the species are able to store and pass on culturally acquired memories to future generations symbolically, verbally, graphically and three-dimensionally – in books, art, on film, tape, and in other ways too numerous to mention. Cultural evolution, in the form and scope possible only to us, is therefore equivalent to what Lamarck believed to be possible genetically.

Thus in addition to genetic memories implanted in all species by evolutionary processes and by learning all that can be learnt in one generation from direct experience, we have an extended cultural memory that can be passed from one generation to successive ones. Elephants are said to have a prodigious memory. Feelings like grief are even attributed to them. But their acquired memories last only a lifetime. No elephant has ever written an autobiography, created a work of art, recorded the thoughts and actions of its own or past generations and speculated about or predicted the future. The same is true of dolphins whose intelligence is often compared to that of man. The preservation of cultural memories and the ability to leave such legacies to future generations are unique to us.

Physical survival – nourishment, shelter and reproduction – may be enough for other species but it is not enough for human beings. Many people never discover this, and some only when it is too late. The fact that there is more to life than physical survival is a reason for the widespread fear of death and for menopausal or male mid-life crises when children have left home and become autonomous. At that point earning a living, keeping house or sexual reproduction are no longer major concerns for many. The idea that 'there must be more to life' is pushed powerfully to the forefront of many people's consciousness. Those whose essential needs are met feel the need for a change in the direction of their lives. But you need a reasonably full stomach before any question of purpose greater than physical survival can become meaningful. Therefore human survival depends not only on the availability of the essentials of life, but also on the development of conscious awareness as a consequence of cultural evolution and learning.

Many species reach absolute limits sooner or later in their evolution. Some, like cockroaches, bees, sharks and alligators, reached those limits millions of years ago because they fulfil limited, yet essential roles in nature. Their adaptive capacities are therefore extremely restricted and species-specific (i.e. limited to an expansion of instincts that concern only their species' physical survival needs), yet environmentally vital. Any further evolution in such 'finished' species would upset the balance of nature. For example, a significant mutation in bees (e.g. if they learnt to feed on anything other than nectar) might cause havoc in the pollination of flowering plants. With the human species it is the other way round. We may or may not have reached the end of our physiological evolution, but we will cause irreversible damage to ourselves and the earth's environment unless we change radically in psychological, cultural and technological terms. Our aim should be to achieve a dynamic, rather than a static balance. If such a behavioural evolution does not take place, we and most other species (except perhaps cockroaches) and the earth as we know it will suffer severely. Nature is certain to redress imbalances caused by our current values and lifestyles, but it will do so to our cost. Learning to behave appropriately therefore goes to the heart of the question of intelligence, learning and long-term survival.

As I said, the learning process is central to evolution; hence we can assume that the implicit 'purpose' of nature is the evolution of a self-aware species that can learn. Many scientists, however, do not accept that nature is purposive. Yet to speak of nature without purpose, even though it has made possible the evolution of a purposive species, is to make nonsense out of language and meaning. The demonstrations given in Chapter 5 (showing that randomness limits chance and that subjective processes – feedback – predominate in nature) should be proof enough that purpose is implicit in nature; in other words, that there is a natural order without the need for an intervening God. Elsewhere I have shown that nature is essentially co-operative and not competitive as is generally believed and that natural laws of cause and effect determine meanings and ethics.[AA] All of these phenomena are signs of an innate purposiveness in nature.

## Learning Failure

If learning is the purpose of life it seems strange that the question of how we learn best has never been satisfactorily answered. Conventional methods of education are usually ideologically biased and unscientific, irrespective of the evidence produced in their favour. Learning failure is on the increase today, despite huge sums spent on mass and private education and a vast accumulation of knowledge. The more years they spend in schools and universities, the less students seem to understand. A 1989 Carnegie Foundation Report on the state of US education paints a depressing picture of declining numeracy and an increase in functional illiteracy. These trends are not unique to the United States but are global and have been apparent for a very long time.[3] A 1990 Economic and Social Research Council study showed that one in three British secondary-school children believe that the sun revolves around the earth and that sound travels faster than light. 'Some of their teachers who sat the tests did no better.'[4] A 1989 newspaper feature about US education described a possible consequence of this trend. It reported growing fears that there will soon be a dearth of people with sufficient skills to staff the factories and offices of the future.[5] To some extent that is already true in many industrialized nations, East and West.

As a result, President Bush, concerned about the state of American education, convened a state governors' conference in 1989 to study the problem. According to another newspaper, the governors and their expert consultants, themselves products of a US education, concluded that:

> . . . one in five Americans are [*sic*] functionally illiterate [in 1989] – 20 percent of the 15,000 adults tested were unable to write a cheque without an error so serious that it was uncashable. Forty percent could not work out how much change they were due from a simple transaction in a shop . . . one in five Americans between the ages of 18 and 24 could not find the United States on a map of the world . . . David Kearns told the *New York Times* that America's educational system had 'the makings of a national disaster' . . . The ideas put forward at the governors' meeting in Virginia will sound familiar to followers of the British debate; . . . more competition.[6]

As all of this indicates, the same fears are expressed and the same remedies are offered in Britain. But competition in education and in our societies is largely responsible for these learning failures. Greater competition will make them worse. Learning is a co-operative enterprise. Further, when you consider that only the adult population has the right to vote, that social issues can be understood only by reading, reflection and informed discussion, and that many adults in the Western world are functionally illiterate (in other words, they can read but cannot understand what they read), the quality of future governments is bound to be very poor. We are endangering our future as a result of wrong educational methods.

## Competitive Learning and Education

Before we can learn we must be interested in a subject and understand that learning means to play with ideas and materials – 'doing something with a purpose for the sake of the thing itself'. As shown later, goals and purposes define freedom itself. That is why young children learn fastest and best, for they have not yet been indoctrinated with the misguided notions that learning means doing as you are told or that it is a passport obtained by competitive examinations to earn and consume more than those who fail. Education can never be successful when learning has no purpose or merely serves economic ends. It must fail if it is coerced, done only for a reward or to avoid penalties or punishment and when it is competitive, except in a qualitative sense.

Education has long been thought of as a quantitatively competitive enterprise. That is to say, the more conventional knowledge you remember the more tests you pass, the higher your score, the more paper qualifications you gather and the more intelligent and competent you are believed to be. Qualitative competition (co-operation with the self, with others and with nature in order to achieve excellence, perfectibility and, it is hoped, error-free results) can help individuals and cultures reach beyond what are believed to be human limitations. Such limitations are imposed only by the wrong forms of conditioning and competition. For as long as quantitative competition and operant conditioning remain the cornerstones of modern education, its products will continue to be functional illiteracy, innumeracy and a lack of creativity.

## A Brief History of Modern Education

Anything that is worth knowing about learning has been proposed or tried somewhere in the world.[7] It is therefore impossible to say anything new about it except to demonstrate, by means of combinatorial analysis, the methods by which every form of learning, teaching, training, conditioning, computer programming and the causes and consequences of all of these can be modelled and defined (see Appendix D). This discovery can turn psychology and education from a maze of vague theories into a reasonably exact science. It also facilitates making value judgements about which methods of education work best under what circumstances and foreseeing the consequences of each. This analysis also discloses the causes of learning failure.

Historically, conventional education is based on methods from which few people seem to have learnt anything. At the same time, isolated individuals have had brilliant intuitions which they have reached by *deconditioning* themselves. Such people, rare as they are and even when results they achieve speak for themselves, could be argued with for as long as there was no totally objective yardstick for evaluating the causes and consequences of learning and its failures. Such a yardstick now exists (see Appendix D).

Conditioning underlies all learning and behaviour. But there is a big difference between the right and wrong forms of conditioning; between those that work only in the short term (i.e. training), and those that work throughout life (i.e. learning to think independently). The difference between learning as a result of external coercion (i.e. carrot or stick) and internal motivation (i.e. interest) is that only the latter allows us to be free to reach a self-determined, worthwhile goal by various routes which can then lead on to new goals. Additionally, few people seem to understand that unconditional freedom leads to the same results as carrot-and-stick training, i.e. total mindlessness. Self-motivated learning does not require psychologists who claim to measure intelligence, or career-guidance counsellors whose aptitude tests are part of an institutionalized arsenal of control and manipulation.

Essential questions and answers about learning must take into consideration those concerning freedom. For without purpose and self-determined goals there can be no freedom, learning or any long-term satisfying future. The avowed purpose of modern education is to enable adults to compete economically and for status. But while competition may be an incentive (i.e. a carrot), it leads to rote performance that only assures employment in the short term. It does not stimulate the long-term learning needed for a satisfying life or for the society of today and tomorrow.[8]

Education should be competitive only in a purely qualitative sense, in which case a student is in competition only with him- or herself and never with others. Everyone should win in proportion to effort, interest and performance. Those who refuse to learn or perform to the best of their abilities should be the only losers. But that is not how the aims of education have been perceived through the ages. Education has always been believed to be a race that begins as early as possible and ends with graduation from apprenticeship, schools, universities, and with employment.

In 1658 John Evelyn's son, Richard:

> ... had learned all his catechism at two and a half years old; he could perfectly read any of the English, Latin, French, or Gothic letters, pronouncing the first three languages exactly. He had, before the fifth year, or in that year, not only skill to read most written hands, but to decline all the nouns, conjugate the verbs regular, and most of the irregular; ... got by heart almost the entire vocabulary of Latin and French primitives and words, could make congruous syntax, turn English into Latin, and vice versa, construe and prove what he read, and did the government and use of relatives, verbs, subjunctives, ellipses and many figures and tropes, and made considerable progress in Comenius' Janua; begin himself to write legibly and had a strong passion for Greek. The number of verses he could recite was prodigious ... Strange was his apt and ingenious application of fables and morals, for he had read Aesop; he had a wonderful disposition to mathematics, having [learnt] by heart diverse propositions of Euclid that were read to him in play, and he would make lines and demonstrate them ...[9]

This sad little boy died at the age of five. When coming across examples of such extreme precocity we must ask, what were the purposes of such a life and training? This child's feats were far from unusual at that time. Philippe Ariès in *Centuries of Childhood*[10] cites other examples. Any 'supergrow' parent of today would be delighted to settle for less. Richard Evelyn could hardly have had time to play, understand or apply what had been drilled into him before his untimely death. Little girls were rarely given any chance to be precocious because, until this century, they were not allowed to learn anything other than household, maternal or dilettante skills. We must ask ourselves why parents push children to achieve adult standards of performance at early ages? None of these children seems more intelligent than anyone else when it comes to anything other than their prodigious feats. In fact, in adulthood they are often remarkably inept human beings.

Significantly, pre-sixteenth-century European children were usually treated as miniature adults as soon as they could walk. Punishment was considered an essential ingredient of education. It is horrific therefore, but not surprising, that middle- and upper-class children of that day were educated as if they were delinquent adults. Even children's transgressions were punishable until the beginning of the twentieth century by sentences no less harsh than those meted out to adult offenders:

> John Robinson, the Pilgrim Teacher, said in his essay on *Children and Their Education*: '. . . Surely there is in all children (though not alike) a stubbornes and stoutnes of minde arising from naturall pride which must in the first place be broken and beaten down so that the foundation of their education being layd in humilitie and tractableness other virtues may in their time be built thereon. It is commendable in a horse that he be stout and stomackfull being never left to his own government, but always to have his rider on his back and his bit in his mouth, but who would have his child like his horse in his brutishness?'[11]

This is a perfect description of operant conditioning.

A new outlook on education began to dawn by the middle of the sixteenth century. It became apparent that an extended period of infancy and childhood was required as a preparation for increasingly specialized and mechanized jobs. More efficient methods seemed necessary to train (but not educate) children in narrower fields than heretofore. This gave birth to a literature about and for the education of children. Erasmus's *Zuchtbüchlein* (*Book of Manners*) of 1537 was among the first to address itself to the education of children below the age of ten. Before then hornbooks, the Catechism, the Bible, *Aesop's Fables* and the Greek and Roman classics were deemed appropriate literature for the children of the well-to-do and those destined for the professions. Comenius's *Orbis Pictus* (1658) began a trend towards training children for specialized employment by means of information broken down into bite-sized portions through pictures as well as words, a forerunner of nineteenth- and twentieth-century educational mass production.

I have treated the evolution of children's literacy elsewhere.[12] Philippe Ariès traces the cultural aspects of education from the fifteenth century onwards.[13] He describes the beginning in European cultures of a new awareness of childhood as a preparatory, but not yet as a developmental stage. As the pressures on children to be little adults lessened, so the number of precocious infants shrank. Yet home, Church and State concerned themselves less with providing guidance that might elicit a child's special talents and interests in an unfolding sense. Instead they concentrated on increasingly rigid forms of training for specialized employment. The former vision of children as recalcitrant miniature adults was replaced by one that regarded them as irresponsible, if temporary, mental retardates who needed training if they were to become docile, task-specialized and increasingly de-skilled employees – a trend that continues today.

From the late eighteenth century up to the twentieth, Johann Pestalozzi,[14] Friedrich Froebel,[15] Maria Montessori,[16] Alfred North Whitehead[17] and John Dewey[18] suggested educational methods that were believed to be more child-oriented. Their ideas had far-reaching, if not necessarily beneficial, effects. Instead of being punished for not learning, students were rewarded for doing as they were told. But this merely replaced the stick with the carrot. In the case of Dewey, any emphasis on individual excellence was discouraged. Group adjustment and permissiveness were favoured in education – a poisonous brew of freedom without goals and peer-group conformity that reached a climax in the 1960s. This led straight back to near total conditioning as now found in most of today's schools, universities and the world at large.

In this century education assumed the characteristics of something into which children needed to be coaxed rather than forced; a preparation for, rather than the business of life. Only once was a public effort made to understand and apply the principles of true learning, but it was unfortunately restricted to early childhood education. Britain's 1966 Plowden Report,[19] based on the work of Jean Piaget,[20] correctly identified the *open classroom* as one of the best methods of early learning. It was misapplied because the totally conditioned training of parents and teachers prejudiced them against it. Therefore they did not understand what was involved. For example, in the United States the Plowden Report recommendations were interpreted to mean classrooms literally without walls, within which the most didactic teaching methods were often used. The resulting chaos soon proved this misinterpretation of an excellent idea to be as insane as it sounds in retrospect, although the results were predictable from the start. The open classroom was intended to give maximum choice to each student to reach any desirable, self-determined, if guided goal – but it was not meant to be *open* in a literal sense. Even where the open-classroom concept was applied intelligently, it lacked follow-through at higher levels of education, thus negating the gains made in early years.

## Education for Work

Society is roughly divisible into four classes: the privileged (upper and upper-middle), the administrative and academic (the bureaucratic and professional), skilled labour (middle and lower-middle), and the unskilled and poor (the lowest). Up to the seventeenth century, the education of privileged children was perhaps more strenuous than that of today's university students. They were required to remember and recite vast amounts of information to gain their credentials and assumed adult roles as soon as they reached puberty. The same was true for apprentices in the arts, crafts, trades and professions. The children of the poor graduated to adult labour as soon as they were physically able, and often before due to dire necessity, as they still do in many Third World countries.

In the past, most work that needed to be done consisted of rote performance, machine-minding or back-breaking labour. Human workers – the 'megamachine' described by Lewis Mumford[21] – were mechanical or semi-mechanical adjuncts to relatively primitive tools and machines, densely concentrated on farms, in mines, factories, offices and schools. Such concentrations of labour demanded high levels of conformity to the group, subservience to autocratic slave-masters, managers, supervisors and trainers, to group-think and to the means of production. Conformity and an extinction of personal responsibility were enforced by the favoured methods of education, by a demand for credentials, by high specialization and by psychological testing that screened out non-conformists. This prejudicial selection process still takes place in schools and colleges and is reinforced by government and private employers.

There were exceptions: for example, the early craft guilds assured a high standard of excellence until they became exclusive. But exclusivity leads to corruption because it engenders the wrong form of competition (quantitative rather than qualitative), which became institutionalized in industries, trade unions and education as we know them today. These practices left little room for autonomy and self-expression. They mechanized what should have remained organic processes. They are reflected in today's educational systems, despite the fact that mass employment in labour-intensive mass production of the kind that still exists in certain industries will disappear almost entirely in the foreseeable future. Perhaps and regrettably these earlier, mechanistic and inhuman methods of learning and production were painful evolutionary necessities. The preconditions for the possibility of responsible freedom from blind obedience and rote performance seem to have demanded various forms of slavery. It seems to have made little difference whether these de-humanizing industrial processes were rationalized by the economic ideologies of the right, left or centre, or by priests, psychologists or educators. The consequences were the same. Neither Karl Marx nor Adam Smith could foresee what is now clearly inevitable (i.e. that many of the means of production no longer depend on mindless labour). Both these men were the products of conditioning and acculturation that had changed only in insignificant details and very slowly for centuries. Now that it is possible to use appropriate technologies instead of heavy manual labour, we have the potential for responsible (i.e. goal-defined) freedom.

In every post- or late-industrial society (and by this I mean the pre-electronic industrial societies) methods of production were wasteful of human and material resources. Now many of these are economically untenable because machines perform purely mechanical tasks better and more submissively than human beings. Education that prepares people to obey and perform without thought (i.e. for purely mechanical production) conditions them to become increasingly mindless, apathetic or robotic, hostile and rebellious in outlook and character, or to seek escape in drink, drugs, apathy or violence that blot out the purposeless aspects of their lives. The educational system itself and its human products become increasingly dependent, unstable, neurotic, corrupt and inefficient, as reflected in industries, governments and most modern cultures. It is totally out of date.

The relationship between mechanistic forms of production and education for tasks best performed by robots (human or mechanical) was first ritualized early in this century by the industrial psychologist F.W. Taylor[22] and the behaviourist J.B. Watson[23] in the US. Like Pavlov,[24] they systematized what had been practised in one way or another for centuries. Only rare Gestalt and humanistic psychologists like A. Maslow[25] tried to reverse these trends.

It is not difficult to predict the nature of work and

employment in the foreseeable future, but our educational systems have yet to adapt to these new realities. Our cultures are therefore reaching a crisis point. Already much rote labour in production and associated white-collar occupations have become obsolete because machines can perform them more efficiently, safely and profitably than we do. A new role for education is therefore in the making. Many agricultural and industrial processes, from certain aspects of farming to raw materials extraction, energy generation, mass production, assembly, administration and distribution can already be done by computer-controlled machines which are supervised and maintained by a minimum of skilled human workers. Un- or semi-skilled labour may soon be limited to those tasks for which there are no ecologically defensible or profitable mechanical alternatives (like some aspects of the building trades).

Skilled labour will inevitably be restricted to work that can be done only by human hands and brains for scientific, practical, social, ecological, health or aesthetic reasons. Innovation, teaching and caring occupations will always remain in human hands because no machine can set its own goals, discover anything new, teach, learn or care. At best it can mimic human behaviour or model options that may have been overlooked by the human beings, but only after the original work has been done by hand. Genuine innovation, creativity and caring always require originality, improvisation, co-operation and kindness. In industry skilled human labour will also be needed where the closest tolerances are required because even the most precisely manufactured parts (e.g. micro-chips) must usually be fitted or assembled by hand to other components produced by machines.

Many administrative routines are already handled efficiently by machines in the office and at home by those who use word processors, fax machines and computers. But de-centralization and the return to a cottage industry orientation also call for an increase in individual responsibility and self-discipline if anything is to work as it can and should. So an educational system is needed that helps students think for themselves, learn and work on their own with little or no supervision and be accountable and inner-motivated, rather than dependent as at present. The teaching, service and caring occupations will need an ever-increasing number of independent workers because of rapidly ageing populations and because better facilities are needed to re-educate people of all ages to take advantage of new opportunities and to face the responsibilities of the societies of the future.

These conditions demand a willingness on the part of young and old, employed and unemployed, to learn new skills and acquire new interests, goals and attitudes, especially in the West. Eastern and Third World countries, while currently still dependent on labour-intensive industries, will eventually achieve similar levels of automation. Only agriculture is likely to become less mechanized in the West for health and ecological reasons (e.g. the inevitable abandonment of 'factory farming' that has given us 'mad cow' disease among other afflictions). In any event learning and re-education can no longer be reserved for the young and the unskilled; it will become a theme for life and play a central role in any global economic, ecological and ethical reformation.

Few Western children of today achieve economic, academic or any other kind of maturity and independence with puberty. On the contrary, dependency usually reaches well into the second and third decades of life. Could it be that modern generations are less intelligent than those of former times, or that fewer demands are made on them? Are today's children less capable than those in the Middle Ages or the Renaissance? Or is it that skill levels needed for today's employment have increased so that an education extended into man- or womanhood has become a vocational necessity? Hardly. For the energy and skills required to be a medieval farmer, trader, craftsman, artist, musician, mathematician or academic, while different, were qualitatively and quantitatively as or perhaps more demanding than those of today. The main thrust of education then largely consisted of memory training, because access to stored information was restricted (books and libraries were not publicly accessible). An educated adult prior to the nineteenth century may have possessed less specialized knowledge, but he knew as much or more than his modern counterpart because the emphasis was on a more general education and apprenticeship. (For example, painters had to be chemists and mix their own pigments, while carpenters seasoned their own wood and prepared their own glues.)

IQ and aptitude tests used by twentieth-century psychologists and educators create group conformity and artificial distinctions between an intellectual or social in-group (the supposedly educable and intelligent) and those who do not fit that mould (those with manual and other non-academic aptitudes) are generally labelled unintelligent and ineducable. The latter are condemned to inferior status because they do not conform to an artificial and entirely spurious norm. Differences in perceptual style, like originality, manual dexterity, visual acuity or a musical ear are not accounted for in IQ tests[26] or recognized as signs of potentially valuable applications of natural intelligence.

In fact, the lack of visual education is largely responsible for much of today's learning failure. We may assign any meaning to whichever words we use and therein lies the danger of an exclusive preoccupation with verbal learning. For before we can extract the meanings of concepts, we must be able to visualize and imagine (i.e. see in the mind's eye) causes, consequences and the operations that bring both about, rather than simply rely on conditioned experience and conventionally assigned, verbally defined meanings. The inability of most people today (other than very young children) to see in the mind's eye or hear in the mind's ear is caused by an education that steers them away from these ways of thought into verbalization (without image analysis) or calculation (without a geometric or graphic basis). But critical analysis and an understanding of the patterns and meanings that underlie words, numbers or behaviours is impossible without these abilities. This even extends to feelings, for without empathy (i.e. placing yourself in the shoes of others) we become anaesthesized, selfish, hostile, unimaginative, and lack foresight.

In medieval times no distinctions existed between verbal and other learning because most adults were illiterate and had to rely on their senses to learn. Those who had the opportunity could learn what interested them – by apprenticeship, in monasteries or in loosely organized academies. People could also learn independently as late as the nineteenth century. The eighteenth-century explorer Captain James Cook is an excellent example. He had little formal education and came from a lower-class family. As a boy he was apprenticed a seaman, taught himself navigation and became a first-rate geographer, astronomer, what would today be called an ethnographer and a comparative anthropologist. He was also a shrewd psychologist and sociologist; entirely unprejudiced in his approach to unfamiliar people and cultures; highly literate and numerate. People like Cook were by no means rare in the past but are virtually non-existent today. They were generalists with great expertise in one or more specialities – often self-taught. But with increased specialization in every occupation (by now you must obtain a degree before you are believed to be eligible for employment), credentials are all that matter and performance counts for relatively little. This is especially true in non-academic subjects like photography where a good eye, a minimum of equipment, dedicated practice and experience are all that is needed. Even worse than the pseudo-intellectualizing of arts and crafts is the professionalization of non-subjects like 'media studies' that elevate TV- and film-watching to a spurious academic discipline. Hence inefficiency and a general lack of creativity prevail in most endeavours, all due to operant conditioning. As a result most people today are bored and boring, only able to repeat what they saw on last night's TV.

The dependency on mechanical forms of teaching – on computers, calculators, teaching machines and audio-visual media – has degraded the learning process even further. Today's computer experts and teachers confuse learning with performance, process with product. Artificial intelligence (discussed in Chapter 8) is one of the most pernicious examples of such conditioning, for it is still believed today by many people in- and outside the sciences that computers can learn and as a result may some day equal or surpass human intelligence. This mistaken belief stems from the conviction that programming (i.e. operant conditioning) underlies all learning. But any learning must first be done, and every problem solved, by brain or hand before it can be automated, tested by computer or turned into a product. For example, after any new scientific discovery has been made by brain and hand, it is often faster and more efficient to test findings by computer. Errors may then be found and corrected. But a computer can never spontaneously produce answers other than those for which it has been programmed, nor can it find and correct errors on its own. It also cannot calculate beyond the limits of its memory store, visualize or imagine. Computers are indeed useful (this book was written on one), but they can never supplant the human brain. Automated teaching may amuse students, but it 'programs' them and does not help them learn. These methods are merely old wine in new bottles.

The rabbi who traditionally offered a Hebrew student a lick of honey when he got the answers right achieved the same results as the schoolroom martinet who punished students for giving wrong ones. The rabbi's method may seem kinder, but the effect of reward or punishment is the same. Neither student learns anything except that it pays to follow the dictates of teachers, audio-visual aids or computers, to avoid punishment, to believe anything even when it is wrong, to give expected answers and never think for oneself. Any form of operant conditioning by man or machine defeats the purpose of education. The Latin roots of the word 'education' (*ex ducere* – to lead out) convey its true meanings.

## Conditioning

The causes and consequences (i.e. the meanings) of the

various forms of conditioning become predictable only when analysed by means of combinatorial methods (see Appendix D). As I said in Chapter 3 and repeat in Chapter 7, human decision-making involves a complex set of sensory-motor information that is ultimately reduced to a *yes* or *no*, *on* or *off*, or a question mark (i.e. what is it?). Sensory certainty (e.g. sight and hearing) demands a single neural conclusion, with an awareness of other possibilities that are ignored or suppressed for practical, valuative, aesthetic or genetic reasons. However, this is not true for muscular certainty. The brain gives a single command but muscles translate this into compound action. Physical actions require a dual neural conclusion – the simultaneous *push* and *pull* of complementary sets of muscles. Therefore the neural network processes two kinds of information – sense impressions and muscular data. Both are inter-connected; sensory data feeding into the muscular system and vice versa.

So in organic systems any sensory push *or* pull decision is passed on as a push *and* pull command to different muscles. The decision as to whether to push or pull depends on purpose and is genetically determined (i.e. reflexive) or voluntary. For example, the iris in the human eye is conditioned genetically to contract or expand, depending on the amount of light that falls on it. That result is achieved by some muscles that pull and others that push simultaneously. Iris contraction is purposive for as long as the eye functions normally; the purpose, in the absence of any volition, is to screen out excess light. Muscular action always involves reflex arcs (more than a single reflex), as the neurologist C. Sherrington discovered early in this century.[27] These are generated by a genetic program, by sense impressions or by intentions wherever volition is involved. But a machine, while it may perform reciprocal actions like a piston's push *or* pull, does not involve reciprocal dual action or a reflex arc. In the machine, a single stimulus or command is invariably followed by a single action. This shows that machines differ from organisms even in terms of physical operations.

A mechanism is purely reflexive in a binary on *or* off sense, and therein lies a profound difference between man and machine. The latter has neither purposes nor intentions other than those programmed into it by its human master. It performs push *or* pull alternately, as commanded, but never both together as a forceful compound action. In fact, mechanisms need protection from *backlash* – pull when the piston pushes and vice versa. The pull action is non-existent when the piston of a reciprocal piston engine pushes. But, as said earlier, in the human body positive push *and* pull actions take place simultaneously when the objective is to push *or* to pull. Even as simple an action as bending or straightening a leg involves first a single neural decision and then a complex of simultaneous reflexive muscular push *and* pull actions not found in any machine.

There are further differences between man and machine that concern learning – something no machine can master. We do not really know anything until it has become reflexive as a result of learning and practice. Then we no longer need to think before we speak or act. At that point whatever thought or action is required becomes automatic and requires no further conscious awareness (see Diagram 7). Once any thought or action becomes reflexive there can be no self-awareness or consciousness of implications, even if that action is wrong. In other words, it is as easy for right as for wrong forms of conditioning to become habitual and reflexive, and therein lies one danger of uncritical learning.

Driving a car involves reflexive conditioning. Once the driver of a car is experienced and fully conditioned, he or she no longer needs to think about when or how to change gears or handle the steering wheel, accelerator pedal, brake or clutch in ordinary situations. However, a driver who only drives reflexively (i.e. mechanically and relatively objectively) can be a menace as soon as anything unusual occurs within or outside the car – someone stepping off the kerb unexpectedly, the car going into a skid or distractions caused by a passenger. When a driver drives purely mechanically (without visualizing and imagining

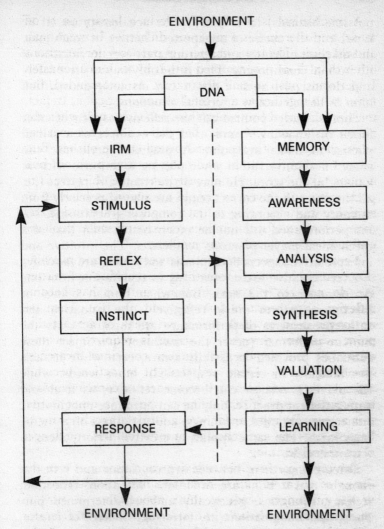

*Diagram 7*: The processes of learning, conditioning and environmental input are shown here in a vastly simplified diagram. Reflexes and instincts are shown on the left, subconscious side of the diagram; the ability to learn on the right, conscious, half. Once anything is learnt and practised often enough (including bad habits or wrong information), it is then transferred to the conditioned, reflexive and instinctive side.

possible hazards) he is likely to be accident-prone. If he is subjectively aware of unexpected changes in conditions, he will react instantly and appropriately even in violation of his normal conditioning. That is the only way to drive safely and defensively. Such a driver can instantly decondition him- or herself in new or critical situations.

Samuel Butler pointed out the reflexive aspects of other forms of 'knowing'[28] and used the example of a skilled pianist to make his point. A practised performer can carry on a conversation while playing a concerto without looking at the score. He may be mechanically perfect (i.e. all the notes in the correct tempi are played precisely from memory and according to the composer's notations), but his performance will not be much better than that of a mechanical player-piano or synthesizer. The intuitive and interpretative aspects of emphasis and feeling are lacking.

Every creative artist varies his interpretation from one performance to the next. But when human beings or machines perform music reflexively, the valuative and subjective aspects of performance are missing. Only the human performer (never the machine) can inject these subtleties provided he is fully aware, even while he acts mechanically in certain respects. In other words, while the player's *technique* can become reflexive, as it should with sufficient practice, only he can introduce imaginative, subjective subtleties, meanings, and variations on a theme (e.g. Jazz). The same applies to creative performances in any other field.

Intervening, then, between sensory input and reflexive thought and actions are intentions, attention, reflection, feelings, intuitions, genetically and self-determined purposes and imagination (i.e. foresight). These, of course, affect the learning process inasmuch as they involve value judgements even when, with practice, the purely mechanical aspects of what has been learnt become reflexive and totally conditioned. In the absence of subjectively critical and valuative decision-making, any performance from playing a piano to making love tends to become mechanical.

# Operant Conditioning

Operant conditioning has been institutionalized in all cultures since time immemorial. When individuals or groups of people condition themselves or let others condition them for long enough and with sufficient reinforcement (either by expectation of a reward, fear of punishment, by imagined unconditional freedom or by mindless imitation) they can be forced (or allow themselves) to become psychologically or physically dependent, self-destructive and a menace to others. Gitta Sereny's study of Franz Stangl, a World War II Gestapo concentration-camp commander, and his victims demonstrates the frightening power of operant conditioning.

> 'Why', I asked Stangl, 'if they [Gestapo concentration-camp guards] were going to kill them [their victims] anyway, what was the point of the humiliation, why the cruelty?' Stangl replied: 'To condition those who actually had to carry out the policies.' [Of the 'final solution' and the brutal killing of millions of people] he said, 'To make it possible for them to do what they did . . .'[29]

But it must also be remembered that, apart from isolated Jewish rebels like those in the Warsaw ghetto, millions permitted themselves to be led to slaughter without demur. Like their torturers they were conditioned to do as they were told, to believe that if they kept a low profile they might survive and that the Germany of Bach and Goethe could never be guilty of atrocities. They were wrong because they were corrupted by their conditioning. Throughout history and especially today, those who allow themselves to be conditioned – victims and their victimizers – co-operate in their mutual destruction.

Operant conditioning works for training the mentally handicapped, domesticating wild animals, creating human monsters like Stangl, or brainwashing people to be willing victims. It penalizes those who allow themselves to be victimized and can destroy them, unless they free themselves from their externally- and often self-imposed psychological fetters. Operant conditioning can turn naturally intelligent human beings into imbeciles. It is also, in effect, the only method for programming computers. Obviously computers can be neither punished nor rewarded. However, a computer program consists of a list of instructions that the machine must follow slavishly. It cannot do otherwise. It cannot perform any routine outside its program, exactly like a human being who has been conditioned by operant means with reinforcement. The difference is that human beings can decondition themselves by acts of will despite reinforcement, or they can become deconditioned gradually when reinforcement ceases for long enough. But neither is possible for computers.

Pavlov's dog salivated when a bell rang even when no meat was offered because it had been conditioned to associate the bell with food. That is known as a conditioned reflex. Consumers and voters who uncritically believe advertisements, commercials, religious, political, scientific or any other form of propaganda are no different from Pavlov's dog. Their reasoning powers can be destroyed and their humanity anaesthetized by perceived promises or threats. In time their responses become conditioned so that they no longer think independently. The same is true of every individual who obeys any authority without questioning its authenticity. There is nothing in our genes that predisposes us to believe falsehoods, no matter how we may be conditioned or how seductive or threatening those who seek to condition us may be.

Pavlov's dog could not help himself; nor was he a believer. He reacted reflexively and without thought because his genetic endowment gave him no choice. But we are able to question the authenticity of the actual or symbolic 'bell' and the motives of those who ring it. We are unique in so far as we can either decondition ourselves or, like Pavlov's dog, wait until all reinforcement ceases (i.e. if the bell rings and no reward is offered for long enough, conditioned reflexes are eventually extinguished). But once we have been successfully indoctrinated by religious, political, commercial or academic programming, it can take a very long time before conditioned (i.e. reflexive) thoughts and behaviours extinguish themselves. Even then it requires great effort for us to rediscover our humanity, imagination, reason and independence. For to allow yourself to be conditioned to believe what may be palpable falsehoods means to have resigned from the human race and to have assumed the characteristics of a machine or Pavlov's dog.

Like Freudian psychiatry, *behaviourism* – the belief that all learning consists of stimulus/response, carrot-and-stick training and that only observed behaviour is worthy of study by psychologists – has had a disastrous influence on twentieth-century perceptions. The object of behaviourism (of which operant conditioning is a central feature) is to manipulate people, presumably in their own best interests. The late B.F. Skinner, a highly regarded US spokesman for this school of psychology, reveals his motives through his own words, as shown in the quote that heads this chapter.

Aversion therapy, as practised by Hans Eysenck and those who share his views, is a variation on the same theme. As the writer Peter Schrag states: 'If one zaps a rat often enough on its way to get food pellets [by forcing it to walk across an electrified grid that gives it unpleasant shocks], one can teach it to starve to death.'[30] That is how some behaviourists claim to 'cure' people of what they deem disturbed behaviour ranging from bed-wetting to homosexuality.

P. London, in his book *Behavior Control*,[31] erroneously attributes the invention of operant conditioning to industrialization. People had been conditioned to believe falsehoods long before that. The only thing that has changed is that modern methods of conditioning are more efficient, thanks to a realization that the carrot – the inducements of unfettered free enterprise and consumerism (i.e. total freedom) fed by mass production and the stupefying mass media – often works better than the stick. In many respects London is correct, despite his distorted conspiratorial view of history:

... contemporary behaviourism is rooted ... in the prosaic soil of rationalized factory production ... The object was not merely to downgrade the worker's skill – to wrest it away from him – but to give management the mystifying paraphernalia ... with which to enhance the legitimacy of control ... A similar system had to be adopted in school. [He then quotes from a 1916 book on school administration:] Our schools are, in a sense, factories in which the raw products [children] are to be shaped and fashioned into products to meet the various demands of life ... [32]

London also debunks the diagnoses of certain disorders that twentieth-century psychologists and psychiatrists insist are genetic in origin rather than caused by conditioning. Some psychologists' findings support race and class prejudices about human intelligence, or excuse intolerable and irresponsible behaviour like alcoholism and other forms of addiction by claiming that genetic predispositions or disease are responsible. Such ideas have been promoted in one or another form by B.F. Skinner,[33] Arthur Jensen[34] and R. Herrnstein[35] in the US, and Hans Eysenck[36] in Britain. They have found corroboration in the discredited statistics of Cyril Burt[37] and other psychologists about whom London writes: 'Through the tests [IQ, aptitude and psychological profiles] the practitioners create wholly new categories of deficiency and diseases which had never existed in the real world ...'[38]

Certainly some motor and neurological disorders are caused by genetic flaws or environmental damage. More often they are due to self-conditioning or conditioning imposed by others. For example, many of today's mind specialists usually discount the role played by incessant TV watching in causing a shortened attention span and lack of self-discipline. Instead they attribute intolerable anti-social behaviours to scientific-sounding (but meaningless) afflictions like *minimal brain dysfunction* and *hyperkinesis*. Then they treat the symptoms with drugs like Ritalin. Other psychologists hold the environment entirely responsible for irresponsible and criminal behaviours, blaming parents, childhood trauma and unhappy experiences that we should be able to overcome with maturity. Lest it be thought that modern psychology is a Western aberration, the same behaviourist and psychiatric methods are used elsewhere not only in the treatment of dissidents and the mentally disturbed but also in education. Educators and behavioural experts in the former Iron Curtain countries remain as dedicated to operant conditioning as most liberal European and US psychologists. Yet N. Bongard, a Russian cyberneticist, was far more aware of the dangers of operant conditioning than his Western colleagues when he wrote:

> For some time it seemed that the performance of the brain was known in general terms. Especially after the studies of I.P. Pavlov of conditioned reflexes, it was thought that by combining a large number of conditioned reflexes of different orders, behaviour of any complexity could be created. Many psychologists, even as late as fifteen years ago [and still today], could risk saying, 'Give us a sufficient number of blocks capable of producing conditioned reflexes, and we will build a system that will adapt to external conditions in the course of training. This system will behave expediently under conditions that vary within a wide range.' Can it be that conditioned reflexes are the required basic building blocks for constructing thinking machines? ... conditioned reflexes are not units upon which to base an understanding of thinking processes, because they perform only very primitive functions, namely the coincidence of certain events with respect to time.[39]

Bongard was only partially right. He might have gone further and shown, as I have done, that an integrated, combinatorial accumulation of binary pathways, like the central nervous system, generates conditional branching of incredible complexity (trinary, quatrinary . . .). Thus a very complex model of behaviour can be built by a combination of our inner and the outer world, based entirely on binary principles. Hence we can speak of free will without fear of contradiction, especially when we relate such a myriad of combinatorial possibilities to an even larger sum of possibilities in the external environment. We would run out of time in our galaxy if we were to try to exercise all options offered even by the game of chess, an analogy that is dwarfed by the complexities of life. But we can also curtail our free will by submitting to operant conditioning, in which case we reduce our decision-making options to a few out of the welter of possibilities that are available to us. No other options than those for which we have conditioned ourselves or have allowed ourselves to be conditioned can then occur to us.

The aim of operant conditioning is to achieve absolute control, to get individuals to follow commands without question. Behaviourists and followers of Pavlov believe that operant conditioning with perpetual reinforcement (punishment, reward and mindless repetition) is the best or only way to learn.

Operant conditioning with reinforcement as the main technique of teaching is so deeply entrenched that even educators who disown it tend to adopt it subconsciously. They have allowed themselves to be conditioned to such an extent that they cannot recognize the contradictions in what they think, say and practise. Examples of such double-think are legion. Most schools of psychology endorse operant conditioning in one form or another, even though this is emphatically denied, because they subscribe to the wrong principles.

These, then, are the favoured methods of teaching and learning within and outside educational institutions that affect the sciences profoundly. They have remained more or less the same for generations except that the stick is periodically supplanted by the carrot or, equally disastrously, by total freedom. The main forms of operant conditioning with reinforcement can be summarized as follows:

- Reward-based conditioning (carrot) in which the student, employee or other individual receives positive feedback in the form of pass-marks in tests, diplomas or degrees, employment, salary rises, bonuses, titles, emoluments, grants, golden handshakes, various forms of advancement, tenure, pensions or bribes. It demands conformity to a current norm. In animal experiments or with young children, rewards may consist of favourite food, sweets, presents, praise or approval in order to assure a given behaviour or result. In relationships between parents and children, lovers, friends, husbands or wives, the reward may take the form of psychological or material bribes without which the recipient would not act as desired. In today's politics, as in advertising, the object of conditioning (i.e. propaganda and promotion) is to raise false expectations of one sort or another.

- Punishment-based conditioning (stick) in which subjects are threatened with negative feedback in the form of pressure, failure, demotion, lack of advancement, being sacked, forcible restraint, isolation, physical or psychological pain or torture, or the withholding of pay or other rewards if an individual fails to act in a prescribed manner. These methods are also used in political and advertising campaigns where they induce or trade on real or imagined fears. Aversion therapy, electric-shock and other physio-chemical forms of treatment are some of the medical tools of this form of operant conditioning.

- Total freedom without goal definition. This method leads directly to total conditioning (i.e. no choice, except perpetual repetition within a closed feedback loop). Total freedom is not generally understood to be a form of operant conditioning. Most forms of addiction like drugs, alcohol, tobacco, food, gambling or any kind of anti-social or psychopathic behaviour that has no genetic origin are products of freedom without responsibility. Politically, any expectation of freedom without advance goal-definition inevitably leads back to authoritarian control.

- Aping or parroting without conceptual understanding is a method of conditioning that is often confused with learning. Many animal species are very good at mimicry. And when the results seem appropriate to us (as when apes living on the African coast wash fruit in salt water), they actually serve as self-reinforcement for misinterpretations of the learning process. But, like a parrot's imitation of human speech, there can be no understanding of meanings. What is acquired by pure imitation cannot be transferred to other, related situations.

In humans, all forms of operant conditioning involve short-term methods of training, propaganda or programming (including self-conditioning) and require constant reinforcement. Operant conditioning of any kind leads to inner conflict, depression, apathy, rigid conformity and dogmatism (i.e. no perceived choices), or to anarchy (rebellion, revolution, violence, insanity or criminality). No learning is possible under any of these conditions.

Obviously a certain amount of conditioning, rote repetition and even mimicry can support genuine learning. Learning to read is a good example. However, young children cannot become functionally literate by parroting the letters of the alphabet by rote (for example, the children's TV show 'Sesame Street' pretends to make pre-schoolers literate and numerate by operant conditioning techniques[40]). That is how most children are taught today. Hence the high level of functional illiteracy in all our societies. No child has ever learnt how to read and understand in this way.

The essential preconditions for genuine literacy are stories frequently told and read to children at early ages, regular purchases or borrowing of children's books from libraries, seeing adults and older children read regularly at home, and curtailment of TV watching. A desire to read can be fostered only when books are treasured sources of entertainment and information. Children will then want to read; they will virtually teach themselves to do so after the method has been pointed out to them. Watching TV by the hour, once it becomes habitual and a substitute for stories, books and active play, stifles literacy, especially at early ages. (A child who watches an average of three hours of TV per day, starting at the age of three (and many children sit for much longer in front of their TVs, videos, arcade game consoles, computers and, starting now, also their 'virtual reality' machines) will have spent 13.5 years of his or her life of uninterrupted, sixteen-hours-per-day TV watching by the age of seventy-five. This figure allows for eight hours of sleep, but no time out for meals, play or any other activity.) That is the main reason for the decline in literacy in Western societies, reflected in science education as much as in everything else. The same is true for numeracy. As reported in the *International Herald Tribune*: '. . . many American students cannot make the grade in demanding graduate and postgraduate levels because they have not received adequate training and motivation, especially in the sciences, from kindergarten through college.'[41]

No one can learn unless he or she wants to. But in order to learn properly, given today's world, we must first de-condition ourselves. This involves breaking inappropriate habits of thought and behaviour and supplanting them with appropriate ones. Finally, the freedom to learn demands worthwhile goals. For example, anyone used to a tropical or temperate climate who finds himself in polar regions will survive if he lets go of the habits of a lifetime, learns directly from the Eskimo or discovers on his own what they know. But transport a dogmatist or a chimpanzee to Greenland and neither will last very long. The same, of course, would apply to a traditional Eskimo suddenly arriving dressed in furs and seal skins in Miami, Cairo or New Delhi.

A good example of the effects of conditioned and uncon-ditioned behaviour is provided by what happened to Amundsen and Scott, the Antarctic explorers of 1905. Amundsen was a Norwegian, and Scott a British naval officer. Each was commissioned by his co-patriates to be the first to reach the South Pole. It was, of course, stupid to turn exploration into a nationalistic competition but both reached their goal although Amundsen arrived first. The latter and his team returned safely after great but endurable hardships. All but one member of Scott's crew, including their leader, perished on the ice.

Amundsen had visited Greenland in advance of his trip to the Antarctic and learnt survival skills from the Eskimo: how to build igloos, about sleds, huskies, pemmican, skis, snow shoes and other essential polar equipment. He found out about the various kinds of snow, ice and other conditions from those who knew how to survive in them.

Scott suffered from the prejudices of his time and class and believed that native wisdom was not to be trusted. Only one member of his expedition knew how to ski and only he survived. Scott insisted on taking along Shetland ponies (instead of huskies), tinned food that burst in sub-zero temperatures and motor-driven sleds that failed to withstand polar conditions. Not one of his team understood arctic survival skills. They suffered miserably and while one must be sympathetic, Scott's ignorance and the stupidity of those who trusted his judgement were deplorable. They created their own fate (as we all do) by their inability to learn and make the correct value judgements. They died unnecessarily. An arrogant refusal to learn independently or from those who know was Scott's undoing and that is always the product of operant conditioning. Scott's heroism against the adversity he created is still held up for emulation in Britain and elsewhere. But his was typical of disasters caused by operant conditioning and the wrong forms of competition. These should be far more useful lessons than appeals to patriotism.

The effects of operant conditioning on popular and scientific perceptions affect all aspects of our lives. They are reflected in every culture, East and West. Demonstrably wrong ideas have become deeply embedded in our psychological make-up. It may take centuries to dislodge them, except for those who make a conscious effort to decondition themselves.

Current teaching and learning methods, rather than helping young and old learn and adapt to rapidly changing technologies, insist on standardized intelligence tests that fail to take into account different individual, cultural and environmental conditions. Examinations, rather than testing for interests, adaptability and a willingness to learn, purport to show that some people are more intelligent than others. The presumption is that any race, group or social class other than our own is stupid. But it is difficult to be more intelligent than the Eskimo, as Scott discovered to his and his party's cost. It is equally difficult to be more stupid than we are when it comes to living successfully in our own environment, as we can see all around us (for example, wars, oil spills, mindless pollution and the creation of other lethal social and environmental hazards). Intelligence is not demonstrated by tests and the passing of examinations but by appropriate behaviour in all circumstances.

The point is that we all share the same central nervous system; the combinatorial neural network which we use to process information. Disregarding genetic defect, disease or gross environmental damage, and aside from skeletal and muscular differences, organic weaknesses or strengths, all of us have the potential to process the same information in a similar manner. Hence each of us is potentially equally intelligent, yet individually unique, depending on internal and external variables and opportunities. However, the major differences between individuals, as far as intelligence is concerned, are interests, intentions and how efficiently we use our common intelligence; in other words habits of thought and behaviour.

## Custom and Habit

A quite different form of conditioning is a required part of learning in the sense that once you have learnt something (including how to learn) it becomes habitual (i.e. reflexive) and you no longer need to think about it. There is a great difference between factually based conditioning and operant conditioning designed to inspire conformity and instil beliefs not founded on fact. To 'believe' anything merely because it is fashionable or convenient – whether it is a scientific theory, a metaphysical imposition or anything else – means to be a willing victim of someone's delusion or greed for money and power.

Pseudo-sciences are as prone to fashion as the clothing industry. My favourite example that links both concerns the 'training bra', a US fad of the 1940s and 1950s. It was no different from the belief in selfish genes, big-bang or chaos theories. Manufacturers advertised training bras as essentials for six- and seven-year-old girls to prepare them for womanhood. Notable US psychiatrists endorsed them to help little girls overcome the supposed trauma of budding breasts. Psychologists wrote PhD theses and popular articles on this subject and middle-class mothers believed them. They went to great lengths to save their pre-nubile daughters from mammary deprivation until this fad eventually died and other equally silly ones took its place.

One cannot help wondering what these children were in training for. Even more interesting is what happened to the psychiatrists and psychologists who endorsed the training bra. Did any admit their error and reverse themselves when this piece of insanity had run its course? It seems more than likely that they looked through the pages of fashion magazines and drug manufacturers' catalogues to see what other things (like 'training pills' in the form of sweets) they might endorse next. The point is that charlatan scientists and their gullible victims are equally to blame. One could not exist without the other.

## True Freedom

Total freedom (i.e. no restraints whatsoever; the cry of the 1960s) leads directly to total conditioning, as is easily demonstrated (see Appendix D). In order to have and enjoy true freedom you need to define a benign goal. You are then free to pursue it by any legitimate means. These are the conditions of freedom and define it. Or, to put this another way, true freedom opens up the options for choosing any one of the best routes to a worthwhile goal. We are then free to choose whichever we prefer, provided it is benign.

This is not a moralistic, philosophical or theoretical precept. It is based on an analysis of the combinatorial neural network. The liberation of the Iron Curtain countries and the liberalization of the Russian regime in the 1980s illustrate this point. Neither has led to real freedom because its conditions are not understood there any better than elsewhere. For most people here and there freedom has meant access to video recorders, the material blessings of the so-called free world, and unrestricted freedom to spend and consume. Liberation has not really changed the quality of life; in many respects it has made it worse. In the USSR, Romania and Poland and Yugoslavia, as in other countries liberated by Gorbachev's *glasnost*, the new freedom from oppression has caused endless political disputes between various groups. Its main product seems to be a reversion to factionalism, racism, religious fundamentalism, opportunism and nationalism. None of the people in these regions appears to have any goal other than to turn on one another, complain, renew ancient ethnic feuds and grudges, create religious or political divisions along classical sectarian lines or demand unqualified freedom or a new state discipline to replace the old. The traditional competitive orientation of the populations and bureaucracies of these countries has not been replaced by an essentially co-operative one (which is what Gorbachev seems to have had in mind) that could lead to individuality, personal responsibility and common goals (i.e. the conditions of freedom). Gorbachev has shown the USSR and former Iron Curtain countries the way, but they insist on clinging to ancient divisive habits. They will not learn because they are totally conditioned. They cannot find the means to make use of their freedom because they have found no goals to replace those that were formerly imposed on them.

What holds true for nations is equally true for individuals. In the West, most of us believe that we are free, but that is true only for the few who can afford to satisfy the material needs of existence and are working towards worthwhile ends. Freedom of choice is meaningless without well-defined goals and a willingness to learn how to reach them autonomously.

In former times children were conditioned to follow in their parents' footsteps, which often led to a good deal of unhappiness. Today, most families and schools urge students to keep their options open and not to commit themselves to a career until after graduation. Some fortunate young people know what they want to learn and be. They are the exceptions. Most flounder through school, hoping to 'find' themselves in college or employment. These students are in a double-bind. They suffer near total conditioning in the classroom (i.e. they do as they are told), yet are given total freedom without goal-definition as far as their futures are concerned.

Most of today's graduates know that they are likely to be thrown on the scrapheap of unemployment or retirement at early ages. Learning ends with formal education and training for those who lack or never find their purpose. Rapidly changing technologies quickly make obsolete whatever they have been trained to do in school or on the job. The promised benefits of early retirement have proven hollow, especially when leisure without purpose and mindless consumption are the sole aims in life. The answer is an education that enables people to discover what interests them; to learn and relearn perpetually, so that their options expand continuously throughout their lifetimes. This is the meaning of and the path to a realization of freedom.

## Goal Definition

Education should show students how to set short-range goals and how to reach them. They will discover their longer-range goals once they become conditioned to learn with a purpose. Rather than disciplining or bribing students or leaving them entirely at sea, teachers should teach them how to discipline themselves and define who and what they want to be. Learning without self-discipline and purpose (i.e. total freedom) is as futile as learning to do as you are told. Both lead to the same ends. This point is illustrated by Bertrand and Dora Russell's disastrous School on Telegraph Hill, symptomatic of the 'advanced' thinking of the 1930s and Russell's flawed philosophy; an educational misadventure which has been mercifully forgotten. Their school was totally permissive and children as young as five and six were encouraged to do what they liked without purpose or restraint. Some never washed or changed their clothes. These children's innate sense of and need for order was undermined. Russell believed that no order at all was better than an imposed one. He never realized that dictatorship and chaos are opposite sides of the same coin. Equal damage is done to children and adults when they are given total freedom without self-originated goals or are controlled in an authoritarian manner. It is therefore critically important to make value judgements about purposes and goals. To put it very simply, in order to have a true purpose you have to know and understand what you are doing, why you are doing it and what the consequences will be.

But some people are solely concerned with *how* things work (e.g. scientists and technicians); others with causes and consequences (e.g. philosophers). Without an understanding of all three (i.e. causes, consequences and the operations that bring both about), we can never get to meanings. For example, we can see the consequences of learning failure all about us. But we seem totally unaware of the causes or the operational methods that can lead to learning success for everyone who wants to learn, depending on interest and effort.

## Education for Unemployment

Education of the right sort can elicit human qualities that might otherwise remain dormant. It can hone logic, reason, analytic skills and craftsmanship in the widest sense. Learning can open opportunities, stimulate autonomy and new interests and increase perceptual, social, intellectual and physical co-ordination. It can arouse ethical and aesthetic senses. Learning can enhance problem-solving and decision-making abilities. It enables individuals and groups to discover their goals and reach them creatively. It increases the short- and long-term options for everyone's future and provides the learner with foresight, imagination, the ability to discover causes, understand operations, predict consequences, extract meanings and make correct value judgements. These are the ways to foster an efficient use of natural intelligence.

Educational strategies determine the quality of life for everyone. Education can either stimulate independent thought and responsible action or irresponsible conformity to an unsavoury standard. Most of today's education means rote learning and a preparation for rote performance in jobs that deprive the individual of will, autonomy, responsibility and options. Conformity is typical of animal species that have evolved to a point of absolute balance with nature (a good thing for bees and ants but fatal for human beings), or of species and cultures heading towards extinction. The latter has happened again and again in our history – in ancient Egypt, Greece, Rome, to mention but a few societies that went into decline as a result of their conditioning, never to recover.

Today's pressures for conformity in education and life-style are almost global and could be culturally fatal for generations to come. Current trends in education prepare people for consumption, obsolescence, heightened competition, early retirement, or a lifetime of dependency and under- or unemployment. Apathy, disillusionment or hostility are inevitable consequences of authoritarianism, as much as of anarchic freedom without goals. People are conditioned to accept these as inevitable conditions of life but they are intolerable and unnecessary.

Consumerism, lack of realizable goals, expectations unrelated to performance, an unwillingness to learn throughout life and a continuing devaluation of craftsmanship in favour of a 'cowboy' approach to success are the by-products of modern education. Today most people work for money alone, an attitude that is responsible for many of our economic and psychological problems. Exceptional individuals who do their work out of interest as well as to make a living are a minuscule minority that is usually considered eccentric.

When the wrong forms of conditioning become globally endemic, as they have, they are difficult to dislodge. Most people accept the status quo and can see no other way of solving their problems. Some cultures, like Western ones in the 1960s, tolerate or encourage futile or misdirected protest. But most youthful protesters matured to become opportunists and hypocrites like the elders against whom they had rebelled. They knew what they were against, but never discovered what they might have been for. Many of today's middle-aged and soon-to-be elderly wheeler-dealers are the ineffectual drop-outs, drug addicts and hippies of the 1960s, 1970s and 1980s. Those who thought they were free – but had no purpose – have become all the things they claimed to despise. Tom Paine, the eighteenth-century libertarian, may have said, 'Give me liberty or give me death', but liberty without purpose is another form of death.

There is no question that we will ever return to labour-intensive production in industry. Nor is it possible to support the unemployed out of the public purse for ever or to make work for those who perform only mechanically, unless we reverse the trends in automation. Or, if we proceed on the road to further robotization without massive re-education, we will be faced with ever-increasing juvenile delinquency, riots, football and other forms of hooliganism, apathy, mental-breakdown rates, drug addiction, crime or open rebellion. Or governments may feel tempted to opt for increased militarization of the police and other forms of regimentation. Industry's freedom to automate without social and educational adjustments to these new circumstances can lead directly to what George Orwell proposed in his book *Nineteen Eighty-Four*.

To avoid this prospect we need an educational system that differs radically from the one we have. It must stress individual responsibility, accountability, autonomy and a regard for consequences on the part of the bureaucracies in government, industry, agriculture, education, and especially in the sciences.

The computer technologies force such a reorientation on us. There is an urgent need to reconsider what we mean by learning if a proper use is to be made of them. The lack of understanding of the human learning process is demonstrated by a prevailing, if waning belief in artificial intelligence (see Chapter 8). Human learning is still believed to depend more on cognition (amassing encyclopaedic information) and stimulus/response rather than on autonomously establishing relationships between different bodies of information. Learning is therefore mistakenly assumed to consist mostly of memorizing isolated facts and repeating them, rather than of analysis, classification, synthesis and valuation. Subjective value judgements are suspect in an age dedicated to relatively objective methods.

The diploma-mill aspects of modern education, viewed as preconditions to employment even in non-academic fields, have helped debase learning further. Sheer accumulation of knowledge or experience (it is also possible to draw the wrong conclusions from the right experiences) do not guarantee understanding. Comprehensive knowledge within too narrow a speciality creates a closed feedback loop common to all forms of operant conditioning. Those who entrap themselves in it tend to remain blind to consequences – like Pavlov's dog – in any frame of reference other or larger than their own.

Examples are legion. Game theory,[AA] the relationship between randomness and chance (see Chapter 5), the search for the pattern structure of prime and composite numbers (see Appendix E), the principles of time and navigation (see Appendix C) and those of learning (see Appendix D) are useful examples. Despite a history that goes back hundreds of years and a vast literature, these subjects have never been understood as they could have been if people had thought logically, clearly and independently.

Learning style not only determines our future personalities and achievements, but also whether or not we can free ourselves from all the wrong-think, cant and hypocrisy with which we are bombarded in the modern world. The only limitations to human learning are genetically imposed. All human beings – children, men and women of all the races of mankind, rich or poor, from 'good' families or 'bad' – are potentially equally intelligent and can learn equally well depending on their interests, strengths or weaknesses (a one-legged man clearly cannot learn to be a long-distance runner) provided they free themselves from their wrong conditioning.

## The Combinatorial Model of Learning

The combinatorial neural network model of learning (as far as it has been extended in Appendix D) shows that it is possible to make clear distinctions between relatively subjective and objective aspects of operant and other forms of conditioning. It provides a totally objective method for assessing causes, consequences and the operations that bring both about – the meanings of what is learnt, how it is learnt and of the learning process itself. It shows how far machines can mimic human intelligence and what their innate limitations are. The optional branching and dataflow possibilities within any system, open or closed, are also demonstrated in detail.

This model defines the logic that underlies all forms of conditioning irrespective of application. Without the ability to learn we would remain stuck in ignorance, error and incompetence. The combinatorial neural network model resolves many unanswered questions and explodes some of the most insidious longstanding myths. Every expansion of the model reveals new subtleties that can only be extracted in time and predicted in general terms on the basis of present-day knowledge. An enlargement of this paradigm can lead to deeper and more revealing insights into the organic aspects of the so-called 'black box' of the human psyche: how we learn best, most rapidly and with the greatest benefit and satisfaction, and how and why we fail to learn and what the consequences are in either event. Any reformation of the sciences or of human societies depends on it.

# 7
# Stirring the Primeval Soup

'Consider that we are alternately astonished and amused at the reports of talking porpoises. How then should we view the prospect of a group of atoms that is astonished and amused? . . . That the phenomenon called life should emerge from inanimate stuff is remarkable enough. That superimposed upon a cooperating group of organs there is consciousness is astounding.' R. Bellman[1]

One of the fundamental questions in biology and psychology has been how intelligence emerged from mindless inorganic matter swimming in the primeval soup. Yet so far no one has suggested criteria for defining human or any other kind of organic intelligence. In the previous chapter I used combinatorial analysis to describe the differences between various forms of conditioning. Here, using the same methods, I discuss the valuative, non-mechanical aspects of conscious awareness and demonstrate that they define the evolution of human intelligence.

But first it is useful to compare human with animal intelligence and with what is today believed to be *machine* or *artificial intelligence*. Once we know what only we can do and what animals and machines cannot do, then we are on the way to understanding what makes us potentially intelligent.

The main schools of thought in the neurological,

behavioural and computer sciences attribute intelligence – human, animal or machine – to cognition and stimulus-response. Cognition means acquiring knowledge on the basis of sensory input and memory. Stimulus-response is simply another term for operant conditioning or programming. The supposition is that human intelligence and behaviour are solely the products of our genes, central nervous system and experiences. The expression of human intelligence is thought to consist entirely of mechanical responses to external stimuli like pleasure or pain, hunger or satiation, heat or cold. This is true up to a point for us as much as for other species but, contrary to the conventional wisdom, we are able to exercise a far higher, non-mechanical intelligence than they. For if human intelligence consisted of nothing but genetically programmed and environmentally conditioned responses, then we would always be at the mercy of our conditioning. We would indeed be nothing but biological machines.

Organic behaviour in a purely mechanical sense means that when electro-chemical impulses arrive at any synapse (a junction of nerve fibres or nodes), a quantitative reaction is transmitted to other nerve cells and converted into sensations, thoughts or actions. It is generally felt that all three depend more on the strength and quantity of the input than on its qualitative interpretation. Hence the human central nervous system is believed to function like a thermostat (see below and Chapter 8). As pointed out earlier, Roger Penrose, a mathematical physicist, suggests that sensory information might be distributed via synapses on quantum principles.[2] In either case, human intelligence is approached from an inanimate, mechanistic perspective. Danah Zohar writes in a similar vein, except that she believes that fundamental particles possess some kind of consciousness[3] – a metaphysical proposition. However, unlike a thermostat (externally controlled) or quanta (bundles of particles), the expression of human intelligence is not purely quantitative, reactive or a God-given faculty. It is the result of an evolution of self-awareness and of interactions of the self with the external environment, guided by feelings, reason, foresight and value judgements. These are determined not only by external conditions, but by internal ones.

A thermostat turns a heating system on or off if it has been programmed to do so at a given temperature. It reacts only to externals on the basis of a quantitative change. If the external temperature exceeds the thermostat's setting, it responds with a *no* (i.e. off); if it falls below that setting, by a *yes* (i.e. on). The thermostat can make no allowance for your wearing a sweater or having exercised, so what might at other times be too cold can be too warm. It is programmed unconditionally. The central nervous system also operates on binary *yes* and *no* principles, but it reacts conditionally to quantitative and qualitative change (i.e. on the basis of feelings, intentions and value judgements) and these alter the direction of the dataflow in the brain. Unlike a thermostat, therefore, human intelligence is largely self-determined even when reactions depend on a mixture of internal (subjective and qualitative) and external (relatively objective and quantitative) circumstances.

Stimulus-response and operant conditioning regulate only some aspects of human behaviours, but they dominate most plant and animal behaviours and are the sole criteria for programming computers. Qualitative decisions – for example, what constitutes ethical or unethical behaviour under which circumstances, an appropriate sense of humour or tragedy or the ability to make distinctions between relatively objective and subjective choices – require an inner consciousness as well as global and self-awareness.

To rephrase this in its simplest analogous terms, a suitably programmed computer (given a huge memory and an infinity of time) or an algorithm (i.e. a sequence of operations expressed as a mathematical formula) can generate all combinations of moves that lead to victories, defeat, draws or stalemates in any game of strategy. But neither a computer nor an algorithm can make a value judgement as to why or how these outcomes occur or which is *superior* (i.e. error-free).[AA] What enables human beings to make such judgements has at various times been called the soul, mind, psyche, character or personality. It makes no difference which label is used. For value judgements to be made and acted upon there needs to be a potential that enables us to order options and select priorities. This can be done on the basis of feelings, an analysis of cause and effect, self- and global awareness, and the power to direct the dataflow in our central nervous system. Aware value judgements are not only matters of *more* or *less* but of quality. As Descartes surmised, if some other species has such capabilities, they function at extremely primitive levels and cannot be compared to the kind of value judgements only we can make. Computers can make no valuative analyses of any kind.

In species other than man most actions and reactions, including changes of mind or behaviour, are the results of genetic, neural/sensory or external environmental conditioning. A plant always turns towards the sun for light and sinks its roots in search of moisture. This is its level of *awareness* which depends entirely on its genetic inheritance and the external environment. But there is no human gene or there need be no external compulsion to account for any change of human behaviour within the range of possibilities available to us. Genes and the environment only provide us with options. Any change of mind or change of direction of the dataflow in the human central nervous system can be brought about by external conditions or by internal feelings or logic. Awareness, conscious feelings and reason can therefore override our genetic (to some extent) and environmental (totally) conditioning.

Consciousness (in the sense referred to above) is a motivating force that can only be understood or expressed metaphorically. An aware human value judgement can be made in the absence of external influences (i.e. by using our feelings, reason and free will) or on the basis of the right or wrong forms of conditioning. In other words, our physiological and psychological constitution allows us to make choices on the basis of characteristics that other species do not share.

# Towards a Classification of Intelligence

The main criteria for defining human intelligence are:

- The genetic, physiological and sensory potential to invent and manipulate symbols (languages, two- and three-dimensional images and tools) and to think and express ourselves symbolically.
- The ability to decondition ourselves, make autonomous choices, recognize errors and learn autonomously so that we can:
  make or recognize rules and limits, extract meanings and differentiate between subjective and objective value judgements (i.e. think in a totally objective manner);

  analyse, classify, synthesize and make generalizations on the basis of logic, intuition, experience, trial and error;

  remember and transmit cultural memories to future generations.
- Inner-, external-, other-, global- and self-awareness, conscience and a sense of responsible freedom.
- Pattern recognition.
- A sense of conditional right and wrong, ethics, humour and tragedy.
- Appropriate behaviour in all circumstances.

Human intelligence cannot be measured by IQ tests nor defined by the prejudicial value judgements on which most modern psychology is based. The uniqueness of individual interests and aptitudes, differences in sensory and muscular/motor strengths and in environmental opportunity, health and energy levels make it impossible for a superior or inferior intelligence to be identified in this way. We all share the same central nervous system with individual variations. Some of us see, hear or co-ordinate better than others. But these differences only affect performance and how we apply our innate intelligence. Learning to become a mechanic, salesman, manager, artist or scientist involves the same neural principles. Therefore, despite what some psychologists may claim, racial or class differences in human intelligence do not exist. Our intelligence is limited only by gross genetic or environmental damage, the wrong forms of conditioning (see Appendix D) or a lack of opportunity. The latter can, however, be overcome by human energy and will.

Although we have a number of words that distinguish between different degrees of intelligence, they have never been classified according to definable criteria. I suggest that every expression of intelligence can be *reflexive*, *instinctive*, *conjectural*, *intuitive*, *inferential* or *global*. These terms describe shorter or longer neural chains and the lesser or greater conditional branching involved in learning and decision-making.

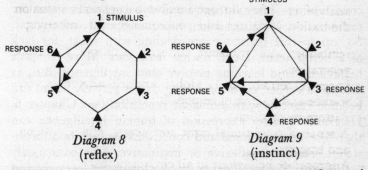

*Diagram 8*
(reflex)

*Diagram 9*
(instinct)

Diagrams 8 and 9 show the differences between reflex and instinct. In Diagram 8 there is a simple relationship between input at 1 and response at 6. Although there are other options, they cannot be exercised because the dataflow (represented by the arrows) prevents it. In Diagram 9, although each path (e.g. from 1 to 3 to 4 to 5 to 6 and back to 1) is still binary, the dataflow offers 'conditional branching'. In other words, there is choice. The dataflow can go directly from 1 to 3 to 5 and back to 1. Instincts can be modified but reflexes cannot.

A *reflex* consists of a one-to-one jump to a conclusion. It is equivalent to a very short chain of neural strands so that the reaction is near instantaneous. The next more complex operation – *instinct* – involves longer neural chains, greater conditional branching, a correspondingly larger amount of data and a potential for modification as a result of experience, trial and error or conditioning. The longer the neural chain, the greater the number of optional branches involved in decision-making. That is why reflexes are relatively difficult to alter and instincts can only be modified to some extent (see Diagrams 8 and 9). For example, tapping a knee-cap triggers an automatic knee-jerk reflex in a healthy individual. But the pecking instinct of pigeons can be modified by operant conditioning that trains them to peck a ping-pong ball over a net. (Note that the following diagrams are vastly simplified combinatorial geometric representations – see also Appendices A and D.)

*Reflex* and *instinct* are subconscious quantitative reactions and are derived from genetic, environmental or self-conditioning. They do not involve a conscious valuative examination of causes and consequences (i.e. meanings). So, up to this point we are dealing with what, for lack of a better term, I call *reactive intelligence*. More complex behaviours and learning involve *active* intelligence. But, as discussed earlier, even something that is actively learnt can become reactive with sufficient repetition (see Chapter 6, Diagram 7). Any expression of human intelligence can therefore be intentional and consciously active, or subconscious, reactive, reflexive or instinctive. The consciously active aspects of intelligence involve long-term foresight and a perpetually growing store of memories and informational chains, until practice and habit allow reflexive jumps to conclusions to be made.

Beyond instinct, the next longer chain is described by the term *conjecture* (see Diagram 10). This involves a conscious awareness of probable causes, consequences and operations that bring either about. (For example, the causes of playing a game are the players' intentions to *want* to play. The possible outcomes – victory, defeat, draw, stalemate or an interrupted game – are the consequences. The operations consist of strategies, tactics and moves that bring about a desired outcome.) Conjecture is always uncertain because it is founded on inadequate information. It is the

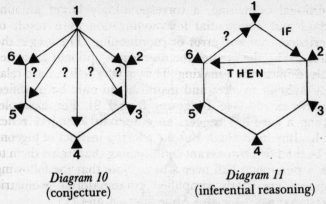

**Diagram 10**
(conjecture)

**Diagram 11**
(inferential reasoning)

Diagram 10 demonstrates the principle of conjecture. The dataflow can go anywhere from 1, but the conclusion is in doubt. Feedback is unlikely and uncertainty prevails. Diagram 11 shows the process of inferential reasoning. The dataflow, starting at 1, excludes some of the possibilities. This always involves making assumptions. By these means it is possible to arrive at the right or wrong conclusions with or without feedback to the self.

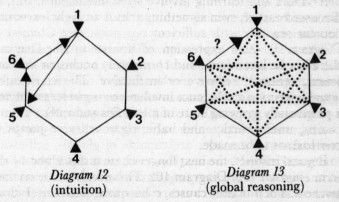

**Diagram 12**
(intuition)

**Diagram 13**
(global reasoning)

Diagram 12 shows the operation of intuition. In essence it represents a jump to a conclusion – right or wrong – without considering everything, e.g. from 1 to 5, and then provides feedback to the self (1) via 6 like a reflex. Global reasoning (Diagram 13) includes all knowable factors with or without jumps to a conclusion and leads to relative or absolute certainty (i.e. feedback to 1 – the self).

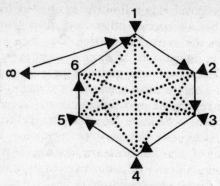

*Diagram 14*
(goal-defined learning loop)

Diagrams 8–13 concern decision-making and are therefore closed. Learning, however, demands constant openness to new input and an ability to change one's mind when any new data requires it. New goals can be extended to infinity once any earlier one (6 in this instance) is reached.

basis of most theorizing and can lead to right or wrong conclusions.

The next higher level is *inferential reasoning* (see Diagram 11) and involves a conjectural jump to a conclusion. *Intuition* (see Diagram 12) is yet another form of reflexive thought. The highest form of human intelligence is *global, goal-defined* and involves perpetual learning (see Diagram 14).

All human beings, unless suffering from severe genetic or environmental damage, are capable of global-, self-aware and goal-defined learning. However, even this highest form of intelligence represents *jumps to conclusions* because no matter how much is considered or how long the neural chain might be, the information is incomplete except in relatively rare instances. None the less, each operation, from reflex to global learning, involves progressively more information, a greater number of synapses, an enlarged neural net and greater optional branching. This is convergent with what the Swiss psychologist Jean Piaget described as schemata formation in the young child (i.e. a linkage of neural nets).[4]

Conjecture (i.e. considering a limited, incomplete number of facts) is possible for species other than man that rank relatively high on the evolutionary tree. But any kind of logic that involves more than a limited number of facts – like intuition, inferential and global logic – is a purely human attribute. These human methods of thought can be based on internal representations (imagination), observation (experience), pattern recognition (see Chapter 8), symbolic communications (language, imagery or technology) or a combination of any of these. Before learning can take place or discoveries be made, reflexive or instinctive habits of thought must not yet exist (as in young children) or be de-conditioned. But, as said before, what is learnt can become reflexive or instinctive as soon as it turns into firm knowledge.

Irrespective of the subject to which it might be applied, learning increases knowledge, understanding and reflexive certainty, enlarges the neural net employed to process information and increases the number of options involved in the decision-making process. Options are also increased when known facts or beliefs are reconsidered from a new perspective. Thus the use of intelligence consists not merely of an accumulation of facts, but enables the learner to discover and manipulate old or new facts or ideas and their meanings, establish relationships between them, decide what the options are, choose the best ones and encode all of this in a shorthand symbology that facilitates thought and its expression. Human intelligence is therefore exercised and nourished as a result of a perpetually enlarged external frame of reference coupled with a greater and more efficient exploitation of inner resources. Understanding depends on how what is learnt is represented internally by means of symbols (facilitating pattern recognition), how it is assessed and integrated with existing and new knowledge, and how it is expressed and acted upon.

Humanity does not invent the universe. We can only discover, classify, analyse, synthesize and become aware of its meanings. We can arrange and rearrange the possibilities that nature provides and choose between them. That is the limit of our intelligence and creativity. Only nature is truly creative for it provides the building blocks of which we and it are composed. Nature creates the conditions for our evolution from which we can choose those that are advantageous, ethical and aesthetic and avoid whatever may threaten our existence and further development.

The *expression* of intelligence in any species (as distinct from intelligence itself) is at the mercy of its genes. It depends on the faculties provided by the DNA, the central nervous system, skeletal features, muscles, limbs, optional branching and a potential for learning. Animals cannot articulate a wide spectrum of sounds because they have no larynx or its equivalent. Their capacity for discovering and using symbols, tools or other artefacts is limited by their ability to manipulate found or converted materials. Finally, species can perceive the world only via whatever senses they possess. In other words, what nature provides determines the exercise of *quantitative* (cognitive, stimulus-response) and *qualitative* (valuative) aspects of intelligence. While any direct comparison between animal and human learning ability is bound to be imprecise, the limits of what each species can express and do define its potential intelligence. This is especially true for learning, for here the boundaries of what and how much can be learnt are fairly clear. Isolated examples are usually given to show that chimpanzees can learn and teach their young (e.g. to wash food), but it seems most likely that such discoveries are fortuitous. What is considered to be learning is no more than imitation. The young of higher species certainly play (a precondition to learning), but such play is limited to the exercise of physical survival skills that are elaborations of instincts and IRMs.

To summarize, qualitative aspects of intelligence depend on options for the dataflow within the central nervous system, relative to sensory/muscular complexity, the environment, an awareness of choices and the ability to exercise them. The ability to interpret options and make valuative choices requires internal representations (visualized thought), the analytic capacity to extract meanings in a totally objective manner (i.e. to differentiate between relatively objective and subjective choices) and then to synthesize, articulate and express all of this symbolically (linguistically or pictorially).

Species other than man are unable to extract meanings (i.e. the natural laws of cause and effect). They cannot create complex metaphors (e.g. languages or games) or the means to represent them internally or express them symbolically (i.e. think about or communicate them). The level of intelligence attributable to various species therefore depends on their awareness and ability to make and use artificial symbols. (Even our use of tools is a symbolic act. For tools are just figurative extensions of our senses and limbs.) Thus, unlike other species, we are not merely affected by our environment or affect it in a purely biological and material sense (i.e. quantitatively); eventually we also affect it qualitatively in ways of our choosing. It has taken our civilizations only a few thousand years to reach this point. As we can see all about us, the sciences and the technologies have played a large role in this and the effect they have had on the environment has often been unintelligent and disastrous, especially in the past few centuries. Something is certainly wrong with how we use our intelligence. It is therefore useful to examine the main components of human intelligence one by one.

## The Genetic Basis of Intelligence

The genetic characteristics of all organisms are made up of identical amino-acid combinations. These acids form genetic triplets, strung together as shorter or longer chromosomal chains. Chromosomes, in combination with the proteins they synthesize, determine the nature of every cell. Each contains special instructions for forming particular sensory and other organs that combine to make up the organism, whatever it may turn out to be. Therefore biological systems can be said to be self-programmed.

We can now point to an actual programme tape in the heart of the cell, namely the DNA molecule. Even more remarkable is the fact that the programmed activity in living nature will not merely determine the way in which the organism reacts to its environment: it actually controls the structure of the organism, its replication, and the replication of the programmes themselves. And this is what we really mean when we say that life is not merely programmed activity but self-programmed activity.[5]

Genes and chromosomes are the repositories of biologically inherited memories. As already pointed out, it is possible that the universe is made up of memory particles that, as they affiliate, turn into information and eventually into matter. Whether or not this is actually so, the processes by which sentient life comes about are described in stylized form by Diagram 15. It shows that the environment creates and then feeds memories and information into the genetic system in a uni-directional manner (i.e. no feedback to the environment is possible in one generation). The organism as a whole and the environment are totally interconnected and there is perpetual feedback from one to the other.

It therefore seems likely that an informational matrix is thus created that eventually results in life. But the innate evolutionary thrust towards awareness (see below) assures an eventual evolution of species that are able to learn.

... it has been suggested that a bacteriophage or virus, with a DNA chain, say 200,000 long, has in its molecular instruction book 60,000 words, which would be roughly 300 pages of an instruction book written in English. The instruction book for a bacterium would be 10 to 100 times larger than this. And for man ... each somatic cell is not so much a book as a very large encyclopaedia with forty-six volumes ... – [with] an average of about 20,000 pages for each [volume] ... It presumably supplies [only] the instructions for the structural ... organization and functioning of the main types of cell.[6]

These processes furnish the information for every organism's construction and internal functions, the interactions between its various parts, and between those and an external larger environment. The result is an ever-widening network of memories, information and options and more complex methods for processing them. These *combinatorial* relationships make for precise replication, whether they form a molecule, a gene, the DNA, a cell, an aggregation of cells, an organ, a whole organism or a group of organisms. Variations are provided by mutation, task specialization, natural selection and adaptation. This has led to the evolution of different central nervous systems which are none the less generated by the same amino-acid, gene, chromosomal chain and protein combinations that form all specialized cells, organs and species.

Evolution ultimately results in conscious awareness for the following reasons. The genetic and neural interconnections within any organism more complex than viruses are extremely rich. The genetic possibilities alone offer a vast number of options. When viewed combinatorially (see Appendix A), the number of possibilities explodes exponentially (i.e. geometrically) with the increase of even

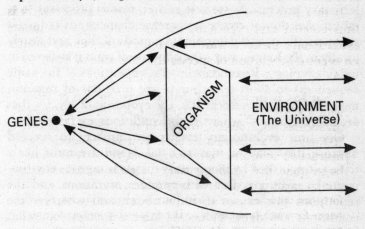

*Diagram 15*

No matter what the smallest particles may be – dark matter or memories – the amino acids that form genes are certainly derived from the environment. They contain information that enables different organs and species to evolve. These affect the environment and are affected by it in turn. The directions of the information-flow within this system and its possible combinations are shown here in stylized form.

one single gene. When the external, environmental possibilities are added to the internal ones, the numbers grow
astronomically. Inevitably choices must be exercised to
shrink the options down to manageable proportions so that
timely and adaptive decisions can be made. The behaviour
of all organisms would remain perpetually unpredictable if
emerging awareness and limitation of choice were not part
of the evolutionary process. Choice – whether limited by
conditioning as in plant and animal species, or relatively
free as for us – serves as a filter that creates stable and
predictable behaviour (i.e. that which is survival-oriented).
This is why, as I showed in Chapter 6, total freedom is as
damaging as any other form of operant conditioning and
why genuine freedom requires us to limit possibilities by
establishing benign goals.

There is a good deal of randomness involved in this evolutionary process. As we saw earlier, *random* processes (e.g.
mutations) do not create or increase chance, but reduce it
substantially over indeterminate periods of time and nearly
totally in the longest run – the opposite of what is believed in
today's biology. Redundancies (i.e. repetitions of the same
sequences) in short-term bursts are products of randomness. They assure success (i.e. the evolution of species that
are able to survive) wherever the conditions are favourable.

One-time evolutionary events are unlikely to succeed
because they may or may not 'take' and are most likely
to be extinguished by momentary disadvantageous environmental conditions. But with random mutations and the
repetitions this causes to come about, and wherever the
conditions are right, sooner or later a species somewhat
like man must eventually evolve that is consciously aware
of itself and the universe. Inorganic nature, unconscious
of itself, is none the less perpetually creative in generating
a sum of possibilities of which the products are life and
conscious awareness. Therefore random aspects of nature
would seem to be self-organizing and purposive in an
evolutionary sense, a conclusion rejected fiercely by most
scientists today because it smacks of religious fundamentalism although theology has nothing to do with it.

The universe generates a seemingly infinite sum of finite possibilities divided into relatively objective (concluded) and subjective (perpetual feedback) categories (see Appendices A and D). The subjective options predominate by far, once more than four memories or facts are considered. This matrix of possibilities is implicitly biased in favour of the emergence of a species that has the potential for making valuative choices (i.e. man) and able to limit the sum of possibilities to essentials. Therefore, the thrust of the evolutionary process is towards ever greater self-organization and self-awareness of what would otherwise remain a hodge-podge of unconscious possibilities.

## The Sensory Basis of Intelligence

There are two kinds of sense data: external and internal. The external is what we experience; the internal what we visualize in the mind's eye, hear in the mind's ear, or feel, smell or taste in the imagination. We use this sensory information as the basis for our thoughts, actions and dreams. They are symbolic of our internal perceptions of an outer world: 'The kind of datum from which scientist and philosopher alike must start is exemplified by I-perceive-the-taste-of-an-apple.'[7]

We can experience only via our senses, at times aided by instruments that enable us to experience qualities that lie beyond what we can see, feel, hear, smell or touch. Even an imagination that transcends experience depends on sense impressions. Yet the world around us does not necessarily exist in the forms we attribute to it, because we can experience it only via sense organs that are peculiar to us. But to doubt the existence of any reality, as philosophers like Bishop Berkeley and Bertrand Russell have done, is to make nonsense out of the impressions it makes on our senses, even though they may only reflect reality symbolically and metaphorically.

Stated in its simplest terms, reality consists of resistance to or penetrability by experience. Reality impinges on us as a result of sense impressions. The nature of experience can therefore be described as something that *interferes* with our bodies or organs of perception which reflect, absorb or resist penetration to a greater or lesser extent. The same reality therefore has informational content that can assume different forms (for example, colour-blind individuals and some animal species experience redness as shades of grey) and can assail our senses in ways to which other individuals or species may be actually or relatively blind. For example, bats lack a sensitive visual sensory system, so they emit sounds that bounce back and *interfere* with their perceptions and enable them to identify obstacles, mates, predators or food.

Every species can resist or absorb experience to varying degrees, but this depends on its physical characteristics and the force of impact or penetration. The meanings of any single experience are conditional depending on the species that it affects. These, then, are the limits of subjective experience common to all species. But human understanding depends not only on what we can sense but also on how we analyse and value it. We, unlike other species, have the means for reaching totally objective conclusions. For example, light enters our eyes; sound our ears. But colour – redness – is not part of the physical characteristics of a rose. What we identify as such is a characteristic of a portion of the spectrum of light reflected by the rose petal's surface, converted by our visual system into what we identify symbolically as the colour red. Redness exists only in the eye of the beholder, yet the light datum that *interferes* with our retina and is converted into what we call redness is a material reality. It can be doubted, as it has been, but to do so ends any rational discussion of experience, reality or science.

All physical and psychological information – whether we sense it directly (by sight or hearing), internally and aesthetically (by feeling), logically (by using reason), scientifically (via instruments), or in the imagination – can be experienced, thought about, synthesized or communicated symbolically only if we are aware. We can express it verbally or numerically and model it graphically in one, two or three dimensions. But the representation of human experience is still only symbolic of a greater reality that may differ from any that we or any other species directly perceive. To repeat, our experiences are only as real to us as our senses permit (as they are to every other species). But we (unlike other species) can analyse, think about and express our experiences symbolically. Irrespective of how we perceive things, we can extract the meanings of what we receive via our senses by isolating their causes, consequences and the operations that bring them about. Our universe is thus governed by meanings that, as far as is known, only we can consciously extract and articulate.

Therefore sensory information can be described in general terms (but only by us). In other words, we can abstract from our experience and make generalizations that apply to us as much as to other species or to conditions that lie beyond direct experience. A dog or a frog cannot know or imagine how we perceive the world. Only we can establish that the whole spectrum of light as perceived by any species can be refracted in a prism or expressed mathematically, including those portions to which we or they may be blind (e.g. infra-red and ultra-violet). And even the latter can be made visible by means of special instruments.

Animal species also experience the world, but what they perceive concerns only their day-to-day survival; they can recognize immediate consequences (like getting an electric shock from a live wire) but cannot connect cause and effect in circumstances other than those for which they are genetically conditioned. Animals cannot be consciously aware of principles or their meanings, or convert them into generalizations. For example, meat may have one kind of symbolic meaning for a predator and another for a herbivore that might be a predator's potential prey. How a tree appears to an insect, bird or mammal depends on the survival needs of the species. It is unlikely that any species other than man perceives a tree poetically or scientifically; even if it could, it lacks the means to communicate such perceptions. To species other than man, a tree can have no symbolic value as a thing of intrinsic beauty, as having a particular molecular structure, as a producer of oxygen or as potential raw material for chemicals or tools. A beaver may use logs to build a dam, but it does so instinctively.

A child born without senses, limbs and means of expression cannot learn. He or she cannot experience symbolic reality and lacks the means of expressing his or her innate intelligence. But that does not mean that she/he is unintelligent. The same would be true of a new-born that has all its faculties but is raised in total isolation. However, once given a minimum of sensory experience, a two-year-old who loses most senses as a result of illness or accident can develop a rich internal life and express it by whatever means are at hand. The best example of this was Helen Keller who was struck deaf, dumb and blind by illness at an early age, yet became remarkably well-educated, sensitive and able to express her feelings and acquired knowledge with great subtlety and dexterity.[8] The multiplicity of our senses (sight, hearing, smell, taste, touch and balance) provides redundancies, so that should some or most fail at some future time it is still possible to imagine sights, sounds, feeling or smells and expand on earlier sensory experiences. But a minimum of sense impressions must be built up during earlier years if such an inner awareness is to blossom after any sensory faculties may be lost. Therefore sensory organs in themselves do not enable us to make value judgements or be intelligent. Nor does lack of education or cultural deprivation make us unintelligent. But either can limit our frames of reference and ability to express our intelligence.

It is generally accepted that direct sensory perceptions are subjective and that scientific ones (presumably based on yardsticks more precise than sensory evidence) are more or less objective. But scientific observations are also predominantly subjective because they are accessible to us only via our senses. This is the relationship between the observer and what is observed. It was defined by Einstein's special theory of relativity but, as I have said, could equally well be described as conditional determinism.

Human intelligence is therefore characterized by an ability to infer the whole from sensing and symbolizing its parts. It is derived from the capacity to be consciously aware, make intentional value judgements, sense, think about, analyse, synthesize and express ourselves symbolically, learn autonomously, extract principles and override our conditioning. Thus we can become conditionally free (exercise free will and choose individual goals) within limitations placed on the sum of all possibilities by nature (natural law) or by aware human value judgements (intelligence). The criteria I have listed either do not apply to species other than man or apply only to a very limited extent, for none is able to extract or symbolize natural laws or act on any other than those for which it is genetically programmed. Certainly no machine or computer, now or in any future, can have these essential characteristics. There may be other intelligent species in the universe but even if they match our level of intelligence or surpass it, theirs must be based on the same or similar criteria as those that apply to us.

## The Role of the Neural Net

The human central nervous system (called the neural net in computer science) is a product of genes, chromosomal chains, cells, nerve fibres and their junctions. It is the wiring diagram for human feelings, intentions, thoughts and behaviours. A vast network of neural strands that converge on synapses (junctions or switches) connects sensory and other organs and muscles and passes memories and information from any one to most others (note: the central nervous system is not fully integrated; for example, the brain is insensitive to touch).

The neural net works on binary principles, offering alternative options to the dataflow as a result of its conditional branching. It provides trinary, quatrinary, quintrinary and greater choices, yet the information it processes is ultimately reduced to binary *yes* and *no*, *on* and *off*. Genetically conditioned behaviours offer only a limited number of reflexive or instinctive options with which we are born (e.g. the sucking or grasping instincts). Further choices evolve through maturation and conditioning (both operant and that which leads to true learning; see Chapter 6). The central nervous system is equivalent to a programmed computer only in so far as genetically and environmentally conditioned reflexes are concerned. We are free in all other respects subject to learning, always depending on limits imposed by the laws of nature and those we impose on ourselves.

As I have said before, the dataflow in the central nervous system consists of memories that are passed across synapses by neuro-transmitters. These are electro-chemical and mechanical processes. But other-than-mechanical forces are involved when conscious awareness, changes of mind or de-conditioning come into play. No organs that trigger these have ever been identified. They can be traced back only to pre-existing or newly constructed memory networks that make up the individual's psyche, personality and character with which we are born but which can be modified through conditioning.

The richness of neuron (and genetic) connections, relationships and optional branching relative to and in combination with any external environment, make possible the uniqueness of every individual within our species. This is not true for insects, for example, where one worker bee or ant is virtually an exact replica of the next, especially when it comes to behaviour. They adapt to a changing environment instinctively and up to a point. They die out if such changes are so radical that they cannot cope. We have far greater powers of adaptation, for we can see much further into the future than any other species, evade the consequences of all but the most drastic changes or adapt to new circumstances. All of this depends on an awareness of possibilities and on autonomous value judgements that limit them. This is something other species cannot do to any significant extent. There is therefore an even greater qualitative than quantitative leap in the evolution of our species.

Our central nervous system and the external environment

represent the sum of all possibilities as far as we are concerned. How large these sums are depends on how large a portion of the central nervous system we bring into play and how much of the external environment is considered; also by the options we perceive and the choices all of this generates. While the possibilities for our individual and collective futures are created by these complex interactions, we must still make value judgements to limit the sum of all possibilities and then decide which future to select for ourselves. These decisions can provide us with foresight and predictive powers limited by an event-horizon (see *Winners*[AA]) that learning pushes perpetually further into the future. The sum of possible options in that future is calculable in any given environment up to certain limits. These are the limits of human understanding and foresight.

How possibilities and options are generated can be demonstrated combinatorially (i.e. as relational patterns of behaviour) and classified into four main categories. Each of these can be subdivided further into groups, families and individually unique states. The criteria by which these states can be classified are determined by the characteristics of the dataflow. The various states thus created define themselves and follow natural laws of cause and effect (see Appendix D). This is perhaps the most persuasive demonstration of what making value judgements involves, and why it has no physiological or bio-chemical basis.

The sum of all possibilities accounted for by the neural net's interaction with the environment can now be modelled on any computer. But no computer (or animal) can sort, classify and identify the meanings of these categories. This is something that only we can do. It depends on pattern recognition and an awareness of what each pattern means. In sum, the neural net is a totally objective model of all forms of inorganic and organic behaviour.

The first combinatorial neural net category (see Diagram 16) consists of a closed, finite and totally conditioned system without feedback that describes relatively objective processes. The second category represents feedback within

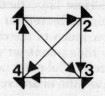

*Diagram 16* (Category 1)

*Diagram 17* (Category 2)

Diagram 16 describes one-time, non-repetitive acts and behaviours, like those of a calculator that has not been programmed or a mentally handicapped individual who cannot remember and needs to be told each time how to perform some simple task.

Diagram 17 symbolizes a perpetual feedback loop in a closed environment; equivalent to a programmed computer or an individual who has been trained (i.e. conditioned) to perform the same task repeatedly without variation.

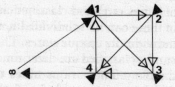

*Diagram 18* (Category 3)

*Diagram 19* (Category 4)

Diagram 18 shows a perpetual feedback loop to any other than the starting terminal. This is equivalent to a computer program that needs debugging or a drug addict whose habit benefits only his supplier.

Diagram 19 describes goal-defined learning with feedback to the self in a perpetually enlarged environment. No machine is capable of this feat.

NOTE: To understand these diagrams and the principle of conditional branching, it is necessary to trace the arrowed pathways from '1' (the self or the starting-point) to every possible conclusion (i.e. the dataflow possibilities). Every enlargement of these diagrams increases the optional branching at an exponential rate. See Appendix D for a full expansion of all combinatorial possibilities when four facts are considered (i.e. when n = 4).

a finite system and defines relatively subjective processes (see Diagram 17). The third consists of confinement within a closed, less-than-all-inclusive feedback loop, as a result of total freedom which achieves the same results as operant conditioning (see Diagram 18). The fourth and last category is symbolic of a perpetually expanding learning loop with feedback – the totally subjective aspects of human thought, learning and behaviour (see Diagram 19). The first three categories represent inorganic (mechanical) behaviour even in organisms. The fourth is exclusively human and applies to true learning and conditional freedom that extend to infinity and feed back to the self.

All organic decision-making is reflexively or instinctively valuative in so far as survival is concerned. These judgements enable species to react as appropriately as they can to whatever conditions they encounter. But we are far more adaptable than any other species and can make critical value judgements unrelated to physical survival. Our valuative faculties enable us to appreciate nature aesthetically, study its phenomena scientifically, manipulate it technologically, discover its meanings and choose our future from the sum of all possibilities. In addition, we can create an infinite number of symbols to communicate whatever we discover from one individual and generation to the next. These abilities provide our species with a progressively growing store of cultural and scientific information about ourselves, the world and the larger universe beyond, and hence the possibility of a progressively more efficient use of our intelligence.

## Awareness

The biologist W.H. Thorpe speaks of an evolution of awareness in different species:

> . . . we shall come to the conclusion that, as we proceed downwards from man through the animal series, the lower we go the less useful and helpful the concept of an 'experiencing self' becomes. When we reach the lowest

animals the relevance of the idea of self-consciousness
becomes vanishingly small ... Thus it may be that the
development of the very mechanism which is essential for
reproduction was itself the basis for the later evolution of
self-perception.[9]

Thorpe did not distinguish between different levels
of awareness. None the less, there are at least five
different kinds: awareness of externals (like danger or
food); awareness of others (a basic condition for sexual
reproduction, child-rearing and social intercourse;) internal
awareness (hunger or pain); global awareness (considering
all possibilities in a perpetually growing environment); and
self-awareness (like recognizing yourself in a mirror and, at
a higher level, self-knowledge).

A crystal has no awareness of options. Many grow
symmetrically according to patterns laid down for them
by their molecular structures. They are totally 'conditioned'
(i.e. 'programmed') and have no choice. Much the same is
true for viruses – the intermediate step between inorganic
matter and organic life. A virus lives in suspended animation
and comes to life only by its attachment to an organic cell. It
is possible to speak of an elementary level of outer awareness
even at this primitive level of life because a virus can adapt
to changing conditions (mutate). As cell combinations grow
in number and complexity, behavioural options increase
enormously. The simplest organisms, like amoebae, are
only aware of externals (like food) and immediate consequences (like obstructions), but never of causes. Inner
awareness evolves with further evolution. Even apes are
only externally and internally aware, conscious of others
and of consequences. We seem to be the only species on
earth able to be fully aware of cause and effect, to be globally
and self-aware and conscious of a long-term future.

Somewhere along the line of evolution a stage is reached at
which instinctive internal and external pattern recognition
of similarities and differences in members of the same
species allow sexual reproduction (i.e. other than simple
cell-division or self-fertilization). This signals an awareness

of *others* that seems to run parallel to the evolution of elementary forms of territoriality, co-operation, nurture and self-defence. How else could a species recognize predators, likely mates or its own young until they become independent? But for most species such species-specific pattern recognition is achieved as a result of IRMs, as where fledglings can tell the difference in silhouette between parents and predators. (The first evokes an automatic 'gaping' response and the second cowering in the nest.) But in some 'higher' species such instinctive pattern recognition has evolved further into a more independent form of other-awareness – concern, affection or fear that is not entirely dependent on IRMs. But no species other than man seems to be aware of the universe or the psychological self.

Eventually psychological evolution in species other than man approaches a stage that is often confused with the concept of culture. In other words, instead of being able to act only within very limited options a species can make what may appear to be ritualistic choices. But these still lie within the possibilities generated by instinct and impulses guided by other than reason, with some minor exceptions.

In mankind this capacity has evolved into patterns of autonomous behaviour. Any form of awareness depends on pattern recognition which is reflexive and instinctive in most species, but which in man has evolved also into reflective and valuative thought and behaviour. We can perceive a vast sum of possibilities and choose options as a result of learning. Thus to all intents and purposes we can exercise free will. Even at the most primitive level we do not respond to external and internal stimuli without some reflection like: do I eat until I can eat no more? Do I eat now or later? Do I share or keep all I can hunt or gather to myself? Is one action preferable to another, given the perceived choices and the consequences? This is the awakening of consciousness and conscience.

Animals in the wild are conditioned genetically to be perpetually aware of predators and food. Domesticated species are so thoroughly conditioned (genetically by selective breeding and behaviourally by means of operant conditioning) that their options are reduced to those we want them to exercise. Much of their instinctive awareness is extinguished in favour of artificially conditioned behaviours. Domesticated animals are therefore far less aware than their relatives in the wild. But neither category has global and self-awareness. If they did, their family relationships might be as enduring as our own. As it is, once an offspring reaches maturity in most animal species other than man it takes its place as another adult for territorial, mating and feeding purposes even as far as parents or siblings are concerned.

Reflexive behaviour means that conditioning is total so that one acts without choice. Instinct means to be able to modify genetic conditioning in a limited way. But reflection means that one may consider a vast number of possibilities before making a conscious decision. Therefore there can only be aware consciousness where conditioning – genetic or cultural – can be extended significantly or overridden so that de- and reconditioning can take place. Only then is it possible to speak of intelligence, learning and acting on the basis of newly conditioned and behavioural reflexes. And so we come full circle because, as I pointed out earlier, what initially requires reflection eventually becomes reflexive through repetition and habit. Equally, as we have seen, to operate on the basis of the wrong premises and conclusions can become as reflexive as acting on the right ones. In other words, both can become conditioned behaviours.

Confusion between conditioned and aware behaviours in man and animals runs through the literature on evolution, biology, ethology and anthropology. Most psychological experiments are conducted with captive wild or domesticated animals in the belief that they can learn as we do. But they are trained by operant conditioning and any result thus obtained has no bearing on questions of intelligence as the term is defined here. In other words, you cannot deduce the criteria for a definition of human intelligence by studying the behaviour of other species or that of mentally handicapped human beings (on the basis of which standard IQ tests were designed by Binet and others).

The options provided by an animal's central nervous

system and physiology are severely restricted compared to ours. Animals do not learn as we do. Their instincts can only be modified by conditioning. An ape trained to use symbols may do so correctly to obtain a reward or avoid punishment. It would never do so spontaneously and for the sake of the thing itself (i.e. in play) or teach its young to do the same. Only we create symbols out of interest or psychological need. Only we can stimulate learning ability or stifle it in our children. There is therefore a sharp dividing line between the intelligence of man and that of any other species.

Chimpanzees have sufficient manual dexterity to use found materials as tools (sticks, for example), but they do so only in response to internal or external stimuli (like hunger or operant conditioning). They cannot discover, ritualize and store symbols or pass them on to future generations. At best they can 'ape' one another. Symbolically speaking, every generation of chimpanzees would have to rediscover the wheel for itself if any ancestor of the species had ever hit upon it. Porpoises are believed to possess an aware intelligence but that is pure speculation; there is no proof that they can think symbolically or communicate their inner world or anything that lies beyond their instincts or direct experience to one another or their young.

Computers are not aware of anything. They can be made to react to externals to whatever extent is provided by sensors, implanted memories and programmed instructions. None the less it has been claimed that they can *recognize* patterns, when in fact they can only match them. Genuine pattern recognition (for example, picking out your mother in a crowd, even when her back is turned) is impossible for computers. It can, however, be simulated if many variations and angles from which an image can be regarded have first been stored and are then matched on a probabilistic (i.e. statistical) basis. For even if a computer were to match the number of neural pathways and the conditional branching in our brains and were given simulated human sensors and servo-mechanisms, it would still lack purposive inner-, other-, global and self-awareness or intentionality. It therefore could not originate symbols or extract meanings from experiences or from the imagination, make value judgements or express them spontaneously.

A computer can match given patterns, but it cannot autonomously (i.e. without instructions) recognize or understand them or their meanings. It cannot de-condition itself or learn. Without these capacities a brain – human or artificial – cannot understand or even learn from its errors. As I stress repeatedly, making autonomous value judgements (which includes the ability to be self-aware and correct errors autonomously) is perhaps the highest form of human awareness; one that is not shared by other species to any significant degree, or by machines. These then are some of the important differences between computer data-processing, animal and human intelligence that are usually overlooked or glossed over.

## Self- and Global Awareness

Let us narrow our consideration of awareness and consider an example of supposedly intelligent machines – the so-called smart missiles that can find a range of targets. Such weapons cannot change their minds independently, become pacifists, abort or self-destruct. Conversely, any number of self-determined (in other words, not pre-programmed) options are available to self-aware human beings, none of which is open to a computer-guided robot or missile. A useful example that illustrates a fundamental difference between human and so-called machine intelligence is the late Grey Walter's mechanical turtle (*Machina speculatrix*), a forerunner of sensor-directed and servo-mechanically operated robots.[10]

Grey Walter, a leading neuro-physiologist who headed Bristol's Burden Neurological Institute, perfected this machine in 1956 and endowed it with a simple neural network, two sensors (a touch-sensitive shell and electric eye) and a mechanism for moving about (wheels on universal joints driven by a battery-powered electric motor). It can avoid obstacles. When its batteries run low it returns to an electrical outlet, plugs itself in and 'feeds'. But it is not aware of hunger or of the consequences of not recharging its batteries. It does all of this because it has been programmed to do so and has no option to do otherwise. (For example, it cannot go on a hunger strike.)

When it encounters a mirror in which its photo-electric cell is reflected, it cannot say to itself: 'Aha; here is another like myself', or 'Here is an enemy', or 'That is my own reflection.' It reverses its motor and backs away until the reflected light reaches a level so low that it no longer registers. It then moves forward once more towards the mirror and the process repeats itself again and again until its batteries run low. That is its program. It has no choice and never makes an autonomous decision. It could not occur to it to approach closer to investigate, inspect the light source or the image, try to make friends or defend its territory against a presumed enemy, nor could it decide that it was 'seeing' itself. It is unaware. In these respects it functions like totally conditioned, dogmatic, primitive or superstitious human beings.

Very young children and primitive people who have never seen themselves reflected in a mirror may react like Grey Walter's mechanical turtle. But they may be aware of an enigma that they can resolve. Even some animals may look behind the mirror to see who might be hidden there, or try to touch it. Primitives who have never seen a mirror before — unless too frightened and superstitious to investigate further (believing that a mirror is some kind of magic) — will realize sooner or later that what they see is not three-dimensionally real; that it has no independent existence, and eventually, that it is an image of themselves. In other words, by trial and error and if they are aware of the options, they have the capacity to reach a correct conclusion. At that point no further awareness is needed, for henceforth an acceptance of mirrors and their meanings becomes habitual and reflexive. The individual has reached the correct conclusion and is no longer puzzled or frightened.

This anecdote shows that evolution, adaptation and learning lead to an awakening of self- and global awareness of the external environment. However, that awakening is also the point at which self-determination and free will (relatively unlimited options) enter the evolutionary process. These are the potential characteristics of man. I say 'potential' because many people remain unaware and act purely on mechanical principles.

Self- and global awareness depend on the ability to step outside one's conditioning and to establish new relationships that go beyond programming. Even genetic conditioning (for example, breathing, heart-beat and other organic processes governed genetically by biological clocks[11]) can be overridden up to certain limits (see also 'jet-lag' solution, Appendix C). Human choices therefore do not only depend on the options provided by the central nervous system and an external environment, but also on valuative decisions. It would do us no good to have this huge number of choices unless we could limit them by setting self-determined goals. For, as I said earlier, we would sink into apathy or go mad if we tried to exercise all options that are available to us (i.e. the total freedom model of behaviour from which we now suffer the consequences; see Appendix D). Global and self-awareness therefore serve two purposes. They make us conscious of an ever-expanding sum of possibilities and of the need to discover rules of behaviour and natural laws of cause and effect that define meanings and place limits on a vast number of possibilities.

To summarize: the principle common to all forms of consciousness is an awareness of causes and consequences and the conditions that bring them about, relative to time, place, circumstances and human behaviour. Human behaviour is part of the circumstances because whether we behave appropriately (i.e. intelligently) or not creates the consequences. This not only defines the meaning of meaning and conditional freedom, but also that of intelligence, consciousness, conscience and learning.[AA]

# Memory

Memory is also an important component of awareness and

intelligence. But there are two types of memory as far as we know: inorganic and organic. A mould is an example of the former. It 'remembers' what is impressed on it until it wears out or is broken. A rubber band 'remembers' and snaps back to its original shape until it loses its elasticity and 'forgets'. Computers, magnetic discs and tapes can have memories implanted in them which remain until they degrade, are corrupted or wiped out. The memory of organization is structurally embedded in inorganic matter, as in some crystals. Here particles replicate their own structure in a purely repetitive, symmetrical, quantitative and mechanical manner. Free crystalline particles suspended in a super-saturated solution could be said to 'remember' and 'recognize' others like themselves. These forms of memory are inorganic and passive.

The concept of inorganic memory as the substructure of information is central to computing. This has not been sufficiently explored in terms of its larger meanings. But while memories can be stored in computers, on tapes or discs and these can be said to remember, they cannot do so permanently, voluntarily or selectively. More room can be made only by wiping out a computer's memory and losing previously stored information, or by removing a disc and starting again with a clean one. In any event, disc and tape memories degrade in time and are eventually lost. As a result a computer cannot learn.

Organic memory involves genes and chromosomes that replicate themselves, although their substructure is chemical and inorganic. Embedded in them are elementary memories essential for evolutionary organization. I discussed in Chapter 5 the possibility that memory particles might be the basis of so-called 'dark matter'; one-dimensional components of two-dimensional information and three-dimensional matter. At higher levels of organic evolution memories trigger reflexes that enable every generation to recognize and react to identical patterns (IRMs, like silhouettes of parents and predators, spots of colour, plumage, or behaviour that may indicate a suitable mate). But, as we have seen, with increased genetic and neural complexity, permanent cultural memory unique to man enters the evolutionary equation.

There is a significant difference between mindless (reflexive and instinctive) and aware (reflective) physiological and psychological memory; between memories embedded in the genetic code or triggered by IRMs and those acquired by conditioning of one kind or another. As we climb the evolutionary tree, IRM-triggered memories, wrongly labelled cultural by many ethologists, play increasingly important roles. For example, worker bees direct one another to flowers, shrubs and trees by dancing near the entrances to their hives. The dance indicates exactly where nectar is to be found. We do not know the ratio between IRM-triggered reflex, instinct and conditioning when it comes to such bee behaviour. But an adaptive, genetically inherent program to perform and recognize this dance is embedded in the genes of every worker bee. Such genetically stored memories are common to every species. In animals IRM-triggered survival skills can be varied only within limits provided by existing instinctive sensory/motor options. A bee performs the same dance in variations dictated by external circumstances. It cannot decide suddenly to perform it for reasons other than pointing the way to a source of nectar. Some bird species can vary their songs within limits imposed by their genetic program. This may seem like a primitive form of creativity. But to my knowledge no bird has ever written a symphony.

Machines can process certain kinds of information faster than human beings. But they are finite and inorganic memory processors. Continuous evolution varies and expands instinctive behaviours in organic species. But an elaboration of IRM potentials far beyond instinct seems to be an exclusively human characteristic. We alone among the species can learn indefinitely, record and store culturally-acquired information and preserve it for the future. Human learning is potentially infinite, thanks to a combination of genetic and cultural evolution of which the act of autonomous remembering is an essential component. A fading human memory is only caused by brain damage, disease, physical injury or old age. Even then, it may well be that the memories themselves remain intact and that only the retrieval mechanism is damaged. In any event, once human memories are recorded they become the permanent property of mankind for all of the foreseeable future.

In this context it is useful to repeat that no species, other than ourselves, has the ability to create and transmit concepts, facts and their meanings from one generation to the next. Cultural memory, even if forgotten, can always be reconstituted by succeeding generations of human beings. We are therefore freed from one of the constraints of genetic evolution – its inability to transmit acquired characteristics – for cultural evolution demands that a symbology can be invented, reinvented or stored and communicated. Such symbols are maps of our inner and outer world and of how we perceive both. Animals also have internal maps of the outer world or else they could not find their way about in it. But such maps are limited to feeding, territory, migration and reproduction. We, far more than any other species, live in a universe represented by symbols that stand for meanings in a much larger context. Only we can transcend our genetic and psychological conditioning and can carry forward a constantly expanded historic record of cultural memories that shape the quality of life for future generations.

Our learning capacity thus endows us with a potential for psychological and cultural continuity and development. There once were two possible directions for the psycho-cultural evolution of our species. The first and most favourable would have led to dynamic balance, diversity, individuality and perpetual change. But such an essentially co-operative and symbiotic psychological orientation in our earliest history seems to have been replaced by a competitive one.[AA] We have reached the point at which the Hobbesian 'war of all against all' and our attempted victory over nature have become globally endemic. This would indicate that we have regressed in terms of our psychological evolution which has led to the kind of uniformity, cultural stagnation and total conditioning found in a beehive or anthill. We will have to reverse this trend before we can go forward once more or else, as seems possible, we may lose our human characteristics or become extinct.

Nature provides us with all the options there are. We choose those we prefer or leave them in the hands of chance. Our future is therefore limited only by the constraints imposed by our genetic heritage, time, space and even more so by conscious global and self-awareness and the will to learn. We are the species that can not only ask the questions, but also find (or evade) the answers.

## Symbols

It is generally believed that the ability to make tools distinguishes us from other species and that this is the reason for our special intelligence. However, this is not a cause but a consequence. Tools are symbolic extensions of our limbs and brains. Symbols are the building blocks of thought and imagination. Therefore the ability to create symbols – language, images, writing and tools – results from our capacity to choose, make abstractions and critically aware value judgements about ourselves and the external environment. We can visualize and manipulate these symbols internally (in our brains) and externally (by gestures, language, images and use of tools). However, we can also create them mindlessly without making value judgements, and that is where human difficulties begin – in the sciences as in the technologies. The correct judgement as to which symbols and tools are useful, when and at what psychological, social or environmental cost, is one of the measures of human intelligence.

Some species use tools and artefacts for various purposes (for example, beavers construct dams and birds build nests). As Köhler demonstrated in the first quarter of this century, some chimpanzees can use sticks to get bananas that are out of their reach.[12] But while this indicates that species other than man can express themselves symbolically and convert found materials for use as tools, none can do so beyond limits imposed by instinct and IRMs; nor can they teach their young skills that can only be transmitted symbolically.

For example, the efforts to teach chimpanzees to communicate by means of symbols are meaningless in so far as they involve a symbology that no animal could ever discover for itself or teach to its young. While some species may be trained to acquire such skills in captivity by carrot and stick, they are non-species-specific and foreign to their ways. The animal's imitation is reflexive (i.e. acquired by operant conditioning) rather than reflective (acquired by independent thought) and therefore is not self-aware. To attribute self-awareness to animals is a form of anthropomorphism. For animals cannot conceptualize ideas or invent symbols that convey meanings to others except in a very limited way. Warning, flight or fight, submission, territorial, hunger, pain, mating and other sounds and gestures lie within instinctive, IRM-triggered ranges for which they are genetically programmed. Their repertoire can even include sounds or gestures made for purely playful reasons, but these are elaborations of instincts rather than autonomous acts.

One of the first serious studies of animal communications was made by R. L. Garner in 1892,[13] who recorded the sounds made by Capuchin monkeys on an early gramophone and discovered some of their meanings. He found that these were directly related to physical need and self-protection. More recently, US psychologists have claimed that chimpanzees can be taught primitive sign and symbol languages. The three best-known experiments were conducted by R.A. and B.T. Gardner,[14] H. Terrace[15] and D. Premack[16] between the 1960s and 1980s. Each used different methods, but operant conditioning was the common thread that ran through these and other attempts to 'teach' animals to communicate symbolically. So far none of our nearest evolutionary neighbours – chimpanzees or other apes – has demonstrated any ability to create a symbology spontaneously or pass on to its young what it has learnt or been taught by human keepers.

Stephen Walker summarizes these studies[17] and shows

that it is one thing to elaborate IRM-triggered instincts and redirect them by means of operant conditioning (as did B.F. Skinner when he trained pigeons to play ping-pong), and another to invent a semantic (i.e. meaningful) symbology (e.g. ping-pong balls, bats, nets, tables and the rules needed to play this game). To train animals to use and respond to symbols is an expansion of genetically conditioned capabilities, enforced by operant conditioning. But to invent a symbology requires de-conditioning, imagination and foresight of a high order. Human intelligence – as differentiated from animal intelligence – therefore consists of an ability to extract and synthesize meanings, to visualize and imagine sounds, and to create abstract symbols that represent these experiences and communicate them to others. Since any language requires agreement as to grammar, syntax and meanings among those who speak it, a shared symbology also demands a high order of co-operation.

The same applies to other aspects of awareness. To imagine what something feels like without having actual contact with it is a related capacity, showing that we can create internal feelings symbolically without having the actual sensory experience. This enables us to empathize and foresee consequences – the preconditions for conscience, responsibility and foresight.

Man's ability to create symbols owes its origins to the same survival needs that cause lions to roar or sparrows to chirp. But in man these abilities have developed much further. We owe this in large part to a larynx that makes speech possible and to a manual dexterity and co-ordination that allow us to create two- and three-dimensional symbols. These were the consequences of a genetic and central nervous system more complex and options more varied than those of any other species.

The psychologist Carl Jung was among the few to recognize that symbolic representation is a leap that sets us apart from all other species.[18] We are capable of autonomous and aware, rather than purely instinctive and conditioned, behaviour. This allows us to define and express our intentions with great subtlety, to reason in- and deductively, to trace events back to their causes and to foresee consequences. Again, long-term foresightedness requires setting and recognizing self-imposed limits that can only be expressed symbolically. Thus we alone among the species create our own future. These characteristics define our intelligence which is directly attributable to self-awareness and a unique capacity to develop a symbology far richer than any required for purely territorial, defensive or reproductive needs. It enables us to think about and express ideas that lie beyond the comprehension of any other species. Human understanding is limited only by will and time.

## Responsibility and Conscience

Human intelligence is therefore defined by self- and global awareness, conscience and potentially appropriate behaviour in all circumstances. Despite claims by biologists,[19] sociologists and psychologists, we are not entirely at the mercy of our genes, conditioning or the environment. As I pointed out earlier, the tendency today is to claim that insanity, criminality, compulsive alcoholism, gambling and other forms of addiction and anti-social behaviour are attributable to genetic and environmental causes. Instead we are or become whatever we want to be (barring gross genetic defects or irreversible environmental damage), either by default (i.e. by a refusal to think independently and assume responsibility for ourselves), by caving in to the carrot, the stick or the delusion of unconditional freedom, becoming enslaved by our environment, or by thinking for ourselves. In all but the last case we allow our future to be created for us by others and by failing to exercise our autonomy.

Only human beings enjoy free will, based on the fact that we have more options than we could ever exercise within the limits of conceivable time.[AA] Thus any comparison between human intelligence and that of other species is inappropriate. Only we can create a symbolic model of the combinatorial matrix that includes intentions, foresight, causes and consequences, the processes of adaptation, conditioning and learning, awareness and other characteristics of the so-called black box of the human psyche. Only we can model the dataflow within our brains, or demonstrate how it interacts with the external environment. These invisible processes determine our personalities, achievements and future. How we combine genetic, environmental and cultural memories – a matter of giving direction to the dataflow in our brains – is each human being's unique responsibility. We alone among the species can define ourselves in every generation.

Intentions, will, learning and their meanings are limited only by the options we perceive. These are the non-material aspects of subjective existence formerly said to lie beyond scientific analysis. The relationships between these internal factors, relative to the external world, condition the quality of our lives and the use we make of our common intelligence. These psychological factors determine which options we exercise and how creative or dogmatic we will be in the pursuit of knowledge and improvements in the quality of our lives.

# 8
# The Bubble that Burst

'Artificial intelligence; It's Here!' *Business Week*, 9 July 1984[1]

Once it is believed that man is nothing but an organic machine, then it may seem logical to assume that a machine might some day be able to think. This myth found expression in 'artificial intelligence' (AI), a concept to which some of today's scientists in computing, cybernetics, psychology, linguistics, medicine and economics still subscribe.

In 1982 the Japanese announced their Fifth Generation computer research project that promised artificial intelligence (computers that think) by 1990. In February 1984 an article I had written called 'Why the Computer Has to be an Idiot', published in *The Times*,[2] evoked a storm of objections from computer and other scientists. The artificially intelligent computer was to be the wave of the future and a source of enormous research funding by governments, defence departments, NSA (the US National Security Agency) and the CIA. Dozens of books and papers are still being published on this subject (more recently in the guise of connectivity, neural networks and parallel computing), making the same absurd 'scientific' and technological claims. Courses in artificial intelligence are still taught in polytechnics and universities. But in early 1990 Japan quietly abandoned its unsuccessful Fifth Generation project. No scientific journal or newspaper and only a few computer magazines mentioned this fact after touting the idea for years. Indeed on 1 July 1990 the *Financial Times* repeated the AI myth in a major article, at the same time completely ignoring what should have been one of the scientific and technological news items of that year.[3]

Believers in AI are divided into two schools – 'strong' and 'weak'. Weak AI suggests that computers might help us understand human intelligence. This is rational. But the idea of strong AI flies in the face of reason. It is based on the belief that computers will eventually be able to make diagnoses, decisions, forecasts and solve problems as well as and possibly better than we do. At various times it has been announced that they can do so already (see the quote that heads this chapter). Here I examine the the absurdity of this idea as yet another consequence of the purely mechanistic, materialistic outlook in the sciences and technologies. As Lewis Mumford wrote:

> . . . the condition of man today . . . resembles the pathetic state of Dr Bruno Bettelheim's psychiatric patient: a little boy of nine who conceived that he was run by machines. 'So controlling was this belief,' Dr Bettelheim reports, that the pathetic child 'carried with him an elaborate life-support system made up of radio tubes, light bulbs, and a breathing machine'. At meals he ran imaginary wires from a wall socket to himself, so his food could be digested. His bed was rigged with batteries, a loud speaker, and other improvised equipment to keep him alive while he slept.
>
> The fantasy of this autistic little boy is the state that modern man is fast approaching in actual life, without as yet realizing how pathological it is to be cut off from his own innate resources for living, and to feel no reassuring tie with the natural world or his own fellows unless he is connected to the power system, or with some actual machine . . .[4]

This boy's symptoms, while extreme, are not very different from those of many modern men and women who feel that they are not in touch with reality unless, machine-like, they are plugged in to a Walkman, video, computer, interactive

TV, or 'virtual reality', the promise (or threat) of the future. These are forms of alienation and pseudo-autism found in many societies today.

Strong AI is based on the premises that learning and operant conditioning (i.e. programming) are synonymous; that the DNA is equivalent to a computer's machine code; that human beings lack free will; that the central nervous system operates like a thermostat; that computers are capable of autonomous pattern recognition; that human decision-making works on the basis of fuzzy logic; that meanings can be inferred from context (i.e. frame of reference) and syntax (i.e. the arrangement of words); that forecasting depends on a statistical analysis of the past, and that computers can be taught to make value judgements. By such reasoning man would certainly be nothing but a machine, and computers would indeed have the power to imitate, emulate and possibly surpass human thought and reason.

It is also believed that, once computers are given as many 'neurons' and 'synapses' as we have and encyclopaedic knowledge, they would be able to make inferences faster and better than we can. Finally, it is expected that if computers were provided with enough memory, sensors, servo-mechanisms, raw materials and energy, they could program themselves and reproduce. All of this is, of course, pure science fiction, yet has been taught as computer science in schools, colleges, polytechnics and universities for almost forty years. These beliefs reflect the worst aspects of behaviourist psychology and social Darwinism: that the fittest survive and the spoils go to the strongest, that genes are programmed to make us selfish,[5] and that intelligence can be measured by how much you know – ideas that have poisoned twentieth-century cultures.

When artificial intelligence failed to be delivered in the 1980s as promised, many of its advocates turned to 'expert systems' and claimed that these were stepping stones to its realization.[6] When expert systems did not turn out to be equal or superior to human expertise, AI believers returned to earlier concepts – connectivity, neural networks and parallel computing – by which they expect to achieve AI by the year 2000. With the collapse of Japan's Fifth Generation computer research program in 1990, most who promoted AI in that form for years began to distance themselves from this concept without notice, switching to neural networks. So far only one, Terry Winograd, has honourably admitted his earlier mistake. Yet the search for AI continues unabated.

The number of academic journals devoted to strong AI keeps growing. Dozens of books, PhD theses and articles are still published, heralding the advent of artificial intelligence or announcing that it has already been achieved. Popular science magazines, TV programmes and the press still tout what is clearly impossible and, until very recently, ridiculed or suppressed any dissent. I cannot help wondering whether it will take as long to lay the myth of AI to rest as it did to end the American training-bra madness of the 1950s.

What makes artificial intelligence attractive to doctrinaire academics and politicians is clear: computers can be used as control mechanisms. Whoever controls and programs them and persuades the public that computer decisions are superior to those of mere human beings, has the power to manipulate public opinion. The thinking computer would be the ideal Big Brother, for who could argue with its objectivity and 'superior' intelligence?

B.F. Skinner, quoted in Chapter 5, blatantly admitted that 'people control' is the aim of operant conditioning (i.e. psychological programming), because everyone would benefit from being controlled – the claim of all demagogues. The 'thinking machine' would be the ideal decision-maker, supplanting everyone except those who programmed the master computer. For these reasons governments have poured billions into universities and private corporations in order to discover AI. The US Star Wars program, still being developed despite the end of the Cold War, depends on the realization of strong AI. Computing research programmes in Britain (Alvey), the EEC (Esprit), and Japan (Fifth Generation) were based on the premise that AI is possible. Many nations that support scientific and technological research are still funding similar programmes. In 1990 – just a few months before Japan abandoned Fifth Generation research – Marvin Minsky, a founding father of strong AI who coined the phrase 'man is a meat machine', was awarded the Japan Prize equivalent to the Nobel Prize, for his 'achievements' in this line of research.

Financial and intellectual support of this kind creates a number of related situations. Dogmatic scientists are encouraged to cling to their worst prejudices, and opportunists become believers in order to get a piece of the action. For many scientists the myth of strong AI was an opportunity to earn undeserved high salaries, become stockholders and principals in high-tech enterprises and consultants to governments. Corporations funded with public money to develop AI never delivered what they promised or diverted this money to other purposes, thus defrauding taxpayers and investors. When results failed to materialize, new buzz-words were invented like expert systems, inference engines, connectivity and neural networks to allow this sham to continue in new disguises for as long as possible. All of this may seem bizarre, yet it takes place again and again in much of mainstream science, as we saw in earlier chapters.

# The Mechanization of Calculation

The mechanization of mathematical operations began in China where a decimal system was used well before 330 B.C. Counting rods were employed about 180 B.C., and the abacus became a household calculator in the fourteenth century A.D. But it was in the West that mathematics was automated beyond the capacity of the abacus. The foundations for modern computing were laid by the development of logarithms and log tables by Napier and Briggs, by Pascal's first digital calculator of 1642, and the discovery of the differential calculus by Newton and Leibniz. Leibniz had also developed a stepped-wheel calculator at a reputed cost of 24,000 dollars, an enormous sum at that time. Subsequently Müller, a German Captain of

Engineers, built what was reported to be a fully functioning calculator in 1735, using Leibniz's methods. But Charles Babbage's nineteenth-century calculating machines – the Difference and Analytic Engines – were the forerunners of adding machines and today's computers. Even at that time Lady Lovelace (Byron's daughter, a mathematician and Babbage's friend) stressed that a 'thinking' mechanism was out of the question:

> Considered under the most general point of view, the essential object of the machine being to calculate, according to the laws dictated to it, the values of numerical coefficients which it is then to distribute appropriately on the columns which represent the variables, it follows that the interpretation of formulae and of results is beyond its province, unless indeed this very interpretation be itself susceptible of expression by means of the symbols which the machine employs. Thus, although it is not itself the being that reflects, it must yet be considered as the being which executes the conceptions of intelligence.[7]

Babbage used punched cards (based on binary principles) to feed information into his machines, an idea he borrowed from Jacquard, the French inventor of mechanical tapestry looms. However, the operating system of Babbage's incomplete Difference Engine (a reconstruction of which can be seen at London's Science Museum) was decimal. It was used during his lifetime only to establish life-expectancy tables for insurance companies, a trivial application considering its power. But it inspired Odhner, a Swede, to improve on it in 1878, and H. Hollerith, an American, to use a calculator based on similar principles for the computation of the 1890 US census.

In 1913 T.V. Hudson had refined the Difference Engine and developed the Burroughs adding-machine. The same principles, with periodic improvements, were applied to the design of cash registers manufactured towards the end of the nineteenth and the beginning of the twentieth centuries. Some of their manufacturers branched into producing typewriters, another essential development for the future of computing. In 1926 Dr J.L. Comrie adapted Babbage's methods to mechanize computations for the *Nautical Almanac* and the *Moon Tables* (both previously calculated by hand and containing a great many inaccuracies), thus enhancing navigational precision and safety at sea. Mechanical improvements in calculating machines were made between the two world wars. The transition from mechanical calculator to electronic computer took place shortly before, during and after World War II. As usual, the scientific foundations had been laid in peacetime but war provided the spur for rapid technological exploitation.

In 1936 Alan Turing, a British mathematician, wrote a thesis that affected the course of World War II and the future of electronic computing.[8] He showed how binary numbers can encode any symbol. (These processes were described more lucidly than Turing had in a 1984 *Scientific American* article.[9]) Turing's working model built in 1937 incorporated the ideas of George Boole, the nineteenth-century mathematical logician. It represented a departure from the cams, mechanical switches and decimal mechanisms employed by Babbage. Because the human central nervous system works on binary principles (see Chapters 6 and 7) Turing persuaded himself that his discovery laid the basis for a universal machine that would eventually equal or surpass human intelligence. Andrew Hodges, his biographer, summed up Turing's understanding of human intelligence and learning: 'His model of "intelligence", using chess and mathematics as its paradigm, was one which simply reflected the orthodox view of [relatively] objective science . . . The education that he [Turing] had in mind was of the public school variety, by the carrot and stick . . .'[10]

During World War II Turing worked at Bletchley, Britain's secret cryptographic installation, where he made major contributions to the breaking of German enigma codes. This enabled Britain to stand virtually alone against Germany until the USSR and the US entered the war. At the end of the war he devoted himself to the development of a mechanical brain, the principles of which he discussed in a much-quoted article published in 1950.[11] In it he described what is now called strong artificial intelligence and asked: 'Can machines think?' He suggested that they would soon be able to do so. In another article Turing addressed himself to the problem of competition, for he was convinced that winning in chess, economics and war defined the height of intelligence and that competitive principles applied to winning games as much as to learning and general problem-solving.[12] These articles provided the intellectual underpinnings for what is now known as strong AI.

Turing was a poor chess player, had no business experience and was not well informed about economics or education. His experience of war was limited to the sheltered environment of Bletchley. But that did not prevent his theorizing about these subjects. Like Donald Michie, his one-time junior colleague and chess companion, he believed in the superiority of the winner in any enterprise and considered the computer's evident ability to follow orders and to win on occasion at noughts and crosses, draughts (checkers) or chess to be signs of machine intelligence – a profound perceptual error.[AA] Turing committed suicide shortly after the war, but Donald Michie, today Director of Glasgow's Turing Institute, was persuaded that Turing was correct because a noughts-and-crosses machine Michie built out of matchboxes succeeded in beating him.[13] The absurdity of this idea is obvious. Yet Michie remains a fervent champion of AI:

> Can machines think? The short answer is 'Yes': there are machines which can do what we would call thinking, if it were done by a human being . . . for the time being we are going to have to define intelligence in machines in the same way that Justice Potter Stewart described pornography: 'I can't define it but I know it when I see it.'[14]

## The Computer as a Metaphor for Thought

The post-war era was followed by a brief period of intellectual questing before the Cold War signalled a renewal of the arms race, the fostering of applied, rather than pure research, and economic recovery based on planned obsolescence, consumerism and rearmament. Qualitative value judgements go out of the window when such standards prevail. These trends stimulated all sorts of competition: to develop the biggest nuclear bomb, the largest universities and laboratories, the most competitive economic systems and conglomerate corporations; to be the first in space, to build the most powerful computers and, of course, to be the first to discover artificial intelligence.

This last idea found favour in the cut and thrust of bureaucratic government and corporate managements, in war departments and in grant-hungry universities, all devoted to fierce competition, winning at any cost, domination, control and avoiding individual responsibility. As a result, a change had occurred in the kind and quality of science practised prior to World War I and for a short time thereafter. The essentially humanistic attitudes of scientists like Einstein, Eddington and Haldane gave way once again to increasingly materialistic and mechanistic ones, despite humanistic pretensions. That academics and the military might promote such ideas because they believed in them or to assure themselves of research support, highlights the danger of conditioning and the corruption of science.

The post-war discoveries that affected computing most included Norbert Wiener's principles of cybernetics,[15] von Neumann and Morgenstern's *Theory of Games and Economic Behaviour*,[16] von Neumann's computer architecture, Claude Shannon's information and communications theory,[17] von Bertalanffy's general systems theory,[18] and Grey Walter's theories about robot behaviour.[19] It is worth summarizing the ideas of these men, for their work laid the foundation for today's computer science.

Shannon demonstrated the relationship between noise, resistance in circuits and information flow. As Grey Walter showed some years later, what was true for electrical circuits seemed analogous to what takes place in the central nervous system. Sherrington's earlier synaptic theory[20] indicated how reflexes are processed in biological systems via axons and synapses that connect the complex network of neurons in the human brain – the wiring circuits for human decision-making and action. By 1952 Grey Walter had built two robots, one of which I described in Chapter 6, that appeared to mimic some of the purely mechanical and reflexive functions of the human central nervous system. Many of today's industrial and other robots are elaborations of these machines.

Von Bertalanffy was a biologist. His general systems theory is vital to understanding the difference between human intelligence and computing because he was perhaps the first to pose questions concerning the relationship between open (subjective learning) and closed (finite, relatively objective, inorganic mechanical) systems. The open and closed systems question has troubled science for centuries and is still a matter of debate in mathematics (for example, the definition of infinity), physics (the many-body problem), and in biology, computing and general problem-solving.

Norbert Wiener coined the word *cybernetics* to describe the relationship between human and machine behaviour, regrettably equating one with the other. Plato first used the term and attributed it to Socrates: 'Cybernetics saves souls, bodies and material possessions from the gravest dangers.'[21] On the other hand, Ampère defined it in his *Essay on the Philosophy of Science*[22] as meaning steersmanship and external political control. In Plato's sense the term meant inner and self-control; in Ampère's it meant control from without – a vital difference that goes to the heart of the man-machine question.

In establishing this new discipline, Wiener laid what he hoped was the basis for a unification of the physical, biological and social sciences, long dreamt of by philosophers. Regrettably Wiener failed to appreciate the fact that human behaviour is part mechanical, reflexive and instinctive (e.g. eye-blink, breathing, heart-beat, etc.) and part other-than-mechanical, reflective and valuative. It is only the latter that can be said to be intelligence. Wiener was a bundle of contradictions for, after denouncing von Neumann and

Morgenstern for their definition of competition as rational behaviour, he devoted a part of his most important work to the development of a mathematical method for winning at chess.[23] Like Babbage, Turing and Shannon, Wiener fell victim to culturally conditioned prejudices. Here again the game and competitive questions recur as they do in most areas of human intelligence and behaviour.[AA]

## Post-war Computing

While Britain had laid much of the groundwork in computing, parallel developments took place in the US. Mark I, the first modern computer, was planned at Harvard University in 1939 and completed in 1944. It was followed by Mark II and both were built with substantial aid and standard adding-machine parts supplied by IBM. These computers were used to prepare mathematical and ballistics tables for the US army during World War II. ENIAC, a more advanced general-purpose computer, was completed in 1946 at the University of Pennsylvania. It was followed by even more powerful machines in Britain and the US which were given acronyms like EDSAC, EDVAC, UNIVAC and one, built in 1952, named MANIAC. This last machine contained a new computer architecture (i.e. the organization of the functional units that form the heart of the computer) designed by a team that included von Neumann. It remained the industry standard until recently.

Early computers were cumbersome, slow and very expensive. The cost of building, operating and maintaining them restricted their use to government agencies, universities and large corporations. Eventually the transistor replaced the valve and was succeeded by the silicon chip, which in turn may shortly be superseded by new technologies now in the making. These developments enlarged the computer's memory a thousand-fold, speeded up number crunching and made word processing and graphics possible. They also helped miniaturize these machines and cut their costs drastically, making micros, minis, portables and programmable calculators generally available, for the shorter the connecting wires inside the computer, the faster the data is processed and transmitted, so that the most powerful computers became smaller and faster.

By 1977 eight million instructions-per-second could be achieved on publicly available computers. By 1984 memory capacity had reached 1 million pages of information, each available at a fraction of a second. By 1989, brute-force factorization of a 100-digit number became possible in three weeks of continuous operation of thirty parallel-linked mainframe computers. In 1990 it was announced that INMOS, the British semiconductor maker, planned to introduce transputers that make possible BIPS (billion instructions-per-second). Today's lap-tops can do the work formerly done by mainframes.

Memory storage, even more than processing speeds, is a severe limitation in today's computing. For every command or byte of information must first be encoded into binary digits before it can be stored and processed in the machine, and this can take up a great deal of memory space. For example, the number 16777213 is stored as 111111111111111111111101, using three times as much memory as the decimal version. When it comes to storing words and graphics the memory problem becomes even more acute because every letter of the alphabet, line or shape is made up of binary digits. Therefore shorthand codes are needed so as not to exhaust the computer's memory with instructions alone. From the early 1950s dozens of artificial languages have been devised to economize on memory space. Data compression also helps, but can never achieve the economy and richness of symbolic representations within the human brain.

Yet the myth of AI persists because people believe that an accumulation of knowledge (cognition), stimulus/response (input/output) and calculation speed equal understanding. Indeed, computers can follow instructions to the letter but they do not have the faintest idea of what they mean. Human beings, on the other hand, can accept or reject information and commands by thinking for themselves, depending on their understanding of meanings (i.e. causes and consequences) and their ability to make aware value judgements (distinguishing right from wrong). They can also refuse to execute orders that are inhumane. To do any less means to be less than human; to do as much is more than any machine can do.

## Strong AI

In 1956 John McCarthy, while an assistant mathematics professor at Dartmouth College in the US, obtained the first grant to research the possibility of AI from the Rockefeller Foundation. He, Marvin Minsky, Allen Newell and Herbert Simon, together with colleagues, students and AI groupies, percolated through the US academic system, including influential academic and technological bastions like the Massachusetts Institute of Technology (MIT), Carnegie-Mellon and Stanford Universities. They published innumerable papers, articles and books, lectured and denounced critics, held artificial intelligence conferences, seminars and workshops, and gave press conferences at every opportunity, as they still do. McCarthy coined the term *artificial intelligence* and, like Ross Ashby, a British believer in the thinking computer, insisted that: '. . . Machines as simple as thermostats can be said to have beliefs, and having beliefs seems to be a characteristic of most machines capable of problem-solving performance.'[24]

The unsubstantiated claims made by these and other academics excited the media and converted many journalists who repeated them uncritically. They exerted considerable influence on the public, major corporations and defence-related think-tanks like the US Science Research Institute, the RAND Corporation and government agencies. All of this took place at a time when increased East/West tensions and growing US military involvement in Vietnam caused the Pentagon to seek new 'winning' strategies and weapons systems. The idea of intelligent computers and robot soldiers seemed a highly attractive concept to militarists and they backed it massively. It was also profitable to defence contractors who saw AI as a new way of stimulating increased military spending and profits.

The 'game' approach to strategic and tactical decision-making is still used widely by economists, business and government managers and the military. The belief in the qualitative superiority of the winner was bolstered by academic devotees of AI who spent a great deal of time and money trying to devise winning strategies for draughts, chess and even poker, without understanding the principles that underlie games of strategy and chance.[AA] The game analogy was used to provide what was claimed to be proof for artificial intelligence because computers seemed able to win games played against human beings now and then. They were therefore believed to be capable of matching and at times surpassing human intelligence. But none of these scientists and computer experts had the faintest idea of what game-playing is all about or why and how we win, lose, draw or achieve a stalemate.[AA]

In Britain, where it all began with Turing's famous article, many academics, encouraged by what was taking place in the US, took up the cry of AI in the 1950s and 1960s. They included Gordon Pask,[25] Stafford Beer,[26] Donald Michie[27] and Ross Ashby, a neuro-physiologist who became enamoured with robotics and cybernetics. Ashby wrote one of the first textbooks on cybernetics and another, *Design for a Brain*,[28] in which he gave birth to the idea that thermostats have feelings, a theme echoed later by John McCarthy.

Ashby's theories are still taught, but he had failed to grasp that homeostasis (i.e. balance) is achieved by the brain's ability to make not only quantitative but also qualitative value judgements; hence he concluded that the brain is a purely mechanical control system. He also did not differentiate between human, inner-directed self-control (i.e. self-rewarding feedback in an open system), and the limited, stimulus/response and outer-directed feedback of biological reflexive behaviours (i.e. feedback within a closed system) similar to those of machines. At the Third Congress of the International Association for Cybernetics in 1961, Ashby was reported to have said in an address that:

> ... contrary to popular belief that the computer is a constrained device which can only do what it is told, and that the human brain is a free agent with wide powers of choice, just the opposite is more nearly true. That the brain does what it is supposed to do, is relatively a complete slave to the past, and is no more free than a high-speed aircraft is free: whereas the computer is the first free complex organism in history: free from intrinsic structure – almost a *tabula rasa*. It is the first extant example of a non-organized system: all others having been eliminated by evolution.[29]

Ashby was not alone in such reckless philosophizing. Many other academics still remain blind to the fact that total freedom without constraints leads to the same consequences as operant conditioning – entrapment in a closed feedback loop from which there is no escape except by de-conditioning. The irresponsible claims of US and British computer experts throughout the 1960s and early 1970s caused the British Government of the day to ask Sir James Lighthill, a prominent mathematician, to report on the possibility of artificial intelligence. Lighthill came out strongly against AI.[30] His reasons were that in order to 'think' a computer would have to consider all 'combinatorial' possibilities (i.e. not only the sequence of facts – the permutations – but also the relationships between them). When the relationships between any body of relevant facts are considered, the number of possibilities explodes at a rate so great that the fastest computers of the future would run out of time in our galaxy, even when it comes to relatively simple strategic games. Lighthill called this the 'combinatorial explosion'. But even he did not understand the semantic and valuative aspects of combinatorial mathematics. These are discussed in some detail in Appendices A and D. Lighthill's critique was quantitative rather than qualitative. His objection, though only partially correct, was sufficiently persuasive to end government support of AI research in Britain for the next few years.

Notwithstanding Lighthill's dismissal of AI, Margaret Boden, then a Sussex University Reader in Philosophy and Psychology and unencumbered by any mathematical or technological knowledge by her own admission,[31] wrote the Open University textbook on AI, published in 1977.[32] Lighthill is mentioned only in two disparaging footnotes. A spate of popular books written in a similar vein was published in Britain and the US in following years, with titles like *The Super-Intelligent Machine*,[33] *Electronic Life*,[34] *Are Computers Alive?*[35] and *Science Fact*.[36] Works like *End*[37] and *No Ghost in the Machine*[38] are still being published.

Professor Frank George, formerly at Brunel University, was a consultant to the British and US military, the Department of Industry, and author of half a dozen books on cybernetics. He remained an advocate of strong AI and was influential in spreading this gospel on both sides of the Atlantic. He was unambiguous about the future of thinking machines:

> Today we are confronted with one of the most intriguing problems ever faced by Man. It is that we seem to be moving towards the point where we can manufacture human beings artificially ... We are absolutely serious about a machine-in-evolution or a machine species, and not just a machine ... Given the 'thinking machine', the machine species follows easily enough.[39]

It is also worth quoting *Science Fact*, typical of a genre of fiction that pretends to science, edited by Professor George. The quoted article was written by the late Dr Chris Evans, psychologist, computer scientist and author, in the turgid style often employed by champions of AI:

> Perhaps in the vastness of outer space there exist other civilizations with beings stupendously in advance intellectually to our own, and perhaps in due course the super-intelligent machines that we have created will go out and meet them. If they do they will find a friendly, rather than a hostile reception. For it seems to me to be inevitable that the creatures who *dominate* other solar systems in other galaxies

will be like those who will come to *dominate* our own. They too will be machines.[40]

Evans, like Turing and Michie, was infatuated with winning and the computer's powers to defeat and dominate human game-players. As a computer consultant to the BBC he influenced a wide audience.

Meanwhile the idea of artificial intelligence had found fertile soil in Japan, a country in which operant conditioning with reinforcement runs through all social, economic, political and educational institutions. If such a development could have been realized it would have given Japan's computer and robot-guided industries a considerable competitive edge over the rest of the world. The Japanese are determined winners. With the publication of Japan's 1982 Fifth Generation report, pressure from academics and the eagerness of electronics firms like ICL, Plessey, Racal and Ferranti to finance their proprietary product development out of the public purse, the British Government was pushed into a reconsideration of the Lighthill Report.

## The Fifth Generation

The term *Fifth Generation computing* was coined by Japan's Ministry of International Trade and Industry (MITI) in a 1982 report announcing its planned £500–1,000 million support for hard- and software AI research over the next ten years. This triggered a competition between Japan, the US, Britain and other EEC countries to be the first to develop artificially intelligent computers. MITI's report stated its goals unequivocally:

... To realize basic mechanisms for inference, association, and learning in hardware and make them the core functions for fifth generation computers ... to prepare basic artificial intelligence software to fully utilize the above functions ... To take advantage of pattern recognition and artificial research advancements, and realize man-machine interfaces that are natural to man ...[41]

Professor Tohru Moto-oka, a member of the forty-man team assembled by MITI to research AI under the direction of Dr Kazuhiro Fuchi, was even more explicit:

> We'll be trying to set up in the machine an associative memory like the one in the human brain. In the present-day computers you can find a memory only if you know the address! . . . In the mind, things don't work that way . . . We have to teach the computer to extract the real ideas that are being expressed in the words it hears, and then transfer that idea into another language.[42]

Tohru Moto-oka elaborated these ideas in a book co-authored by Masaru Kitsuregawa, published in 1985, reiterating the aims of MITI and the promise that the realization of artificial intelligence was just a matter of time.[43]

In November 1984, two years after MITI's announcement, Japan unveiled its initial AI results at a Tokyo conference where it claimed to have succeeded in its search, while debates were still going on in the West on how best to proceed. For the first time doubts were raised about the possibility of building machines that might match or surpass human intelligence.[44] None the less, AI research in Japan and elsewhere continued unabated.

Japanese efforts in the AI world championships were centred, like everyone else's, on producing hardware that is faster than a Josephson Junction (the fastest processor so far) and on colossally large databases, in the mistaken belief that data-processing speed and encyclopaedic knowledge spell intelligence. (If that were the case then every encyclopaedia would be intelligent.) Artificial intelligence was supposed to have been achieved with DELTA, a twenty-gigabyte database installed on four dual processors. By 1985 DELTA developed serious problems. This setback was not admitted by Kazuhiro Fuchi, who declared the Fifth Generation project to be on target and himself satisfied with the progress made to date. Still, MITI's AI research funding was cut and personnel loaned to it by contributing corporations were withdrawn. Meanwhile, in the basement of MITI headquarters in Tokyo giant squid nerve cells (axons) were being grown in attempts to build an 'intelligent biocomputer': '. . . an information processing system functionally resembling the brain.'[45] Scientists at Bell Telephone Laboratories and the Massachusetts Institute of Technology in the US and Imperial College in London conducted similar experiments in attempts to create organic computers that think. According to Professor Joseph Albery at Imperial College, '. . . the all-thinking bio-computer is a mere thirty years away'.[46]

US computer scientists and researchers like the aforementioned John McCarthy, Marvin Minsky, Allen Newell, Patrick Winston, John McDermott and Edward Feigenbaum, spurred on by the Japanese, accelerated research purporting to demonstrate intelligent behaviour on the part of computers. They claimed to have found convincing evidence to prove that human beings are nothing but machines. On the basis of alleged, but unsubstantiated 'proof', a large segment of the academic and government establishment was persuaded yet again that human thought and decision-making are purely mechanical processes that can be replicated and possibly surpassed by machines.

The experts of the 1960s and 1970s developed programs showing that computers can do interesting things – some faster and better than human beings. They also discovered that once a computer with built-in optional branching is given sufficient information, it can find alternate ways to solve problems, provided the problem is defined for them and at least one answer already exists. In other words, they demonstrated what should have been obvious – that every problem has more than one solution, some as good as and others better than those we already know. This became known as 'theorem proving' and provided yet another supposed demonstration of AI.

Marvin Minsky was surprised that when he entered one of Euclid's theorems into his computer it produced a different solution, as good or better than Euclid's own. Donald Michie was equally impressed.[47] Here, they argued, was a machine that could out-perform a master geometer.

Neither seemed aware that there is a considerable difference between a human being who sets his own goal, defines a problem and finds a solution, and a machine that generates variations on a given theme. Without Euclid's awareness of the existence of geometric problems and his discovery of a single solution for each, his theorems could not have been entered into Minsky's computer. Without Euclid's solution, Minsky would not have recognized a variation of it when it was generated by the machine.

Another 'proof' of AI was 'natural language understanding'. In 1972 Terry Winograd published his PhD thesis describing a program he had developed – SHRDLU – that supposedly enabled a computer to understand and converse in English about constructions with children's building blocks (a 'block world' domain, in computer jargon).[48] Subsequently Winograd reversed himself and disavowed his findings. He is the only one of the AI fraternity to have admitted his mistake as early as 1976.[49] But from the day his original claims were published to the present, virtually every book on artificial intelligence has genuflected to his 'success', paying no attention to his repeated disclaimers. Even Roger Penrose, a critic of artificial intelligence, seemed unaware of Winograd's disavowal as recently as 1989.[50]

In the face of the massive failures of computer-derived US strategies applied in the Vietnam War, academic promoters of AI revised their claims and promised to do better in the future if given greater research support. In 1977 Edward Fredkin, Professor of Computing at MIT, stated:

> In order to produce a machine that thinks better than man, we don't have to understand everything about man. We still don't understand feathers, but we can fly . . . In the distant future we won't know what computers are doing, or why. If two of them converse, they'll say in a second more than all the words spoken during the lives of all the people who have ever lived on this planet.[51]

By 1980 the subject of artificial intelligence gained such

credibility in the US that *The New York Sunday Times Magazine* published a two-part series on this subject:

> A machine *who* could think, reason, make logical deductions, remember past experience, solve present problems by recognizing analogous situations, would not such a computer hold the capacity that has always distinguished man from other forms of life . . . Now, however, some of the world's philosophers, mathematicians, electrical engineers and computer scientists are working to create machines that do just that . . . As a result, artificial intelligence researchers are developing computers that can listen to spoken sentences and *grasp their meanings* . . . [My italics; Marvin Minsky was quoted:] 'There are people who think that evolution has stopped and that there can never be anything smarter than man.'[52]

Dozens of books were written that elaborated the AI theme, like *Machines Who* [sic] *Think* compiled by Pamela McCorduck, a journalist who promoted these ideas and sought to disparage the few critics.[53] Another, *The Fifth Generation* published in 1983, was written by McCorduck in collaboration with Edward Feigenbaum.[54] In it they extolled the virtues of AI and helped increase US paranoia about the possibility of losing to the Japanese the race to discover it first. The authors promised benefits of which the following is typical:

> The geriatric robot is wonderful. It isn't hanging about in the hopes of inheriting your money – nor of course will it slip you a little something to speed the inevitable. It isn't hanging about because it can't find work elsewhere. It's there because it's yours. It doesn't just bathe you and feed you and wheel you out into the sun when you crave fresh air and a change of scene, though of course it does all those things. The very best thing about the geriatric robot is that it *listens*. 'Tell me again,' it says, 'about how wonderful/dreadful your children are to you. Tell me again that fascinating tale of the coup of '63. Tell me again . . .' And it means it. It never gets tired of hearing those stories,

just as you never get tired of telling them. It knows your favorites, and those are its favorites too . . .[55]

Feigenbaum's enthusiasm was not untinged by self-interest, for he was one of many academics who became founders of new companies set up to exploit the artificial-intelligence craze. US military and multi-national corporations involved in defence contracts invested heavily – the first by infusion of research funds and the second by stock purchases in a spate of newly-founded AI companies. 'There's such a tremendous rush to own a piece of AI that we were a multi-million-dollar company before we opened our doors.' (Larry K. Geisel, academic and President, Carnegie Group.)[56]

International Resource Development Inc., a US market-research organization, predicted in 1983 (in a report that sold for $1,650) that artificial intelligence revenues would exceed $8.5 billion by 1993.[57] Similar claims were made for expert systems [58] and, most recently, for neural networks.[59] *International Business Week* was able to report in 1984, quoting some of the AI academics, 'It's ironic. Three years ago, AI was flaky. Now it's hot and everyone wants in' (Randall Davis, Professor of AI at MIT.)[60] and: 'This is the age of euphoria for AI. It's like being at Kitty Hawk when the Wright brothers' plane took off.' (Patrick Winston, Director of MIT's AI Laboratory.)[61]

Feigenbaum founded IntelliGenetics Corporation of Palo Alto, California, a company that floated a $1.6 million stock offer in 1983, despite a $700,000-plus loss during the preceding year. General Motors invested $3 million in Teknowledge Inc. – yet another company in which Feigenbaum was a prime mover – for a 13 per cent share. Thinking Machines Corp. was founded by Marvin Minsky and his academic colleagues, and had on its board of directors Frank Stanton and William Paley, founders and former chief executives of the CBS broadcasting and TV network. John McDermott and his friends at Carnegie-Mellon University formed Carnegie Group Inc. More than forty such corporations existed by 1984 and many more have been formed since then, each headed by academics, most with intriguing names like Cognitive Systems Inc., Symbolic Inc., Computer Thought Inc. and Artificial Intelligence Inc.

The US Defense Department's Advanced Research Projects Agency (DARPA) allocated $250 million to launch its Strategic Computing Program (i.e. Star Wars) that expected to develop 'super-intelligent machines', with up to $1 billion promised to see the project through to a successful conclusion. Most of this money was funnelled into AI corporations like those mentioned. But the link between universities, industry, government and the military in the attempted development of intelligent computers and robots is illustrated dramatically by the Microelectronics and Computer Technology Corporation (MCC). This was founded by a consortium of twelve US corporate giants and had a $75 million annual budget. It was headed by Admiral 'Bobby' Inman, former chief of DARPA, the Pentagon agency that put up the R&D money to make all this possible. Much the same applies in Britain and elsewhere.

## Dissenters

Public critics of AI are relatively rare, even today. Among the earliest of these was Mortimer Taube who was roundly denounced for his heresy and who died in 1961 shortly after the publication of his book.[62] Herbert Dreyfus, another dissenter on philosophical grounds, made the mistake of allowing himself to be drawn into the computer chess debate without understanding the game. He was challenged to play against a computer – and lost.[63] According to his critics this disqualified him from being taken seriously.

Joseph Weizenbaum, an MIT computer scientist, believes that AI is a possibility but that it should not be allowed on ethical grounds. His objections are none the less valid.[64] He, like other critics of AI, has not yet tumbled to the 'computers are intelligent because they can win games' fraud and therefore tends to concede that they might, some day, acquire pseudo-intelligence. However, Weizenbaum's famous ELIZA program is still one of the most persuasive demonstrations of the fact that computers merely regurgitate variations of whatever has been programmed.

Weizenbaum's ELIZA program (named after Eliza Doolittle in Bernard Shaw's play *Pygmalion*) is a spoof that fools many people into believing that it provides authentic psychoanalyses because the machine successfully mimics a classical psychiatric technique. The ELIZA program holds a mirror up to the 'patient' and responds by feeding back variations of what he types in. The machine has been programmed with standard questions and in a format that incorporates whatever words the patient uses into its next question, without having the faintest idea what it or the patient is talking about. The result can be sufficiently convincing to delude the unwary into believing that the computer is sympathetic or critically helpful. But the patient is simply talking to him- or herself.

The ELIZA program also responds with irrelevancies when the patient fails to provide it with the vocabulary it needs in order to respond, or when the database in the computer's memory is insufficient. A number of these irrelevancies are stored and regurgitated when no other response is possible, so that they seem spontaneous when they appear on the screen.

Anyone who is not fooled by the pretended seriousness or feigned inquisitiveness of the program (e.g., 'What do you mean by "I hate my mother?"') or its fake objectivity and interest ('Tell me more about why you hate your parents?'), can soon reduce the computer to respond with nothing but gibberish (for example, 'Do you play the nose flute?' or 'What do you think of Adolf Hitler?'). Such inappropriate replies are signs of stupidity, insanity or deliberate obfuscation when made by human beings. But the computer is neither sane nor insane, intelligent, stupid or deliberately disconcerting. It simply does what it is told to do and cannot do otherwise. What is extraordinary is that, despite Weizenbaum's published explanations of his elaborate and instructive practical joke, psychologists and psychiatrists insist that ELIZA is a legitimate psychoanalytic tool that can understand the meanings of a patient's history or behaviour and can think and reason.

The American philosopher John Searle is one of the most severe critics of AI. His BBC Reith Lectures of 1984[65] and his 1990 article in the *Scientific American* are among the most cogent attacks on the AI mythology. He faults computer scientists and artificial intelligence experts because they insist that meaning resides in the structure of syntax (i.e. in the arrangement of words and phrases) and context, or is a matter of opinion. But unfortunately he never defines how human beings extract meanings, an oversight that is general in philosophy and linguistics. All of the foregoing bears directly on the general translation problem – another solution sought by artificial intelligence aficionados. Despite strenuous efforts supported massively by Japan, the EEC and the US, computer and linguistics experts will never realize the chimera of a universal language translation program or computer.

In Britain, the only recent published objections to AI come from Roger Penrose[66] and Jeremy Campbell.[67] Campbell objects mainly on humanistic grounds. Penrose is convinced that strong AI is impossible because computers cannot make value judgements, although he does not define what constitutes a value judgement. At the same time he takes issue with John Searle because Penrose believes that the extraction of meanings has nothing to do with intelligence or with making value judgements. However, it is impossible to make value judgements without semantic precision (i.e. without knowing the meanings of ideas and concepts). For example, unless you know what winning, losing, a draw or a stalemate mean causally, consequentially and operationally as far as intentions and feelings are concerned, you cannot make a value judgement about any of these outcomes.[AA] Regrettably, Penrose also believes that the central nervous system operates along the lines of quantum mechanics (see Chapter 7). As I said earlier, this is an example of attempts to understand human intelligence from a specialist perspective in particle physics when this can only be done successfully the other way round.

Aside from these and a small handful of other critics like Lewis Mumford[68] and Theodore Roszak,[69] this is the sum of informed public dissent from what has become the established wisdom. It is puny, given the massive propaganda in its favour and the importance of the issues that are involved. Undoubtedly other people in- and outside the sciences realize that strong AI is a mirage but they are a silent minority, often unaware of what is really at stake.

## Expert Systems

As I have shown, Japan's Fifth Generation programme and the fears this aroused brought about fierce competition in industrialized countries which sought to be the first to develop AI. In Britain it was promoted as the potential salvation of an ailing electronics industry. In the US it was seen as the ultimate weapon in defence of the 'American way' against Japanese economic hegemony and Communism (and more recently against Iraq that proved to be a boon for US defence industries suffering from the end of the Cold War and the current economic depression). In Britain a twelve-man public committee and a smaller advisory one to the Cabinet Office were formed in 1982, with members drawn entirely from industry. The public committee was named after its chairman John Alvey, then Director of Research for British Telecom, and its unsurprising verdict rendered in 1983 found against Lighthill and for AI.[70] But because that ultimate goal seemed beyond reach at that time, 'expert systems' were invented as an intermediate step.

An expert system is a computer program that supposedly encapsulates the expertise of a specialist. There are now so-called expert systems in chess, chemistry, medicine, oil and natural gas exploration, machine fault-finding, teaching and management decision-making. But the term itself is misleading, for every computer program could be considered an expert system of a kind. None the less this has become part of the AI jargon, along with 'knowledge engineering' – another label for systems analysis. Tim

Johnson, author of *The Commercial Application of Expert Systems Technology*, defines an expert system as '... a set of computer programs which emulate human expertise by applying the technique of logical inference to a knowledge base'.[71]

It was believed that expert systems would be intelligent, diagnose, predict, understand, and give reasons for what they were doing because they are rule-based. No one ever questioned whether the computer programs said to achieve all this were given the correct rules. The British Government implemented the Alvey Report with massive funding to industry and universities. One computer per classroom for primary and secondary schools was proposed and proved a boon to manufacturers. Academics were unhappy because most Alvey funding went to industry and AI was being pre-empted by commercial interests. The British computer industry had succeeded in getting a free ride on the taxpayers' coat-tails in the name of AI, although it was expected to make contributions out of corporate funds. At least half of Britain's largest (and least innovative) electronics corporations' product development was underwritten by the Government under the guise of knowledge engineering, expert systems and artificial intelligence. The Turing Institute was given the single largest academic Alvey research grant to study the predictability of 'idiosyncratic aspects of human behaviour'. That research has seemingly so far produced no viable results. Could any behaviour be more idiosyncratic than belief in artificial intelligence?

Sir Clive Sinclair, Britain's computer and electric car-manufacturing genius, remained undeterred by the failure of his peers to discover AI. Going it alone, he started his own independent Metalab research centre, staffed with fifty Cambridge scientists devoted to discovering computers that think in a human way. According to Sinclair:

I think it certain that in decades, not centuries, machines of silicon will arise first to rival and then to surpass their human progenitors. Once they surpass us they will be capable of their own design. In a real sense they will be reproductive. Silicon will have ended the carbon monopoly.[72]

Having reduced higher education budgets by £100 million and cut more funding at primary and secondary school levels, the British Government gave back in the form of computer education less than half of what it had taken away, while making a £150 million present to the computer industry. The Departments of Industry, Defence and Education were joint sponsors of the Alvey programme, but their funding produced nothing by way of artificial intelligence. By 1986 the Alvey Committee had fallen into obscurity. It was replaced by another, consisting of academics and industrial managers who suggested a new research project. The Government was to provide £300 million, of which £135 million was allocated to the EEC's ESPRIT (European Strategic Program for Research and Development in Information Technology) project begun in 1983. From 1986 onwards, ESPRIT focused on artificial intelligence and expert systems. It funded a Siemens-Bull-ICL co-operative centre near Munich which promised completion of an artificially intelligent business decision-making expert system by 1990. This project seems to have sunk without a trace after eating up large amounts of cash. EUREKA, an acronym for yet another EEC science and technology support program, will presumably involve itself in AI and expert systems through the 1990s with further massive infusions of taxpayers' money.

Arthur D. Little, management consultants, estimated in the early 1980s that worldwide corporate and government spending for expert systems should reach $11 billion by 1990. A more conservative forecast by International Resource Development Inc. predicted that by 1993 there would be a global outlay of $8,835 million, whereas in February 1986 *Computing* magazine suggested that the European market alone would expand from $73 million in 1985 to $3.823 billion by 1990. None of these predictions materialized.

At this time few expert systems are available commercially. Those that are come in two forms. The first are tailor-made programs that can cost up to £100,000 each. The second are expert systems 'shells', each of which provides the procedural framework for a number of related applications. Some shells can be bought off the shelf from £50 to £4,000 and can run on standard micros and minis, whereas the more ambitious ones require mainframe computers.

While the idea of artificial intelligence has by now come in for a certain amount of scepticism, expert systems have hardly been questioned despite their limited successes. The main problem is that no distinction is made in computing between purely mechanical (finite, closed) and organic (open) systems. Expert systems have their uses when applied to inorganic (closed) processes, but organic (open) problems can never be solved by these means. Therefore, when expert systems techniques are seen as economically attractive alternatives to the creative exercise of human skills or intelligence in business, war and peace studies, education, translation, scientific research, medicine or psychiatry, they lead to a corruption of the decision-making process.

As shown elsewhere, omniscience in any subject is usually impossible.[AA] Expertise is therefore generally incomplete and depends far more on an understanding of principles, global and self-awareness or intuition, than on knowledge of all the facts. Because such an orientation demands understanding more than knowledge, a true expert can jump to correct conclusions provided he has enough facts at his fingertips. On the other hand, experts other than those who are globally aware and intuitive tend to perpetuate the established wisdom, no matter how wrong it may be. None of this is reassuring when it comes to trusting specialists, knowledge engineers and the expert systems they create.

For example, no knowledge engineer has ever asked whether there might be a difference between finding faults in a diesel-electric locomotive and medical diagnosis, or between a rote performer and a creative individual. (One is an assembly-line worker who can be replaced by a robot. The other is irreplaceable except by other creative human beings who are prepared to learn.) Knowledge engineers believe that creativity is simply a matter of arrangement and variation, of exhausting the brute-force sum of all possibilities (the monkey-at-the-typewriter principle), and that learning is a matter of operant conditioning. Knowledge engineers who try to formulate expertise of which true experts are no longer consciously aware and therefore find difficult to explain, often debase understanding and craft to probabilistic guessing or rote performance that can be mechanized and mimicked by a machine. The expertise required to diagnose, predict and prescribe for organic systems can never be delegated to machines.

Some expert systems work better than others. But whether or not a process works is not a test of its efficacy or value. As I said earlier, operant conditioning with reinforcement 'works', but it makes most people stupid. None the less, operant conditioning has its uses. The same is true of expert systems. Their usefulness depends on the appropriateness of the application. But even then such computer programs must be monitored by human beings and subject to human control.

The literature on expert systems is extensive. However, the books and articles dealing with this subject repeat the same success stories of a small number of programs, many of which are nearly two decades old and have been shelved for reasons that are usually not given. DENDRAL was one of the first programs to be called an expert system. It identifies chemical molecular structures and its performance is based on knowledge developed by human experts. The program does not allow a computer to make discoveries. It only provides a catalogue of what is known and conditional branching enables the computer to generate all possible variations. This, then, is a computer program that performs rote tasks successfully.

DELTA or CATS 1 diagnoses faults and suggests possible remedies in the maintenance of diesel-electric locomotives. It is a computerized maintenance manual based on

530 rules deduced from interviews with top engineers. It leads the user through step-by-step 'if ... then' repair procedures once a fault has been identified. There is nothing novel about such a service manual, except that this one is computerized and provides faster access to information than a book. It is the medium that is new and not the message. These conventional diagnostic procedures may speed up fault-finding but do not replace maintenance engineers, any more than a car-repair manual replaces a skilled garage mechanic.

Another family of expert systems deals with geological surveys. These help find underground mineral, gas and oil deposits. Their locations have been traditionally established by seismic resonance, a method discovered by J.C. Karcher in 1917. Karcher's techniques have since been refined but they remain unaltered in principle. The success rate for finding oil by this method is between 10 and 20 per cent. In other words, when the seismic survey suggests that a trial well might be worth digging, one or two out of ten wells drilled may produce oil in commercial quantities. PROSPECTOR mechanizes Karcher's methods. Its success rate is the same as that achieved in pre-computer days and its advantage lies solely in that it can display more information faster than was possible before. More locations can therefore be tested in greater detail and in a shorter period of time, but the same number of trial wells still need to be drilled.

These are expert systems that work, albeit in limited applications. None of them display what in human beings would be considered intelligence, although they encapsulate the knowledge of those whose expertise they reflect.

## Medical Expert Systems

Computerized medical diagnoses typify the flaws in the scientific method. They deal only with symptoms (i.e. the operations) without considering causes and consequences. This, of course, goes to the very heart of the problems of modern medicine. For to treat symptoms of illnesses like the common cold, cancer and mental disorders means to plaster them over without curing anything for as long as causes remain unknown or are insufficiently understood. Treating symptoms may alleviate discomfort, but a responsible physician tries to look further and deeper in order to discover and treat causes. The best a computer can do is to compare lists of programmed symptoms to those that are entered by the patient or diagnostician and then to suggest treatment. At worst this is quackery; at best, damage control that offers relief from suffering.

Medical expert systems are therefore extremely dangerous if used as substitutes for a conscientious physician's hands-on expertise. Besides, they are much slower than human diagnosticians. More than 50 per cent of human illness is probably psychosomatic, behaviourally, or environmentally caused. Further, the best medicine is preventive. No computer program could ever assess a patient's physical and psychological states or the circumstances in which he might live or work. The symptoms of congenital heart disease and those brought about by a stressful occupation or private life may be the same, but the treatment in each case should be very different. The distinctions that need to be made require sensitive diagnoses and penetrating insights based on personal contact between patient and physician. Going by the book (or a computer program) is no substitute.

Additionally, an increasing number of physicians combine conventional and alternative medicine. Which of these may be appropriate and when requires diagnoses more complex and subtle than any 'if . . . then' probabilistic diagnosis that may be enough to find faults in a diesel-electric locomotive. A medical diagnosis may include an assessment of a patient's will to live or his ability to change his behaviour, occupation or environment. Very often the best a conscientious physician can do is stimulate the self-repairing aspects of the human system. A patient has the right to an intuitive and global, rather than a rote diagnosis and to be treated as an individual rather than as a machine.

The existing tendency towards high-tech conveyor-belt medicine encourages the development and use of expert systems. Even at today's level of mechanical monitoring of patients (the excuse given is that it is less expensive and more reliable than nursing care), there have been cases where the medical staff relied on unattended monitors with fatal results. Computer diagnoses may seem attractive to inexperienced, over-worked and tired junior doctors or medical bureaucrats. Pressured young housemen may prefer referring to a computer rather than seeking the advice of consultants or talking to patients. Reliance on medical expert systems, except in unusual circumstances, could therefore stand in the way of the development of human expertise and responsibility. Who would be responsible for mistakes made by a machine's diagnosis: the physician whose expertise formed the basis for the program; the knowledge engineer who formulated the rules, options and inferences; the programmer who encoded them or the physician who relied on them? This raises legal questions that remain unanswered. Professor J.A. Campbell of Exeter University suggests that because the technology is complex and relatively untried, no one should be held to account for computer diagnostic errors. This is typical of the irresponsibility that surrounds the advocacy of expert systems.

CADUCEUS is a probabilistic medical diagnostic program said to cover 500 different diseases and more than 3,500 symptoms. It is alleged to incorporate more than 80 per cent of all knowledge in internal medicine. Like PUFF, MYCIN and other such programs, CADUCEUS is a computerized textbook that lists clusters of symptoms assumed to be associated with particular disorders. Such a program may be useful in medical schools and in situations where medical expertise is unavailable (for example, in a space capsule), but it hardly represents sound medical practice in most other situations.

Feigenbaum cites the case of an electrocardiograph (ECG) manufacturer whose machines, like any produced by his competitors, are accurate 75 per cent of the time.[73] The

25 per cent error is due to medical ignorance and individual human or mechanical variations. This manufacturer hoped to increase his share of the market by 30 per cent and his company's annual earnings by several million dollars by turning his ECG machines into computerized medical expert systems. He estimated that he could recover the cost of development in less than a year and believed that diagnostic accuracy could be increased by 10 per cent. Such a belief appears to have no basis in fact except as a promotional claim that is virtually impossible to verify. It is most likely an advertising hype that increases the manufacturer's profits and costs to physicians, patients and the state, but does not increase diagnostic efficiency. Such gimmickry fuels inflation and impoverishes everyone, except the producers of expert systems.

Expert diagnostic systems have even been used in psychiatry. A physician at London's Maudsley Hospital has 'perfected' a psychiatric diagnostic expert system that achieves an alleged 80 per cent success rate,[74] the same percentage of 'cures' as those he claims for his own personal treatment. Yet what constitutes a correct psychiatric diagnosis or cure is highly questionable because both are still matters of controversy even among the experts.

Medical and psychiatric diagnostic and prescribing machines might eventually take the place of machines that, in addition to telling your weight, used to dispense astrological forecasts on railway station platforms. Public medical diagnostic machines would be a boon to hypochondriacs and pharmaceutical companies and bring medicine out of the surgery and into the marketplace. This is where medical quackery began and to which it might return with the introduction of expert systems.

## Teaching Machines

Teaching and learning systems are among the most questionable applications of expert systems. There are two different approaches: Computer Assisted Instruction (CAI) and Computer Assisted Learning (CAL). Both have their uses in the training and rehabilitation of the mentally and physically handicapped. But the rationale for programmed teaching and learning as a preferred method of general education is grounded in the behaviourist school of psychology, of which the late B.F. Skinner was a spokesman. In *The Technology of Teaching*,[75] he shows that CAI and CAL have their roots in classical, Pavlovian operant conditioning.

Sydney L. Pressey developed a series of intelligence-testing machines in the US during the early 1920s that required children to press buttons to give rote answers to programmed questions. Teaching machines seemed attractive to governments that sought to economize on public education. They usually favour training rather than teaching children and young people to learn. Mechanized teaching continues to gain ground, represented as an educational revolution in the United States in the 1960s. It gave birth to O.K. Moore's Talking Typewriter, among other machines. Another, designed by Skinner, dispensed sweets when children gave the 'right' (i.e. the expected) answer by pressing the appropriate button – a direct application of Pavlov's famous dog experiment. The successes originally attributed to TV 'educational' programmes like *Sesame Street*, similar to those made for teaching machines and CAI, have been shown to be based on fraudulent research evaluations.[76] It turns out that they actually damage children's learning abilities as I predicted they would nearly twenty years ago. The harm done by rote-learning machines and programs that are used as substitutes for hands-on, human interactive learning is only now beginning to surface, as the second and third generations of children mature who received their early schooling sitting in front of TV sets. Any assessment of the damage done by CAI and CAL lies in the future.

The use of calculators in primary and early secondary school grades is yet another example of the danger of the mechanization of education. Children who have not learnt first to manipulate geometric shapes and numbers by hand can never learn or understand the concept of numbers (i.e. they are innumerate), even when they get the answers right by pushing buttons. Mechanized teaching methods and expert systems used in the classroom are manipulative and encourage rote learning and rote performance, even when the educational philosophy that goes with it is larded with the turned-on 'de-schooling' jargon of the 1960s.

The patterns that emerge from this examination of representative examples of expert systems allow them to be classified into useful, cosmetic and potentially harmful categories. At best, they facilitate or speed up rote labour. They cannot replace human expertise or serve as substitutes for human skills or intelligence. We are in deep trouble when rote performance is confused with learning or creativity. In game theory, psychology, language translation and prediction even human specialist expertise is questionable when meanings are not understood.[AA] This lack of understanding is common in other areas of so-called expertise because experts tend to follow in each other's footsteps and pass conventional knowledge on to students without testing or questioning the premises, methods or meanings on which it is based.

## Machine Translation

Computer scientists working in this field have been encouraged in their search for general machine translation by the fact that it is already possible up to a point, provided it is limited to defined and unambiguous vocabularies, grammars and syntax. Many of the world's intelligence agencies – GCHQ, NSA, the CIA and others – use computers to translate diplomatic, military and technical information. Industries with international markets use them for user manuals. But such translations require a great deal of editing by hand. Machine translations can lead to misunderstandings unless the meaning of every transactional word and phrase in one language can be matched to identical ones in another. Literary and poetic language, dialect, idiom, popular sayings, slang or humour can never be translated by machine. None of this, however, has prevented fruitless research and attempts to achieve such a pipe dream:

... 'We have not yet been able to build that universal understander,' said Roger Schank of Yale University, one of the leading researchers in the field. 'The language is simply too vast, there are too many meanings attributed to words,' said Roger Kittredge of the University of Montreal, a specialist in machine translation. Not that people aren't trying. Projects are under way in the United States that seek to have machines do text analysis, write summaries, answer questions about stored information and translate from one language into another. But there is considerable disagreement on how the problem should be approached. Some researchers say that they should determine how people do these things and then get computers to imitate them. Others say that is both unnecessary and wrong ... in one experiment a machine was asked to translate the sentence: 'The spirit is willing, but the flesh is weak' into Russian. Its translation: 'The vodka is good, but the meat is rotten.' ... 'Meaning is really in the mind of the reader and not on the paper,' said Evan Grenias, who heads IBM research in this area. The IBM program avoids the question of meaning for the time being and seeks only to analyze the text.[77]

If such opinions were to prevail no one could possibly know what anyone else was talking about, even when they spoke the same language. For more than a common vocabulary, the only ways for people to understand one another are via analyses and agreement as to what transactions actually mean in a given frame of reference. Without analyses of causes and consequences and agreement as to the true meanings of concepts we would all be speaking different languages, even when we use the same words. John Searle seems to be the only philosopher today who has come close to understanding this simple fact. But even he does not seem to know the meaning of meaning.[AA]

## The Creative Computer

It has even been suggested that computers can be creative in the arts[78] and that they can be programmed to write novels indistinguishable from those written by people.[79] But this reflects a misunderstanding of what is involved in creative work. Given a number of sub-plots and themes, a dictionary and a grammatical and syntactic program, a computer can produce a huge number of variations. It cannot, of course, add anything out of its own experience or imagination. Who needs a computer to do what hack writers have done for centuries? But unlike a competent hack, the computer cannot make any judgement as to which might be the most commercially viable version of its output. Where skilled human beings can churn out such trash with a minimum of trial and error, the computer would produce reams of gibberish before a usable variation emerges; a proposition foreseen by Jonathan Swift more than two hundred years ago (see Chapter 2). But even this would require considerable editing by hand before it could become a saleable commodity.

The difference between creative and hack performances or brute force (trying everything once) is exemplified by the example of an infinite number of marble blocks exposed to the wind and rain. The weather might turn one of these into Michelangelo's David, sooner or later. It could equally produce a Henry Moore sculpture, the statues on Easter Island, or forms that have not yet been thought of. Yet in the absence of intentional pattern recognition and purposive craft we could not consider the wind and the rain to be creative agents. Having formed what we might consider a masterpiece, the weather would continue to carve and destroy it in the same mindless manner in which it was brought into being. Recognizing the finished product of creativity and knowing when to stop are as important as its exercise.

If the computer could be a substitute for the artist, it would also be able to replace the creative scientist. Few scientific discoveries are the results of pure chance or brute force. Instead they are usually the products of selective, dedicated logic, observation and experiments. These are processes in which human feelings, intuition, global logic, jumps to conclusions, self- and global awareness, purposive action and valuative pattern recognition play essential roles, none of which computers can match.

## Pattern Recognition

Penicillin would have remained undiscovered without Sir Alexander Fleming's awareness of the problem and his recognition of a possible solution once it was generated. A sudden insight into what may have been a closed book in the past, an experiment that produces an unexpected result or one that is a fortuitous accident is never a chance event. The most important aspect of any discovery is that the discoverer has a purpose, is able to make value judgements and recognizes the *meanings* of what he has discovered or found.

As I have said, all human and animal behaviour is based on pattern recognition. Recognition means prescience because it is impossible to 'recognize' anything unless it was foreseen. Some behavioural patterns in organisms exist prior to birth (like IRMs); others are added through nurturance, maturation, play, autonomous learning and conditioning. Innate and acquired patterns are deeply embedded in the central nervous system, triggered by and matched to those in the outside environment depending on a combination of various forms of awareness and consciousness. The combinatorial possibilities are so great that no two human beings are alike. Human behaviour is therefore not merely a mechanical response to stimuli from the outside environment, but reflects an awakening of self- and global awareness, consciousness and conscience.

The product of these processes is an individual who differs from all other human beings in significant respects but has enough in common with them for social, sexual and economic intercourse. Machine behaviour, however, depends solely on a match between memories, commands and servo-mechanical input implanted by the human programmer. A computer cannot make any independent, intentional, purposive contribution, reflect or 're-cognize'. It has no innate, species-specific, archetypal or genetic memory accumulated through mutation, evolution and adaptation and no awareness of any kind. Therefore it can merely match images by approximation. Since it has no will it cannot choose between options. And although it might be able to construct a duplicate of itself, no evolutionary change could take place between one generation and the next without human intervention. The computer is a clean slate in every generation, awaiting its users' precise instructions. That is what makes it a useful, unthinking tool.

## Neural Networks in Computing

K. Zuse, a German electronics engineer, developed a computer one year after Turing's PhD thesis appeared, but, unlike later US and British machines, it lacked conditional branching and hence could only follow orders precisely (i.e. the German military ideal).[80] However, conditional branching in conventional computers generates variations that can achieve surprising results (see above; Minsky's proof for one of Euclid's theorems). The 'behaviour' of computerized control and guidance systems allows for many variations unless severely limited by programming. Given unlimited optional branching and external environmental variables, these conditions can create a nightmare of compounded 'accidents' as they have on more occasions than are publicly admitted. The bigger and faster concept of AI computing that is not constantly monitored by human beings, combined with a growing information glut and programming bugs, could be a recipe for disasters greater than those we have suffered in the past (for example, Three-Mile Island and Chernobyl), instead of giving us artificial intelligence or expert systems.

Conditional branching in modern computers simulates mechanical aspects of the human brain (i.e. reflexive jumps to conclusions). But the use of human intelligence depends on autonomous (i.e. unprogrammed) valuative choices as to the direction of the dataflow through the neural net's branches. This process cannot be matched by any machine. None the less, it has come to be believed that the neural network approach to artificial intelligence will succeed where other attempts have failed.

I have discussed neural nets earlier in a mathematical, philosophical and biological context (see Chapters 3 and 5). Here a very brief history of the concept is outlined in so far as computing is concerned. (The geometry of neural networks is explained elsewhere.[AA]) In Appendices A and D, I show how neural networks can be used to model the combinatorial aspects of every form of conditioning, programming and learning in causal, consequential and operational terms. Such a model appears to allow us to analyse what takes place in the human brain in analogous terms. But this model, like any other, is not a substitute for the real thing. On the contrary, it demonstrates that artificial intelligence is impossible, now or in any other future. None the less, the search continues in universities and elsewhere for neural networks that will make computers think and reason independently.

The idea of neural networks was first proposed in 1943[81] and again in 1957, but abandoned in favour of conventional AI research that led to dead ends by the late 1980s. Meanwhile the trend is to return to the neural network concept on to which claims made for AI are grafted.[82] But neural network research as defined in today's computer science is simply AI in a new disguise and will certainly fail for the same reasons. Institutions like Bell Laboratories, MIT, Stanford University, California's Institute of Technology, Sussex and Brunel Universities, London's Imperial College and MITI in Japan, among others, have simply continued looking for artificial intelligence, using a new jargon. In the journalese of AI promotion, the state of expectations in neural networks was summed up in 1987:

... apprehensive desk jockeys discovered that, despite closetloads of AI software, their IBM PCs were still as dumb as a toaster. Now, however, a radically new form of computer architecture and a revolutionary conception of synthetic thought are bringing the prospect close to reality:

- In Baltimore, a bucket of [computer] chips is teaching itself to read.
- In Cambridge [Mass.] and San Diego, blind wires are learning to see in three dimensions.
- In Pittsburgh, terminals are talking to each other.
- And suddenly in laboratories across the country [US], formerly dreary and docile computers are becoming quirky, brilliant and inscrutable.[83]

A *New Scientist* article, published in 1988, said: 'If computers are organized more like brains, will they behave more like brains? . . . The goal is to build a neural computer or "neurocomputer", in which processors take on the role of neurons . . .'[84]

Igor Aleksander, head of an information technology unit at London's Imperial College, claims to have been at work on neural network research for the past twenty years. He is co-developer of Wisard, a pattern-matching system (erroneously described as a visual recognition method) that, unlike the human optical system, works on probabilistic principles. Aleksander expressed the absurd hope that neural networks will lead to 'an improvement in natural language understanding machines',[85] a goal sought by AI researchers since the 1950s. By 1988 it was claimed that 180 companies were at work world-wide developing neural network projects, twenty of which marketed products that are supposed to make computers intelligent.[86]

In the light of these perpetually repeated self-delusions or entirely unwarranted claims, it was therefore not surprising that the Pentagon allocated $2–3 billion to neural network research in 1989. The sum of £350,000 was provided by the British Government to Imperial College in that same year in the hope of discovering a computer that understands (i.e. decodes the meanings of) what it 'sees', 'hears' and prints out – the thinking computer, the machine-man, and the apotheosis of exclusively mechanistic and materialistic sciences and societies.

Whenever positive demonstrations show that AI is impossible, believers and academic opportunists drag out the old saw about human flight having been considered impossible only 200 years ago. But we must accept that some things are simply impossible, now or in any future. Besides, human flight is still impossible. Flight can be emulated by machines, subject to human control, but this is very different from the autonomous flight of birds and insects. I venture to predict that no human being will ever fly like either, as demonstrated by the Greek legend of Icarus. Like genuine non-mechanical human flight, a machine that thinks or makes decisions like a human being is and always will be impossible for all the reasons given. But the search for the thinking machine is not just a costly error or research racket. It is indicative of a deep-seated psychological malaise that affects most of us today.

The AI concept, sponsored by governments, industry and academics worldwide, provides the basis for the continuation of a disastrous religious, philosophical, scientific and educational tradition. AI researchers may have been severely shaken by the collapse of Japan's Fifth Generation project but they survive by ignoring this fact. Indeed in the sciences, technologies and education this is something we can no longer afford, given the state of the global economy and ecology. As this book goes to press, a convincing revelation is Japan's planned *Sixth Generation* computer research program to discover neural network artificial intelligence. There is a possibility of a massive contribution of US millions.[87] If this fails to achieve its promised objectives, as it must, we can probably look forward to the seventh, eighth and further generations of computers that their sponsors hope and believe, perhaps subconsciously, will replace or enslave us completely. Those whom the Gods would destroy they first drive mad.

The mechanistic idea of AI in new disguises is therefore still widely touted as heralding a social and economic millennium by those who are too blinkered to learn or who hope that the AI fraud will pay their way until retirement. No doubt we will see the end of strong AI sooner or later. The real question is, how long will it take to reverse the psychological damage done by our corrupted and corrupting hard and soft sciences of which the man-machine myth and strong AI are symptoms rather than causes?

# Conclusion

In my previous book I showed that there is a new and unconventional way of looking at human behaviour that is highly predictive.[AA] Here I have applied what seems to be the grand unification theory (GUT), defined by the combinatorial method, to today's sciences and technologies. My object has been to encourage others to apply it to whatever interests them most.

This method has so far produced a number of novel results – the unravelling of the game enigma, of the semantic, learning, many-body, prime-number and time problems, and, most important as far as all branches of science are concerned, the relationship between randomness and chance. In addition, it has led to the proposal of a number of theories that still need to be tested. The method appears to work for anything to which I have applied it, suggesting that it is a general one because it allows us to extract meanings.

The demonstrations indicate that today's scientific method is severely flawed, concentrating as it does on the 'how' to the exclusion of the 'why'. The result has been the promotion of essentially mechanistic, purely materialistic, rather than subjective and human-centred solutions, many of which may work in the short run but are disastrous in the long term.

Perhaps the most satisfying and optimistic conclusion to be drawn from what I have discovered is that there is always more than a single solution to every problem, some better than others and more right than wrong ones. The combinatorial method indicates that there exists a far greater number of possibilities in every field of endeavour than is generally suspected, providing us with immense diversity and opportunities for the future. Thus if we choose one of the correct options in any application we could stand on the threshold of a new beginning.

# Appendices

The demonstrations given in the Appendices should enable anyone with a basic background in mathematics to test many of the contentions made in this book. Greater detail is provided in cited papers.

*Appendix A* discusses differences between combinatorial analytic methods and conventional ones. The mathematics are given in *Winners*,[AA] but the geometry is shown in Appendix D.

*Appendix B* illustrates the 'memory and information as fundamental particle theory' that may explain the 'dark matter' in the universe, as discussed in Chapter 5.

*Appendix C* deals with the three-dimensional nature of time/space, showing that time is not a fourth dimension in a literal, geometric sense. Navigation, mapping, targeting and jet-lag applications demonstrate that time, relative to space and motion, is three dimensional like everything else in the universe.

*Appendix D* shows that the combinatorial method provides the geometric definition for all forms of programming, conditioning and learning. As a result, we can now trace the operations of every kind of conditioning, its causes and the consequences to which each leads in a scientific manner.

*Appendix E* describes work-in-progress and a new approach to the prime-number problem. The distribution of primes (i.e. numbers that are divisible only by 1 and by themselves) and their composites (i.e. any prime number multiplied by one or more other primes) are shown to follow precise geometric, repetitive patterns, each unique for every prime and its composites but all containing common character-istics. This is one demonstration of the kind of order that underlies seeming randomness. It also reduces drastically the number of operations required for factorization and for the establishment of primality.

# Appendix A:
# The Combinatorial
# Method

Combinatorial methods (geometry, mathematics and analyses) underlie all claims made in this book. They permit deep insights into causes, consequences and the operations that bring both about. The geometry, maths and the classification method are given in *Winners*[AA] and are partially shown here in Appendix D. But some comments are required to explain the differences between combinatorial methods and more conventional ones that involve only permutations.

Combinatorial analysis also shows the possible relationships between the workings of systems relative to any external environment, whatever that may be. This method appears to work for everything. Hence the claim that this may be the Grand Unification Theory. This enlarges the sum of possibilities and transactions that can be isolated and considered. Relationships of any kind can be represented by means of directed graphs as I have done in this book. These can be quantified by means of combinatorial mathematics and generalized algebraically as shown in *Winners* (see Appendices A and B)[AA]. The internal relationships (e.g. intentions that are always causal) are invisible in reality, but can now be modelled and explained in terms of their operations and consequences. I have applied this method to games of strategy and chance and analogous human behaviours, to semantics[AA], to learning and conditioning (see Appendix D), to prime numbers (see Appendix E), to the so-called many-body problem in physics, the DNA, the central nervous system and computer programming. In each instance I have found that combinatorial analysis either confirms existing knowledge or provides new answers to questions that remained unresolved until now. Combinatorial analysis makes it possible to look at small systems as a whole in a way that was previously impossible, and to isolate representative examples for detailed analysis of systems too large to be considered as a whole. This appears to be a model of the universe as we perceive it. Combinatorial methods seem more powerful than any others that are used in modern science.

Currently permutations are believed to constitute a sum of all possibilities. Permutations permit a systematic and finite rearrangement of any given sequence of facts or events. For example, the letters ABCD or the numbers from 1 to 4 can be rearranged permutationally in only twenty-four different ways (e.g. ABCD, ACDB, ADCB . . .). All possibilities can be said to have been calculated and exhausted once every permutation is accounted for. But this is an incomplete series for several reasons. The permutational sequence as a whole is considered but not its parts. Permutational calculations for four facts (ABCD) exclude A, AB, BA, ABC . . . However, viewed combinatorially, four facts or events generate a finite sum of 256 possibilities, a considerable enlargement (see Appendix D) that can provide deep insights into otherwise hidden processes.

For example, in the game of noughts and crosses the standard permutational sum (362,880) includes only games played to the last turn. (The mathematical expression is 9!, representing $9 \times 8 \times 7 \ldots \times 1$) These calculations exclude games that end earlier for any reason. The actual number of permutations, including partial ones that are never accounted for conventionally, should be larger than two times and smaller than three times 9!.

Even this larger permutational sum of all possibilities does not describe anything of value. The permutations of possible moves and counter-moves reveal nothing about the players' strategies and intentions (i.e. their invisible, black-box behaviours) that are crucial in predicting the outcome of any game or gamelike relationship.

But the combinatorial method – by means of a considerable enlargement of possibilities to 618,475,290,624 – discloses not only how both players make their moves in this game, but also why; the causes and consequences of their intentions, tactics (plans) and strategies (moves), whatever these might be for all possible games from the first turn to the last. This method has been known but not classified or understood until now. It generates not only all permutations for any given set of events (ABCD, as shown above), but also those for every smaller set that is included (e.g. A, AB, ABC . . .). Additionally, every permutation within this combinatorial sum of possibilities repeats a number of times, creating a high number of seeming redundancies. Why this should be so was never understood previously. However, the classified combinatorial method shows that internal and external variations in the dataflow (i.e. the changes in the direction of the arrows on the diagrams shown in Appendix D) make for subtle differences that cannot be extracted and analysed by any other method.

With classification of combinatorial sums (see Appendix D and *Winners*[AA]) every repeated permutation can be shown to be individually unique. That uniqueness depends on the options the dataflow provides, defined by conditional branching in the system and the possible relationships between 'internal' and 'environmental' factors and their permutations. Each diagram in Appendix D is a directed combinatorial 'graph' in which the arrows determine the conditional branching and possible options for the direction of the dataflow in any infinite series of finite systems (any systematically ordered or random series of events, like ordered or shuffled packs of cards or particles).

However, classified combinatorial methods pose problems for the conventional scientist and mathematician. Most seem to have a vested interest in and prefer to stick to methods they know (even when these might be flawed), rather than learn something new. At the same time most non-scientists and mathematicians are put off by mathematics and prefer other methods for arriving at conclusions. This is understandable, for there is no reason for everyone to be mathematically inclined. The truth, as far as we can ascertain it, can be reached by a path so wide and varied that it includes intuition and feelings as well as language and numbers. Numbers happen to be the most precise yardstick we have and that is why they are useful for scientific analysis. Anyone who claims an interest in the sciences can penetrate and understand the combinatorial method, but only by working and applying it.

# Appendix B:
# The Three-dimensional Universe

Current theories in physics suggest that between 90 and 98 per cent of all matter in the universe is invisible and consists of so called 'black matter'. This implies that we can physically sense only a tiny fraction of reality. The substructure of energy and matter may consist of what I call 'memories' and 'information'. This, in essence, is a view of the universe suggested by information theory.

Thus one-dimensional memory particles might be the invisible energy source of the universe and its fundamental building blocks. By their combination and recombination they could be the basis of all two-dimensional information and three-dimensional matter in the cosmos. Such a theory may account not only for space, energy and matter, but also for intangible and invisible aspects of nature, including time, awareness, conditioning, programming, learning and behaviour[AA] (see also Appendix D).

None of this is as far-fetched as it may sound. We know that amino-acid combinations contain information that combinatorially translates itself into genes, chromosomes, protein and eventually into cells, organs and organisms. It is therefore reasonable to suggest that the same principle might be true for all evolutionary processes of nature – inorganic and organic.

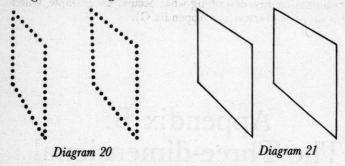

*Diagram 20*     *Diagram 21*

Diagram 20 shows an arrangement of one-dimensional particles. While invisible, they can be represented as a series of dots that occupy points in space but have no width, length or breadth. If we consider them as individual 'memory' particles they have no meaning until they affiliate with others. This is rather like any letter of the alphabet that has no meaning until it is affiliated with others and thus becomes a word. Diagram 21 shows that with affiliations in particular ways, one-dimensional memories can turn into a two-dimensional information slice (a line, a square or any other two-dimensional shape that has no material substance).

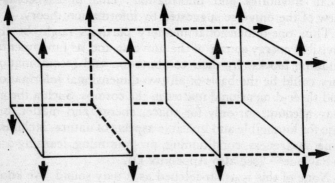

*Diagram 22*

Diagram 22 shows how two two-dimensional information slices can be joined to represent three-dimensional space and matter.

This model may perhaps describe what happens in nature. Two-dimensional data slices are added to form an extended three-dimensionality, describing what occurs, for example, when time is an added factor (see Appendix C).

# Appendix C:
# The Three-dimensionality of Time

The principles of navigation are used here to demonstrate the three-dimensionality of time, that the arrow of time always points towards the future (no matter what a clock may show), and the principles that underlie relative certainty and uncertainty. These demonstrations are directly related to aspects of relativity, quantum theory and causal/consequential analysis. They indicate that all of nature is three-dimensional and precise. Only our lack of knowledge, wrong analytic and diagnostic techniques, as well as our instruments and methods of measurement (e.g. statistical analyses) create uncertainties.

Time can be represented one-, two- or three-dimensionally. Elapsed, subjective (clock) time is two dimensional (i.e. it is pure information and has no three-dimensional characteristics). But time used to establish any location or position in space, relative to motion (on earth this is the inertial dead-reckoning method of navigation), is part of a three-dimensional space, time and motion continuum. Space, motion and time are inseparably interlinked. Without space there can be no motion and without both there can be no time.

The mistaken idea that time is a fourth dimension is based on the fact that when you establish any fixed position in space you need three co-ordinates (one each for height, length and width). These are represented in Diagram 23. It is erroneously believed that time is described by extra co-ordinates added at right-angles to the original three (see Diagram 24). This, while a fourth factor, does not constitute a fourth geometric dimension. Therefore the concept of a greater-than-three-dimensional universe is a fiction.

As discussed in Chapter 5, the concept of a multi-dimensional universe (i.e. greater than three dimensions) may be due to a mistranslation of Einstein's work. Whatever the cause of this misunderstanding may have been, a great many people today within and outside the sciences believe that time is a fourth dimension in a geometric sense. However, this is impossible. Our universe is entirely three dimensional and even its invisible components (e.g. time or psychological factors) can only be represented geometrically in one-, two- or three-dimensional terms. Any factors added to the three co-ordinates of space do not alter its three-dimensional characteristics, but create an extended three-dimensionality. This is demonstrated by the following:

Time relative to motion in space from any point of departure to a present or future position in a particular heading is best represented three-dimensionally. Inertial

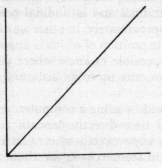

*Diagram 23*
Three-dimensional space
co-ordinates

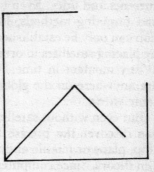

*Diagram 24*
The so-called 'fourth'
dimension

and dead-reckoning navigation would not be possible if this were otherwise. These three-dimensional characteristics of time, space and motion do not seem to have occurred to anyone from the time of the earliest map-makers and navigators to the present.

As James Jeans said (see Chapter 5), navigation can be a useful analogy for Heisenberg's uncertainty principle. Absolute navigational or positional certainty in practice is impossible because even the most accurate instruments of measure have a built-in error of plus/minus .5 of whatever unit of measure is used. However, absolute theoretical precision and certainty are possible, provided the theory is complete.

In the past, and prior to radio-direction finding, navigation by radar or satellite, various methods were used to fix positions on earth. The most common one consisted of establishing latitude by measuring the sun's position above the horizon at noon and then comparing it to sun tables in which the sun's position is given at that hour for each day of the year at any latitude. It was not until the end of the seventeenth century that relatively precise methods for establishing longitude were first discovered.[1] Before then, approximate longitude was established by calculations involving elapsed time from the point of departure, compass heading and estimated speed, relative to winds, currents and tides. Even today, using satellite navigational and targeting methods, longitudinal and latitudinal position can only be established approximately. In other words, by placing satellites in orbit, the position of which is known at any moment in time, it is possible to know where you are anywhere on the globe, but only up to an accuracy of some yards.

But even without satellites and by using a computer, you can discover the precise local time directly beneath any ship, plane or missile and then know exactly where you are – in theory. Since computers and atomic clocks are about as accurate as anything can be at present, we can now establish local time to the nearest micro-second. But additional information is needed for positional accuracy, including

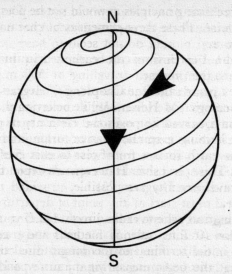

*Diagram 25*: Three-dimensional longitudinal space time spiral

speed of travel, heading, countervailing influences (tides, winds and currents), altitude and trajectory in the case of planes or rockets. We can enhance our navigational accuracy indefinitely as we discover better information and more precise instruments to measure these various factors. None the less, time is the key to position-finding. Only a full understanding of the basic principles involved in navigation provides accurate dimensional characteristics of time relative to space and motion in any context.

Inertial and dead-reckoning navigational methods depend on the intersection of long- and latitudinal time/space co-ordinates at any point on earth or in space, relative to the direction and velocity of motion. In order to demonstrate this principle, it is necessary to define the geometry of longitudinal time (see Diagram 25) relative to the earth's rotation starting from any point of departure, and latitudinal time (see Diagram 26) relative to the flattening of the earth at the poles, easterly or westerly heading, speed of travel and other variables. A different co-ordinate matrix is needed for navigation beyond the earth's atmosphere, but the same time principles apply in space. The following diagrams demonstrate these principles but are not geometrically precise.

Longitudinal earth time can be defined in the following manner. Imagine yourself travelling at 500 m.p.h. from either pole towards the equator along 0° degree longitude (i.e. the Greenwich Meridian). While believing that you are travelling in a curved line over the earth's surface you are actually describing a spiral, relative to longitudinal time, because the earth rotates from west to east every twenty-four hours. This spiral shrinks or expands depending on the speed of travel (see Diagram 25).

This spiral must start at any point of departure and end at the destination, wherever that might be. If you departed from London (0° longitude; 51.1 north) and travelled due north, the initial terminal of this longitudinal time spiral would lie at the beginning of your journey and work its way round the globe in a northerly direction towards your destination.

However, latitudinal earth-time is defined by headings in westerly or easterly directions. Imagine yourself starting from London and travelling in every westerly *and* easterly direction at 500 m.p.h. All points at which you could arrive after one hour's travel will form an ellipsoid of which the point of departure is the centre (because the earth flattens towards the poles – see Diagram 26). Had you started at the Equator and travelled west and east in all directions, the possible points of arrival after one hour at any given speed would be described by a nearly circular figure.

Now let us superimpose the longitudinal and latitudinal time graphs (remembering that we are travelling at 500 m.p.h. for demonstration purposes, for the longitude and latitudinal time configurations would change at greater or lesser speeds). Depending on your point of departure (London in this instance), heading (south-west to New Orleans), and countervailing influences after one hour's travel, you are wherever the spiral and ellipse intersect. Longitude and latitude are then established all along the way on the basis of time at that moment and place directly under the plane.

If a computer is programmed with this configuration, and allowing for continuous entry of variables like changes in speed, heading, lateral and vertical motion, a continuous track will be recorded consisting of points where the spiral and ellipse intersect. This, then, will give you long- and latitude at intervals of your choosing.

If we departed from London by plane at a known time and flew to New Orleans (see Diagram 27), the intersection of the spiral and ellipsoid would provide the local time (and hence position) directly beneath the plane as precisely as our knowledge of countervailing influences and the accuracy of our instruments allow. The computer could display or print out a second-to-second or minute-to-minute positional track on an appropriate map or chart.

All of this and the necessary peripherals can be built into any computer. Using this system, a ship could theoretically 'kiss the dock' with the windows of the bridge blacked out, or a plane could land blind in total fog or at night without landing lights and not miss the runway – were it not for the unknowns and built-in instrumental error concerning the measurement of speed, winds, tides and other variables. However – and this is the point of this demonstration – time, like everything else in the universe, extends the essential and unalterable three-dimensionality of space,

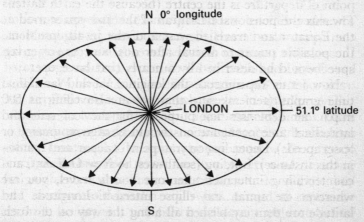

*Diagram 26*: Latitudinal time definition

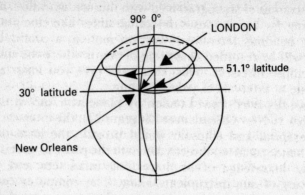

*Diagram 27*: Combined longitude and latitudinal time fix for travel from London to New Orleans. Note that the longitudinal time spiral here represents 3,728 miles per 7.27 hours and that 90° longitude is distorted for clarity's sake

subject to Einstein's theory of relativity. Further, uncertainty is a measure of our ignorance and instrumentational inexactitude and not a characteristic of the universe. These principles are elaborated elsewhere.[2]

# Jet-lag and Time Disorientation

The three-dimensional definition of the time-space-motion continuum also reveals the cause of the jet-lag problem. Inconclusive studies to discover the cause and cure of jet-lag have been conducted in all countries that have operated trans- or inter-continental airlines since World War II.[3]

The solution of the jet-lag problem also confirms the main theme of this book: the inadequacy of scientific methods that concentrate on the study of symptoms (i.e. operations) without consideration of causes and consequences. As a result, millions have been wasted in fruitless studies of metabolic rates and other physiological variations in human, day/night related bio-rhythms. The jet-lag problem may seem trivial, but it is typical of much larger issues.

In the US it was realized only as late as 1965 that north–south flights, while fatiguing depending on duration, could not possibly induce jet-lag. Even then this discovery was preceded by extensive flight, metabolic, anal temperature, heart-beat and other clinical tests (i.e. looking at symptoms), when common sense could have revealed the time-related cause.[4] A \$2 million 1980 NASA research effort was still inconclusive about the causes of east–west flight jet-lag.[5] The methods used in these studies were inappropriate and largely nonsensical because the causal, three-dimensional characteristics of time and its psychological and physiological effects on organic systems were not understood. The symptoms of jet-lag are products of local time conditioning. But it was never considered how time conditioning could be deconditioned and readjusted to the time-zonal habits prevailing at any destination. The most impractical and potentially dangerous jet-lag 'cures' like sleeping pills and other inappropriate treatment of symptoms are still periodically proposed.

Jet-lag (the consequences) badly affects some pilots, cabin crews, astronauts and most long-distance flight passengers. A variation of this syndrome causes stress in night workers. Jet-lag can cause pilot error and accidents. When flying for more than four hours east or west at great speeds, those who live by the clock (like pregnant women, many elderly people, and those who need regular medication) may suffer acute psychological and physiological disturbances. On arrival at their destination those who are prone to jet-lag can become physically ill, irritable, drowsy and restless, and their sleep, hunger and metabolic cycles can be severely affected. Their ability to make critical judgements can be disturbed for days and sometimes weeks, and people may suffer difficulties caused by additional stress like personal and on-the-job crises and foreign languages, currencies and ways of life. They can also become accident-prone. Jet-lag can therefore cause serious problems.

There are any number of ways to ameliorate jet-lag so that it has minimal or no effect, except for people on medication, or those who live slavishly by the clock. But this can be done only by understanding the causes. One of the simplest (although not entirely effective) methods is to set your watch on departure to the current time at the point of destination and eat and sleep aboard according to that time. Another is to adapt to the time zone that prevails at your destination a day or two before departure and to eat and sleep according to that schedule until your arrival. A third and most effective method would be an on-board clock programmed to tell the time directly beneath the plane in flight, so that passengers eat and sleep (and the cabin would be lit or darkened) according to the time told on this clock. Passengers would slide into the new time zone with minimal or no jet-lag on arrival. The reduction of jet-lag would be considerable on any western flight of four or more hours' duration, but less so on easterly flights because here clock time is shrunk rather than expanded. The shrinkage of clock time is more difficult to compensate for than expanded time. (I have designed and copyrighted a program for such a clock and a personal watch.)

The Russians use one version of this jet-lag amelioration technique that works only for pilots and cabin staff who are greatly inconvenienced by it.[6] On landing, crews must stay at a local hotel where they turn day into night and continue to live according to Moscow time. Obviously this is impractical for passengers.

The British Pilots and Navigators Guild agreed that my jet-lag solution is indeed the best one possible, but said that it was not likely to be implemented because airlines profit by competing with one another by offering frequent meals, selling wines, spirits and duty-free goods, and showing films at inappropriate times, thus making jet-lag worse for everyone. It seems that they have a vested interest in not ameliorating jet-lag for their passengers. Further, the BPNG felt that cabin-crew unions would resist the required changes in working conditions, even though this might mean less work and the elimination of jet-lag for them;[7] proof that operant conditioning makes people resistant to learning and change, even when it is in their own best interest. It is worth noting that de-conditioned, undogmatic adults, those not suffering from the aforementioned conditions, and many young children usually have no trouble adjusting to time-zonal differences caused by long-distance flight without psychological or other aids.

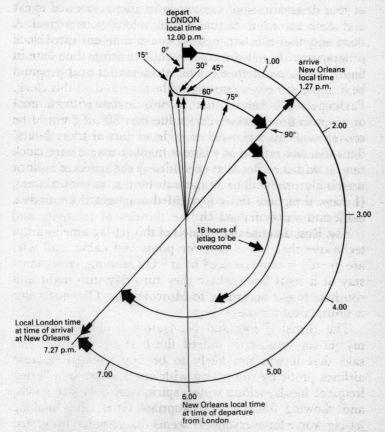

*Diagram 28*: The amount of jet-lag suffered and the required passenger adjustments concerning on-board eating and sleeping times are shown, relative to the elapsed times of flight for the postulated 500 m.p.h. trips from London to New Orleans and return. Note the apparent reversal of clock time between 0° and 30° longitude.

The conditions that lead to jet-lag are illustrated by a representative flight from London to New Orleans, plotted as a two-dimensional time graph derived from the three-dimensional demonstration given earlier (see Diagram 27). For the sake of simplicity, the average speed of the aircraft is presumed to be 500 m.p.h. throughout and, for the purposes of this demonstration, variations in speed, rates of climb and descent, wind direction and velocities are ignored. Naturally flights in other directions at different speeds and of longer or shorter duration require different calculations using the same methods. The mathematics and program that apply are given elsewhere.[8]

Diagram 28 shows that in this instance clock time appears to flow backwards for the first 30° of flight, even while subjective, elapsed time flows forward as always. This demonstrates that whatever a clock may demonstrate (e.g. it will slow down at speeds near the speed of light or seemingly reverse time in other instances, as shown here), the arrow of time flows forward throughout the universe, subject to laws defined by the theories of relativity and conditional determinism.

# Appendix D:
# The Combinatorial Neural Network Applied to Learning and Conditioning

Combinatorial geometry provides a model of how and why we think because it represents every form of conditioning and programming, including the strategies required for learning. In conventional science a model serves to explain a concept as the double helix is thought to represent the DNA and isobars the weather. In the combinatorial neural network model this process is reversed, for whatever it explains is generated by rather than imposed on it. It seems to confirm what we know but also provides insights that fly in the face of the established wisdom.

The geometric and mathematical principles that underlie the combinatorial neural network are detailed in Appendices to *Winners*[AA] and outlined in Appendix A. The geometric aspects are demonstrated below in Diagram 31 in which four 'facts' are arranged as a directed combinatorial graph.

Each arrow, reversed in turn in relation to all others in succeeding patterns that make up this graph, provides the combinatorial sum of all possibilities. A finite sum of sixty-four such patterns is generated in diagram 31 when '1' is used as the starting point for every pattern (or 265 when all four numbers are used in such a manner), a considerably enlarged sum compared to the permutational one. As explained in Appendix A, the combinatorial sum includes all permutations, but each repeats a calculable number of times. Every redundant permutation is unique in so far as choices for the dataflow are concerned because of optional branching. This method also permits relationships to be established between 'internal' and 'external' conditions in any context, for example that between any sequence and the rest of a pack of fifty-two playing cards or between an organism and its environment.

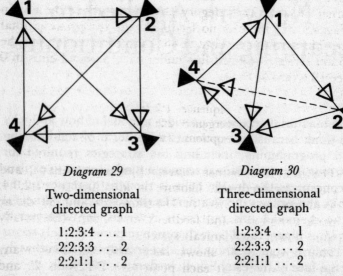

| *Diagram 29* | *Diagram 30* |
| :---: | :---: |
| Two-dimensional directed graph | Three-dimensional directed graph |
| 1:2:3:4 . . . 1 | 1:2:3:4 . . . 1 |
| 2:2:3:3 . . . 2 | 2:2:3:3 . . . 2 |
| 2:2:1:1 . . . 2 | 2:2:1:1 . . . 2 |

The numbers beneath the diagrams are criteria for analyzing dataflow

I have chosen four factors for demonstration purposes because, as the physicist Eddington thought, four factors are the minimal number required to reach any meaningful conclusion. But, as he admitted, he did not know the reason why: 'We use four numbers [in any analytic coordinate system concerning relationships] because it turns out that ultimately the structure [we wish to analyse] can be brought into better order that way; but we do not know why this should be so.'[1]

What escaped Eddington is that the number four is the first in the hierarchy of numbers that can be represented either two- or three-dimensionally in geometric terms – as a square divided by diagonals (see Diagram 29) or as a three-sided pyramid (see Diagram 30).

To return to an explanation of Diagrams 29 and 30: these are *feedback* dataflow patterns.

Dataflow criteria for *feedback* apply only to Category 2 (see patterns below the black line in Diagram 31). The three dots after each line indicate feedback to one or another corner or node. In Category 1 (patterns above the line in Diagram 31) there is no feedback, the *convergence* is total (i.e. four arrows converge at one or another node) and the option series (the third line under each pattern) ends in 0 (see Diagram 31):

$$\text{sequence: } 1:2:3:4 \ldots$$
$$\text{convergence: } 2:2:3:3 \ldots$$
$$\text{options: } 2:2:1:1 \ldots$$

- The first line defines *sequence* (i.e. permutation), and closure or feedback. Closure is identified by 1:2:3:4, feedback by 1:2:3:4 ... Diagrams 29 and 30 define perfect sequence and feedback in a closed (i.e. totally conditioned, mechanical) system.
- The second line shows *convergence*; i.e. how many arrows converge at each point (see Diagrams 29 and 30) in the order given in the sequence line (see above). The information contained in the arrows converges on 1, 2, 3 or 4. These convergences have definable meanings, depending on context. This is therefore a second self-defining criterion for analysing conditioned behaviours, their causes, operations and consequences, modelled by each of the sixty-four patterns in Diagram 31.
- The third line defines the number of *options* for the continuation of the dataflow (e.g. 3:2:1:0 for closed

patterns and 1:1:2:2 . . . for feedback ones) in the given sequence (see above). Note that all graphs with feedback feed back to 1 with relatively rare exceptions (see Diagram 31, H7 and H8). Closure means termination and zero options for continuation of the dataflow and only applies to Category 1).

The four factors of any sequence in these representations stand for:

1   the self that affects or is affected by the environment, a machine that can only be conditioned, or a human being who only thinks or does as he or she is told.
2   Any letter of the alphabet, number, word, sentence, book or subject.
3   A different, but related letter, word, sentence, book or subject.
4   The conclusion, outcome, goal, objective or consequences in a closed or feedback situation (e.g. winning, losing and conventional stalemates are closed situations in games or in any other context; a draw of which the meanings are understood can lead to perpetual feedback in any enlarged universe of discourse).

Diagram 31 models the combinatorial sum of all possibilities for 4 facts, when 1 is the starting point. This sum is four times larger when any other point (2, 3, and 4) is also used as the starting point. As shown by the heavy black line separating Diagram 31, this sum can be divided into 2 categories (closure and feedback). Additionally, these two categories can be divided into families (see below) that are not identified on Diagram 31 for reasons of space.

Applying this combinatorial, analytic method to conditioning of any kind, each graph and family of graphs models the possible relationships between whoever or whatever is to be conditioned (the self: 1), what is to be trained or programmed (2 and 3) and the objective (his, her or its goal or the consequences: 4) – in other words 'how' and 'why'. The arrows (i.e. the external ones at each point and those that lie on diagonals and that lead internally from point

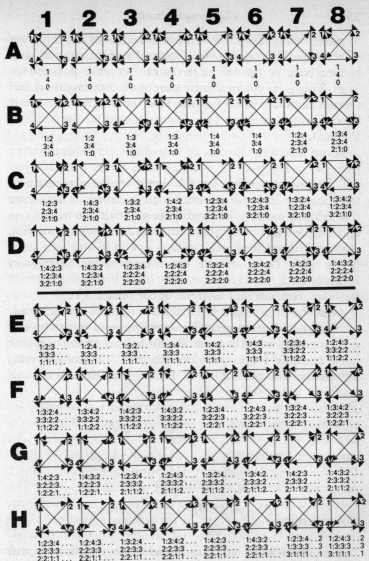

*Diagram 31*: The sum of all combinatorial possibilities for every form of conditioning or programming involving four factors. This graph is divided into two categories: Category 1, closed patterns (above the line) and Category 2, feedback patterns (below the line). These two categories can be subdivided into eleven families (see below).

to point) show the possibilities of external input, direction of dataflow, the available choices for continuation and convergence, or closure or feedback. No other possibilities exist. This is therefore a finite sum of all combinatorial and relational possibilities for any form of programming and conditioning involving four factors including the self and the goal.

If you follow the arrows on any of the sixty-four different patterns in Diagram 31, starting with 1 (i.e. the self), you will find more options for the directional continuation of the dataflow in some patterns than in others. This shows that certain patterns of conditioning provide more options and others fewer ones. Some come to an absolute stop (i.e. closure without feedback); others continue and feed back to the self. These criteria are shown in the three lines beneath each pattern. They are the self-defining criteria for interpretation and analysis of the meanings.

All of the foregoing defines forms of operant conditioning, training or programming. However some of the sixty-four patterns shown in Diagram 31 can be turned into genuine open learning loops, provided there is autonomous goal definition, the possibility of future goal definition, and feedback to the self (see Diagram 32).

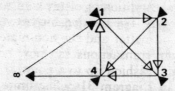

*Diagram 32*: The learning pattern

This method of analysis mimics the dataflow in our central nervous system relative to the external world of experience, providing us with all the options there are in any given context. This is a domain-defined, infinitely expandable, combinatorial and relational model, based on genetic, evolutionary and neural principles. It can be used to define the meanings (i.e. causes, consequences and the operations that bring both about) for any form of conditioning. The vast number of options thus generated can be confusing, just as it would be if we were to 'mind' everything that goes on around us. This is one reason why the analysis of conditioning methods is limited here to four facts and why I describe only each of the eleven families rather than all sixty-four individual patterns or states (see below).

One of the properties of this model is that it seems to reflect the relationship between relatively objective (closed) and subjective (feedback) processes and options. The graphs above the heavy line in Diagram 31 lead to *closure*; those below the line to *feedback*. With any enlargement of this paradigm (i.e. when the number of nodes is increased to 5, 6, 7 . . .) the proportion of subjective (feedback) to relatively objective (closed) patterns increases exponentially (i.e. geometrically). Thus it can be shown that in any complex system, subjective options outnumber relatively objective ones by far.

All of reality is divided into these main categories. This approach achieves what Bertrand Russell, Joseph Needham and many others believed to be impossible – geometric demonstrations, mathematical quantification, algebraic generalizations and definitions of qualitative value judgements.[AA] The principles that govern neural networks place the study of conditioning of any kind and learning on a truly scientific basis. The relationship between the tangible material world of matter and the non-material, subjective aspects of human transactions can now be demonstrated definitively in this fashion up to a point.

All patterns in Diagram 31 define finite mechanical or pseudo-mechanical systems (i.e. totally conditioned) ones; none obtains for open, organic ones (i.e. true human learning). True learning requires autonomy and a goal-defined 'open' system with perpetual feedback, as shown in Diagram 32.

Certain aspects of combinatorial geometry have been known for a very long time, going back to *ca.* 500 B.C. in China. However, the dataflow patterns it generates were not classified until now into categories, groups, families and individually unique states, expressed geometrically and mathematically or analysed logically so that their true meanings could be extracted. As a result of classification this is a highly predictive method. In this appendix I apply it to an analysis of every kind of conditioning as described in Chapter 6 and show how causes, consequences and operations of each can be extracted within any given context. With every expansion of this model new subtleties become apparent, but the principles remain the same.

Given this model, it is possible to make value judgements about the kind of conditioning that leads to the best or worst results, depending on circumstances. The goal, conclusion or outcomes are the consequences. How we reach our goals is defined by the operations. Why we reach them depends on causes, consequences and the operations. In practical terms this means, for example, that when two people are faced with exactly the same circumstances, each may interpret them differently, depending on their conditioning (i.e. the direction of the dataflow in their central nervous system). In that case one or the other may be correct or both may be wrong. Even when both are right (or wrong) and agree, they may have reached the same conclusion by different pathways.

It must be stressed that this method of analysis applies only to value judgements based on factual information and not to aesthetic judgements. The latter are not amenable to geometric classification or analysis.

It remains to examine more closely the eleven pattern families shown in Diagram 31, each of which has different characteristics, and some of the self-defined meanings that can be extracted from them. With enlargement of this paradigm (when five or more factors are considered) further divisions (groups, for example) and many more option-families emerge.

## Diagram 31 divided into Families

Category 1 is divisible into five families and Category 2 into six, making eleven families in all. The options generated by the dataflow (i.e. the third line of numbers under each pattern) provide the distinctions between each family.

## Category 1

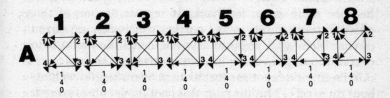

*Category 1*: Family 1
Total convergence; no options

Category 1 consists of concluded patterns of behaviour. With one exception no feedback is possible and even then only in limited circumstances.

This family describes a situation in which the individual is totally controlled by the environment and, as a result, cannot react. There is no interaction or feedback. In terms of human behaviour these states symbolize autism, acute depression, deep coma or total isolation – a human reduced to mechanical functioning. The environment and the conditions (i.e. lack of options) overwhelm the individual totally and, as a result, he or she cannot act or reacts irrationally. In technological terms, this is like pressing the starting switch of a machine which does not turn over or grinds due to some mechanical malfunction. The engine is totally non-responsive or responds inappropriately.

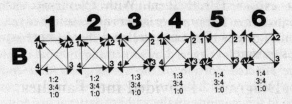

*Category 1*: Family 2
Binary concluded options

This family is symbolic of binary one-way relationships without feedback (1:2, 1:3, etc.) within any universe of discourse. It is equivalent to yes or no, on or off states. In human behavioural terms, this defines a reflexive jump to a conclusion – right or wrong. Again, nothing can be learnt because there is no feedback. It represents one of three possibilities: a jump to the correct conclusion as a result of conditioning; a jump to a wrong conclusion as a result of conditioning (nothing has been learnt and the reaction is mindless); or a one-time mechanical operation (switching a light on or off). This diagram does not model physical reflex actions which always require a 'reflex arc' (see Chapters 6 and 7). In any event the *self* has no options for any action other than one, despite the existence of other possibilities. None is accessible due to conditioning. The arrows close off all other possibilities for the dataflow.

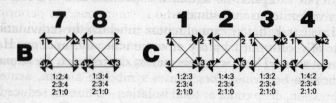

*Category 1*: Family 3
Trinary concluded options

Here more complex behaviour than a binary reflex is modelled. Three out of the four factors are engaged. Note that in two out of six patterns, the correct conclusion (i.e. 4) is reached, but there is no feedback of any kind to the self (i.e. 1) and no continuity. Closure is reached in every instance. These patterns are equivalent to involuntary muscular tics or twitches, purely mechanical behaviour or any other that is triggered by something internal or external to the affected portion of the system, but that comes to a stop with or without having achieved any purpose. To return to the machine analogy, these patterns are equivalent to switching on the starter. The starter turns the engine over a few times (i.e. it is momentarily responsive) but it will not function (i.e. no continuous feedback) because it has flooded or because of some inhibiting external factor.

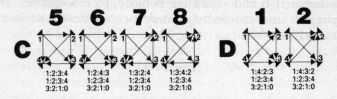

*Category 1*: Family 4
Global concluded options

All four factors are engaged in this family of patterns, but there is no feedback. These are like repetitive computations on a calculator that has not been programmed. All the operations that lead to the same conclusion must be repeated again and again. In behavioural terms this is equivalent to an individual who is conditioned to perform a simple task that he cannot repeat either due to a traumatic loss of short-term memory or some other dysfunction. He needs to be retrained again and again to reach the same conclusion.

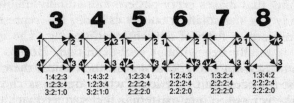

*Category 1*: Family 5
Global concluded options with limited feedback

All four factors are involved in this family and these patterns represent total conditioning as in all other Category 1 and 2 families. But here limited feedback surfaces for the first time. The dataflow provides the options for closure as in Family 4 or perpetual feedback within a recursive loop that excludes one or more of the factors. The purely mechanical analogy is that of a wind-up toy that keeps going until it runs down. Behaviourally, this pattern family stands for reflexive neurotic or psychopathic, mindless, self-destructive and repetitive behaviour or addiction. It can repeat itself indefinitely unless it enters the closed loop or comes to a stop.

## Category 2

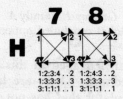

1:2:3:4 .. 2
1:3:3:3 .. 3
3:1:1:1 .. 1

1:2:4:3 .. 2
1:3:3:3 .. 3
3:1:1:1 .. 1

*Category 2*: Family 1
Total freedom

This is the first family in Category 2. All families in this category involve feedback of one kind or another. Every pattern in each family offers different options for the dataflow. This difference in options is a result of optional branching that makes every pattern individually unique.

Family 1 – the smallest one in category 2 – represents total freedom; a form of operant conditioning. The individual is totally free without goal-definition. He has the option to go from 1 to 2, 3 or 4 – all the choices there are without restraint. But no matter which option is chosen, he or she is trapped immediately in a closed feedback loop from which there is no escape. While this model may seem seductive at the start because all options are open, once any choice is made there is then only one option at each successive step, equivalent to no choice at all. The self (1) is always excluded. Hence there can be no feedback to the self (i.e. there is no benefit or profit). It is usually believed that total freedom is highly desirable or that it leads to anarchy. Both views are wrong because total freedom without goal-definition must result in perpetual repetition without benefit to the self or it leads to absolute external control, no choice, total constraint and constant repetition.

In the next family (Category 2: Family 2) only three out of four options can be exercised in each of the six patterns. In two out of six the correct conclusion (4) can be reached. This represents yet another form of operant conditioning, training or programming, equivalent to an 'instinctive' response that allows for a certain amount of modification.

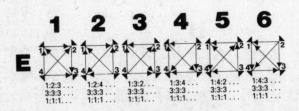

*Category 2*: Family 2
Feedback with limited options

It is possible in any of these families of patterns (in Categories 1 and 2) to 'add' external information (i.e. the external arrows at each point) but, while this may enlarge the database, part of the system is always inaccessible. Category 2: Family 2 is a variation on Category 1: Family 3 patterns (see above), except that here it takes the form of a perpetual, limited feedback loop although one or another factor is inaccessible and there is no opportunity for setting further goals and hence for learning.

The following and remaining four families (separated by black lines) are 'all-inclusive' (i.e. each allows access from 1 to 2, 3 and 4 with feedback to 1). In these respects they are alike. But each differs from the others as far as the internal options for the dataflow are concerned. Consider patterns E7, F5, G3, and H1. Each of these includes all four 'facts'. But at E7 there is one option at 1, one option at 2, two at 3, and two at 4 (represented as 1:1:2:2). At F5 the options are 1:2:2:1; at G1/3 they are 2:1:1:2, and at H1 they are 2:2:1:1. This is still a model of training, programming and operant conditioning because the individual (human being, computer or robot) cannot set his, her or its own goal. He, she or it is trained or programmed and therefore cannot learn. While the optional branching in each diagram provides an illusion of choice (hence artificial intelligence), the system is totally conditioned.

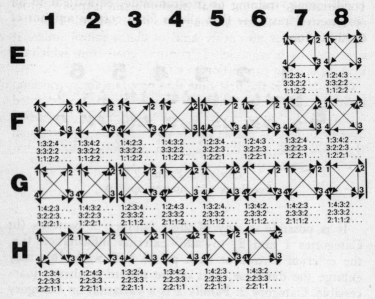

*Category 2*: Families 3,4,5 and 6
All-inclusive feedback

However, whenever any of these diagrams allow extension to infinity at 2, 3 or 4, the individual can choose his or her own goal. He is free to reach it by any possible means and can then set a next goal *ad infinitum*. He is in a position to learn perpetually (see Diagram 32 above).

The patterns of conditioned or programmed behaviours shown in Category 2, Families 3, 4, 5 and 6 or those in any enlarged, yet closed frame of reference (when 5, 6, 7 or more factors are involved in various combinations) can serve as the logic and flow charts for all possible computer programs or training methods. No others are possible irrespective of the number of factors that are involved. This overall paradigm represents an infinite series of finite combinatorial directed graphs. But, as I have said before, learning demands self-originated goals and is something each individual can only do for him- or herself (see Diagram 32). The Category 2: Family 1 diagrams show that total freedom – the supposed goal of democracy – leads ultimately to total control (Fascism, Communism or any other kind of dictatorship) unless it is limited by benign, self-determined goals from which all benefit, each in proportion to effort.

This, then, is the first time that programming, training, learning and the meaning of freedom have been defined geometrically, quantitatively and qualitatively, classified in a manner that allows synthesis and semantic precision (i.e. showing causes, consequences, and the operations that bring both about).

# Appendix E:
# The Patterns of Prime Numbers and Their Composites

'The subject of prime numbers has been one of the most alluring and fascinating aspects of the theory of numbers. The irregular manner [i.e. randomness] in which these numbers occur without any clue to their distribution has been one of the most distracting problems among mathematicians.'
George P. Loweke[1]

At the time of writing, the following consists of work-in-progress. It may have been completed by the time this book has been published. It is but one example among many that exemplifies how efficient combinatorial methods can be. The rapid prime number identification and factorization of composites solution, not given in this appendix, is merely a spin-off of this larger and more important discovery that is adequately, if partially, explained in my previous book[AA] and demonstrated mathematically in its appendices. Given here is one previously unknown, significant, but partial solution to the prime-number problem.

The demonstrations given here and those yet to follow show that prime numbers (those divisible only by 1 and themselves) and their composites (primes multiplied by one another) form an infinite series of repeat patterns (see Diagrams 33 and 34). These allow rapid-calculation algorithms to be extracted that alter and accelerate how we divide any number by any other. Given parameters may eventually provide the algorithms for extremely rapid prime-number testing or the extraction of all (i.e. not just the first) divisors, if any, of any number, odd or even, with minimal iteration.

This method is likely to be so fast and the time taken to calculate all but the largest numbers so short that it does not register on most computer clocks. Therefore the number of calculation steps (and often no additional steps other than the parameter itself are required) reveals the rapidity of the method. Even when more than one step is required, the number of subsequent steps is reduced proportionally as the numbers increase in value. Thus the larger the results (i.e. the factors) or the number to be tested (to see if it is prime), the smaller the proportion of required steps. This may sound self-contradictory but it is not. In time, and with continued testing, additional refinements may be discovered that could speed up the method further, but it seems unlikely that the principles behind the method could be improved. Among other things, the method resolves the pseudoprime, Mersenne $(2 \uparrow k - 1)$, Fermat number $[(2 \uparrow k - 1) + (2k - 1)]$ and integer long-division problems.

Even at this point I can safely predict that these discoveries should eventually alter the very methods used for long division in education, in science, in computing in general, to say nothing of encryption. For mathematicians especially, and here I address myself only to them, these discoveries open the doors wide to future solutions of still unresolved problems concerning integer (i.e. whole number) arithmetic and topology (e.g. 'tiling' problems). The same is true for genetics, in which field the need for a precise mathematical analytic method is known but has not yet been discovered (or recognized). I emphasize 'should' rather than 'will' because all depends on whether mathematicians, computer scientists and geneticists, among others, pay attention to these discoveries, the principles that underlie them, and apply them.

## A Brief History of Prime-Number Mathematics

The first deductive definition (trying to discover the cause by examining the consequences) in the West of prime numbers as an infinite series is ascribed to the Greek geometer Euclid. Later, another Greek, Eratosthenes, discovered a matrix (one of the first 'spread-sheets') that demonstrated inductively (discovering consequences by reconstructing causes and operations) the infinite range of primes and their composites (i.e. products of primes). But neither he nor any mathematician since seems to have discovered the repeat-pattern nature of primes and their composites that emerges from a critical analysis of Eratosthenes's sieve.

Eratosthenes's sieve reconsidered (see Diagrams 33 and 34 below) appears to generate every possible repeat pattern in the universe, each individually unique for every prime and its composites – a far more significant finding than 'fractals' (meaningless, if often pleasing, patterns generated by simple algorithms).

The history of prime-number conjectures, from the alleged discovery of the characteristics of primes by Chinese mathematicians *c*. 500 BC to D.H. Lehmer in this century, is given by G.P. Loweke.[2] In 1909, D.N. Lehmer published a *Factor Table for the First Ten Million* not divisible by 2,3,5, or 7 up to 10,017,000, worked out by hand, presumably with the assistance of an early adding machine.[3] Richard K. Guy lists common short cuts to factorization discovered in intervening centuries.[4] The most informative reference works concerning primes and their composites have been compiled by Paulo Ribenboim.[5] He suspects that they are related to Fermat's Last Theorem and he turns out to be correct.

From G.B. Riemann's hypothesis some statistical postulates about the relative density of primes among natural numbers have been derived. But this hypothesis does not address the pattern structure of primes and their composites or the latter's decomposition.

Identification of primes and decomposition of composites depended until now on what are essentially brute-force mathematical methods (i.e. dividing any odd number by all known primes or odd numbers up to the square root of the given whole number), at times aided by short cuts. Fermat, in the 16th century, came closer than anyone else before him or since to discovering mathematically one other aspect of the pattern structure of primes and their composites (Fermat's Little Theorem). The latter has been re-defined here and provides just one of a number of limits that are the essential pre-conditions to the general solution of the prime-number problem.

Apparently Fermat did not recognize the pattern structure that underlay his mathematical formulation ($2 \uparrow k-1 + 2k - 1$). Another flaw in Fermat's work was that his criterion fitted, apart from all primes, a number of composites which were later called 'pseudoprimes' (e.g. 341, 561, 1,105, 1,729, 2,047 . . .). These, while they seem prime by application of Fermat's Little Theorem, turned out to be composites. Fermat failed to identify this problem. The graphic methods show clearly why pseudoprimes occur (see Diagrams 33 and 34).

Between 1983 and 1990 the discovery of the 'largest known prime' was repeatedly announced, each larger than the next and each isolated by brute-force methods. Up to 1986 the largest known prime was the Mersenne number, $2 \uparrow 216,050 - 1$.[6] Its isolation required three hours of super-computer time and involved brute-force methods and 400 million calculations per second. In January 1991 the most powerful computer so far created, named 'Little Fermat', was announced.[7] It is said to be able to multiply numbers thousands of millions of digits in length. It does so by means of its intricate circuitry, a multi-precision mathematics chip or program, and brute force. If that computer were given this present method of division, it could discover primes and factorize composites of enormous size. Using current short cuts, mathematicians can find only the factors of composites larger than 150 decimal digits for one in a million numbers. Until now there were therefore severe and calculable limits to numbers that could be factorized within reasonable limits of time, even if present-day megamachines were to be linked in parallel. The answer to far greater computing and factorization power (or any other form of long division) must therefore lie in more efficient mathematical methods of data reduction and processing. In 1983 H. Cohen and W. Lenstra announced that they had discovered a rapid method of prime identification. They claimed that, using their methods, it required only eight minutes to establish the primality of a 200-digit number, but they did not reveal their method, presumably for the following reasons.

Since World War II, large prime numbers have found a practical use in encryption. Many of the world's most sensitive documents in government and business are encrypted with the RSA, a patented and expensive technique involving multiplication of large prime numbers. This includes a 'trapdoor', designed to make it still more difficult for messages to be deciphered by those to whom they are not addressed. A document encrypted by these methods can only be decoded by the recipient when the prime numbers that make up the composite number used are known or discovered.

The latest and fastest computers can break most of these codes in record time, but only by brute force. Only government agencies own, control or have access to them. Thus the megamachines of our day already make such codes relatively insecure. Ultimately the most powerful computers may be limited by the speed of light. But what are still believed to be codes sufficiently secure for all practical purposes use composites of 200 or more decimal digits because these may take weeks, months or years of brute-force computing time for illicit decoding on publicly available machines. Even if the use of these encrypting methods were halted, huge data-banks of messages as yet undecoded due to time limitations, held in storage by the major powers' security services, may soon become readable as if they were written in clear text. That will cause a number of embarrassing surprises, given the policies of all governments since World War II (e.g. the 'cold war'), shady business practices by large corporations, and questionable money manipulations by banks.

As Paul Hoffman writes, 'What the field needs is another Euclid ... Until then, we may remain in the curious situation where forces in government and industry [and banking] that depend on secret communications continue to profit from the ignorance of mathematicians.'[8] That state of ignorance may be ended with this present discovery, because primes of astronomical size and beyond (e.g. numbers larger than the number of atoms in the universe) may soon be found and the first, second and other factors of enormous composites isolated extremely rapidly on mini-, micro, lap-top or home computers. (More secure codes are presently in the making by this and other authors.)

## Primes

Every prime number, pseudo-prime and their odd or even multiples can be represented as repeat patterns (see Diagrams 33 and 34). It is important to recognize that here different algorithms are required when the binary order of magnitude (i.e. the exponent) is odd or even. This of course involves making qualitative value judgments about whole numbers, a need that is generally rejected in principle by most mathematicians.

No brute-force methods or conventional short cuts are henceforth required for factorization or prime identification. However, in most cases (but by no means in all), a number of iterative steps are needed depending on the characteristics of the numbers involved, of which certain categories call for different but related sets of limits, parameters and algorithms. The system is conditionally deterministic and dynamic (i.e. it requires algorithms that are perpetually adaptive and change according to given rules), like everything else in the universe. Application of the appropriate algorithms and methods reduces the search for prime factors or the primality of any given odd number to a conditionally absolute minimum number of operations.

An intriguing aspect of this discovery is that it demonstrates that there are always more correct solutions than wrong ones, and that some of the best are better than others out of the sum of all combinatorial possibilities. The method offers so many different approaches to the same or similar solutions that it was difficult to choose what seemed to be the best and fastest from among them.

Finally, this, like all good solutions, opens the door to a plethora of future discoveries in many branches of science (e.g. in mathematics – the possible solution to previously unresolved Diophantine problems like the Goldbach conjecture; in physics – the given resolution to the randomness/chance problem and disproof of aspects of Heisenberg's uncertainty principle; in biology – the mathematical definition of gene and chromosomal structures, among others). These may seem like very large claims, and many still need great care and much work to be resolved. However, they are not unreasonable in view of the fact that any mathematical or scientific breakthrough should be predictive even before all details are known. I am on the way towards solving some of these problems and have solved others already. There is, however, far more work to be done than is possible for any individual, and it may take generations of scientists/mathematicians to make the best use of these new tools and apply them imaginatively in fields about which I know nothing.

As indicated earlier, the method works beyond the brute-force number-crunching capacity of any existing or future computer. This places severe limits on brute-force testing of numbers that lie beyond this limit now or in the future. However, the deductive proof should suffice to turn into a theorem (i.e. a proven fact) what some might claim to be just another theory (an as-yet unproven conjecture that seems to work up to a point and can only be partially demonstrated).

But – and this is an important substantiation of my claim

that induction must precede deduction and that both must lead to the same conclusions – the method discussed here could probably never have been discovered by deduction from the start, without initial induction. Let us use crime detection as an analogy. The conditional variations of a crime may or may not be discovered deductively in time by exhaustive hit or miss methods (as any good detective knows). But that might take forever because the initial causal conditions and their variations cannot be deduced without induction (e.g. reconstruction of causes, intentions and motives for the crime, and the relationships and circumstances of both criminal and victim up to the time of the crime itself). In other words, a criminal may be caught as a result of clues left behind. But clues, tools or weapons tell you nothing about the variety of circumstances that caused the crime to be committed. All you can ascertain with certainty without close inductive analysis are the consequences (who did what) and some of the actual operations (how they did it), but seldom why they did it. This is equally true in science where the why should be as important as the how and the consequences.

Further, no computer could ever have generated this solution. It was extremely valuable to have computers available to test various wrong and right turnings on the way to this discovery. But Euclid, Fermat or anyone else could have worked out the same principle by hand and without computers, had they had the interest or time. This also shows therefore that value judgements are more important than mechanism, and that the human brain is far more powerful than any machine as far as qualitative and quantitative valuative analyses and rigorous logic are concerned.

These demonstrations indicate that a fundamental geometric pattern structure underlies what seem, superficially, to be random processes. They establish that linear methods work best for creating order out of seeming chaos, provided initial conditions (i.e. causes), limits, parameters and consequences are discovered, recognized for what they mean, and clearly defined. The true order of most – and perhaps all – random and seemingly chaotic systems and behaviours in nature, including human nature, is amenable to linear analysis by means of combinatorial methods and logic, reducing chance, probabilities and uncertainties to a minimum. The following also illustrates that utter simplicity underlies the most complex systems. The search for and explanations of such simplicity may be tedious and complex, but in the end the formalisms are simple.

## A Word of Caution

The solution to the general division problem in the near future has serious political and commercial implications. It is currently being tested by sundry computer experts and mathematicians. Too early a publication of my findings could enable anyone to decode highly sensitive government and business messages, past and present, without difficulty. Aside from the havoc this might cause to the relations between the major powers, it could jeopardize my own interests and those of my associates. For these reasons I am not giving the whole solution here, simple as it is. No one could possibly reach such a solution from what I provide here without a great deal of time and effort. However, given that the underlying maths were published in 1989,[AA] any good mathematician should now be able eventually to do what I and my associates have already done. The prime-number solution is embedded yet clearly visible in the published material. It is therefore simply a matter of time before someone else, somewhere in the world, discovers what I have discovered, using my methods.

There are difficulties that many academics in a variety of disciplines may have to overcome when faced with this and related discoveries. Even the methods described here are unorthodox, mathematically speaking, despite the fact that they form a link with the work of Euclid, Eratosthenes and Fermat. Unconventional methods are required whenever conventional ones fail. Only full disclosure will demonstrate just how unorthodox they are. This is why 'outsiders' often succeed where establishment scientists reach dead ends.

Euclidian, linear methods are considered 'old fashioned' and 'out of date' by many modern mathematicians and scientists. They turn out to be wrong. The primacy of Euclid, Pythagoras and many others cannot be disputed. We all follow in their footsteps (or stand on the heads of these great men, to paraphrase Newton).

For these reasons it may be necessary for conventional mathematicians to reconsider some of their perceptions and decondition themselves from the habits of a lifetime before the meanings and the simplicity of this solution become as obvious to them as they are to non-mathematicians. They and governments may have a vested interest in clinging to outdated methods, protecting their past mistakes. But such attempts would certainly frustrate the early resolution of many medical and other scientific and social problems that are as vital to them as to everyone else. Acceptance of radically new ideas is never a problem for free thinkers who are not handicapped by being locked into the wrong conventions. It is possible that others have discovered some of this, but it seems unlikely because of the varied and highly profitable commercial computing applications involved, some of which certainly would have surfaced by now.

## Description of the General Long-division Method

Inductively, the first and all other divisors of composite odd numbers can now be extracted algorithmically (i.e. by means of algebraic formulae based on the method) in a minimum number of steps without brute-force factorization. If the first divisor is small this can often be done in a single step. If it is larger, then a second, third, etc. repeat operation may be required by establishing a succession of a very small number of trial divisors within the given bounds. The number of repetitive operations depends on the relationships between values of k (the power of 2), y (the excess for the given number), those of any first divisor or, if S (the number to be tested) is prime, $\sqrt{S}$. The same can be done deductively.

In any event, and because the value of successive steps increases exponentially, the required number shrinks rapidly in proportion to any increase in the values of p (every divisor) or √S, compared to the number of trials required by brute-force factorization or known short cuts. In other words, the larger the number to be factorized or tested for its primality, the smaller will be the proportion of the number of trial divisors needed to establish primality or to find the first factor – the reverse of what takes place today. It also makes it possible to factorize or establish the primality of S for numbers that could not be considered previously or in any future, even with maximum computer power. The number of brute force trials required is simply too large within reasonable limits of time, given today's methods. The following is only a small part of the process that allowed me to arrive at this solution. In itself it represents a radical departure from the conventional wisdom.

## The Repeat Patterns of Primes and their Composites

Conventions: ↑ reads 'raised to the power'
S = an odd natural number
k = its (binary) order of magnitude
S = 2↑k + y always holds implicitly
y = the excess over that magnitude, thus the equation

p = a trial prime number
f = a (prime) factor of S
q = any natural number
r = any even number

Prime numbers and their composites form repeat patterns (see Diagrams 33 and 34). The repeat-pattern series for every prime and its composites is unique, generating what I suggest may underlie every possible pattern in the universe. This discovery has made it possible to develop the pattern structures that lead to extremely rapid factorization and

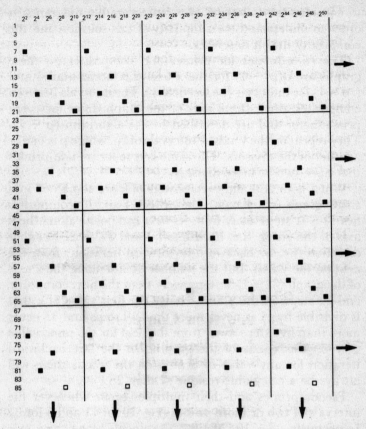

*Diagram 33*: Structure of Primes, Pseudo-primes and Composites
Even powers of 2
for 11 and its odd-number multiples
S = 11
11 = 2 ↑ + 3

identification of primes. It also serves to resolve some of the core problems of whole-number (integer) mathematics; for example the 'pseudo-prime' problem. Pseudo-primes are those odd numbers that, when tested by means of Fermat's Little Theorem, appear to be primes when, in actual fact, they are composites. It is therefore essential to consider the following two representative diagrams in order to understand the simplicity of this solution and the complexity that it describes.

The co-ordinates for primes and composites on these graphs are q(p − 1) for the x axis (i.e. horizontally) and (rp − 1) for the y axis (i.e. vertically). The intervals between composites along the x axis of the graph differ for every prime factor and are described by the algorithm (p − 1). They repeat on the y axis at intervals of 2p, where p is one or another of the divisors. The same is true for pseudo-primes that have two or more divisors.

When both odd and even powers of k are combined in a single graph (not shown), the prime 11 and its composites lies 11 − 1 steps away from its next composite along the x axis of the graph (i.e. horizontally) and 22 away in either direction (i.e. by backward or forward iteration) from the next on the y axis. But the number 31 lies along the x axis of the graph (31 −1)/6 steps away from the next composite and 62 steps on the y axis. Hence the first value of k that is divisible by 11 is never more than 10 steps and 31 never more than five steps away from the next for the same value of y on the x axis of the graph. On the last backward iteration for any value of S or p on the y axis there will always be a calculable residue < than 2p.

Pseudo-primes and their multiples occur whenever the intervals of two or more primes (e.g. 10 for 11 and 5 for 31 respectively – i.e. 10, 20, 30 . . .) coincide along the x axis of the graph. However, pseudo-primes have one additional characteristic. The coincidence of two or more primes and their multiples occurs for them, and for them alone, when modulo [2 ↑ q(p − 1), + r(2p − 1)] provides an integer (i.e. a whole number) solution − an extension of Fermat's Little Theorem. This is the point at which all primes can be shown to be just that, except for pseudo-primes. Hence Fermat's confusion (see k = 8 and y = 85 on Diagrams 33 and 34). Given the impending factorization solution, pseudo-primes should be identifiable and factorized in the same way and as rapidly as any other composite.

Further valuative analyses of numbers are required (e.g.

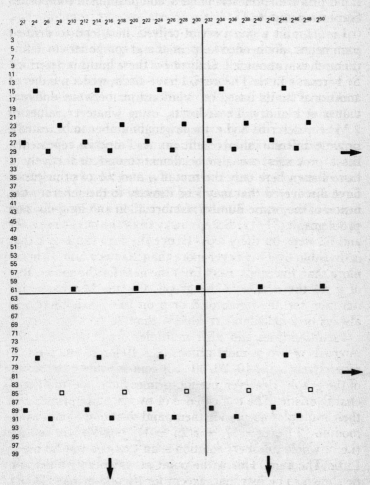

*Diagram 34*: Pattern Structure of Primes, Pseudo-primes and Composites

Even Powers of 2
for 31 and its odd number composites
S = 31
31 = 2 ↑ 4 + 15

that a distinction be made between odd and even powers of k and between certain other number classifications derived from the parameters) before a deeper understanding of rapid prime identification and decomposition of composites becomes possible.

Limits, and a given set of criteria that lead to defined parameters, are needed for primes and composites to define themselves without fail. Only one of these limits is described by Fermat's Little Theorem. I have discovered a number of additional limits based on relationships between different values of k and y. These limits, using whatever values of $2 \uparrow k + y$ describe S (i.e. the original number to be tested), provide different initial conditions. As I mention repeatedly, these processes can also be demonstrated deductively. I have shown here only the first of a number of principles I have discovered that may lead directly to the general resolution of the prime-number, factorization and long-division problems.

# Annotated References

NOTE: To avoid repetition, the AA superscript in the text refers to:

Arnold, A., *Winners and Other Losers in Peace and War* (London: Paladin Books, 1989).

This book includes a full description of neural networks in its Appendices, and provides the geometry and mathematics that define the classified sum of all combinatorial possibilities used here for analysis and prediction. Also included is a glossary of defined terms used in this book (e.g. the three laws of thermodynamics).

## Chapter 1: The Question (pp. 23–39)

1. Eddington, Sir A.S., *New Pathways in Science* (Cambridge: Cambridge University Press, 1935), p. 311.
2. Barrow, J.D. and Tipler, F.J., eds, *The Anthropic Cosmological Principle* (Oxford: The Clarendon Press, 1986).
3. Bohm, D., *Causality and Chance in Modern Physics* (London: Routledge and Kegan Paul, 1957).
4. Prigogine, I., *Order Out of Chaos: Man's New Dialogue with Nature* (New York: Bantam, 1984).
5. Mandelbrot, B., *The Fractal Geometry of Nature* (New York: Freeman, 1982).
6. Penrose, R., *The Emperor's New Mind* (Oxford: Oxford University Press, 1989).

7. Gleick, J., *Chaos* (London: Heinemann, 1988).
8. Lysenko, T.D., *Heredity and its Variability*, trans. T. Dobzhansky (New York: Columbia University Press, 1946). See also Huxley, J., *Soviet Genetics and World Science* (London: Chatto and Windus, 1949).
9. Delgado, J.M.R., 'Permanent Implantation of Multi-lead Electrodes in the Brain', *Yale Journal of Biological Medicine*, 1952, Vol. 24, 351–8.
10. Penrose, R., op. cit., see also Zohar, D., *The Quantum Self* (London: Bloomsbury, 1990).

## Chapter 2: Nothing But a Machine (pp. 40–66)

1. Rignano, E., *Man not a Machine* (London: Kegan Paul, 1926).
2. Chapuis, A. and Gélis, E., *Le Monde des Automates*, limited edition (Paris: 1928), 2 vols.
3. Gimpel, J., *The Medieval Machine* (London: Victor Gollancz, 1977).
4. Lieh Tzu, 'The Book of Master Lieh' (5th to 1st centuries B.C.), in *Science and Civilization in China*, by Joseph Needham, Vol. 2, *History of Scientific Thought* (Cambridge: Cambridge University Press, 1956), p. 53.
5. Chapuis, op. cit.
6. Swift, J., *Gulliver's Travels; A Voyage to Laputa*, 1727, Part III, Ch. 5.
7. Brewster, D., *Letters on Natural Magic* (London: John Murray, 1832).
8. *The Gentlemen's Magazine*, Vol. 18, 1758, pp. 9 and 109.
9. —, Vol. 24, 1754, p. 196.
10. —, Vol. 82, 1812, p. 440.
11. *The Monthly Magazine* or *British Register*, No. 5 of Vol. 25, 1 December 1808, p. 469.
12. Schodt, F.L., *Inside the Robot Kingdom* (Tokyo: Kodansha International Ltd, 1988).
13. Barnes, J., 'Is It Made in Japan – or Stolen in California?' (London: *The Sunday Times*, 27 June 1982).

14. Descartes, R., *Principia Philosophiae* (Amsterdam: 1644); trans. and ed. by E. Anscombe and P.T. Geach (London: Thomas Nelson and Sons Ltd, 1971).

15. —, 'Letter to More', 5 February 1649, in *Descartes, Philosophical Letters*, trans. and ed. by A. Kennedy (Oxford: The Clarendon Press, 1970).

16. Mumford, L., *The Myth of the Machine: 2, The Pentagon of Power* (London: Secker and Warburg, 1971), pp. 87, 98.

17. De la Mettrie, J.O., *Man a Machine* (Leyden: Elie Luzac, 1748); first English edition (London: G. Smith, 1750). French–English edition (LaSalle: Open Court, 1912).

18. Anon., *Man More than a Machine* (Leyden: Elie Luzac, 1748) (attributed to de la Mettrie).

19. Frantzen, *Denial of Man a Machine* (Leipzig: 1749).

20. Tralles, *On Man's Machine and Soul* (Leipzig: 1749).

21. Hollmann, *Refutation of Man a Machine* (Berlin: 1750).

22. De la Mettrie, J.O., *Natural History of the Soul* (The Hague: 1745).

23–8. —, *Man a Machine*, op. cit.

29. Lange, F.A., *The History of Materialism* (London: Kegan Paul and Co., 1925, introduction by Bertrand Russell), p. 49.

30–1. Rignano, op. cit.

32. Needham, N.J.T.M., *Man a Machine* (London: Kegan Paul and Co., 1927).

33. —, *Science and Civilization in China*, 7 vols (Cambridge: Cambridge University Press, 1956).

34. Diderot, D., *Encyclopédie ou Dictionnaire Raisonnée des sciences, des arts et des métiers*, 12 vols (Paris: 1751–65).

35. Needham, N.J.T.M., interview with, Channel 4 TV, produced by M. Burgess (London, 13 August 1988).

36. Needham, N.J.T.M., 'Mechanistic Biology and the Religious Consciousness', in *Science, Religion and Reality*, ed. by Joseph Needham (London: The Sheldon Press, 1925), p. 225.

37. —, 'Mechanistic Biology', op. cit., 36.

38. —, *Man a Machine*, op. cit., 32.

39. —, *Order and Life* (Cambridge: Cambridge University Press, 1936).

40. Haldane, quoted in Needham, N.J.T.M., *The Sceptical Biologist* (London: Chatto and Windus, 1929), pp. 72–3.

41. Del Torto, J., 'The Human Machine', *Neurotica*, Spring 1951, Vol. 8, 21–35, p. 32.

42. Midgley, M., *Wickedness – A Philosophical Essay* (London: Routledge and Kegan Paul, 1984).

43. Dawkins, R., *The Selfish Gene* (Oxford: Oxford University Press, 1976). Note: in this book Dawkins sets out to 'prove': '. . . what our own selfish genes are up to, because we may then at least have the chance to upset their design, something which no other species has ever aspired to'.

44. Midgley, M., op. cit., p. 42.

45. Dawkins, R., *The Selfish Gene*, new and revised edition (Oxford: Oxford University Press, 1989). Note: the author states: '. . . we animals are the most complicated and perfectly-designed pieces of machinery in the known universe . . . Like successful Chicago gangsters, our genes have survived, in some cases for millions of years, in a highly competitive world.' However, Dawkins now takes cognizance that somewhere, somehow, co-operation plays a role in this evolutionary process. He has come to this conclusion as a result of a book, *The Evolution of Cooperation* by R. Axelrod (New York: Basic Books, 1984), that purports to show the main springs of co-operation. Although based on the imaginative work of Anatol Rapoport, Axelrod's book is a hodgepodge of contradictions. As a result, Dawkins is still married to his original theme, modified by yet another myth.

46. Mumford, L., *The Condition of Man* (London: Martin Secker and Warburg, 1944).

47. —, *The Myth of the Machine: Technics and Human Development* (New York: Harcourt, Brace and World, 1966). See also Mumford, L., *The Pentagon of Power*, op. cit.

## Chapter 3: Stubbing Your Toe on the Philosopher's Stone (pp. 67–100)

1. Descartes, R., *Philosophical Writings*, trans. and ed. by E. Anscombe and P.T. Geach (The Open University: Nelson University Paperbacks, 1970), p. 51.
2. Durant, W., *The Story of Philosophy* (New York: Simon and Schuster, 1927).
3. Russell, B., *A History of Western Philosophy* (London: George Allen and Unwin, 1946).
4. Jeans, J., *Physics and Philosophy* (Cambridge: Cambridge University Press, 1942).
5. Heisenberg, W., *Physics and Philosophy* (London: George Allen and Unwin, 1959).
6. Kant, I., *Critique of Pure Reason*, trans. by N.K. Smith (London: Macmillan, 1929).
7. Lorenz, K., *Studies in Animal and Human Behavior*, Vol. 1 (Cambridge, Mass.: Harvard University Press, 1970).
8. Descartes, R., *Philosophical Writings*, op. cit.
9. Ibid.
10. Burt, C., *The Subnormal Mind* (Oxford: Oxford University Press, 1977); see also by the same author, *The Gifted Child* (London: Hodder and Stoughton, 1975).
11. Butler, S., *The Note-Books of Samuel Butler*, ed. by Henry Festing Jones (London: Jonathan Cape, 1921).
12. Simons, G.L., 'Whatever Turns You on', *Guardian*, 8 July 1982, p. 17.
13. Ibid.
14. —, *The Simons Book of Sexual Records* (London: Star Books, 1975).
15. —, 'Whatever Turns You on', op. cit.
16. Hawking, S., *A Brief History of Time* (London: Transworld, 1988).
17. Yates, F., *The Art of Memory* (London: Penguin, 1970).
18. Plato, quoted in Russell, B., op. cit.
19. Russell, B., op. cit., p. 149.
20. Ibid., p. 297.
21. Walter, G., *The Living Brain* (London: Duckworth, 1953), p. 180.

22. Penfield, W. and Roberts, L., *Speech and Brain Mechanism* (New York: Atheneum, 1960); see also Penfield, W. and Rasmussen, T., *The Cerebral Cortex of Man* (New York: Macmillan, 1950).
23. Penfield, W., *The Mystery of the Mind*, 1975.
24. Popper, K.R. and Eccles, J.C., *The Self and Its Brain* (Berlin: Springer-Verlag, 1977).
25. Lange, F.A., op. cit.
26. Ibid.
27. Cohen, C., *Materialism Restated* (London: Pioneer Press, 1927).
28. Ibid.
29. Ibid.
30. Russell, B., *An Inquiry into Meaning and Truth* (Harmondsworth: Penguin, 1973).
31. Eddington, Sir A.S., *Science and the Unseen World* (London: George Allen and Unwin, 1929), p. 18.
32. Ibid.
33. Needham, N.J.T.M., *Man a Machine*, op. cit.
34. —, quoted in Cohen, C., *Materialism Restated*, op. cit., p. 66.
35. Russell, B., *A History of Western Philosophy*, op. cit.
36. Hawking, S., op. cit.

## Chapter 4. In the Name of God (pp. 101–131)

1. Cohen, C., op. cit.
2. Pascal, B., *Pensées* (pub. posthumously, 1670).
3. Leibniz, G.W., *Monadology*, 1720.
4. Spinoza, B., *Ethics*, 1677.
5. Boyle, R., 'A Disquisition about the Final Causes of Natural Things', 1688, in *Science and Religious Belief, 1600–1900*, ed. by D.C. Goodman (John Wright and Sons in association with the Open University Press, 1973).
6. Priestley, J., *Letters to a Philosophical Unbeliever* (Bath: 1780).
7. Newton, I., 'Four Letters from Sir Isaac Newton to Doctor Bentley, Containing Some Arguments in Proof of a Deity' (London: 1756).

8. Holbach, Baron P.H.D. von, 'Système de la Nature' (London, 1770) in *The System of Nature*, trans. Samuel Wilkinson, 3 vols (London: 1820).

9. Paley, W., *Natural Theology; or Evidence of the Existence and Attributes of the Deity, Collected from the Appearances of Nature* (London: 1819, orig. 1802).

10. Huxley, T.H., *On the Reception of the 'Origin of Species'*.

11. Schrödinger, E., *Mind and Matter* (Cambridge: Cambridge University Press, 1958).

12. Thorpe, W.H., 'Biology, Psychology and Belief', 1961, in Eccles, J., *The Brain and the Unity of Conscious Experience* (Cambridge: Cambridge University Press, 1965).

13. —, *Purpose in a World of Chance, A Biologist's View* (London: Oxford University Press, 1978).

14. Ibid., cites Whitehead, A.N., *Process and Reality, an Essay in Cosmology* (Cambridge: Cambridge University Press, 1929).

15. Ibid.

16. Augros, R. and Stanciu, G., *The New Biology* (Boston: Shambala, 1987).

17. Malinowski, B., 'Magic, Science and Religion', in *Science, Religion and Reality*, ed. J. Needham (London: The Sheldon Press, 1925).

18. Godwin, J., *Athanasius Kircher* (London: Thames and Hudson, 1979).

19. Yates, F.A., *The Art of Memory*, op. cit., chap 8.

20. Yates, F.A., *Giordano Bruno and the Hermetic Tradition* (London: Routledge and Kegan Paul, 1978).

21. Smuts, J.S., *Holism and Evolution* (London: Macmillan, 1936).

22. Durant, W., op. cit.

23. Bettany, G.T., *Encyclopedia of the World's Religions* (London: Bracken Books, undated, original pub. 1890).

24. Frazer, J.G., *The Golden Bough* (London: Macmillan, 1975).

25. Mumford, L., *My Works and Days – A Personal Chronicle* (New York: Harcourt Brace Jovanovich, 1979).

26. Joad, C.E.M., *The Testament of Joad* (London: Faber and Faber, 1933).
27. —, *The Recovery of Belief, A Restatement of Christian Philosophy* (London: Faber and Faber, 1952).
28. Ibid.
29. Chardin, P.T. de, *The Phenomenon of Man*, with an introduction by Sir Julian Huxley (London: Collins, 1961).
30. Ibid.
31. Kehoe, A.B., *The Paradox of the Western World*, unpublished MS (Milwaukee: 1985).
32. Chardin, P.T. de, op. cit.
33. Asimov, I., Warrick, P.S. and Greenberg, M.H. (eds), *Machines That Think* (Harmondsworth: Penguin, 1983). Editors' introduction to 'Farewell to the Master' by Harry Bates, p. 93.

## Chapter 5: The Blinkered Sciences (pp. 132–182)

NOTE: In addition to the cited works on relativity, quantum, time, chance and chaos theories, the following books and articles may be of interest to the general reader:

Relativity:
Einstein, A., *Relativity, the Special and General Theory*, trans. R.W. Lawson (London: Methuen and Co., 1920).
Reichenbach, H., *The Philosophy of Space and Time*, trans. M. Reichenbach and J. Freund (New York: Dover, 1956).
Rosser, W.G.V., *Introductory Relativity* (London: Butterworth, 1967).

Quantum Theory:
Bohr, N., *Collected Works*, in *Nuclear Physics*, Vol. 9, ed. E. Rüdinger (Oxford: North Holland Publishing Co., 1986).
Broglie, L. de, *Matter and Light in the New Physics* (New York: Dover, undated, original pub. 1937).
Gribbin, J., *In Search of Schrödinger's Cat* (London: Corgi Books, 1985).

Heisenberg, W., *The Uncertainty Principle and Foundations of Quantum Mechanics*, eds W.C. Price and S.S. Chissick (London: Wiley, 1977).

Jeans, J., *The New Background of Science* (Cambridge: Cambridge University Press, 1933).

Planck, M., *Treatise on Thermodynamics* (London: Longmans Green and Co, 1927); see also by the same author: *Where is Science Going*, with introduction by A. Einstein, trans. J. Murphy, (Oxbow Press, 1981; original pub. 1933).

Time:

Freeman, E., et al., eds *Basic Issues in the Philosophy of Time* (New York: Exposition Press, 1974).

Gedda, L., et al., *Chronogenetics* (Springfield, Illinois: Thomas, 1979).

Landsberg, P.T., *The Enigma of Time* (Bristol: Adam Hilger Ltd, 1982).

Priestley, J.B., *Man and Time* (London: Aldus Books, 1964).

Smart, J.J.C., ed., *Problems of Space and Time* (New York: Macmillan Publishing Co., 1964).

Terry, B., *The Theory of Time* (New York: Exposition Press, 1974).

Whitrow, G.J., *The Nature of Time* (Harmondsworth: Penguin, 1975).

Zeman, J., ed., *Time in Science and Philosophy* (Prague: Academia, 1971).

Chance:

Bell, E.T., *Men in Mathematics* (London: Victor Gollancz, 1937).

Bernoulli, J., *Ars Conjectandi* (Basel: 1713).

Cardano, G., *The Book of Games of Chance* (1663).

Born, M., *Natural Philosophy of Cause and Chance* (Oxford: The Clarendon Press, 1949).

Hopkins, M., *Chance and Error: The Theory of Evolution* (London: Kegan Paul, 1923).

Monod, J., *Chance and Necessity* (London: Collins/Fontana, 1974).

Pascal, B., *Pensées*, trans. A.J. Kreilsheimer (New York: Penguin, 1966).

Chaos:

Barnsley, M.F. and Demko, S.G., eds, *Chaotic Dynamics and Fractals* (New York: Academic Press, 1985).

Peitgen, H.O. and Richter, P.H., *The Beauty of Fractals* (New York: Springer, 1986).

Saperstein, A.M., 'Chaos – A Model for the Outbreak of War' in *Nature*, Vol. 309, 1984, pp. 303–5.

Sparrow, C., *The Lorenz Equations, Bifurcations, Chaos, and Strange Attractors* (Heidelberg: Springer Verlag, 1982).

Stewart, I., *The Challenge of Chaos* (Harmondsworth: Penguin, 1988).


1. Eddington, A.S., *Science and the Unseen World* (London: George Allen and Unwin, 1928).
2. Hawking, S., *A Brief History of Time*, op. cit.
3. Krauss, L., *The Fifth Essence* (London: Vintage Press, 1989).
4. Hawking, S., op. cit.
5. Bohm, D., op. cit.
6. Prigogine, I., op. cit.
7. LaPlace, P.S. de, *Essay*, 1819.
8. Eigen, M. and Winkler, R., *The Laws of the Game* (London: Allen Lane, 1982).
9. Inglis, B., *Coincidence* (London: Hutchinson, 1990).
10. Hawking, S., op. cit.
11. Davies, P., *The Cosmic Blueprint* (London: Unwin Paperback, 1987).
12. —, ibid.
13. Hawking, S., op. cit.
14. —, ibid.
15. Jeans, J., *Physics and Philosophy* (Cambridge: Cambridge University Press, 1942).
16. Hawking, S., op. cit.
17. Hoyle, F. and Wickramasinghe, C., *Evolution from Space* (New York: Simon and Schuster, 1981).
18. Gleick, J., *Chaos* (London: Heinemann, 1988).

19. Ibid.
20. Lorenz, E., 'Deterministic Nonperiodic Flow', in *Journal of Atmospheric Science*, Vol. 20, 1963, pp. 130–41.
21. Dawkins, R., *The Blind Watchmaker* (London: Longman Scientific and Technical, 1986).
22. Gleick, J., op. cit.
23. Ibid.
24. Krauss, L., op. cit.

## Chapter 6: You Can Take a Horse to Water (pp. 183–225)

1. Skinner, B.F., quoted in P. Schrag, *Mind Control* (London: Marion Boyars, 1980).
2. Thorpe, W.H., *Purpose in a World of Chance*, op. cit.
3. Arnold, A., *Teaching Your Child to Learn from Birth to School Age* (New Jersey: Prentice-Hall, 1971).
4. Lees, C. and Driscoll, M., 'One in Three Children Thinks Sun Goes Around Earth', London, *The Sunday Times*, 22 April 1990, p. 1.
5. Fiske, E.B., 'Growing Gap in Worker Skills Alarms Corporate America', *International Herald Tribune*, 26 September 1989, p. 9.
6. Rachman, R., 'Schools Set Bush His Toughest Test', London, *Sunday Correspondent*, 1 October 1989, p. 13.
7. Atkinson, C. and Maleska, E.T., *The Story of Education* (New York: Bantam, 1964).
8. Arnold, A., *Teaching Your Child to Learn from Birth to School Age*, op. cit. In the chapter 'The Electronic Mother', the history of 'Sesame Street', the supposedly educational TV programme for pre-schoolers is detailed from its beginnings to its dubious claims of success.
9. Earle, A.M., *Child Life in Colonial Days* (New York: The Macmillan Co., 1899), p. 178.
10. Ariès, P., *Centuries of Childhood* (Harmondsworth: Penguin, 1979).
11. Earle, A.M., op. cit., pp. 191–2.

12. Arnold, A., *Pictures and Stories from Forgotten Children's Books* (New York: Dover, 1969).
13. Ariès, P., op. cit.
14. Silber, K., *Pestalozzi: The Man and His Works* (London: Routledge and Kegan Paul, 1960).
15. Froebel, F., *The Education of Man*, trans. W.N. Hailman (New York: D. Appleton and Co., 1909).
16. Montessori, M., *The Discovery of the Child* (New York: Ballantine Books, 1972).
17. Whitehead, A.N., *The Aims of Education and Other Essays* (London: Williams and Norgate, 1950); see also by the same author, *Science and the Modern World* (Cambridge: Cambridge University Press, 1926).
18. Dewey, J., *The Quest for Certainty* (New York: Minton, Balch and Co., 1919); see also by the same author, *How We Think* (Boston: D.C. Heath, 1909).
19. *Children and Their Primary Schools*. A Report of the Central Advisory Council for Education (England), 2 vols (London: HMSO, 1966).
20. Piaget, J., *The Origins of Intelligence in Children* (New York: International Universities Press, 1956); see also by the same author, *Biology and Knowledge* (Edinburgh: Edinburgh University Press, 1971); also in *Discussions on Child Development* – Meetings of the WHO Study Group on the Psychobiological Development of the Child (Geneva and London: 1953–6), 4 vols (New York: International Universities Press, undated).
21. Mumford, L., ops. cit.
22. Taylor, F.W., *The Principles of Scientific Management*, printed for private circulation (New York: Harper and Bros, 1911).
23. Watson, J.B., *Behaviorism* (Chicago: 1958).
24. Pavlov, I.P., *The Essential Works of*, ed. Michael Kaplan (New York: Bantam Books, 1966); see also by the same author, *Reflexes* (London: Martin Lawrence, 1929); *Lectures on Conditioned Reflexes* (London: Lawrence and Wishart, 1964).
25. Maslow, A., *The Farther Reaches of Human Nature* (Harmondsworth: Pelican, 1973).

26. Walter, G., *The Living Brain* (London: Gerald Duckworth and Co., 1953).

27. Sherrington, C., *The Brain and Its Mechanism* (Cambridge: Cambridge University Press, 1933); see also by the same author, *Man on His Nature* (Cambridge: Cambridge University Press, 1933), and *The Integrative Action of the Nervous System* (New Haven: Yale University Press, 1906).

28. Butler, S., *Life and Habit* (London: Wildwood House, 1981).

29. Sereny, G., *Into that Darkness* (London: André Deutsch, 1974), p. 101.

30. Schrag, P., *Mind Control* (London: Marion Boyars, 1980).

31. London, P., *Behavior Control* (New York: Harper and Row, 1969).

32. Cubberly, E.P., *US School Administration*, 1916, quoted in P. London, op. cit.

33. Skinner, B.F., *Beyond Freedom and Dignity* (Harmondsworth: Pelican, 1973).

34. Jensen, A.R., 'Environment, Heredity and Intelligence' (Cambridge: Harvard Educational Review, Vol. 39, Winter 1969).

35. Herrnstein, R., 'I. Q.', Boston, *The Atlantic Monthly*, September 1977, pp. 43–64.

36. Eysenck, H.J., *Race, Intelligence and Education* (London: Temple-Smith, 1971); see also by the same author, *The IQ Argument* (New York: The Library Press, 1971); see also Eysenck, H. J. vs Kamin, L., *Intelligence, The Battle for the Mind* (London: Pan Books, 1981).

37. Burt, C., op. cit.

38. London, P., op. cit.

39. Bongard, N., *Pattern Recognition*, ed. J.K. Hawkins, trans. by T. Cheron (New York: Spartan Books, 1970; orig. title: *Problema Uzanavaniya*, Moscow: Nauka Press, 1967).

40. Arnold, A., op. cit. (see 3. above)

41. DePalma, A., 'Foreign Scholars: Made in USA' (Paris: *International Herald Tribune*, 30 November 1990).

## Chapter 7: Stirring the Primeval Soup (pp. 226–264)

Note: In addition to the cited works, the following books and articles on brain mechanisms and memory may be of interest to the general reader:

Brain Studies:
Gregory, R.L., *Eye and Brain*, third edn (London: Weidenfeld and Nicolson, 1977).
Luria, A.R., *The Working Brain* (Harmondsworth: Penguin, 1973).
Pietsch, P., *Shuffle Brain* (New York: Houghton Mifflin, 1981).
Popper, K.R. and Eccles, J. C., *The Self and Its Brain* (Heidelberg: Springer Verlag, 1977).
'The Brain', *Scientific American* (New York: W. H. Freeman & Co., 1979).
Wooldridge, D.E., *The Machinery of the Brain* (New York: McGraw Hill, 1963).

Memory
Feindl, W., *Memory, Learning and Language* (Toronto: Toronto University Press, 1959).
Pribram, K.H., ed., *Memory Mechanisms* (Harmondsworth: Penguin, 1969).
Rapoport, D., *Emotions and Memory* (New York: International Universities Press, 1967).

1. Bellman, R., 'Mathematical Models of the Mind' in *Journal of Mathematical Bioscience*, Vol. 1, No. 2, 1967, pp. 287–303.
2. Penrose, R., and Zohar, D., op. cit.
3. Ibid.
4. Piaget, J., op. cit.
5. Higgins, L., quoted in Thorpe, W. H., *Purpose in the World of Chance*, op. cit., p. 25.
6. Thorpe, W.H., op. cit., p. 23.
7. Eddington, A.S., *New Pathways in Science*, op. cit.
8. Keller, H., *The World I Live In* (London: Methuen, 1933).

9. Thorpe, W.H., *Purpose in the World of Chance*, op. cit.
10. Walter, G., op. cit.
11. Ibid. See also Latil, P. de, *Thinking by Machine* (Boston: Houghton Mifflin Co., 1957).
12. Köhler, W., *The Mentality of Apes* (Harmondsworth: Penguin, 1957; orig. pub. 1925).
13. Garner, R.L., *The Speech of Monkeys* (London: William Heinemann, 1892).
14. Gardner, R.A. and Gardner, B.T., 'Two-way Communication with an Infant Chimpanzee', in A. M. Schrier and F. Stollnitz, eds, *Behavior of Non-human Primates*, Vol. 4 (New York: Academic Press, 1971).
15. Terrace, H., *Nim* (London: Methuen, 1980).
16. Premack, D., *Intelligence in Ape and Man* (Hillsdale: Lawrence Erlbaum, 1976).
17. Walker, S., *Animal Thought* (London: Routledge and Kegan Paul, 1983).
18. Jung, C., et al., *Man and His Symbols* (London: Aldus Books/W. H. Allen, 1964).
19. Dawkins, R., op. cit.

## Chapter 8: The Bubble that Burst (pp. 265–308)

1. 'Artificial Intelligence; It's Here!', *Business Week*, 4 July 1984, pp. 52–60.
2. Arnold, A., 'Why the Computer Has to be an Idiot' (London: *The Times*, 14 February 1984).
3. Tyler, C., 'Make Way for the Thinking Machine', (London: *Financial Times*, 30 June–1 July 1990). The article was based on the book by the same author: *Benefits and Risks of Knowledge-based Systems* (Oxford: Oxford University Press, 1990).
4. Mumford, L., *My Works and Days*, op. cit.
5. Dawkins, R., op. cit.
6. Hewett, J. and Sasson, R., *Expert Systems 1986*, Vol. 1, USA and Canada (London: Ovum Ltd, 1986).
7. Menabrea, L.F., *Taylor's Scientific Memoirs*, Vol. III, pp. 666–731, trans. and annotated by the Countess of Lovelace; Bibliothèque Universelle 82:10, 1842;

reprinted in Bowden, B.V., *Faster than Thought* (London: Sir Isaac Pitman and Sons, 1953).

8. Turing, A., *On Computable Numbers, with an application to the Entscheidungsproblem*, Proc. London Math. Soc., 2: 42: 230: 1937, corrected in Proc. London Math. Soc., 2: 43: 544: 1937.

9. Hopcroft, J.H., 'Turing Machines', New York, *Scientific American*, May 1984.

10. Hodges, A., *Alan Turing – The Enigma* (London: Burnett Books, 1983).

11. Turing, A., 'Computing Machinery and Intelligence', *J. Mind*, October 59: 433–60: 1950.

12. —, in Bowden, B.V., *Faster than Thought*, op. cit., Chap. 25, pp. 286–310.

13. Michie, D., *On Machine Intelligence* (Edinburgh: Edinburgh University Press, 1974).

14. Michie, D. et al., eds, *Machine Intelligence*, Vols 1–7 (Edinburgh: Edinburgh University Press, 1968–72).

15. Wiener, N., *Cybernetics* (New York: Wiley, 1948).

16. Neumann, J. von and Morgenstern, O., *Theory of Games and Economic Behavior* (Princeton: Princeton University Press, 1953).

17. Shannon, C. E., and Weaver, W., *The Mathematical Theory of Communication* (Urbana: University of Illinois Press, 1949).

18. Bertalanffy, L. von, *General Systems Theory* (Harmondsworth: Penguin, 1973); see also by the same author, *Robots, Men and Minds* (New York: Brazilier, 1967); and *Perspectives on General Systems Theory*; see also Cohen, J., *Human Robots in Myth and Science* (London: Allen and Unwin, 1966).

19. Walter, G., op. cit.

20. Sherrington, C., op. cit.

21. Plato, *Gorgias*, 511.

22. Ampère, J.J., *Essay on the Philosophy of Science, etc.*, 1838.

23. Wiener, N., op. cit.

24. McCarthy, J., 'Ascribing Mental Qualities to Machines', in *Philosophical Perspectives in Artificial Intelligence*, ed. M.D. Ringle (Brighton: Harvester Press, 1979).

25. Pask, G., *The Cybernetics of Human Learning and Performance* (London: Hutchinson Educational, 1975).

26. Beer, S., *Decision and Control* (London: Wiley, 1966).

27. Michie, D., op. cit.

28. Ashby, R., *An Introduction to Cybernetics* (London: Chapman and Hall, 1956); see also by the same author, *Design for a Brain* (London: Chapman and Hall, 1954).

29. —, Address, in *Communication 33*, Report on the Third Congress of the International Association for Cybernetics, Namur: 11–15 Sept, 1961 (Brockenhurst: The Artoga Research Group, Sept 1961).

30. Lighthill, J., *Artificial Intelligence: A Paper Symposium* (London: The Science Research Council, April 1973).

31. Boden, M., personal communication.

32. —, *Artificial Intelligence and Natural Man* (Hassocks: The Harvester Press, 1977).

33. Berry, A., *The Super-Intelligent Machine* (London: Jonathan Cape, 1983).

34. Crichton, M., *Electronic Life* (London: Heinemann, 1983).

35. Simons, G., *Are Computers Alive?* (Hassocks: The Harvester Press, 1983).

36. George, F.H., ed., *Science Fact* (Great Missenden: Topaz Books, 1977).

37. Close, F., *End* (Harmondsworth: Penguin, 1990).

38. Cotterill, R., *No Ghost in the Machine* (London: Heinemann, 1989).

39. George, F.H., *Man and Machine* (London: Paladin, 1979); see also by the same author, *Computers, Science and Society* (London: Pemberton Books, 1970), and *Cybernetics* (London: Hodder and Stoughton, 1971).

40. —, ed., *Science Fact*, op. cit.

41. ICOT, *Outline of Research and Development Plans for Fifth Generation Computer Systems* (Tokyo: Japan Information Processing Development Centre, 1982).

42. Tohru Moto-oka, in Ramsay, D. and Willenson, K., 'The Fifth Generation Challenge' (New York: *Newsweek*, 9 August 1982).

43. — and Kitsuregawa, Masaru, *The Fifth Generation Computer: The Japanese Challenge*, trans. F.D.R. Apps (New York: Wiley, 1985).

44. Johnstone, B., 'Japan Unveils Fifth Generation (London: *New Scientist*, 8 November 1984) pp. 10–11; see also Watts, D., 'Japanese may Regret "Intelligent Computer" Hype' (London: *The Times*, 20 November 1984).

45. Ball, J., Johnstone, B. and Nakaki, S., 'The New Face of Japanese Science' (London: *New Scientist*, 21 March 1985).

46. Williams, I., 'Can Computers Come Alive?' (London: *The Sunday Times*, 16 June 1985).

47. Michie, D., op. cit.

48. Winograd, T., 'Understanding Natural Language', *J. Cognitive Psychology*, 3: 8–11: 1972.

49. —, *Understanding Computers and Cognition* (US: Ablex Publishing Co., 1985).

50. Penrose, R., op. cit.; the author, although disagreeing with the possibility of a realization of AI, cites Winograd (op. cit.) as one of its claimed successes. Boden (op. cit.) and many other authors have done and continue to do the same.

51. *Business Week*, op. cit.

52. Stockton, W., 'Creating Computers that Think', two-part series (New York: *New York Times Sunday Magazine*, 7 December 1977).

53. McCorduck, P., *Machines Who Think* (San Francisco: W.H. Freeman & Co., 1979).

54. Feigenbaum, E. and McCorduck, P., *The Fifth Generation* (London: Michael Jospeh, 1984).

55. Ibid.

56. *Business Week*, op. cit.

57. *Artificial Intelligence*, Report No. 552 (Connecticut: International Resource Development Corp., June 1983); see also *The Artificial Intelligence Report*, Premier Issue, August 1983, 1: 1: January 1984, 2: 1: January 1985 (Palo Alto: Artificial Intelligence Publications); and Yorick Wilks, ed., *Artificial Intelligence Abstracts*,

1: 1: January 1987; Barr, A., Cohen, P.R., and Feigenbaum, E.A., *The Handbook of Artificial Intelligence*, 4 vols (Wokingham: Addison Wesley, 1989).

58. Hewett, J. and Sasson, R., op. cit.

59. Grossberg, S., *Neural Networks and Natural Intelligence* (Cambridge: MIT Press, 1988); see also Anderson, J.A. and Rosenfeld, E., *Neurocomputing* (Cambridge: MIT Press, 1988); Arbib, M.A., *The Metaphorical Brain 2* (New York: Wiley Interscience, 1989); Hech-Nielsen, R., *Neural Computing* (Wokingham: Addison Wesley, 1990).

60. *Business Week*, op. cit.

61. Ibid.

62. Taube, M., *Computers and Common Sense: The Myth of Thinking Machines* (New York: Columbia University Press, 1961).

63. Dreyfus, H. L., *What Computers Can't Do: A Critique of Artificial Reason* (New York: Harper and Row, 1972); see also Dreyfus, H.L. and Dreyfus, S.E., *Mind Over Machine* (Oxford: Basil Blackwell, 1986).

64. Weizenbaum, J., *Computer Power and Human Reason* (San Francisco: W.H. Freeman and Co., 1976).

65. Searle, J., *Minds, Brains and Science* (London: BBC Publications, 1984).

66. Penrose, R., op. cit.

67. Campbell, J., *The Improbable Machine* (New York: Simon and Schuster, 1989).

68. Mumford, L., op. cit.

69. Roszak, T., *The Cult of Information* (New York: Pantheon Books, 1986).

70. *A Program for Advanced Information Technology: The Report of the Alvey Committee* (London: HMSO, 1982); see also Commission of the European Communities, eds, *Esprit '85, Status Report*, Parts 1 and 2 (Amsterdam: Elsevier, 1986), and Mehta, A., 'Ailing after Alvey' (London: *New Scientist*, 7 July 1990) pp. 24–5.

71. Johnson, T., *The Commercial Application of Expert Systems* (London: Ovum Ltd, 1984).

72. Bird, J., 'Sinclair's Fifth Symphony' (London: *The Sunday Times*, 4 November 1984).

73. Feigenbaum, E., op. cit.

74. Carr, A.C. and Ancill, R.J., 'Computers in Psychiatry' *J. Acta Psychiatr. Scand.*, 67: 137–143, 1983; see also Carr, A.C., Ghosh, A. and Ancill, R.J., 'Can a Computer Take a Psychiatric History?' *J. Psych. Medicine*, 13: 151–158, 1983.

75. Skinner, B.F., *The Technology of Teaching* (New York: Meredith Corp., 1986).

76. Arnold, A., *Teaching Your Child to Learn*, op. cit.

77. Dembart, L., 'Language: Computers Still in Kindergarten' (Paris: *International Herald Tribune*, 3 February 1982).

78. Michie, D. and Johnstone, B., *The Creative Computer* (London: Viking Press, 1984).

79. Yazdani, M., 'Building Knowledge-Based Systems in Prolog', talk given at an 'Expert Systems' conference (London: The Polytechnic of North London, 10 September 1983).

80. Ceruzzi, P.E., *Reckoners, A Prehistory of the Digital Computer from Relays to Program Concept, 1935–1945* (Westport: Greenwood Press, 1983).

81. Ferry, G., 'Networks on the Brain' (London: *New Scientist*, 16 July 1987); see also Tank, D.W. and Hopfield, J.J., 'Collective Computation in Neuronlike Circuits' (New York: *Scientific American*, December 1987).

82. Ricciardi, L. and Scott, A., eds, *Biomathematics in 1980*, Workshop on Biomathematics: Current Status and Future Perspectives, Salerno, April 1980 (New York: North Holland Publishing Co., 1982).

83. Supples, C., 'Efforts to Duplicate Human Wetware' (Paris: *International Herald Tribune*, 3 March 1987).

84. Redece, M. and Treleaven, P., 'Computing from the Brain' (London: *New Scientist*, 26 May 1988).

85. Aleksander, I., quoted in 'Viewpoint' (London: *Business Computing and Communications*, February 1988).

86. *Informatics*, January 1988; and New York: *Scientific American*, special issue: *Trends in Computing*, Vol. 1, 1988, and Vol. 265, No. 6, December 1991

87. Sanger, E.D., 'Big Science Needs Big Money', *International Herald Tribune*, October 17, 1991.

## Appendix C: The Three-dimensionality of Time (pp. 320–330)

1. Taylor, E.G.R., *Heaven Finding Art* (London: Hollis and Carter, 1956).

2. Arnold, A., *Inertial Dead Reckoning Mapping, Navigation and Targeting* (London: 1981).

3. Hauty, G. and Adams, T., *Pilot Fatigue: Intercontinental Jet Flight 1; Oklahoma–Tokyo* (Oklahoma City: Federal Aviation Agency, March 1965); see also by the same authors: *Phase Shifts in the Human Circadian System and Performance Deficit during the Periods of Transition: I. East–West Flight, II. West–East Flight* (Washington: Federal Aviation Agency, December 1965); also Mohler, S.R. et al., *Circadian Rhythms and the Effects of Long-Distance Flights* and Siegel, P.V. et al., *Time-Zone Effects on the Long-Distance Traveller* (Washington: Federal Aviation Administration, September 1969).

4. Hauty, G.T., and Adams, T., *Phase Shifts of the Human Circadian System and Performance Deficit During the Period of Transition, III. North–South Flight* (Oklahoma City: Federal Aviation Agency, December 1965).

5. 'NASA Will Study Effects of Erratic Sleep on Pilots' (Washington: *The Washington Post*, 17 October 1980, p. A21.

6. Private communication, The Guild of Air Pilots and Air Navigators, London, 10 March 1982.

7. Ibid.

8. Arnold, A., *Jet-Lag: Time De- and Resynchronization* (London: 1981).

## Appendix D: The Combinatorial Neural Network Applied to Learning and Conditioning (pp. 331–345)

1. Eddington, A.S., *The Nature of the Physical World*, op. cit., p. 231.

## Appendix E: The Patterns of Prime Numbers and Their Composites (pp. 346–360)

1. Loweke, G.P., *Prime Numbers* (New York: Vantage Press, 1982).
2. Ibid.
3. Lehmer, D.N., *Factor Table for the First Ten Million* (Washington, D.C.: Carnegie Institution of Washington, Publication No. 105, 1909).
4. Guy, R.K., 'How to Factor a Number', *Proc. of the Fifth Manitoba Conf. on Numerical Mathematics*, 1–4 October 1975 (Winnipeg: Utilitas Mathematica Publishing Co., 1976); see also Selfridge, J.L and Wunderlich, 'An Efficient Algorithm for Testing Large Numbers for Primality', *Proc. of the Fourth Manitoba Conf. on Numerical Mathematics*, 1–5 October 1974 (Winnipeg: Utilitas Mathematica Publishing Co., 1975).
5. Ribenboim, P., *13 Lectures on Fermat's Last Theorem* (New York: Springer Verlag, 1979); see also by the same author: *Book of Prime Number Records* (New York: Springer Verlag, 1988).
6. Hoffman, P., *Archimedes' Revenge* (London: Penguin Books, 1988).
7. Berry, A., '"Rat's Nest" computer thinks big on numbers' (London: *Daily Telegraph*, 2 January 1991).
8. Hoffman, P., op. cit.
9. Arnold, A., Pickard, R. and Sippel-Dau, T., 'The pattern structure of primes; algorithms and computer programs for rapid prime identification and decomposition of composites into prime factors' (London, 1992, in preparation).

# Name Index

Note: Bold face page numbers indicate name given in the References

# Subject Index